RUNNING MATES

RUNNING MATES

-- -- -- -- -- -- -- -- --

JOHN FEINSTEIN

VILLARD BOOKS · NEW YORK · 1992

Library of Congress Cataloging-in-Publication Data

Feinstein, John.
    Running mates / John Feinstein
       p.   cm.
    ISBN 0-679-41220-4
    I. Title.
    PS3556.E433R86   1992
    813'.54—dc20   91-37129

9 8 7 6 5 4 3 2

First Edition

With thanks and love,
this is for my sister, Margaret,
and my brother, Bobby,
who will always be my
running mates.

CONTENTS

The first streaks of sunrise were just appearing on the horizon when the unmarked car pulled up to the basement entrance of the State House.

The timing, he knew, was perfect. It was still dark and there wouldn't be a soul around except for the lone guard sitting at the information desk. Arriving at this hour wasn't even that unusual; his regular work shift began in less than an hour anyway.

He climbed out of the car, shivering slightly in the early morning chill, and popped open the trunk. He lifted out a large bag, quietly eased the trunk closed, then walked in the door, the bag slung over his shoulder. If a civilian came strolling in carrying a bag this large at six o'clock in the morning, the guard would stop him.

Not a cop, though. With a casual wave, he walked by the guard, an old man who barely looked up from whatever it was he was reading. He climbed the steps that led first to the main floor of the building, then to the second floor, not bothering to look up as he went past the huge painting of George Washington resigning his commission, which hung on the landing between the two floors.

At the top of the steps, he turned right and glided around the corner to the entrance to the House of Delegates spectator gallery. He was wearing sneakers, so as not to make any clacking sounds on the floor. He had counted on the old guard not noticing that little detail.

He pushed opened the door to the gallery—nothing was ever locked in this building—and quickly made his way down to the front row. The work didn't take long.

He had been instructed in great detail about the placement of the guns. Tossing them inside the paneling in the balcony wasn't enough. They had to be placed in such a way so that someone could reach inside, pull them out, and be able to fire in one motion. If it took more than five seconds, that would be too long.

He placed the first gun, then the second, then the third, moving gingerly along the front row of the balcony, glancing around every now and then on the off chance that one of the two state troopers working in the governor's office might have gone for a walk and heard him.

The entire process took twenty minutes. When he was finished, he stuffed the now-empty bag deep inside the paneling, behind the last gun. Then he took off his gloves, stood up, and looked around. The sun was almost up now; a few early rays were coming through the skylight. He looked at his watch: six-forty. He had just enough time to go back downstairs, drive around the block, and park in front. In just a few minutes, he would walk in the front door to report for his seven o'clock shift.

Never once did he think about what he was doing or what he was putting into motion. He had been paid: that was what mattered. The politics of it didn't concern him one bit. They paid him in cash. As long as someone wanted to do that, he didn't ask questions.

It was six-fifty when he pulled away from State Circle. He still had time to get a cup of coffee before work.

▬ ▬

Ten minutes later, the phone rang in Bobby Kelleher's room at the Annapolis Marriott. He groaned, reached his arm out, and put the receiver to his ear without saying anything.

"Good morning, Mr. Kelleher," a disgustingly lively voice said in his ear. "It's seven o'clock and the temperature is thirty-three degrees. Have a nice day."

"Glub," Kelleher answered and buried his head in his pillow. He knew he had to wake up. He had a breakfast meeting at seven-thirty. Then he remembered what day it was and picked his head up, suddenly awake.

Barney Paulsen's speech was today. He was going to write a kick-ass front-page story. He rolled out of bed, walked to the sliding glass door, and pulled the curtains. The rising sun streamed in, forcing him to blink. He pushed the door open and walked out onto his balcony.

He looked down at Annapolis Harbor, which was slowly coming to life, and smiled. "What a beautiful day," he said aloud. "What a goddamn beautiful day this is going to be."

He shivered for a moment, then went inside to take his shower. This was one day he didn't mind starting early.

RUNNING MATES

CHAPTER 1

THE REPORTER

At the moment that he was interrupted, Bobby Kelleher had just about everything he could want in life.

He was seated in one of the comfortable high-backed chairs in the House of Delegates lounge, the morning sun slanting off the nearby window, providing brightness as he read the newspaper. The paper was spread out in his lap, open to the story about the previous night's Virginia–North Carolina basketball game in Charlottesville. Virginia had come from six points down to pull the game out in the last minute and Kelleher, like any proud alumnus, was savoring every word. He had just finished reading the game story and was about to stand up to pour himself a second cup of coffee when John Frece interrupted him.

Frece, the *Baltimore Sun*'s longtime political reporter, was standing in the doorway leading from the lounge into the House chamber. At first, Kelleher, wrapped up in the game story, didn't hear him.

"Kelleher! Hey, Kelleher! Earth to Kelleher!"

When he finally looked up from the newspaper, Frece was urgently waving him toward the chamber. "Get in here!" he hissed. "You don't want to miss this."

Kelleher glanced at his watch, wondering if he had somehow lost track of the time. He couldn't imagine what could be going on at ten-thirty on a Thursday morning that would cause Frece to come racing into the lounge. The first hour of each day's House of Delegates session was strictly routine, which was why Kelleher was in the lounge reading the paper and drinking his coffee.

It was his favorite time of day. Even if he had been out late the night before, his hangover—helped by the coffee—was usually gone or fading. He could enjoy the sports section, the style section, even sneak a glance at the comics, since he would have already gone through the political sections of all the other local newspapers to make sure no one had come up with a story he and his partner, Maureen McGuire, didn't know about.

On the mornings when he found one of those stories, there was no time to sit and read in the lounge. He had to rush out to work, to dig up *something,* since he and McGuire knew the first thing they would hear when they talked to their editors would be the seven most dreaded words in journalism: "Did you see the story in the . . . ?" The only possible response to that question was either to shoot the rival story down—which was usually impossible—or to have found another twist to the same story. If the *Sun* or *The Washington Post* or the Washington *Times* or the Annapolis *Capital* broke a story, Kelleher and McGuire knew about it by eight in the morning—at the latest—and would spend the next three hours chasing it down. It was important to be prepared for the seven dreaded words.

That didn't happen to Kelleher and McGuire very often. They had been *The Washington Herald*'s team in Annapolis for three years, and even though the *Sun* and the *Post* always had more people covering the legislature, Kelleher and McGuire didn't get beaten too often.

Once he had made certain there was nothing political he had to check out, Kelleher would head to breakfast, usually with a source, and then to the House lounge. He and McGuire had decided this year to split the two houses of the legislature. He had the House, she had the Senate. The House met in the morning while the Senate was in committee meetings; in the afternoon the proceedings were reversed.

The new setup was perfect for both reporters. Kelleher liked having 141 different delegates to choose from each day; working a room, or preferably a bar, was one of his great strengths. McGuire was better at developing sources slowly and methodically. The Senate, with just forty-seven members, most of them older and more cautious than the members of the House, suited her fine. Kelleher loved working the bar scene at night; McGuire despised it.

John Frece was the most low-key of the reporters covering Annapolis. He had been on the beat twelve years and was known among his colleagues for his astonishing ability to cut through the hieroglyphic-like language of any bill and figure out what it would actually mean if it ever became law. He was not a man given to hyperbole. If he thought something on the floor was worth seeing, Kelleher wasn't going to argue with him.

So, with a sigh of regret, he tossed the paper aside, drained the dregs of his coffee, and followed Frece through the double doors.

Even after six years in Annapolis, every time he saw it, Kelleher was struck by the hugeness of the House chamber. But this morning it looked no different to him than it did during any other midsession morning. Pages, in their bright-yellow jackets with the Maryland state crest on them, scurried up and down the aisles, delivering coffee or messages or copies of bills to delegates. A number of delegates stood in the far back corner, whispering to one another or sneaking a cigarette. The two galleries, one directly overhead, the other at the back of the chamber, were almost full.

Speaker Fred Weiland was about twenty feet to the left of the double doors on the podium, dressed, as always, in a conservative blue suit and red-striped tie. Kelleher was firmly convinced that Weiland had been born in that same outfit. The State House media always sat to the right of the podium, facing the delegates just as Weiland did. The difference was that Weiland stood several feet above everyone else, wielding a gavel. The members of the media had to wedge themselves into small wooden school desks, designed, Kelleher was certain, to make them feel as uncomfortable, physically and psychologically, as possible.

Kelleher never sat at the school desks. Instead, he used the railing that separated the media from the podium, always sitting on it with his head resting against the wall. This galled Weiland, a conservative Democrat from the Eastern Shore who had no use whatsoever for the media. At one point, shortly after he had been elected speaker, he had ordered the state troopers who handled security in the legislature to keep Kelleher off the railing. They had done so—apologetically—until Tom Kenworthy of *The Washington Post* had mentioned the railing ban in a column note as an example of how petty Weiland could be. Embarrassed, Weiland claimed that he knew nothing about the ban and Kelleher was promptly restored to his unusual seat.

Kelleher had the unpleasant suspicion that if he were to spend too many more years dealing with issues as monumental as whether or not he could sit on a railing, he was going to lose his mind. Now, rather than push his way through the reporters at the school desks, he stood in the corner with Frece.

"So what's the big deal?" he asked.

"Just watch," Frece said. "And remember, you owe me dinner."

Weiland had just recognized Wendell Hoxledeer, the resident House gadfly. Every legislative body in America had a gadfly, but no one could play the role quite like Hoxledeer. He had run for office seven times in three different Maryland counties, running three times as a Democrat, three times as a Republican, and once as a Libertarian. Somehow, two years earlier, he had gotten himself elected as a Democrat out of Anne Arundel County. Already, the local Democratic party was raising money to ensure that it would rid itself of Hoxledeer in next year's elections.

"You brought me in here to listen to *Hoxledeer*?" Kelleher said, looking at Frece incredulously. He was beginning to suspect a prank.

Frece didn't answer. Instead, he handed Kelleher a copy of a bill proposal. House Bill No. 321 was titled, "A bill to make the piano the official musical instrument of the state of Maryland."

Kelleher giggled. Typical Hoxledeer. But weirdo bills, especially Hoxledeer weirdo bills, did not usually get Frece's attention. A year ago, the House and Senate leadership had gotten together and decided to pass a Hoxledeer resolution to try to get him to stop screaming that there was a leadership conspiracy against him. Resolutions were harmless things anyway. Unlike a bill, which created law, they were merely statements made by the legislature.

Most resolutions were congratulatory: "The House of Delegates congratulates the cheerleading squad of Chestertown High School for its participation in the national cheerleading finals," or "The Senate of Maryland sends its sincere best wishes to former Senator Joe Smith in his new endeavor as owner/operator of Joe Smith's Fine-dining Deli and Disco."

Hundreds of resolutions offering best wishes or condolences or congratulations were whisked through the House and Senate each year, all of them passed unanimously and extremely quickly. There were also resolutions deploring wars and bombings and kidnappings and earthquakes. The Maryland Legislature was second to none when it came to deploring death, deprivation, and disaster—natural or otherwise.

Hoxledeer had played football at the Naval Academy for a year before being expelled for cheating on an exam. Kelleher's favorite of Hoxledeer's many idiotic resolutions had been one that "strongly urged" the athletic departments at the Naval Academy and the University of Maryland to settle the differences that had ended their football rivalry almost thirty years before and begin playing again. The leadership figured, why not? and had passed the resolution—with forty-seven no votes in the House by delegates who refused ever to vote yes on *anything* Hoxledeer proposed.

Now Hoxledeer wanted to make the piano the official musical instrument of Maryland. Kelleher read the bill proposal until he reached the line that said, "Whereas it is an accepted fact around the world that the piano makes the most beautiful music of any instrument ever invented . . ."

Clearly, Hoxledeer had never heard the Virginia pep band play "Auld Lang Syne"—sans piano. Still baffled, he handed the bill back to Frece. "It might be worth a sentence," he said. "But dinner? No way."

Frece laughed. "Come on, Kelleher, think for a second. You did the same Hoxledeer profile we all did two years ago."

Not quite the same. Kelleher's profile had been the only one Hoxledeer had attacked, in a speech on the floor urging his fellow members "to boycott the vicious and malicious reporter from *The Washington Herald*." He had then ripped up a copy of the *Herald* and held up a letter to the editor, canceling his subscription. Naturally, the attack had made Kelleher a hero for a day. He couldn't really blame Hoxledeer, though. His lead on the piece had been, "When Wendell Hoxledeer speaks, nobody listens."

Kelleher smiled, thinking back on the story. Then it hit him. "His wife," he said, snapping his fingers. "His wife's a piano teacher!"

"The brain hasn't gone completely dead yet," Frece said, nodding approval. "Dinner at Middleton's."

"Riordan's," Kelleher said. Middleton's was considerably more expensive. "If they pass the stupid thing, it's worth Middleton's."

Frece tipping off Kelleher to a story like this one was not uncommon. The Annapolis reporters were intensely competitive when it came to breaking real news stories, but on something cutesy or funny, a story that might be worth ten or twelve inches in the newspaper, they generally traded with one another.

With 188 legislators to cover, not to mention the governor, his cabinet, and the dozens of lobbyists and activist groups, no paper—even the *Sun*,

which sent six reporters to the session—could catch everything. So if you helped a friend out on Tuesday, the odds were the tables would be turned by Thursday.

Hoxledeer was speaking now, standing at his desk near the back of the chamber, holding his microphone too close to his mouth as always, his words bouncing off the walls.

"And so I say to you, Mr. Speaker, this bill is strictly a matter of law and nothing else. The majority leader's attempt to place it in his own committee is yet another example of his mean-spirited approach to any legislation I propose. . . ."

"One moment, sir," Weiland said, breaking in. Hoxledeer paused in mid-tirade. "The gentleman is fully aware of the rules of this body, and he knows the chair will not, under any circumstances, tolerate derogatory comments made by one member about another. I would remind the gentleman of this, as I have done in the past."

Weiland had decided that to call Majority Leader Roger Foulkes "mean-spirited" was derogatory. Kelleher thought "imbecilic wimp" might be more fitting, but he wasn't the presiding officer. *Robert's Rules of Order* allowed any presiding officer plenty of latitude, and Weiland was using it. If someone called Foulkes—or even Hoxledeer, for that matter—frivolous or silly or an imbecilic wimp, Weiland could let it ride so long as no name was mentioned. *Robert's* was very firm on that subject: no member was to refer to another by his actual name during any kind of debate.

"Does this mean the chairman will do the same for me when derogatory comments are made by other members of this House?" Hoxledeer asked.

"It does, sir," Weiland answered, a note of anger creeping into his voice. "Just as it has always done in the past, regardless of the nature of the gentleman's speech."

That was cutting it pretty close, derogatory comment–wise, but Weiland had the gavel. Hoxledeer got the message.

"I beg your pardon, Mr. Speaker," he said. "May I continue?"

"Please do, sir," Weiland said, formal as ever.

Hoxledeer's argument was logical but pointless. Foulkes was recommending that the piano bill be placed in his committee—Economic Matters. That way, he could bury it there so it wouldn't even come up for a public hearing. The last thing Foulkes wanted was to waste a half day of a committee's time on a parade of piano teachers testifying to the wonders of ebony and ivory. Hoxledeer wanted the bill placed in his own com-

mittee, Constitutional and Administrative Law. That way he might be able to trade a couple of votes with other committee members and at least get the bill to a hearing.

Foulkes knew that was exactly what Hoxledeer was thinking and he was about to recommend it be sent to Economic Matters when it came up for first reading. Every bill introduced in either the House or the Senate had to go through three "readings" before it could be passed. First reading simply announced its existence. It was then referred to a committee, where it either died or was passed. It would then come back to the floor for second reading. Amendments might be tacked on but second reading was essentially confirmation that the committee had passed the bill. Third reading was when the real vote took place, one that was recorded on the two electronic boards that dominated the side walls of the chamber.

If the bill passed one house, it then went to the other, where it went through the same process. If the Senate amended a House bill (or vice versa) it then had to go to a conference committee of House and Senate members so they could agree on final language and then send it back to each for one final vote. Often, conference committees were used to kill bills during the final days of the ninety-day legislative session. That was way down the road from here, though. This was day forty-four of the session, a routine first reading of a meaningless bill that would never get out of committee.

Fred Weiland didn't want the House bogging down for an entire morning on a Hoxledeer bill, especially since a large chunk of the afternoon was going to be wasted—in his view—by Governor Barnard A. Paulsen's annual midsession address to the legislature. He glanced at his watch as Hoxledeer droned on, not wanting to break decorum by interrupting but not wanting this to drag on too long either.

Hoxledeer was winding up. "And so, in closing"—a mock cheer went up from some corners; Weiland gaveled for quiet—"let me say this to my colleagues: do not judge this bill on merit now. Judge it only on *where* it should be judged. Clearly, that place is in Constitutional and Administrative Law, not Economic Matters. Mr. Speaker, fellow members, I thank you."

He sat down as a few people in the gallery clapped. Kelleher peered up, wondering if Hoxledeer's wife was present. There was a TV light shining toward the podium and he couldn't make out any faces.

"Clerk will read the bill," Weiland said.

"House Bill number three twenty-one," the clerk said tonelessly.

"Mr. Speaker."

"Chair recognizes the majority leader."

Foulkes, standing at his seat in the front row, had tiny beads of sweat on his balding forehead. It was warm for February outside, about fifty degrees. But Foulkes always sweated, especially if he sensed a TV camera lurking. "Mr. Speaker," he said, "recommend HB three twenty-one be referred to Economic Matters."

"All in favor?" Weiland asked.

A chorus of ayes responded.

"Opposed?"

One loud nay rang out from the back of the chamber. Hoxledeer. Of course.

"The ayes have it," Weiland said. "HB three twenty-one is referred . . ."

"Mr. Speaker."

Weiland glared at Hoxledeer, who was on his feet again.

"Chair recognizes the bill's proposer," he said.

"Request a roll-call vote, Mr. Speaker."

A loud groan went up. No one *ever* requested a roll call on a bill referral. No one except Hoxledeer.

"Request is denied," Weiland said firmly. "The voice vote was quite clear and quite one-sided. The chair will *not* waste any more of the House's valuable time with these antics, sir. Bill three twenty-one is referred to . . ."

"Mr. Speaker."

Weiland froze at the sound of another interruption, not believing that the ice in his voice had gone unnoticed. Only this time it wasn't Hoxledeer. Not by a long shot. It was James Immel, the chairman of the Ways and Means Committee, one of the two or three most respected members of the House.

Like Hoxledeer, Immel was from Anne Arundel County. The similarities ended there. When Big Jim Immel spoke, *everybody* listened. He had been in the legislature twenty-six years—the last fourteen as Ways and Means chairman. Weiland was truly puzzled when he looked out to the floor and found that it was Immel on his feet.

"Um, yes, I mean, *yes,* the chair recognizes the chairman of Ways and Means?" he said, a large question mark in his voice.

"What the hell is *this*?" Kelleher whispered to Frece.

Frece didn't answer. As soon as Immel stood up, the reporter had pulled out his notebook. Kelleher did the same—just in case.

"Thank you, Mr. Speaker," Immel said, his basso voice even lower, it seemed, than usual. "Mr. Speaker, there is no need for me to chronicle here my feelings or the feelings of my entire local delegation about the antics of this bill's proposer." He was right on the edge of a derogatory comment, but Weiland wasn't about to stop him.

"I would say the odds of this bill ever reaching this floor again are about as good as my chances of playing the piano some day soon in Carnegie Hall." No one even snickered. Immel continued. "But the fact is, this bill has nothing at all to do with economics. It is strictly a matter of *law*, nothing else. Silly law, perhaps, but that is what the committee it is assigned to must judge and I have no doubt *will* judge. But it *is* a matter of law, and while I certainly sympathize with the majority leader's wishes to conduct the business of this body as efficiently as possible, I must also say that I think for us to begin to subvert the process of the constitution for any reason, no matter how legitimate, cheapens all of us and cheapens this body, which we all hold so dear.

"I would, therefore, with all due respect to everyone here, especially my good friend the majority leader, request a reconsideration of where this bill should be assigned. Thank you, Mr. Speaker."

The place was completely silent as he sat down. Even the pages had stopped their scurrying. Foulkes stood rooted to the spot at his desk, microphone in front of his mouth, staring at Immel. His face was pale. Now he was really sweating.

"Mr. Speaker," he said, voice quavering slightly. "In light of the comments made by the chairman of Ways and Means, I would like to withdraw my recommendation and ask that HB three twenty-one be referred instead to Constitutional and Administrative Law."

"All in favor?" Weiland asked, his voice quieter than normal.

"*Aye!*"

"Opposed?"

Not a sound. "Bill is referred to con-ad law," Weiland said. "Clerk will read the next bill."

"Treaty of Paris," Frece hissed at Kelleher, the name of the best restaurant in Annapolis. He was beaming. So was Kelleher. The other reporters had barely moved. To them, Big Jim Immel essentially overruling the majority leader in front of the entire House of Delegates was no big deal. After all, no legislation had been passed or killed. To Kelleher and Frece, though, this was the kind of story that made covering politics worthwhile. It was an example of how unpredictable the process could be, how the routine could become the writable in a matter of moments. Kelleher had been looking for a peg to write a profile of Immel all session; now, out of the blue he had it, courtesy of Wendell Hoxledeer.

Tom Kenworthy, *The Washington Post*'s bureau chief and Kelleher's drinking partner on too many nights, walked over with a huge grin on his face. "So what do you wanna bet my desk has no clue why this is a good story?" he asked.

Kelleher shrugged. "I'm not even going to bother," he said. "With Paulsen's speech this afternoon, I couldn't get six inches out of this today. But I can use it later. Even if I *never* use it, seeing Immel cut Foulkes off at the knees made my day."

"Which might be a story in itself," Kenworthy said. "Might be something up between those two."

Frece shook his head. "Nah, no way. Immel's BS meter just went off. It's not like it was Myron Cutler trying to shove a bill down his throat."

Kelleher had to agree with that one. Senate President Myron Cutler was the only person in the legislature who could cause Immel to lose his cool. Cutler was as conservative as Immel was liberal; he had fought against every piece of civil rights—not to mention women's rights, gay rights, *any* rights—legislation introduced during his thirty years in the legislature. He had been asked in the mid-eighties by another senator, during a floor debate on abortion funding, how he would react if his own daughter's life were endangered by a pregnancy and she could not afford a life-saving abortion.

"That is a foolish question, Senator," Cutler had sneered, "because my daughter is neither a poor Negress nor some white trash and therefore would not be in such a situation."

Cutler's presence in the Senate as presiding officer was another reason Kelleher was happy to be covering the House. He had learned long ago that he could both like and respect people whose political views were different from his own; he had little trouble being fair even to those legislators whose politics he considered Neanderthal. Cutler was different, however. Not only were his politics reprehensible, he was sanctimonious, condescending, and impossible to talk to. The only person Kelleher had ever met who was able to charm Cutler was Maureen McGuire. He suspected that she reminded him of his daughter, which was ironic since Maureen's politics were as far left as Cutler's were right. Cutler was either unaware of that or chose to ignore it. As a result, the *Herald* had a considerable advantage in the Senate; Maureen was the only Annapolis reporter with whom Cutler had so much as a civil relationship.

Thinking about Cutler always made Kelleher's stomach turn a little—which reminded him that it was almost time for lunch. "Well, guys, I'd like to continue this, but I've got to meet someone for lunch," he said to Frece and Kenworthy.

"Sweet Susan?" Kenworthy asked, smiling wickedly.

"No, asshole, strictly business," he said. But he blushed anyway.

Susan Sanders was the new Annapolis reporter for Channel 2 in Baltimore, the kind of blond-haired, blue-eyed TV type that made Kelleher weak kneed and Maureen nauseated. Kelleher had been slowly working his way up to asking her out. He hadn't quite gotten there yet, partly because every time she came near him, Maureen started hissing "bimbo-alert, bimbo-alert."

Kelleher had bantered with her often enough that he was convinced Susan wasn't nearly as stupid as Maureen insisted she was. Either that or he had talked himself into thinking it. He wasn't really sure. The only thing Kelleher did know was that one way or another, he was going to find out soon.

CHAPTER 2

THE SPEECH

*L*unch *was* strictly business. Governor Barney Paulsen was giving his midsession state-of-the-state speech that afternoon. The speech was really nothing more than a public relations ploy by Paulsen and his staff to put budget pressure on the legislature. This was a key year for Paulsen. He would be up for reelection in another eighteen months and this session— his third—was the one in which he needed to put his stamp on something, create an identity for himself.

Largely because of the presence of Meredith Gordy as his lieutenant governor, Paulsen had become known as a women's rights governor. He had spent his first two years keeping the status quo on women's issues in place, recognizing the conservative nature of the legislature, especially with Cutler and Weiland as Senate president and House speaker. Now, though, he was making his move: he had almost doubled the money for abortion funding in his budget; he was proposing much stricter date rape laws, and he was proposing a new cabinet position for someone who would deal strictly with women's issues. Paulsen had done a lot of pre-session vote counting before unveiling this package and thought he could push through most of it. But it was all going to come down to the wire. Giving the legislature a public nudge with a midsession address seemed like a smart idea.

That was exactly the story Kelleher was planning to write this evening.

Rather than simply report what Paulsen said to the legislature—there wouldn't be any surprises there—he wanted to write a story explaining exactly how the speech had been put together, who had been consulted, what had been left out and why, and exactly what the governor hoped to accomplish.

At _The Washington Herald_ this was known as a "Kelleher process piece." Kelleher was fascinated with the process of government and politics. The product didn't really matter to him that much—the so-called who-what-when-where of journalism. He was interested almost exclusively in the _why_. The problem was that _why_ rarely made the front page; who-what-when-where did. Still, Kelleher was stubborn enough to keep trying to produce what interested him—and keep hoping that would get him noticed by the powers that be at the paper.

Kelleher had covered Annapolis for the _Herald_ for six years. He had turned thirty the previous November and had vowed to make this his last legislative session. He knew it was time to move on. His hope was that the _Herald_ would promote him to the national staff for the national elections coming up the following year.

He was realistic enough to understand that might not happen, though. Kelleher was known at the _Herald_ as an excellent reporter and a solid, clean writer. But he was hotheaded, sometimes _too_ passionate about what he was doing. He was famous for telling editors, if they didn't see a story as clearly as he did, that they didn't know what the hell they were doing. By contrast, his partner, Maureen McGuire, played the editors like a violin. Kelleher had learned a lot from watching her in action. She had become his middleman, dealing with the desk as often as possible. That seemed to cut down on his fighting time.

McGuire, everyone agreed, was a rising star. Kelleher already knew from friends at the paper that she was ticketed for the national staff as soon as the session was over. That was fine with him. McGuire deserved to move up. She was good.

But so was he. And, if truth be told, if she moved up and he got left behind, he wouldn't be able to deal with it. He would have to leave, a thought he dreaded more and more as the legislature moved swiftly from the ecstatic opening days in January, days that were one party after another, into the midsession doldrums of February, when bills began to snake their way through committees without making any real news—yet.

When the midsession mark was reached on Friday—the forty-fifth day—things would begin to heat up. The Paulsen process piece, which Kelleher believed would show everyone that he was better plugged into the administration than any reporter in town, would be, Kelleher hoped, the beginning of a hot streak for him. Yet, as he walked from the State House around Church Circle toward Main Street, he couldn't help but have doubts.

It was a beautiful day and Kelleher was again struck by his weakness for this place and for many of the people who lived The Life every winter when the legislature met. To Kelleher, Annapolis was Oz, a world away from downtown Washington and the suburbs that tracked their way around the Beltway. Even now, after six years, he always felt a tingle when he steered his car off Route 50 at the Rowe Boulevard exit and saw the State House dome gleaming in the distance. It was a two-mile drive to the front steps of the State House, past the Naval Academy's football stadium, the Maryland Court of Appeals, and, finally, the House and Senate office buildings. Each time he made that drive, he felt as if he were returning home.

As he pulled up to the stop sign in front of the State House, with the Governor's Mansion looming on his right, Kelleher always felt comfortable. He knew his way around all these buildings; he was, in some sense, a part of it all. He still loved his mornings in the House of Delegates lounge, the legislators milling around, the call to the floor by the speaker, even the saying of the prayer and the passage of the silly resolutions. Kelleher would sit in his chair, sip his coffee, read his newspapers, and feel as if all was right with the world.

What fascinated him about the legislative process was not the laws but the people who made them. Part-time legislatures, he was convinced, were the last of America's melting pots. There were 141 delegates— ninety-eight men and forty-three women; 106 whites, thirty-two blacks, and three Hispanics. There were seventy-three lawyers; twenty-four businessmen/women; nineteen teachers; nine doctors (three of them veterinarians); four dentists; three morticians (two of them brothers); two bar owners; two unemployed heirs to fortunes; two housewives and one househusband; one fireman; one ex-cop.

The Senate's forty-seven members, older and more established in general, weren't as interesting: there were only five women in the Senate and just seven blacks. Thirty of the forty-seven senators were lawyers. Even so, there were two men who had been to jail, one of whom, minority whip

Jon Leonow, was considered the most honest man in the legislature. There were, by Kelleher's unofficial count, nine gay delegates and four gay senators, although none had gone public about their sexuality. Maryland wasn't exactly San Francisco when it came to enlightenment on the subject of homosexuality.

As different as they were—ranging in age from twenty-two to seventy-nine—they all came to Annapolis as dreamers. The majority of them believed they had been elected to make the world a better place and that their effect on the legislature would be swift and complete. A few—very few—actually became "players" in the Annapolis game. Most were quickly buried on committees dredging through bills that didn't matter while learning that to vote against the leadership in either house was virtually to ensure their own failure.

All of them learned that to move along, they had to play along. Tim Maloney, who had come to Annapolis at the age of twenty-two, elected during an anti-machine backlash in Prince Georges County, had explained it best to Kelleher years ago: "You drive down Rowe Boulevard that first day thinking you're going to make history," he said. "You learn very quickly that history has gotten along quite nicely without you for more than two hundred years down here."

Maloney was now in his fourth term and, as chairman of the Prince Georges delegation, he was part of the machine.

To some degree, so was Kelleher, though he would deny it on his deathbed. The reporters who came to Annapolis were not all that different from the legislators. They arrived dreaming of The Big Hit, the story that would make them stars and leave a legacy. All of them thought they knew just where The Big Hit was—the sleazy committee, the chairman taking payoffs, the lobbyist buying votes. And then they found out that nothing was quite so blatant, that the Annapolis Marriott was never going to be mistaken for the Watergate, and that reporters who made it too clear they were searching for The Big Hit were quickly frozen out, not only by sources but by other reporters.

Play along to move along. Certainly there was an adversarial relationship between the Annapolis press and those in power. Whenever any controversy broke out, whoever was in the middle of it—the governor and his staff or someone in the legislature—always blamed it on an overzealous press. More often, though, the only real tension between the press and the legislators took place during the annual basketball game.

Kelleher knew he was guilty of liking a lot of these people. Perhaps that was why he had never come up with The Big Hit—although he liked to believe it was because it just wasn't there to come up with. After all, McGuire, Frece, Kenworthy, and the rest of his colleagues, many of them top-notch reporters, hadn't found it either. And yet, the notion that The Big Hit might turn up if he drank less with the legislators and spent more time in committee meetings gnawed at him.

The best reporter Kelleher had ever known was David Jackson. He had been Kelleher's partner and mentor when he first arrived in Annapolis. Technically, Jackson had never come up with The Big Hit. But the total body of his work was pretty damn close.

David Jackson was a legendary figure in Annapolis. He smoked at least a hundred cigarettes a day and he knew everyone. When Jackson walked into a committee room, chairmen had been known to recess to consult with their colleagues about what it could be that had brought Jackson in to listen. His profiles were often devastating and always brutally accurate. He had sources everywhere. Nothing happened in Annapolis without Jackson knowing it.

Kelleher, who after graduating from college had spent two years at the Richmond *Times-Dispatch* covering the Virginia legislature and a year at the *Herald* as a police reporter, had never met anyone like Jackson. He hung on his every word. "Remember one thing," Jackson had told him. "Never act important. If you do, you scare people and they won't tell you things. Even now, when these guys *know* I'm gonna nail 'em, they talk to me. It's because I don't come off as threatening."

Jackson owned, as far as anyone could tell, one sports coat and one pair of shoes. He always looked like he hadn't slept for a week and was about to fall asleep. A lot of people made fun of him, until they read his stuff. Then, the laughter stopped. One legislator had summed up Jackson simply: "David is a great writer," he said, "until he writes something about *you.*"

Jackson could cut through the BS of the State House faster than anyone, but he also had a light touch, the ability to find humor in a story or situation. He never killed anyone with a hammer. Instead, he used velvet gloves. But the victim was just as dead when Jackson was finished. He was in Moscow now, writing stories that would no doubt win him a Pulitzer Prize someday. Five years after he left Annapolis, it seemed that a day didn't go by without someone beginning a sentence by saying, "Remember that story Jackson wrote about . . ."

Kelleher knew he was a long way from that status. He was good at what he did. He had plenty of sources and he and Maureen almost never got scooped. His profiles and features were solid but not memorable. Too soft or too hard. He still hadn't learned how to kill someone without bludgeoning them. His approach was too black-and-white.

But, slowly, Kelleher was learning how to shade things in gray. As much as he admired Immel, he knew that Big Jim was capable of being a bully. He was friends with Maloney but understood that Maloney had long ago traded in his dreams for the comfort of being part of the establishment.

He reminded himself often of David Jackson's parting words to him as he left Annapolis for the national staff: "If you understand that these people aren't your friends, you'll do well," he had said. "There isn't a politician born who won't lie to you at some point. What you have to figure out is *when* they're lying and, most important, *why* they're lying."

Annapolis was a small town where big things happened. It had the Naval Academy, the State House, and the harbor. That was about it—but little else was needed. During the session, the newspaper put Kelleher and McGuire up in the Annapolis Marriott, which was right on the harbor. Every morning, Kelleher would walk out on his balcony, look out toward the Chesapeake Bay Bridge, and think how lucky he was to work in such a scenic place. At night, after filing for first edition, he would go for a run at the Naval Academy. Running out by the seawall, he would think about how much he would miss these times.

Now, as he cut across Main Street toward The Maryland Inn, he tried repeating his Jackson-mantra about politicians and lies. But it wasn't working. Waiting for him in the hotel's Treaty of Paris restaurant was Alan Sims, Barney Paulsen's chief of staff. If Sims had ever lied to him, Kelleher hadn't caught him. He had known Sims for six years, first as a senator from Prince Georges County and now as Paulsen's man.

In an administration symbolized, Kelleher thought, by the rantings and ravings of Press Secretary Regis (Rocky) Altmann, Sims was not only a voice of reason, he was a voice often willing to tell Kelleher what the hell was going on. Rocky Altmann had been Paulsen's press secretary while Paulsen was the state attorney general. He was an ex-radio guy, someone who thought good reporting meant getting a solid forty-five-second cut from anyone who was available. Real reporting scared and frustrated Altmann, and he did everything he could to shield Paulsen from the print media.

For his part, Barney Paulsen was the type of easygoing guy who was usually willing to answer a question if asked but just as happy not to answer if Altmann told him to take that route. Most of the administration took its cue from Altmann, who particularly despised leaks. No one wanted to risk his considerable wrath, which meant information was always hard to come by.

Altmann had once tried to cut off media access to the second floor of the State House, where the governor, lieutenant governor, and their staffs had their offices. A storm of protest put an end to that idea but Altmann had won at least part of the battle by insisting that, for security purposes, no member of the media could enter the hallway leading to the governor's conference room and his suite of offices unless he had an appointment.

Fortunately, Alan Sims's office was on the far side of the floor, down the hall from the lieutenant governor's office. Often, late in the afternoon, when he wasn't on deadline, Kelleher would wander down there. Sims would pull a couple of beers out of the refrigerator he kept in a corner and they would talk—mostly on background—about what was going on.

Sims knew that Altmann considered him the primary leaker in the administration but he didn't much care. He was the administration's link to the Washington-area legislators. He knew it and they knew it and if Rocky Altmann didn't like it, that was too damn bad. Even so, Kelleher sensed that although Sims liked Paulsen, he had tired of the bunker mentality and was looking to make some kind of move before next year's elections.

That wasn't what this lunch was about, though. Kelleher wanted Sims to fill him in on the machinations and infighting that had gone on leading up to Paulsen's speech. He would use that background as a foundation for his process story. McGuire would write the lead on the speech itself. She was guaranteed a spot on page one. Kelleher's story was not. Still, it was the story he wanted to write.

He bounced down the steps from the hotel lobby to the basement, where the restaurant was located. Treaty of Paris was Kelleher's favorite restaurant in Annapolis. Like the hotel itself, it reeked of history and times past. And the food was excellent.

Mike Blauser, the maître d', was waiting at the bottom of the steps. There were twenty people waiting for tables but that wasn't a problem for Kelleher. Mike Blauser had ridden the bench as a basketball player at Maryland the same way and at the same time Kelleher had ridden the bench at Virginia. When people asked if they had played against each other, they would both shake their heads and say, "No, but we sure glared an awful lot."

Their nonplaying days bonded them. Whenever Maryland and Virginia played, Kelleher and Blauser made the same bet: if Virginia won, Kelleher's next dinner at Treaty of Paris was on the house. If Maryland won, he had to order the most expensive wine on the menu. Kelleher figured it was a no-lose deal. The teams were playing in Charlottesville on Sunday afternoon.

"You driving down Sunday?" he asked Blauser as they walked to the table where Alan Sims was waiting.

"Can't," Blauser said. "My son's turning five. Our bet's on though, right?"

"Oh, yeah. Even though you guys should beat us both games this year."

"Come on! When was the last time that happened?"

"Two years ago."

"Oh, yeah. I forgot."

"I haven't. Getting that wine by on my expenses was tough."

Sims looked up from a menu as they approached. "Big stuff, huh, guys? Maryland–UVA?"

"Big as it gets, Alan," Kelleher said, sitting down. "Not like this silly speech stuff."

Blauser disappeared to get Kelleher a Perrier. He had put on five pounds since the session started. He wasn't about to stop drinking at night, but he figured he could knock off the Cokes during the day. At six-one, 185, Kelleher was only ten pounds heavier than he had been when he had "played" basketball in college. But he didn't want to get any heavier.

"Well, I want to thank you for a miserable morning," Sims said.

"What did I do now?" Kelleher demanded.

"That stuff in your story about Paulsen saying 'er-um' thirty-seven times in his January speech. Rocky went ballistic."

" 'Rocky goes ballistic—film at eleven.' Tell me something new."

"Yeah, but then he found out I was having lunch with you and started into his 'Why give that cocksucker anything?' speech."

Kelleher grinned. He always felt warmed knowing that Rocky Altmann spent time bouncing off walls calling him a cocksucker.

"Look, Bobby, make me a deal. I tell you this stuff and you don't count Barney's 'er-ums' today—at least not in print."

"Done," Kelleher said. That was easy. Counting "er-ums" again would be redundant.

By the time lunch was over, Kelleher was brimming with anticipation. Alan Sims had given him more than simple background; he had given him a real story. Paulsen had shown an advance copy of his speech to Cutler and Weiland. He was throwing down the gauntlet, ending the sort of mating dance that the governor and legislature went through during the first half of every session. Paulsen wanted the so-called "women's" package passed and he was threatening to cut off programs that were important to the two legislators—like building new prisons—if they played legislative games to slow the process down.

"Cutler and Weiland are off the wall," Sims said. "Cutler told Barney he was the most pussy-whipped politician he'd ever met."

"Did he have anyone in mind?" Kelleher said, loving the thought of Cutler being so upset.

"You know he did," Sims said. "In fact, Weiland wanted to know why they didn't just go across the hall and meet with Governor Gordy to save time."

"Can I use that?" Kelleher said, trying not to sound too eager.

Sims shrugged. "Sure. I really don't care if those two assholes guess that I'm the one who told you. Kyler will probably come charging in screaming at me, but that's okay. I enjoy our little shouting matches."

Andrea Kyler was Lieutenant Governor Meredith Gordy's administrative assistant. Like almost every other man in Annapolis, Kelleher had a wicked crush on her, at least in part because she was completely untouchable.

Gordy and Kyler were the real political stars in Annapolis at the moment. Gordy was thirty-four, a willowy blonde who had been number one in her class at both Harvard and Harvard Law School. While in law school, she had met and married Alvin Gordy, the only son of Alvin Gordy Sr., who had made millions producing and selling apples.

The newlyweds had moved to Washington and started their own law firm. The marriage and the law firm had lasted less than three years. Alvin Gordy Jr. wanted to become rich without touching his father's money. His wife thought they should take advantage of his father's financial status to run a law firm that concentrated on pro bono work: helping the homeless, the disenfranchised, the starving. Alvin Gordy moved back West to start his own firm while the divorce was being processed. Meredith Gordy stayed behind, living in their huge home in Potomac while continuing to build the law practice.

Seven years ago, she had been appointed to a seat in the House of Delegates when the Democratic Party had been looking for up-and-coming women. A year later, against the advice of all her friends, she had taken on four-term Senator Briggs Munson for the Senate seat in her district. Gordy not only beat Munson, she got more than 70 percent of the vote. She harped on his pro-life position, noting how out of step he was in the district. As a campaigner she was brilliant: good-looking, quick-witted, charming. If Meredith Gordy got within ten feet of you, you voted for her. It was as if she cast a spell.

Paulsen had recognized this when he ran for governor, so he courted her as his running mate. He was Baltimore; she was Washington. He was old-line Democrat; she was the party's summer storm, flashing across the horizon. He was fifty-four and pot-bellied; she was thirty-two and stunning. Gordy drove a hard bargain, though: Paulsen had to pledge at least three cabinet seats to women, he had to promise to support a package of women's rights legislation, and he had to agree that Andrea Kyler would work as a near equal with his own chief of staff in putting together the budget.

That last promise hadn't sat too well with Alan Sims when he learned of it after agreeing to be Paulsen's chief of staff. Working with Kyler was a little bit like spending your life on a high wire.

Andrea Kyler had been with Meredith Gordy since her early days in the House of Delegates. She had been running the Washington office of FFF—Females for Freedom—when Gordy was appointed, and had left that job to work for Gordy. FFF's main purpose was to identify women who could become significant office holders, help them get elected, and then help move them up the political ladder. But that wasn't all. Four years ago, just before she came to Annapolis to join up with Kelleher, Maureen McGuire had written a series of stories on FFF in which Jamelle Tourretta, the group's president, had admitted that one of FFF's tactics was to use attractive women to seduce male office holders, then use those affairs as blackmail to force the men either to come around on women's issues or to leave office. It was, quite literally, a fucking-sting.

"Is it an admirable tactic?" Jamelle Tourretta had said to McGuire. "Probably not. But if a guy is honorable, he won't get caught. We don't pick on single men, only married ones. And we don't entrap. We just put the opportunity out there, sort of like a piece of cheese, and see if the rats bite. A whole lot of them do.''

After McGuire's story, FFF had announced it would no longer use such tactics, but McGuire had told Kelleher she suspected it still did—just on a more selective basis. Andrea Kyler, he believed, had at one time been one of the seducers, and it was easy to see why the rats would jump at her. She was very tall, about five-ten, with jet-black hair and smooth, olive-toned skin. She had dark, almost black eyes that flashed like lightning when she was angry—which was often. Her disdain for almost everyone on the Annapolis scene was well documented, but she knew how to use the media when she wanted to. If Gordy wasn't available when a TV camera was around, Kyler was. Once, when Kelleher had asked her why she spoke to TV people who she knew didn't have the faintest idea what she and Gordy were about, Kyler smiled and said, "For exactly that reason, Kelleher. If they understood, they might ask intelligent questions. We don't need that to get our message across.''

Once, on a Monday night in Fran O'Brien's, after five large bourbons, Kelleher had asked Kyler if she wanted to dance. Kyler had looked at Kelleher and laughed.

"Maybe someday, Kelleher," she had answered. "But probably not anytime soon.''

The very fact that he had worked up the nerve to ask Kyler was the main subject of conversation among all the reporters for several days. Even McGuire, who disapproved of Kelleher's flirtations at Fran's, thought he had been rather brave. A lot of the male legislators and some of the reporters liked to claim that Kyler was gay, since she was so clearly uninterested in all of them.

Kelleher knew from McGuire that this wasn't true. In fact, according to McGuire, who had first met Kyler during her FFF research, she had been married in her early twenties and had been pregnant twice, only to lose both children to miscarriages. She had been divorced for a long while now but Kelleher thought it would be fascinating to meet the man who had once been married to her.

"Speaking of Gordy," Kelleher said as Sims was paying the check (it was his turn), "what's the word? Is she going to take Barney on next year?''

Sims shook his head. "I really don't think so. I think she's got her eye on Capitol Hill, the Senate. You know, deep down I think she really kind of likes Barney.''

"She probably does," Kelleher said. "Just like we all do. He's not a bad guy, just a boring one."

"Yeah, well, tell that to Cutler and Weiland."

Kelleher laughed. "Not my problem."

"Not mine either," Sims said. "Not for long, anyway."

Kelleher's eyebrows went up. "What's that mean?"

"Nothing, really."

"Come on, Alan."

Sims sighed. "Off the record? I mean *really* off the record? Between us? As friends?"

Kelleher should have said no, absolutely not, I'll find out from someone else. But Sims had just given him a terrific story and, to be honest, any decision he had made about his own political future wasn't that important, at least not right now. He could get him to put it on the record later.

"Off the record, if you promise to tell me for print first," he said.

"You got it," Sims said. He leaned forward and whispered. "I'm running for Congress next year. Whitson's seat. He's going after the Senate. I've been up here eighteen years—I'll be fifty next month—and it's time to make a move."

"You won't miss it?" Kelleher said, a little bit stunned.

"I'll miss you," Alan Sims said, only half joking.

Kelleher stood up. "Maybe," he said, not joking at all, "I'll get to go with you."

He knew Sims was right. The time to leave Oz was very near.

CHAPTER 3

BARNEY PAULSEN

After lunch with Sims, Kelleher made a brief stop at the *Herald*'s office to see if Maureen McGuire was around. She had spent the morning, as she always did, poking around the Senate's five committees.

Kelleher enjoyed working with McGuire. It meant he spent a lot of time listening to the male legislators' crude one-liners about her. McGuire looked like the clean-cut Irish-Catholic girl everybody wanted to date in high school. Kelleher might have wanted to date her too, if she hadn't been his partner and his best friend. Anytime he found himself thinking romantically about her he stopped himself—why ruin a beautiful relationship?

Since a lot of the legislators didn't take their marriages very seriously, they saw no reason for Maureen McGuire—or any other attractive woman—not to be a target. So Maureen spent a lot of time fending off the wolves, one of the reasons why she hated going into Fran's at night. She understood that working the pols' watering hole was part of the job but, unlike Kelleher, it was a part she despised.

The office was empty when Kelleher walked in but the telephone message light was on. Two messages: one to call his editor, Jane Kryton, to talk about his story; the other from McGuire, asking that he bring her running shoes over to the State House with him. She had gone to lunch with a lobbyist at The Lafayette, one of Main Street's chic restaurants, but didn't want to spend the afternoon in a dress and heels.

Kelleher called Kryton back to make sure he still had the thirty-five inches he had been promised for his process piece, especially now that Sims had given him so much good background.

"I'm sorry, Bobby, it's a tight paper," Jane Kryton said. "I'm trying to get you thirty."

"What do you mean, *trying?*" Kelleher said, dismayed as always by the machinations of his editors. "What do they want to give me?"

"Quintal put it down on the budget for sixteen to twenty."

Kelleher could feel blood rushing to his temples. Tony Quintal was the deputy metro editor and Kelleher's number one newsroom nemesis. It was a feud that dated back to Quintal's outrage when Kelleher had been sent to Annapolis over him six years ago. Back then, Quintal had been at the paper nine years; Kelleher one. He went on the desk shortly after that and had somehow now become the number two person on the metro staff.

"Since when does Quintal decide lengths for the Maryland staff?" he asked, trying to stay calm.

"Look, Bobby, I had it down for thirty-five, I had it down to be pitched for page one. He picked up the budget, looked at it, and said, 'Why do we need more than sixteen inches for this sidebar?' I explained to him that it wasn't a sidebar. He crossed out thirty-five and wrote sixteen to twenty."

"You talk to Anthony about it?"

Tom Anthony was the metro editor. "Not yet, but I will before the three o'clock meeting. I promise."

Kelleher sighed. McGuire had coached him to stay calm in these situations and he knew that yelling at Kryton wouldn't do any good. "Okay," he said. "I'll call you right after the speech. Take care of me, Jane. Okay?"

"I'll do the best I can, Bobby."

He hung up. In fifteen minutes he had gone from chirping at the birds as he walked back from The Maryland Inn to feeling sick to his stomach. He picked up McGuire's running shoes and headed back to the State House. The *Herald*'s office was a half block off State Circle, a five-minute walk straight uphill to the back door of the State House. Unlike before, when he had looked all around and marveled at the beauty of the town, Kelleher walked with his head down, seeing nothing. He pulled the door open and walked into the huge main lobby. It was crammed with people, their voices echoing off the high ceilings and walls.

In the middle of the lobby were the marble steps leading to the second floor. Kelleher paused there to see if Maureen was around anywhere. He was five minutes early. Looking up, he spotted her at the top of the steps talking to Andrea Kyler. He made a mental note to ask her if Kyler had said anything about Gordy's role in writing the speech. He waited a couple of minutes, thought about walking up the steps to interrupt; decided against it. Kyler was talking very animatedly and Kelleher didn't want to stop her if Maureen had her on a roll.

When they finally turned away from each other, Maureen bounded down the steps. She had already changed into her pants, which looked funny with high heels. "I didn't know you were already here," she said, looking surprised to see Kelleher.

"Yeah, I started to come up but it looked like you had Kyler going, so I waited."

"*Going?* Not really. She was just giving me her 'all men suck' speech again."

Kelleher laughed. "What did you tell her?"

Maureen smiled. "I told her she was absolutely right, except when it came to my brother and my partner."

Kelleher smirked. "Did she buy it?"

"Only the part about my brother."

"Figures. Come on, let's go. The House is heading in."

The doors leading to the back of the House chamber were about to close, which meant it was still a good fifteen minutes before Paulsen's speech would begin. All the rituals of any joint session of the House and Senate were still to come: the Senate going into session, then walking en masse across the hall into the House; the formal entrance of the lieutenant governor, then, finally, the governor. Kelleher loved all the rituals. He loved knowing that these were traditions that dated back centuries and would never change.

McGuire understood. "Let me go change my shoes and I'll meet you on the floor," she said.

"I may need you to help with the desk," he said. "Quintal's trying to screw me again. He wants sixteen to twenty inches."

"I'll talk to Jane later."

She turned toward the ladies' room, while Kelleher walked past the back doors of the two houses, now being closed by the state troopers who manned them, to the end of the lobby. There he turned left, down the narrow hallway that led to the speaker's offices and the House lounge. Just outside the speaker's office was a security checkpoint.

Tom Wyman, who had been the state-police driver for four different speakers of the House, was stationed there today, so Kelleher didn't have to take out his press ID.

"Where's Maureen?" Wyman asked as Kelleher passed him. Wyman was madly in love with Maureen, not in the crude try-to-put-the-move-on way but in a real, live teenage-boy way. If Maureen ever needed to be rescued from a sorcerer's castle, Tom Wyman was the man. But if by some chance she showed up on Wyman's doorstep tomorrow, he would faint dead away.

"Patience, Wyman, patience," Kelleher said. "She'll be here in about ninety seconds."

He breezed into the House lounge, empty except for a few pages and a long line of reporters at the far door leading to the floor. Whenever the governor spoke, his troopers, a different group than the legislature's troopers, set up a second checkpoint for the media. Usually it took about two more seconds to wave to the governor's trooper as you walked past him. Not today, however.

"What's the deal?" Kelleher said, stopping to pour himself a cup of coffee.

"New trooper," said Tom Kenworthy, who was at the end of the line. "I think he's checking IDs and blood types."

Kelleher shrugged, stirred his coffee, and joined Kenworthy in line. He pulled his ID from his wallet and waited. Most of the troopers were pretty good guys, but there was no doubt the governor's protectors were a lot more hard ass about things than the legislature's guys.

It took nearly three minutes to get to the door. Kelleher could hear the prayer being said inside. The trooper at the door was very blond, very tall, and very young. "How you doing?" Kelleher said, trying to keep things loose. He held up his ID for the trooper to see.

The trooper took it out of his hands, looked at it, looked at him, then handed it back silently. "Okay," he said. "But lose the coffee."

Kelleher looked at him quizzically. "Excuse me?"

"No coffee in the chamber."

"Look, I understand you're new. Coffee is allowed. People send pages out for coffee. Look." Kelleher pointed to a page bringing coffee to Foulkes, who sat in the front row.

"For the delegates. Not the press."

Kelleher was starting to lose his cool. He always carried coffee onto the floor with him. It was one of *his* rituals. What's more, he didn't like some twenty-two-year-old meet-the-new-boss trooper making up rules.

"Who told you that?" he asked, still not raising his voice. Weiland was about to recognize the House doorman, John Tischman, a seventy-three-year-old ex-boxer who had been the doorman for thirty-seven years. Tischman, who had one of the great voices of all time, would announce the arrival of the Senate as if it had just returned from a successful trip to the moon.

"No one had to tell me," the trooper was saying to Kelleher. "*I'm* telling you. You want to come in here, you lose the coffee."

Kelleher felt his face flush. He looked at the trooper's name tag: B. D. Stern. He put the coffee down on an end table a few feet from the door. "Okay, Trooper Stern," he said. "We'll find out later who makes the rules around here."

As he started to step past Stern into the chamber, the trooper put his hand on his shoulder. "Back talk me and you won't get in at all," he said.

Kelleher bit down hard on his lip. He didn't have time for a confrontation. But he and Stern weren't done. He waited until Stern let go of his shoulder, then walked through the school desks to his railing. He sat down just as John Tischman said, "Mr. Speaker, the Senate of Maryland!"

The doors at the back of the chamber opened and in walked the Senate, led by the ineffable Myron Cutler. The delegates stood in a mock semi–standing ovation, some of them booing good-naturedly. It was all part of the ritual. Cutler led the way down the center aisle, with senators peeling off to join the delegates from their districts. He walked through the school desks and paused at the gate leading to the podium.

"I certainly hope you're comfortable, Mr. Kelleher," he said with a sneer in his voice.

"Thank you for asking, Mr. President," Kelleher answered, trying not to sneer in return.

Once Cutler was on the podium and everyone was seated, Weiland declared the House and Senate to be met in joint session. John Tischman, still at the back doors, took center stage again: "Mr. Speaker, the lieutenant governor of the state of Maryland, the honorable Meredith Gordy!"

The doors, closed once the Senate was all in, opened again and in walked Gordy, dressed smartly in a bright blue dress. Kyler and Willie Ervin, Gordy's driver, were a couple steps behind. Willie Ervin was Kelleher's favorite trooper. He had played basketball at George Washington University four years before Kelleher had played at Virginia. The difference was that Ervin *had played*—and well. Every year Kelleher recruited Ervin as a ringer for the press-legislators basketball game and, since Ervin was clearly the best player on the court, every year the legislators howled.

The ovation for Gordy was respectful. She worked her way down the aisle, shaking hands with legislators as she went. Kyler ignored everyone. Kelleher loved the fact that she wouldn't so much as glance at any of the legislators. She wore a red blouse and white pants. Gordy sat down where the House clerk usually sat, just to the right and below the podium.

John Tischman had one more announcement to make. "Mr. Speaker," he boomed, "the governor of the state of Maryland, the honorable Barnard A. Paulsen!"

One last time everyone stood—except, of course, for the media. As Paulsen worked his way down the aisle, pages began weaving through the media desks, handing out copies of the speech, which had been closely guarded until just this moment. As Kelleher sat watching, he heard a voice to his left say, "What's the matter, don't the media rise to pay homage to Barney Paulsen?"

It was Kyler, who had worked her way to the area between the podium and the railing. Kelleher, who had been watching Paulsen, spun his head around, smiling. "I only stand up for Gordy," he told her.

Kyler laughed and was about to answer, when a page came up with copies of the speech. She handed one to Kelleher and then offered one to Kyler. "Isn't it enough that I have to *listen* to it?" Kyler said, sending the poor page off looking as if she had just been told her boyfriend had been drafted.

"Jeez, Kyler, you always pick on children?" Kelleher said, unable to resist.

"Children?" Kyler laughed. "You'll probably be hitting on her in Fran's this very night."

Kelleher shook his head. "Come on, you know that's not my style."

"Looks like *exactly* your style," Kyler answered.

The page was quite blond and quite cute. Also quite seventeen—or younger. The pages were high school students sent to Annapolis for one week to learn about the workings of state government. Many of them returned home with an education that went far beyond the floor of the House or Senate.

Some legislators had no qualms at all about hitting on the pages. In fact one of them, Mickey Currigan, had *married* a page. Maloney had described the wedding to Kelleher. "It was something to see," he said. "On one side of the aisle was the Maryland House of Delegates. On the other side of the aisle was the senior class of James Madison High School."

Kelleher had learned his lesson during his first year in Annapolis. He had asked a woman to dance with him in Fran's one night, figuring she was probably a year or two older than he was, but what the heck. After he had gone off to buy her a drink, David Jackson had grabbed him.

"Who is that you're dancing with?" he asked.

"I have no idea," Kelleher said, a bit drunk and very interested in the young woman.

"Well, you better find out," Jackson said, "because I think she's a page."

Kelleher sobered up quickly. He walked to the table where he had left his dancing partner, handed her the drink, and said, "Are you a page?"

"What if I am?" she answered.

"Thanks for the dance," Kelleher said and escaped, humiliated and relieved. Later that night, he saw the girl leave with one of the governor's lobbyists.

Actually, a page–media member rendezvous had produced one of McGuire's best lines. One morning, sitting in the House after that week's page du jour (so dubbed by the media) had been seen leaving Fran's with Charles Barnes, a Ken doll–look-alike TV reporter, someone had said, "Wow. How do you bring yourself to fuck a page?"

To which McGuire, without looking up, had answered, "Fuck a page, that's nothing. How do you fuck a mannequin?"

Barnes was known from that day forward as "the mannequin," though he never knew why.

Before Kelleher could think of a clever retort to Kyler's latest page put-down, Barney Paulsen arrived at the podium. The only way to describe Barney Paulsen was "ordinary." He was five-ten, with graying hair and a middle-age paunch. His face was a bit craggy, but holding up all right for fifty-six. His only distinguishing feature, at least as far as Kelleher could see, were bright-blue eyes that twinkled when he smiled.

Away from Rocky Altmann, Paulsen wasn't a bad guy. On the campaign trail, he was apt to sit up at night with reporters having a few drinks, especially if his wife, Helen, wasn't on the trip. Helen Paulsen was one of the major pains in the butt of the twentieth century. Paulsen's staff called her ''war department'' because every time she got involved in something, there was bound to be a war over it. Helen Paulsen, who Kelleher could see sitting front and center in the balcony as always, was boring and boorish. Everyone in Annapolis knew that the governor was carrying on a long-running affair with Barbara Nilson, Alan Sims's secretary.

Paulsen shook hands warmly with Cutler and Weiland, whose smiles seemed frozen in place. All three men knew that Paulsen was about to publicly announce his intention to take them on in what would probably be the political battle of their lives. And yet, politics being politics, you might have thought the three were loving brothers reunited after years apart.

Everyone sat down—at last—and Paulsen pulled his speech from his breast pocket. Kelleher leafed through the text. It was eleven pages, double-spaced. Paulsen was about a three-minutes-per-page speaker. Kelleher glanced at his watch: two twenty-seven: Paulsen should be finished by about three o'clock. That would give him and Maureen plenty of time to gather reaction quotes. First-edition deadline was six-thirty, although that could be stretched to as late as nine if something major was unfolding. That wouldn't be necessary tonight.

''I hope I'm not interrupting anything,'' Paulsen said with a smile, looking out into the packed chamber. That was his version of a one-liner. Kelleher began leafing through the speech, looking for the key lines Sims had told him about, as Paulsen began speaking.

''Mr. President, Mr. Speaker, members of the Senate, members of the House, ladies and gentlemen . . .''

The first couple of pages were routine, the usual self-congratulations about what a great session it had been thus far. Kelleher noted that Paulsen looked up at the end of each paragraph, just as his staff had taught him to do.

As Paulsen neared the end of page one—''but there is still much important work left to do these next forty-five days . . .''—Kelleher's attention wandered. He glanced up toward the balcony to see if anyone interesting was in the audience. When Ben Mitchell, Weiland's predecessor, had been speaker, he'd had a remarkable talent for spotting good-looking women from the podium. As a debate raged on the floor, Mitchell would wander over to where Kelleher sat on his railing and, without looking up, whisper, ''Second row, five seats in from the wall, left side.''

Kelleher would look up and, sure enough, a very good-looking woman would be in the exact seat Mitchell had described.

Now, having again spotted Helen Paulsen, he began checking out the audience. Normally the gallery contained a lot of school kids, brought in for a few minutes to see government in action. But when the governor spoke, it was a more adult crowd. Often, if Rocky Altmann thought the gallery wouldn't be packed, he would order staffers to fill the seats to play cheerleader. Kelleher had once spotted fourteen staffers in the balcony (and he couldn't even see half the seats because they were directly overhead) and had written about it, infuriating Altmann.

Kelleher had just seen one of Altmann's secretaries sitting in the second row when he vaguely noted a rise in the pitch of Paulsen's voice.

"And so now the time has come . . ."

He was midway through page three. The rest of the line was "to make the hard decisions." Only he didn't deliver the line because just as Kelleher was starting to turn his attention back to Paulsen, the lights suddenly went out: *Whoosh!*—just like that, the huge chamber was pitched into total darkness. Kelleher heard a collective gasp of surprise and then some firecrackers went off, about six of them right in a row.

Just as they stopped, Kelleher heard what sounded like a moan directly to his left, and he heard Barney Paulsen say something like, "*Aargh*, Jesus, oh, Jesus!" His eyes still adjusting to the darkness, Kelleher jumped off the railing and looked toward the podium. Barney Paulsen was slumped forward, head under the microphone. Kelleher could see a puddle of red forming underneath him.

In a split second he went from confused to terrified. "Oh my fucking God!" he said aloud, realizing that the firecrackers had to have been gunshots. He was suddenly aware of the screaming all around him and, with his eyes now focusing again, he saw Andrea Kyler crouched in front of him, yelling, "Keep her down, Willie, keep her down!" Willie Ervin was lying directly on top of Meredith Gordy. At least Kelleher assumed it was Meredith Gordy, since he couldn't actually see her.

Instinctively, Kelleher jumped onto the podium. He arrived at Paulsen's slumped body just as one of the state troopers did. Without saying a word to each other, they peeled Paulsen off the microphone stand and tried to lay him on his back on the floor. The trooper immediately ripped off what was left of Paulsen's shirt and Kelleher felt himself becoming sick. Barney Paulsen's chest had been blown away. There was bone and blood all over. Kelleher, on his knees, swiveled away at the sight just as he heard a voice screaming at him.

"Get the fuck out of the way, Kelleher! *Move!*"

He looked up and saw Larry Bearnarth, Paulsen's driver, his face masked in complete terror. Kelleher quickly stood up and took a step back to get out of Bearnarth's way. Bearnarth was kneeling over Paulsen, trying to stop the bleeding somehow with his jacket. It was like trying to catch all of Niagara Falls with a coffee cup. And yet, Bearnarth was screaming for help as if Paulsen could still be alive. Kelleher knew that was impossible.

He tried to blink away the horror of what he had just seen and look around the room. Some of the legislators were on the floor, others were trying to get up to the podium to see what had happened. Uniformed troopers, who seemed to have appeared by magic, were holding them back. To his right, Kelleher could see a few of the plainclothesmen blocking the media.

No one was paying attention to Kelleher. To ensure that didn't change, he dropped back to his knees and looked to see what had become of Gordy. She was on the floor, in a sitting position, with Ervin still hovering over her protectively. Kyler was sitting next to her with her arm around her shoulders. The lieutenant governor appeared to be unharmed.

Kelleher crawled over to Gordy. "Everyone all right?" he asked.

"Barney?" Gordy asked.

"Looks bad," Kelleher said. He didn't want to say, "He's dead," partly because it sounded so gruesome, partly because he supposed there was some small chance he wasn't.

"Bobby, you got to get back with the other press," Willie Ervin said. His friend's voice was quite firm. Kelleher nodded.

"Meredith, you aren't hurt, right?" he said, wanting to be sure.

"I'm fine," Gordy answered. She was about to say something else but Kyler interrupted.

"Willie, if Kelleher isn't behind the railing in fifteen seconds I want you to arrest him."

Kelleher knew this was no time to argue. Just as he stood up, the lights came back on. Another gasp went through the room. Kelleher could see now that Weiland had been hit too, but it looked like his injury was just on the shoulder. A trooper was holding a jacket on the wound and Weiland was standing next to the podium, dazed but conscious. Paramedics were arriving on the podium as Kelleher pushed his way back to the other side of the railing.

Some of the other writers were shouting things at him but he couldn't hear what they were saying. Maureen was in the back, near the door. He got to her.

"Are you okay?" She was shouting, almost hysterical.

"Fine, yeah." He looked down and realized he was covered in Paulsen's blood. He hadn't realized what he must look like. "This is Paulsen's blood. I'm not hurt at all."

She grabbed his wrist. "Is he dead?"

Kelleher looked back over his shoulder at the mob scene on the podium. "Has to be," he whispered. "His whole chest is blown away."

He was about to go on when he heard a voice saying, "Clear a path here, clear a path." Several troopers were now leading Gordy, with Kyler on one side of her and Ervin on the other, off the floor through the lounge. Kelleher started to step out of the way, only to get nailed by a swinging elbow as a trooper came by.

"Hey, watch it," he shouted instinctively.

"You watch it, asshole," came the reply, and Kelleher saw his new friend, B. D. Stern.

"That fucker," he said as the Gordy entourage disappeared.

"Forget that," McGuire broke in. "Listen, I'll try to trail Gordy. You call the office. Tell them what happened and tell them the cops might come after you as a possible witness since you were so close. Tell them to get someone on the phone calling Anne Arundel Hospital right away to check Paulsen's condition."

Kelleher had stopped listening. "The question is, who did this?" he said, surprised at the emotion in his voice. "Who the hell would want to shoot Barney Paulsen?"

▬ ▬ ▬ ▬ ▬ ▬ ▬ ▬ ▬ ▬ ▬ ▬ ▬ ▬ ▬ ▬ ▬

CHAPTER 4

GOVERNOR GORDY

As McGuire ran down the hallway in pursuit of Gordy, Kelleher started toward the back stairs, heading to the pressroom to call the office. But as he went past the speaker's suite, he noticed there was no one in the outer office. He ducked in there and quickly dialed his editor's direct line.

Busy. He slammed down the phone and dialed the Maryland-desk number. A copy aide picked up on the fourth ring. Kelleher was on the verge of hysteria by this point. "This is Kelleher, I need Jane," he said, realizing he was shouting.

"She's on the other line. . . ."

"Well, get her the fuck *off* the other line, for God's sake! The goddamn governor of Maryland's been shot!"

"Hold on, hold on," the copy aide said, sounding annoyed at the interruption in his day. He snapped Kelleher on hold. Before Kelleher could blow a gasket completely, Kryton came on the line.

"What's the story, Bobby, how bad is he hurt?"

"I think he's dead, Jane. . . ."

"Whoa, whoa, what do you mean dead? The wire bulletin just said shot."

"What else could they say right now? It's only been ten minutes. I was there, Jane, I saw the guy up close. I mean, he's got no chest left."

"Okay, okay," Kryton said. "But you know we have to confirm it. We can't write he's dead until someone says so besides you."

"I know, I know. Listen, we need people up here and we need someone working the phone, checking the hospital every ten minutes until we can get somebody over there."

"Can't you or Maureen go?"

"Maureen's trying to chase Gordy and I want to stay here awhile and see what I can find out."

"Any suspects? Arrests? How in the world did someone get a gun in there?"

"All good questions. That's why I want to stay here."

"Fine, fine. I'll send someone to the hospital. What else do you need?"

"Anyone and everyone you can find. Weiland got winged, too, though it doesn't look too bad. Jeez, Jane, you knew the guy, why would anyone want to kill Barney Paulsen?"

"I was just saying that to someone. He's not exactly Huey Long."

"Was he the last governor shot?"

"We're double-checking in the library. Certainly the last one assassinated."

"I'll call when I know more."

He hung up just as Linda Tanton, Weiland's secretary, came in. Her face went white when she saw Kelleher. "Oh, my God, Bobby, sit down! I'll call a doctor!"

Kelleher shook his head. "It isn't me. This is the governor's blood. I was on the podium right after."

Her face relaxed briefly. "Do you think he's . . ."

"It didn't look good, Linda," he said softly. "How's the speaker?" It was the first time in his life he had ever expressed concern over Fred Weiland's health.

"Seems okay. They're taking him to the hospital but apparently the bullet only grazed him."

"Anybody else hit?"

"No. It's amazing. Cutler was on the speaker's left and Gordy on the right and neither one of them got touched."

Kelleher took a deep breath. "I better get back in there."

Tanton shook her head. "Don't bother. They've cut off all access to the floor."

"Have they moved Paulsen?"

"Oh, yes. He should be at the hospital by now."

Kelleher needed to get back to the floor. He thanked Tanton and walked back to the security checkpoint. There was a uniformed trooper there, blocking him. "Sorry, sir, no one's allowed in there," the trooper said. "They're still clearing people out."

"Yeah, officer, I know," Kelleher said. He pointed at his bloody shirt. "But look, Tom Wyman ordered me *not* to leave. I was an up-close witness. He gave me five minutes to call my office, then told me to come right back."

The officer wasn't sure, but the bloody shirt sold him. "Well, okay, if Lieutenant Wyman said so then."

Kelleher didn't wait for him to rethink the question. He patted him on the shoulder and walked by, looking for Wyman. Stunned delegates were still leaving through the back door; troopers seemed to have multiplied in droves. He spotted the lieutenant standing next to the podium, talking into one of the wrist walkie-talkies the troopers used.

"Tom, listen," he said, walking up to him.

Wyman held up a hand as he listened to what was being said on the walkie-talkie. Then he turned, eyes blazing. "Who the fuck let you back in, Kelleher? We're trying to get you SOBs the hell out of the way!"

"Whoa, Tom, calm down." Kelleher grabbed Wyman by the shoulders. He had found over the years that, in a moment of crisis, making physical contact with someone you knew often calmed things down. It was a reminder that you were a friend, not the enemy. "Look at me. I've got the guy's blood all over me. I know how bad this is. But help me for one minute. You guys got any idea what the hell happened?"

Wyman shook his head. He looked like he was close to tears. "Bobby, we got *nothing*. All we know is that someone got to the generator in the subbasement and cut the power at exactly two thirty-five. Had to be someone who knew just what buttons to push. We found three submachine guns in the front row of the gallery upstairs."

"Submachine guns? Jesus! How can someone just walk in there carrying a goddamn submachine gun?"

"No one could. They had to have been planted."

"You mean whoever did it goes in unarmed, sits in the front row, grabs the submachine gun that's sitting on the floor, and shoots when the lights go out?"

"Not on the floor. Inside the balcony railing. It looks like someone put the guns inside the railing and they were pulled out."

"Lots of planning."

"No shit."

"Suspects?"

"None. We're checking every person who leaves the building, but with the guns left behind we have no idea what we're checking for."

"Three guns, you said?"

"Yeah."

"Somebody wanted to be sure, huh?"

"But *why*, Bobby? Why Barney Paulsen?"

Kelleher was beginning to feel like Joe Friday. All he could do was stand there and shake his head, baffled. "One more question," he said, not wanting to push his luck too far. "Paulsen?"

"Don't know yet, but Bearnarth walkied from the ambulance that he thought he was going to be DOA. That was a few minutes ago, and we haven't heard anything else. If he was DOA, Bearnarth would have let us know so we could tell Gordy she's going to be governor. Least I think he would."

Kelleher clapped Wyman on the shoulder again. "Thanks, Tom."

Wyman's head drooped. "Hey, no quotes, right?"

"We never talked," Kelleher said, walking toward the side door. It was time for him to try to find Alan Sims.

▬ ▬

As Kelleher walked into the hallway, he was struck again by the horror of the past forty-five minutes. Involuntarily, he shivered, remembering the sight of Barney Paulsen's blown-away chest.

As a reporter, Kelleher had covered his share of murders and fatal accidents. He had talked to relatives of the dead—a task he despised—and he had interviewed the dying for a story he had written about AIDS victims. But he had never been this close to someone in the bloody throes of violent death. If he stopped to think about it, he knew he would feel sick again.

Instead, Kelleher let his reporting instincts take over. Horrible as the shooting was, it was also an unbelievable story, and it gave the reporter in him an adrenaline rush. Pushed by that adrenaline, Kelleher raced down the back steps to the basement. He knew that if he walked back into the main lobby, he would encounter a mob scene; he also knew that there'd be no way he would be able to get to the second floor.

Perhaps, though, no one had thought to cut off the elevator that was supposed to be used only by the governor, the lieutenant governor, and their staffs. No one ever guarded the elevator and maybe, Kelleher reasoned, no one had thought to guard it now.

He walked quickly past the pressroom, which he could see, out of the corner of his eye, was chaotic, and past the guard's desk in the middle of the basement. No one seemed to notice him and, sure enough, at the elevator there was no one around. He pressed the button and tapped his foot nervously. If the elevator arrived with a trooper on it, he was finished.

His luck held. The elevator was empty. He got in, pressed the button for the second floor, and waited, almost holding his breath as it labored upward. When the doors opened, he glanced out to see if the coast was clear. If the elevator had been on the governor's side of the floor, the place would have been swarming with troopers, but it was down a small hallway from the lieutenant governor's offices. No one was around.

Quietly, he walked around the corner, trying not to look toward the security desk, where a cadre of troopers was gathered. As he went past the glass doors of the lieutenant governor's offices, Kelleher angled his body away, just in case someone in there looked in his direction. No doubt Gordy was inside her office under heavy protection.

At the end of the hall he turned right. No one was in Sims's outer office so he walked up to Sims's door and knocked softly. No one answered. He turned the knob, gingerly pushed the door open, and poked his head in. Alan Sims was sitting behind his desk, feet up, a drink in his hand.

He looked at Kelleher and smiled. "I won't even ask how the fuck you got up here," he said.

"You all right?" Kelleher wanted to know. Sims looked like he was in shock.

"I'm great. My boss is dead. Guess that means I have the rest of the day off. What could be better? Pour yourself a drink."

Kelleher ignored the offer. "Are you sure he's dead?"

Sims stood up, walked over to his closet, and pulled a sweatshirt out of it. He tossed it to Kelleher. "Put that on. Get out of that bloody shirt. Yeah, he's dead. I just got off the phone five minutes ago with the doctor at the hospital. He was DOA. You saw him up close. You think he had any fucking chance to live?"

Kelleher didn't answer the question. "So, they've announced it then?"

Sims laughed and picked up the scotch bottle on his desk and poured some more into his glass. "No, they haven't announced a goddamn thing.

Do you want to know why? Make sure you put this in the paper. Rocky Altmann is at the hospital right now telling the doctors he doesn't want the governor's death announced until seven o'clock.

"Do you want to know why again? I'll tell you why. First, he wants to fuck all you newspaper guys and make you miss your first editions. 'Course, he doesn't know you'll just hold the first editions, 'cause he's too fuckin' stupid to know that. Second, he doesn't want Meredith Gordy to become the story on the six o'clock news.

"Can you believe that? He's known Barney Paulsen for twenty years, worked for him for six, and all he can think about right now is screwing the press and Meredith Gordy. What a guy, huh? What a guy."

Sims took a long swallow of his drink and stared at the glass. Kelleher had never seen him like this. But then, Kelleher had never seen Sims at the end of a day in which his boss had been murdered.

"You were on the podium, I saw you," Sims said, looking up. "It must have been gruesome."

"Exactly the right word," he answered.

Sims shook his head and asked the question Kelleher couldn't seem to escape. "Why in the world would anyone want to kill Barney? This guy isn't a Kennedy or a King or even a Jesse Jackson. He's a nice little governor in a nice little state. Nothing more. What the hell could he be involved in that would convince someone to cook up this elaborate plan to kill him?"

Sims had now reached the part where Kelleher came in. "It almost sounds like an inside job from what I heard."

Sims was suddenly alert. "What have you heard?"

Kelleher shrugged as if passing out information that was common knowledge. "Three submachine guns in the gallery, someone pulled the main power switch in the subbasement, guns obviously placed in the gallery long before this afternoon."

Sims smiled, almost, it seemed to Kelleher, in admiration. "You really are good, you sonofabitch," he said. "I happen to know that none of that's been released and the plan is not to release any of it, at least until tomorrow. What else do you know?"

Kelleher didn't want to get fenced in too quickly. "Hang on, I'm the reporter here," he said. "You tell me first."

Sims laughed harshly. "Bobby, this isn't a fucking budget story. I'm not going to play your reporter games today. My boss is dead, I've confirmed that, which'll save you a lot of running around. I'm completely clueless on motive, which you and I know is what this story is all about now. The only thing you didn't mention that I thought you might have noticed is that Jamelle Tourretta was in the gallery.''

Kelleher's head snapped up. He had no idea why Jamelle Tourretta, the president of Females for Freedom, would be there for a Barney Paulsen speech. More important, he had even less idea why her presence would be significant to Sims.

"And?" he said, hoping Sims would tell him more.

"With Barney dead, who becomes governor?" Sims asked. "I mean, total coincidence, I suppose, that she's here. The speech was an important one in terms of women's issues, but it isn't the first time he's come down on their side. Probably means nothing.''

"Hang on here; what do you mean, 'means nothing'? Is she a suspect? Are the cops questioning her?"

"Don't overreact.''

"What do you mean, 'overreact'? *You* brought it up. If she isn't being questioned, how do you know she was here?"

"I saw her with my beady little eyes, walking in just before the speech.''

"You sure it was her?"

Sims snorted. *"Sure it was her?* Kelleher, you ever see Jamelle Tourretta?''

"Actually, no, never.''

"Actually, that was a stupid question for me to ask. If you had ever seen her, you would never have asked me if I was sure it was her. It's impossible to confuse her with anyone else in the world.''

"Why?"

Sims shook his head, stood up, and poured some more scotch. "Jamelle Tourretta is, I would say, about six feet tall. Always wears high heels. Loves to tower over men. She's got flaming red hair, sort of like Blaze Starr—you remember that movie?—and a bodybuilder's body. I mean, she's huge, big shoulders, chest, everything, but she's a goddamn knock-out. I can't believe you've never seen her, Kelleher. What planet you been on?"

"You say anything to the cops about it?"

"Hell, I'm probably adding one plus one and getting five. But I probably will tomorrow, when I'm sober and things are a little bit calmer. If

I were you, though, I wouldn't even think about bringing it up in a story.''

"You *have* been drinking, Alan. I couldn't bring something like that up unless I wanted a serious libel suit. Besides, I'd rather keep it to myself. Just in case one and one *does* equal five.''

Kelleher glanced at his watch. Almost five o'clock. He groaned.

"Deadline, Bobby? You've got a lot of writing to do, don't you?''

"Yeah, I do,'' Kelleher said. He had just thought of one more stop he wanted to make before he went back to the office. "Are you all right? I don't think you should drive home.''

Sims waved him off. "I'm fine. I'm not leaving for a while and when I do, I'll get one of the cops to take me.''

Sims was tighter with the state police than anyone else in state government. Kelleher knew he would have no trouble getting a ride. He turned toward the door. As he pulled it open, he had one last thought.

"Alan,'' he said, "I really am sorry.''

Sims smiled a tired, sad smile at him. "I know you are, Bobby. But not as sorry as I am.''

━ ━

Kelleher walked out of Sims's office feeling profoundly sad and confused. What in the world did Jamelle Tourretta's presence this afternoon mean? He could think of two people who might have an answer to that question, and they were just a few feet down the hallway. The only problem was going to be getting in to see them.

This time when Kelleher reached the glass doors that led to the lieutenant governor's suite of offices, he pulled them open and walked in. He got about three feet before he was stopped by a state trooper he recognized although he couldn't remember his name.

"Can I help you, sir?'' the trooper said in a tone of voice that meant he had no intention of helping Kelleher with anything except a quick exit. Kelleher decided to play it low-key and dumb.

"I'm here to see the lieutenant governor,'' he said, as if it were just another early evening in Annapolis.

The cop regarded him with an amused smirk. "Uh-huh, sure you are. No one told you that media are banned from this floor? No one told you that any comments from the lieutenant governor will come through the press office?''

Kelleher had to stall now until he could think of a way to get help. His best tactic, he decided, was pure bluff. "Look, I don't know about bans or anything," he said. "I got a phone call asking me to come over here to see Gordy. I've got deadline in one hour and if she needs to see me, I'd appreciate it if we could get this over in a hurry. I haven't got time to be screwing around right now."

For the first time the cop looked a little bit baffled. "Who called you?" he asked.

Kelleher had to be careful now. "I'm not certain; the message was on my answering machine back at the office. It sounded like either Kyler or Gordy."

"Wait right here," the cop said. Kelleher's heart sank. He was hoping the cop would take him into Gordy's outer office, where he might push the bluff a little farther. If the cop went inside and consulted with Beth Bevans, Gordy's secretary, he was done. Bevans was the most sour human being in Annapolis. She didn't even like the people she liked. And she *really* didn't like the media. So Kelleher gambled and pushed his luck one last time.

"Look, Officer," he said, trying to sound respectful but a little impatient. "I know you've got orders, but I've got a deadline. How about we just walk in there together so we can both find out quick as possible what the deal is here."

The cop looked him up and down for a second. "You're Kelleher, right?" Kelleher nodded, not knowing if that was going to be good or bad. Apparently it was good. The cop pushed the inside door open and said over his shoulder, "Come on."

The outer office was filled with troopers and secretaries who all seemed to be answering phones. Beth Bevans sat at her desk just outside Gordy's office. She was also on the phone. When she saw the cop and Kelleher approach, she put the phone down quickly. Her eyes were filled with loathing as she turned to the cop.

"Officer Norton, did someone change your orders regarding the media? Why in the world is this person"—she spat out "this person" as if the sight of Kelleher made her ill—"here? In fact, how did he get by the first checkpoint? Are *all* of you asleep on the job?"

Norton glared at Kelleher as if he had been set up. "Miss Bevans, the guy claims he has an appointment with the lieutenant gov . . . with Ms. Gordy."

Bevans looked at Kelleher as if he were the ghost of Barney Paulsen.

"Oh, he does, does he? Who made this appointment for you, Mr. Kelleher, Rocky Altmann?"

Kelleher had to admit that wasn't a bad line. He had to play this to the finish, though. "There was a message on our phone, Beth," he said. "It sounded like Andrea. Or even Meredith, actually. Maybe someone's playing a joke on me. As I told Officer Norton, I really don't have time to be screwing around here if I'm not wanted, but I came because I thought I was."

He looked her right in the eye throughout. Show any fear and Bevans will eat you alive; Kelleher knew that. She stood up. "I will go in and find out if anybody called you, Mr. Kelleher. If you are lying, I'm going to have you arrested right now for unlawful entry. Officer Norton, watch him closely."

Kelleher could feel himself breaking into a sweat. Getting arrested wouldn't bother him all that much; the *Herald*'s lawyers would get charges like that dropped pretty quickly. But if he was off somewhere trying to get out of jail when he should be writing a deadline story on the assassination of the governor, he was going to be in big trouble.

He could hear the conversation now:

"What do you mean *arrested*? What were you trying to do?"

"Get a quote from Meredith Gordy."

"A quote from Meredith Gordy? You got arrested an hour before deadline trying to get a quote from Meredith Gordy?"

Kelleher was trying to think up an answer to that question when Bevans reappeared in the doorway, looking extremely surprised and very disappointed.

"You can go in," she snarled.

Kelleher's heart almost stopped. What was this? Was he being set up to *really* be arrested? "Thanks for your help," he said to Norton, ignoring Bevans. He walked past her into Gordy's office.

Gordy was lying on the couch across from the desk, her shoes off, a towel on her forehead. Kyler was standing in front of the desk, also in her stocking feet, her arms folded. No one else was in the room. Kelleher glanced at the window on the right side of the desk and could see State Circle. He wondered if there was a fire escape outside the ledge he might be able to use.

"So, Kelleher, someone called you and said to get right over here, huh?" Kyler said. "Who do you think it was, me or Meredith?"

Before Kelleher could think up a clever answer, Gordy sat up, pulled the towel off her forehead, and swung her feet onto the floor. "Okay, Andrea, that's enough." She looked at Kelleher. "Sit down, Bobby, and tell me why it was so important to bluff your way in here that you risked getting arrested."

Kelleher had always liked Gordy because there was absolutely no BS in her. Kyler was just as straightforward but there was always a razor in her voice. Gordy was tough without being intimidating.

Kelleher sat in one of the chairs next to the couch. "I'm sorry, Meredith, I really do apologize. But you're going to be governor soon and I really needed to try to ask you a few questions before I write for first edition."

"Wait a second," Gordy said, holding her hand up like a stop sign. "Please don't dance on Barney's grave just yet. I know it looks bad but . . ."

Kelleher interrupted her without thinking. "Hang on, Meredith, what are you talking about? Barney's dead."

Gordy looked at Kyler. "What do you mean? We haven't been told that."

Kelleher knew Gordy was telling the truth. For one thing, lying just wasn't in her makeup. For another, the look on her face made it clear she wasn't playing a game. He wanted to tell her to just pick up the phone and call Alan Sims but he couldn't do that. "Meredith, call the hospital. Ask to speak to the doctor directly," he said.

Gordy reached over and pressed her intercom. "Beth," she said, "get the hospital on the phone. Tell them I want to speak directly to the doctor in charge. And I want to speak to him *right now.*"

She looked at Kelleher again. "Why would the hospital not tell me if Barney was dead?" she said, a touch of anger in her voice. "What the hell is the point?"

Kelleher had no problem telling her the point. "Rocky Altmann's delaying the announcement," he said. "He wants to screw up newspaper deadlines and he doesn't want your swearing in on the news."

"My swearing in—if there is one—*won't* be on the news, that much I can assure you," Gordy seethed. "But if this is true . . ."

The intercom buzzed. "Dr. Ritchie on line one," Beth Bevans said.

Gordy pressed the speaker button on the phone. "Dr. Ritchie, this is Meredith Gordy," she said. "You are the doctor in charge over there?"

"Yes, ma'am, I was," Ritchie answered. The *was* seemed to hit Gordy in the face like a ton of bricks.

"Was?" she repeated. "Doctor, is the governor dead?"

"He was DOA, Miss Gordy. I'm very sorry. . . ."

Gordy broke in: "DOA? That means he was dead two hours ago. Why hasn't my office been informed, for God's sake?"

"Miss Gordy, I apologize. But Mr. Altmann has been insisting we not release anything until seven o'clock. I haven't even been allowed to go out into the waiting room to tell Mrs. Paulsen. She thinks we're still operating on her husband."

Kelleher felt a surge of real revulsion. Helen Paulsen was a certified bitch, but the thought that Altmann would leave her sitting in a waiting room thinking her husband might live when he was already dead sickened him. Gordy clearly felt the same way.

"Doctor, I am *ordering* you to go and tell Mrs. Paulsen the truth right now. You tell Mr. Altmann you just hung up with me. And if he tries to stop you, tell Captain Bearnarth to arrest him immediately."

She slammed the phone down, as angry as Kelleher had ever seen her. She pressed the intercom. "Send Willie Ervin in here right away."

"Yes, ma'am," Bevans answered enthusiastically, no doubt convinced that Ervin was being sent in to arrest Kelleher. Ervin appeared a moment later. "Willie, you can raise Larry Bearnarth on your wrist radio there, can't you?" Gordy asked.

"Right away," Ervin answered and began talking to his wrist. "I'll turn the volume up," he said.

"Ms. Gordy, this is Bearnarth," Kelleher heard a voice say all of a sudden, as if it were inside Ervin's wrist.

"Captain Bearnarth, I just hung up the phone with Dr. Ritchie," Gordy said.

"I know ma'am, he's right here with me. He told me what you want. We're about to do that immediately. Ms. Gordy, I'm really sorry, but I had to follow Mr. Altmann's orders. . . ."

"Don't give it another thought, Captain," Gordy said. "Just get this taken care of as quickly as you can and please let me know as soon as Mrs. Paulsen has been informed. Then bring her back to my office—if she's up to it—or take her home. Whatever she wants."

"Yes, ma'am."

Gordy turned to Ervin. "Thank you, Willie." Ervin took the hint and left. Gordy turned to Kyler. "As soon as we get word that Helen Paulsen has been told, announce that the governor is dead. I will be sworn in at seven o'clock.'' She paused. ''We'll do it in the governor's ceremonial room. Only regular Annapolis media allowed. I'll talk to the press for twenty minutes after I'm sworn in.''

Kyler was making notes on a pad as Gordy spoke. ''Anything else?''

''Yes, see if the troopers can get me something bland to eat. Soup and a hot sandwich or something. I think my stomach's ready for some food.''

She turned to Kelleher. ''I'm actually glad you showed up, Bobby. I always knew Altmann was despicable but I never dreamed he could be so sick. But then, I never dreamed anyone would shoot Barney Paulsen. You seem to be way ahead of me on information. What have you heard?''

Kelleher went through the guns and the power switch, all of which, as he suspected, Gordy knew about. ''There's one other thing,'' he said finally as Kyler hung up the phone, having forwarded Gordy's instructions. He wanted her to be listening when he added his tag-on sentence.

''What's the one other thing?'' Gordy asked when she saw Kelleher hesitate.

''Did you know that Jamelle Tourretta was going to be here today?''

Gordy knitted her eyebrows and shook her head. ''Andrea, did you know she was going to be here?'' Gordy said to Kyler.

''No, no, Meredith, no, I didn't,'' Kyler said. ''First I've heard of it. Um, you saw her here, Kelleher?'' She couldn't look Gordy in the eye as she spoke.

Kelleher saw no reason to tell the truth in reply, especially since he was certain Kyler was lying. ''Yeah, I did,'' he answered. ''She's kind of hard to miss, you know.''

Gordy stood up. ''I wonder why she'd show up and not tell us.'' She turned to Kelleher. ''Do you think there's some significance to her presence?''

Kelleher shrugged. ''Right now everything is significant. And nothing.'' But Kyler's clumsy lie had made Tourretta's presence a lot more significant than it had been thirty seconds ago. Just as clearly, at least to Kelleher, Gordy was telling the truth.

''Well,'' Gordy said, ''who knows why Jamelle was here? I could see why she might want to hear the speech, given what Barney said.'' She paused. ''*Was* going to say, I mean.'' She looked at Kyler. ''I'm surprised she wouldn't call and let you know she was coming. You two are still pretty close, aren't you?''

''We are,'' Kyler said, standing and putting her shoes on. ''I'll speak to her tomorrow and find out why she didn't call us. I better go and start getting ready for the swearing in.''

Kelleher checked his watch again as Gordy stared after Kyler. It was almost five forty-five. He wanted to push Kyler a little bit farther on Tourretta. He had never before seen her even a little unnerved. This was turning out to be a day filled with firsts.

This wasn't the time for pushing, though. He had a little more than an hour to get back to the office, produce a first-edition story, and come back for the swearing in. He hoped McGuire had started to write and that reinforcements had arrived from Washington.

As he stood to leave, Gordy put a hand on his shoulder. ''Why did you ask about Jamelle Tourretta, Bobby? Do you know something?''

Kelleher shook his head emphatically. ''No, I really don't. I just know she was here. Which may mean absolutely nothing.''

''I would hope,'' Gordy said, ''that it means absolutely nothing. Still . . .''

She stopped in midthought. ''What?'' Kelleher asked softly.

''Nothing,'' Gordy said. ''Nothing. Bobby, I have to start writing some kind of speech.''

''Good luck, Meredith,'' he said, turning toward the door.

She smiled a very tired smile. ''Thanks,'' she said. ''I'm going to need it.''

CHAPTER 5

ANDREA

Kelleher walked briskly back to the elevator, took it to the basement, and walked out of the building, his mind racing. He was convinced of two things. One, Andrea Kyler had lied through her teeth about Jamelle Tourretta, and two, he wasn't the only person who knew it. Gordy's distracted look as Kyler left the room convinced him that she thought her confidante was lying, too.

He needed to thrash all of this out later on with McGuire, who knew Kyler better and longer than he did and who also knew Tourretta. For the moment, he had to focus on a first-edition story. He raced up the steps to the office and found four people in it. McGuire was hunched over a computer; Jim Forrestal, the Montgomery County political writer, was looking over her shoulder; Tim Burnett, one of the city-desk police reporters, and Maralee Alexander, another of the local political reporters, were both on telephones.

McGuire looked up as Kelleher dashed in, a look of disgust on her face. "Where the hell have you been?" she said. "The desk wants this story in an hour and we still haven't been able to pin down Paulsen's condition."

"It's stable," Kelleher said. "He's been dead more than two hours."

"How do you know that?" McGuire demanded.

"No time to talk about it now," he answered. "We'll be getting a fax here in the next fifteen minutes announcing that Gordy's being sworn in at seven o'clock. Why don't you move over and let me have a look at that?"

McGuire didn't argue. Each knew the other's strengths and weaknesses and Kelleher's strength was speed. He could crank out a story on deadline faster than anyone else on the paper. McGuire was a crafter, Kelleher a sprinter. He looked at the three paragraphs on the screen, which out of necessity hedged on Paulsen's condition. They were useless. He hit the "kill" button and started again.

"Let me work on this," he said to McGuire. "What do they want from us?"

"Mainly the lead. Forrestal's doing a political sidebar; what it all means, what kind of maneuvering we can expect after the postmortems, all that. I'm also supposed to put together a profile of Gordy with Maralee. Burnett's just working his police sources. The obit is being written in the office."

"Burnett come up with anything?"

"Well, apparently there was more than one gun involved, but we don't know exactly how many. . . ."

He cut her off with a wave of the hand. "Three. Submachine guns. Placed inside the balcony railing sometime earlier. There's more but we'll talk about it later."

"What more?" she wanted to know.

"Later," he insisted, just as the phone rang. He grabbed it: "*Washington Herald.*"

"Bobby, something's moving on the wire right now saying Paulsen's dead." It was Jane Kryton. The fax was clanging, obviously with the same information.

"Yeah, Jane, we know. You'll have a lead in about forty-five minutes."

"Wait, wait, Bobby. There's also something on the wire about more than one gun. . . ."

"I *know,* Jane," he answered, becoming exasperated. "Wait forty-five minutes and you'll know a lot more."

"Okay, hotshot, but it better be good. Watkins is breathing down our necks on this one."

Kelleher hung up. He tried to picture the scholarly J. Wynton Watkins, the patrician executive editor of the *Herald,* breathing down the metro desk's neck. Wyn Watkins usually cared about Maryland politics as much as he cared about the future colonization of Pluto. Now, however, there was blood all over the House of Delegates chamber and Wyn Watkins wanted to know exactly what Bobby Kelleher was going to do for him tonight.

"Asshole," he said under his breath.

"What?" Maureen said.

"Forget it," he said and began to write his lead:

ANNAPOLIS, Feb. 22—Maryland Governor Barnard A. Paulsen was assassinated this afternoon, shot down by submachine fire while he was giving his midsession state-of-the-state address to a joint session of the legislature in the House of Delegates.

Paulsen, 56, was pronounced dead of multiple gunshot wounds upon arrival at Anne Arundel County Hospital. Police said late today that there were no suspects in the shooting and, at the moment, no known motive. Paulsen is the first governor to be assassinated since Huey Long was shot down in the Louisiana House in 1937.

Kelleher sat back in his chair and read for a moment. It was as straight a lead as he had ever written, but that was as it should be under the circumstances. He kept coming back to the words "no known motive." Each time, he thought about Jamelle Tourretta. That was for later, though. Now, he had a story to finish.

It was ten minutes to seven by the time Kelleher sent the story. He had written just under two thousand words in an hour, riding the adrenaline of the day. His certainty that the story was full of details no one else had made him feel good. Reading over his shoulder, McGuire kept letting out little yelps, especially as she came to the parts about Altmann suppressing the news of the death and Kelleher's description of Meredith Gordy stretched out on her couch with a towel on her forehead.

"How in the world did you get all this?" she demanded.

"Took a couple of chances," he said.

"Good ones," she said, patting him on the shoulder.

They told the desk they would check back after the swearing in and press conference. The tentative plan was to do a separate story on that, with some Gordy quotes thrown into the lead up high. "Just remember we close the first at nine P.M." Kryton said. "Not a second later."

They left the other three reporters in the office, since only regular State House press would be admitted to the swearing in, and raced up the hill to State Circle. When they got there, the enormity of what was going on hit Kelleher full blast. The back lawn of the State House had been turned into a TV studio. Minicams were set up everywhere, bathing the entire circle in hot lights. Some reporters were doing live stand-ups, other crews were waiting for their "talent" to come back from the swearing in. Clearly, the number of crews admitted to the building had been limited.

Kelleher could see on a quick glance that many of the crews were national: CBS, NBC, ABC, CNN. All of a sudden this lawn, thirty-five miles and a lifetime from the White House, had become the focal point of the nation's media. He and McGuire were starting up the steps toward the back door when someone called her name. Peering through the lights, Kelleher recognized Herb Younger, who was rumored to be Dan Rather's future replacement at CBS.

Hearing her name, McGuire stopped, spotted Younger, and ran over to say hello. They exchanged a hug and a kiss. Kelleher figured McGuire knew Younger through her brother, Mike, who worked on Capitol Hill. When she came back a minute later, he asked, casually, "He a friend of Mike's?"

"No," she answered with a smile. "He's an old boyfriend."

That one surprised Kelleher, since he didn't think of Maureen as going for pretty boys. He started to ask her about it but she was sprinting up the steps leading to the back door of the State House. There were uniformed troopers posted at the door.

"Sorry, folks," one of them said. "Everyone has to go through the front."

"But we have ID," Kelleher said, somewhat desperately. It was five minutes to seven.

"Sorry. No exceptions."

Kelleher was about to argue but McGuire was tugging on his arm. "Forget it, Bobby. Let's go."

They ran around to the front door. No one was being admitted to the building without ID. Everyone had to go through a metal detector. Kelleher squirmed impatiently as he and McGuire waited for people to be turned away or admitted through the detector. By the time they got into the main lobby, it was exactly seven o'clock. They walked quickly to the bottom of the steps, where they had to pass yet another ID check. At the top of the steps was a third stop.

"Sort of understandable under the circumstances," McGuire said as they headed down the hall to the governor's ceremonial room, where Tom Wyman was posted at the door.

"No need to rush," he said softly. "Everything's running late."

"How's the speaker?" McGuire asked, remembering that Weiland had been grazed.

"Enjoying the attention," Wyman answered. "He's in there with Gordy and Cutler and all the rest of them, getting ready."

The ceremonial room was packed. A small stage had been set up at the front of the room. Hot TV lights bathed Kelleher and McGuire as they walked in. Blinded by the light, Kelleher heard a female voice calling his name. "Bob, Bob Kelleher!"

Once past the lights he could see that the voice belonged to Susan Sanders. People who didn't know him called him Bob, since that was his byline in the newspaper. "Bimbo at six o'clock," McGuire hissed in his ear. Kelleher ignored her and walked back to where Sanders was standing with her crew.

Her blue eyes were shining with excitement as he picked his way through the reporters and crews to where she was standing. "Bob, I saw you up on the podium after the shooting! My God, was it awful? What did it look like up there? Did he say anything to you!"

Kelleher, noticing the heads swiveling toward them, shook his head. "I think he was dead when his head hit the lectern, to tell you the truth," he said. He noticed a couple of the reporters from the local weeklies taking notes as he spoke. "Hey, guys," he said, interrupting himself. "This isn't a press conference."

Bob Milgaw, a writer from one of the Eastern Shore papers who had covered Annapolis for at least a hundred years, waved a hand at him. "Would you let someone go off the record on you like that, Kelleher?"

Milgaw was right. He was standing in a crowded public room and if he was stupid enough to put himself in the role of doctor to try to impress a blonde, the other reporters had every right to quote him—if they thought anything he had to say was important. He kept forgetting that things had changed this afternoon. The stakes were higher now. He had been right there when the governor of Maryland died and that meant an offhand comment could be construed by some people to be news.

"Milgaw, you're right," he said, feeling his face flush slightly. "I wasn't thinking. You have every right to use the quote. I would just appreciate it if you didn't. I don't see how my opinion could be that important."

"Do you really think he was dead, Bobby?" This came from Karen Williams of the *Baltimore Evening Sun*.

Kelleher shrugged. "I'm no doctor," he told her. "Maybe he was still alive in the ambulance. I don't know a thing about ballistics either. It just looked awful bad when the trooper pulled him off the lectern.''

"Actually, you helped pull him off the lectern too, Bob.''

This came from Sanders, still standing right behind him on the platform set up in the back of the room for TV cameras. "Yeah, I guess I did,'' he said. He decided to let it go at that. Andrea Kyler had just walked out of the governor's office at the front of the room and was walking toward the podium. That got the attention of the reporters. Kelleher took out his notebook.

The room quieted quickly. "Ladies and gentleman let me explain to you what will happen here in the next few minutes,'' Kyler began. "Meredith Gordy will be sworn in as governor by James A. Alman, the minister of her church in Potomac. She will then take questions for about twenty minutes. Due to the nature of what has gone on today and the size of this press conference, Tom Stallworth, the president of the Annapolis Political Correspondents Association, will recognize all questioners. Please do not call out a question if you are not recognized. Governor Gor . . . I mean, Ms. Gordy, won't answer anyone unless they have been called on by Tom Stallworth.''

"Do we have to keep our hands folded at all times?''

It was Tom Kenworthy, saying what everyone was no doubt thinking. Kyler glared at him. "Mr. Kenworthy, if you don't like the ground rules, you're welcome to leave.''

"I just don't like being talked down to, Ms. Kyler,'' said Kenworthy, never one to back down from anyone.

"Far be it from me ever to talk down to the media,'' Kyler replied, her voice laced with sarcasm. That got some catcalls and hisses from the suddenly hostile crowd. Kyler looked surprised. She hadn't expected any kind of revolt in Munchkin Land. At least not so quickly. For the second time in two hours, the unflappable Kyler seemed unnerved.

"Tom, I apologize,'' she said, recovering quickly. "It's been a very long day for everyone.'' She paused a moment, then plowed on. "Ladies and gentlemen, the lieutenant governor of the state of Maryland, the honorable Meredith A. Gordy.''

Kyler stepped back from the microphone as the door to the governor's office swung open. Larry Bearnarth led the way, followed by Gordy and Helen Paulsen. Why the late governor's wife would want to witness this, Kelleher couldn't fathom. Tragedy did strange things to people. Behind Gordy and Helen Paulsen came the minister, flanked by Myron Cutler and

Fred Weiland. The speaker's left arm was in a sling; other than that he looked none the worse for wear. Behind them came Willie Ervin. All were as somber as might be expected. Gordy and Helen Paulsen were both in black.

Bearnarth and Ervin peeled off at the podium. Gordy, the minister, Helen Paulsen, and the Senate president and speaker moved onto it. Helen Paulsen carried a Bible and held it for Gordy while she read the oath of office. Cutler and Weiland stood behind her. It occurred suddenly to Kelleher, as he watched, that Myron Cutler was now the number two person in Maryland state government, at least until Gordy nominated a lieutenant governor and he (or she) was approved by the legislature. Kelleher had never given any thought to "a heartbeat away" when it came to Maryland state politics. Now, looking at Cutler, the phrase crossed his mind. Governor Myron Cutler might not be as scary a thought as President Dan Quayle, but it wasn't far from it.

"God bless you, Meredith," Helen Paulsen said as soon as the minister had said, quietly, "Congratulations, Governor."

There was no applause, even from the staffers—some of Paulsen's, some of Gordy's—in the room. In happier times, during gubernatorial press conferences, Rocky Altmann always packed the room with staffers so there would be applause at the appropriate times. Altmann was nowhere in sight. But Alan Sims was, standing in the corner, arms folded, looking completely sober. Kelleher knew better.

As soon as Helen Paulsen and the minister had been escorted to seats, Gordy turned to face the media. "I know you have dozens of questions," she said. "So do I. Unfortunately, I'm like you in that I have questions but no answers. I can tell you there are no suspects in the governor's murder at this time, although the police are working with several pieces of evidence.

"Tentative funeral arrangements have been made. The governor will lie in state here in the main lobby of the State House through the weekend. A memorial service will be held Monday morning during a joint session of the legislature, and he will be buried in Baltimore Monday afternoon. That could change, but at the moment it is what Mrs. Paulsen has requested. The legislature will not meet again until Monday night, at which time I will address the members in joint session about my plans to carry out the governor's budget and legislative agendas.

"I want to thank Helen Paulsen for having the strength to be here this evening. I cannot begin to tell you how much her courage means to me.

This has been a horrible, tragic day for all of us in this state. Maryland lost a great governor, Helen Paulsen lost a loving and devoted husband, I lost a good friend. We are all very tired and very, very sad right now. There is much work to do and a large void to fill.

"I will be happy to try to answer any questions you might have now."

She spoke without any notes, in a clear, strong voice that seemed to resonate around the room. Watching her, Kelleher realized he was witnessing the birth of a political star. By becoming governor in the wake of a baffling assassination, Meredith Gordy would be the center of national media attention. Being a woman, an attractive woman, would add to her mystique. And, perhaps most important, the coolness and the charisma that were so much on display this very minute would immediately make her a name in national political circles.

Those thoughts made him think again about Jamelle Tourretta and Kyler's verbal squirming when he brought her name up. It was a long-standing joke in Annapolis that if Gordy had Kyler's ambition she would be president some day. Ambition was one thing; conspiracy to murder a governor quite another. And yet, someone had to be behind the murder; someone very smart. Kyler certainly fit that criterion.

Kelleher's reverie was interrupted by the sound of Kyler's voice saying, "One last question." The twenty minutes had flown by, although Kelleher, listening with one ear, had not picked up a single question or answer worthy of note. Gordy was committed to Barney Paulsen's programs, would make no changes in the cabinet, had asked all staff to stay on board, including and most notably Alan Sims, "without whom I am convinced the state would cease to function." Sims never even looked up as she talked.

The last question came from John Frece and, as was almost always the case with Frece, it carried just a little more spark than most of the others. "Governor," he asked, "do you find any irony in the notion that because of the way you have ascended to office, your own political career may benefit greatly?"

Kelleher didn't even look at Gordy when Frece finished; he looked at Kyler. He expected to see her glaring at Frece for such a hard-nosed question. Instead, she was staring at her shoes. Gordy, naturally, hit the question out of the park. Rather than pretend that the question had no relevance, as most politicians would have, she took it head-on.

"Politics is an often cruel and always very insensitive game, Mr.

Frece," she said. "All you have to do is look on the back lawn of this building to know that the national media are far more interested in Maryland politics today than it ever would be under less tragic circumstances. My job right now, though, is to do what I can to get this state through this trauma and get this legislature through this session with Governor Paulsen's objectives met. When we adjourn *sine die"*—*sine die* was Latin for "with no future time certain," and was used to describe the end of each year's session—"I will begin to look beyond the next forty-five days both personally and politically. But not before then."

That was it. Meredith Gordy's political coming-out party had been a smash. Kelleher could almost see the "Woman in the News" column in Saturday's *New York Times*, not to mention the ABC News "Person of the Week" feature the next night. Gordy was completely right about one thing, though: politics *was* an often cruel game. The fact that Barney Paulsen would be yesterday's news by next week—if not sooner—was certainly proof of that.

As the press conference broke up, Gordy heading back to what was now *her* office, Kelleher wanted to find Sims. But somehow, he had vanished. Before he could make a move to find him, he felt a hand on his shoulder. He turned to find Susan Sanders there.

"She's pretty good, isn't she?" she said, blue eyes still shining.

"Oh, yeah," Kelleher said. "Star material."

"So what do you think about coming on with us at eleven?" she asked.

"What about eleven?" That was McGuire, who had materialized behind him when he had turned to talk to Sanders.

"Oh, I was going to see if Bob could do a live stand-up with us since he was so close to the podium when the shooting happened."

Kelleher thought McGuire was either going to gag herself or choke him. Instead, she just looked at him. He had hoped, as long as she had shown up, that she might take him off the hook by mentioning how close to deadline eleven o'clock was. No way.

"Susan . . . I'm really sorry," he said. "When you asked before I wasn't really thinking. That's right up against our deadline for next edition."

"What about right after, say at eleven-fifteen or even eleven-twenty? We're expanding the news tonight."

"Well . . . um . . . why don't you call me at the office at about ten-thirty? I'll have a better feel then."

She beamed, sort of glowed, Kelleher thought. "Great." She ran off to talk to her crew.

McGuire started to open her mouth. Kelleher cut her off. "I know, I know," he said. "Don't say a word."

▬ ▬

McGuire, who agreed to answer the phone against her better judgment, didn't even have to make up a story to get Kelleher out of the stand-up when Susan Sanders called at ten-thirty. The truth did quite nicely.

"Susan, we aren't even close to being finished," McGuire told her. "The desk doubled the length on our Gordy profile after they saw the press conference on television, and pushed our deadline back to midnight. We'll probably still be here writing through long after that."

McGuire listened for a minute. "No problem," she said finally. "I'll have him call you first thing in the morning."

She hung up, made a face, and looked at Kelleher. "She wants you to call tomorrow about doing the noon news."

"Tenacious, isn't she?" Kelleher said, smiling. "You don't think she has something other than news-gathering on her mind, do you?"

"Don't flatter yourself, kiddo," McGuire said. "Right now, she looks at you and sees nothing but a giant scoop. And I don't mean ice cream."

Kelleher smirked. "Thanks for the vote of confidence."

Just before midnight, Jim Forrestal and Tim Burnett, who had finished their sidebars, went out for pizza and beer. When they returned, Kelleher practically inhaled three slices, remembering that he hadn't eaten anything since his lunch with Sims. That lunch now seemed to have taken place in another lifetime.

McGuire's prediction about how long it would take to finish writing and rewriting was accurate. Just before two, Kelleher and McGuire sent their two helpers home, since they still had to drive back to Washington. Kelleher finally opened a beer as they sat down to go through the lead— which had grown from fifty inches for the first edition to almost eighty for the last—one final time.

It was an excellent story. McGuire was good at plugging in details and had come up with some very strong quotes from delegates who had been near the podium. Tom Hergennyl, one of the Baltimore County delegates, had described the whole scene better than anyone:

"It was as if the real world disappeared when the lights went out," he said. "One minute we were all sitting there listening to one more speech on one more Thursday afternoon. By the time the lights came back on there was blood everywhere, people screaming and diving for cover. I felt like I had been set down in the middle of a movie set. None of it seemed real."

They sent in their final inserts at two thirty-five A.M. Looking at his watch, Kelleher realized it had been exactly twelve hours since the lights went out. Thinking about that, he felt a surge of exhaustion. He and McGuire had been writing almost nonstop for five solid hours. The _Herald_'s package for the next morning had six stories: the lead on the shooting, the profile on Gordy (now almost sixty inches long), a sidebar on where the police stood in their investigation, a political reaction story, a so-called scene piece that the desk had asked for at midnight that Kelleher had written off the top of his head, and the obituary. There was also a piece done in the office on national reaction to Paulsen's death.

Just before three, they called the office for a final check on their copy. "Hang on a second," Jane Kryton said. "Everything's fine here, but Anthony wants to speak to you."

Tom Anthony was the metro editor. Kelleher liked him as much as he disliked his assistant, Tony Quintal. Anthony enjoyed the editor-reporter byplay and didn't mind if a reporter disagreed with him.

"Bobby, Maureen, you both on?" Tom asked. Assured that they were, he went on. "I just wanted to tell you two what a great job you did today. We saw the _Post_ and the _Sun_'s early editions and they didn't touch you. They didn't have the number of guns pinned down or an explanation of how the power was lost. Neither one. And they weren't even close to having any of that stuff about Altmann at the hospital. Wyn Watkins walked out of here an hour ago chortling. He said he couldn't remember the last time he kicked Ben Bradlee's ass so thoroughly. "That's the good news," Anthony went on. "The bad news is, he wants the two of you down here for a planning breakfast at nine A.M."

"_What!_" Kelleher and McGuire screamed together.

"I know, I know," Anthony murmured. "I tried to convince him to put it back at least until ten. I told him that way you might get four hours of sleep. He just said to me, 'Tell them to go home and watch the last scene of All the President's Fucking Men.' "

Kelleher remembered that scene well. After all, he had seen the movie eight times. In that last scene, standing in his backyard, Jason Robards as

Ben Bradlee—or as Watkins might put it, Jason Fucking Robards as Ben Fucking Bradlee—tells Woodward and Bernstein, "Go home, take a bath. Rest up. Take fifteen minutes. Then get back to work."

Wyn Watkins's message was clear and Kelleher knew he wasn't wrong. The *Herald* might have won the first day's battle, but as long as Paulsen's killers were uncaught the war would get heavier and heavier. Ben Fucking Bradlee wasn't going to be in a very good mood when he read the *Herald* in the morning, and reporters like Kenworthy and Frece would be looking to get even as soon as possible.

"We'll be there, Tom," McGuire said as Kelleher's mind absorbed all of this. "Where?"

"The Willard," Anthony said. "At least you'll get a decent breakfast out of it."

They hung up the phone and looked at each other. Kelleher hadn't even had a chance to tell McGuire about Jamelle Tourretta. This was their first quiet moment of the day. He opened another beer, flipped her one, and filled her in on what Alan Sims had said and on Andrea Kyler's reaction when he had brought up Tourretta's name. McGuire put her feet up on the desk as he talked and put her head back, trying to relax. Kelleher was struck as he talked at how completely worn out she looked. Maureen usually had an energetic aura around her. It was nowhere to be found at the moment.

When he finished, she picked her head up and took a swig of the beer. "You think it's possible Kyler was just surprised?" she asked.

He shook his head. "Unless my ability to read people has completely deserted me, she was lying," he said. "And I think Gordy knew it too."

"The question, then, is why?" McGuire said. "I'll make some calls tomorrow after we get done with the editors. I'll see if I can track Tourretta down and find out why she was there."

"She still talk to you?"

"Oh, yeah. She's not a grudge holder. She never denied anything I wrote about her or FFF."

"Is she as striking as Sims says?"

McGuire grunted, swallowed the last of her beer, and stood up. "You've heard the phrase 'She's too much woman for you'? Well, Jamelle is too much woman for just about anyone. When I was doing the series, I went with her to work out one day. First of all, when she walks in the weight room in her T-shirt and shorts she stops traffic. Then she goes over and starts dead-lifting two hundred and fifty pounds—maybe more, I don't remember—doing ten reps of everything.''

''So you're telling me if she turns out to be involved in this somehow, I shouldn't try to take her out by myself.''

McGuire laughed. ''Not unless you bring Willie Ervin and a couple of his state-police pals with you.''

Kelleher had to admit to himself—not to McGuire—that meeting this woman would interest him. Not in a dark alley, though. ''Come on,'' he said. ''Let's go take a bath and rest up for fifteen minutes.''

━ ━

They walked down Main Street, their steps echoing against the sidewalk. There wasn't a soul in sight. Kelleher guessed there hadn't been much partying in Annapolis that night. When they reached the bottom of Main Street, the moon was hovering over the harbor and Kelleher felt a rush of adrenaline. He knew he wasn't going to be able to sleep; despite the exhaustion, his mind was racing and he felt a guilty exhilaration, so he suggested to McGuire that they turn left instead of right and walk over to the Naval Academy.

''Bobby,'' she said patiently, ''we have to be up and on the road in four hours.''

When he didn't say anything, she knew she couldn't talk him out of going. When *she* didn't say anything, he knew he was going alone.

''Okay,'' he said. ''You go ahead.''

She shook her head, puzzled. ''You'll be sorry in the morning.'' She leaned forward and kissed him on the cheek. ''You're a hell of a reporter, Kelleher. I'll see you in the lobby at seven-thirty.''

''Seven forty-five.''

''Seven-thirty. And if you're late, I won't let you drive.''

McGuire was a notoriously careful driver, so much so that Kelleher got headaches sitting in the passenger seat. ''Seven-thirty,'' he said, knowing when he was beaten.

She turned and walked toward their hotel. He watched until she reached the driveway and disappeared. His partner, Kelleher knew, was his best friend. If they had met in another time and another place, who knew? And yet, watching her walk to the hotel, looking so tired and vulnerable, he felt a surge of feeling for her—a surge he quickly pushed out of his mind.

Kelleher turned and started walking toward the Naval Academy gate. In six years he had never seen the streets of Annapolis so empty. There wasn't a car or another living soul to be seen. Kelleher jammed his hands into his pockets and tried to shove the picture of the dying Barney Paulsen out of his mind. All night, as they had been writing, the sight of Paulsen, his chest completely shot away, kept thrusting itself into his mind's eye. That was another reason Kelleher didn't want to go to bed. He was certain that if he did sleep, he would have terrible nightmares. He was a vivid dreamer, both asleep and awake, and this was not a night to let his subconscious take control of his thoughts.

Normally, when Kelleher ran in the evenings, he jogged past the sentry post at the academy gate with a wave or a nod. The only time there had been any kind of real security at Navy during Kelleher's years in Annapolis had been during the Persian Gulf War. Then, Kelleher had needed a special pass to get on campus for his runs, a pass provided by one of the school's assistant basketball coaches.

At a few minutes before four in the morning, Kelleher assumed he couldn't just amble onto campus. Sure enough, as he walked up, the guard came out of the sentry box to greet him.

"May I help you, sir?"

"I hope so," Kelleher said. "I'm a reporter; I work the State House. Usually I run out by the seawall at about seven each night. Today was a little bit different, though, and I just finished working. I wanted to walk out there for a while. That's all. I'm too hopped up to sleep."

The guard, who had the solid, stocky build of a wrestler, looked Kelleher up and down for a minute. "You have some kind of ID or something?" he asked.

"Sure," Kelleher said, digging into his wallet for his State House press card. The guard held it up to the light.

"*Washington Herald*, huh? Hey, how come your sports section never runs our wrestling results?"

Funny how Kelleher could almost always tell what sport a guy played. He shrugged his shoulders to indicate how sorry he was about the wrestling results.

The guard handed the press card back to Kelleher. "So, were you there when they shot the governor?"

"Yeah, I was," Kelleher said, not eager to provide any details. "It's been a real long day—and night. So, if it's all right . . ."

"Yeah, sure," the marine said, clearly disappointed that the conversation was ending. He probably had another four hours to go before being relieved and would just as soon have some company.

Kelleher walked quickly past Halsey Field House and felt the wind as he approached the seawall. He thought this was one of the most beautiful spots on earth. To his right was the harbor, with the Marriott directly across the way. He could see his room and balcony. The light was on next door in McGuire's room. She hadn't gone to sleep yet either. Directly ahead of him, as he made the turn for the one-mile walk along the seawall, a couple of miles out on Chesapeake Bay, were the twinkling lights of the Bay Bridge. To his left were the Navy practice fields. Kelleher loved running there every evening, especially late in the session when the clocks were changed and the days were long enough that he could finish before sunset.

As he walked past the football team's practice field, he tried to sort out what had gone on in the last thirteen hours. "Think clearly, Bobby," he said to himself. What did he know *for sure*?

First, someone, or more likely some group, wanted Barney Paulsen dead. They had carefully planned his murder: the guns, the power black-out, the shooter—or shooters—arriving early enough to be certain to get seats in the front row.

The question was *why*? The only lead at all, and it was a slim one, was Jamelle Tourretta. Could it be that Females for Freedom had plotted to kill Barney Paulsen to put Meredith Gordy in the governor's office? There was certainly no doubt after tonight that Paulsen's death had cleared the way for her to become a major political star.

Even so, it didn't make much sense. Gordy was bound to continue to rise in the political world without anyone having to resort to murder. What's more, even though Kelleher was no expert on the feminist move-ment, he had read enough to know that over the years, it had been non-violent. Even Tourretta, he remembered from McGuire's series, had pointed out that FFF did not believe in violence on any level.

What had happened in the House of Delegates on Thursday afternoon was a long way from nonviolent. It may have been that Tourretta's pres-ence was sheer coincidence. But if that were the case, why had Kyler seemed to lie about it?

Kelleher had been so wrapped up in his analysis, he barely noticed that the road was beginning to curve left. He looked up and was surprised to see a car pulled off to the side, at the corner of the seawall. Even more surprising were the state-government license plates. Beyond the car, someone was sitting on the wall, legs dangling over the water.

"Hello?" Kelleher said softly, not wanting to startle whomever the wall-sitter was.

He failed. Andrea Kyler almost jumped into the water at the sound of his voice. "Who's there?" she demanded, whirling around, almost losing her balance in the process. She scrambled to her feet. "Kelleher?" She sighed in disbelief. "What the hell are *you* doing here?"

"My guess is, the same thing you're doing," he said.

She had a light-blue winter coat on but had taken her shoes off. When the moonlight hit her face, Kelleher was struck once again by just how pretty she was. Her eyes looked red, as if she'd been crying. She didn't respond to his comment. Instead, she turned back around to resettle herself on the wall. That may have been a hint that she wanted to be left alone, but Kelleher didn't take it. He sat down next to her. For a while they both stared out toward the Bay Bridge, saying nothing.

"So why do you think I came out here?" she said finally.

"Couldn't sleep. Too confused by it all. Wound up. Excited that Meredith's governor but a bit horrified by how it happened."

"A *bit* horrified? Do you really think I'm *that* heartless?"

"Okay, very horrified. I'm sorry."

She was quiet again for a minute or so. "Basically, you're right, though," she said. "I was no big fan of Barney Paulsen. But he never did anything to deserve to die."

It sounded as if she was talking to herself more than to Kelleher. He didn't push it. "How's Meredith?" he asked.

"Amazing, actually. She fainted after we got out of the chamber and felt sick most of the afternoon. But after you came to the office and she found out about what Altmann had done, she turned into a tiger. You saw her at the press conference."

"She really was great."

Kyler laughed suddenly. "I guess, Kelleher, I should thank you. If you hadn't bluffed your way in this afternoon, Meredith might have never snapped out of her depression."

"You know, Kyler, that may be the nicest thing you've ever said to me."

She laughed again. Twice in one minute, a new record. "Kelleher, that *is* the nicest thing I've ever said to you—by far. Of course, if you repeat it to anybody, I'll deny it."

"Your secret is safe with me."

He wondered for a moment if this was the time to bring Tourretta up again. But looking at her in the moonlight, he just couldn't bring himself to do it. The Andrea Kyler sitting next to him—vulnerable, smiling, eyes misty—was someone he could easily fall for. So he swallowed his question and sat in silence.

"What are you thinking?" she asked after a while.

"Nothing, really."

"Liar. Kelleher, how old are you?"

"Thirty."

"A baby."

"Baby? What are you, thirty-one?"

"Next week. I'm a lot older than you though, trust me."

"What's that mean?"

She turned and looked right at him. "Actually, it's a compliment. I think you have the potential to turn out all right, Kelleher. You'll outgrow Fran O'Brien's and TV bimbos and someday, a few years from now, you'll probably turn out to be a pretty good guy."

"What about right now?"

She didn't answer. Instead, she stood up, slipped on her shoes, and put her hand out to help him up. "What's this?" Kelleher asked, genuinely baffled.

"This is going back to my apartment before you freeze to death out here."

Kelleher hadn't even noticed that he was shivering. "Your apartment?"

"My apartment. I need to be with someone right now and, I suspect, so do you."

Kelleher stared at her for a moment, wondering when he would wake up from the dream he was obviously having. He had fantasized about Andrea Kyler on more than one occasion, but the thought of actually going to bed with her had seemed an impossibility. In the corner of his brain a small voice was saying, "Don't do this, she's a news source." It was being shouted down, though, by every other cell in his body. He took her hand and pulled himself up. They walked to her car.

"Never thought this would happen in a million years, did you?" she said when she was behind the wheel, a little bit of the old Kyler creeping into her voice.

"Two million," he answered.

"I like an honest man," she said and started the car.

CHAPTER 6

THE BIG HIT

*T*he alarm went off at seven: Kelleher heard it but for a moment couldn't get his body to move. He lay there, eyes shut, wondering if the alarm was part of his dream. He hoped so. But it kept on buzzing so he opened his eyes. Sure enough, he found himself staring at the curtains in Andrea Kyler's bedroom. He remembered setting the alarm a little more than an hour ago, just in case he fell asleep. He reached out and punched the button to shut it off.

He stretched his arm behind him, then twisted his body around so he could see the other side of the bed. It was empty. "Andrea?" he said, tentatively at first; then louder, "Andrea!"

No response. He thought about getting up to look for her, then thought better of it. He fell back onto the pillows, shut his eyes, and thought about what had taken place when he and Kyler had reached the apartment a few hours ago.

They hadn't talked very much. She had made some hot chocolate and they had sat in the small living room, sipping it until they both warmed up. Then she had gotten up, taken him by the hand, and led him to the bedroom.

Once they were in bed, there had been none of the tentativeness Kelleher usually associated with first-time lovemaking. It was as if both were experiencing some kind of catharsis after the events of the day. The sex was intense and emotional. For close to two hours, they explored each other. Andrea had finally asked what time he had to get up in the morning and he had remembered the breakfast meeting in Washington.

"Oh, God," he said. "I have to leave here by seven-thirty."

"Better set the alarm," she whispered.

That was the last thing he remembered. He had set the alarm, crawled back into her arms, and fallen asleep. He opened his eyes again: seven-ten. Kyler's apartment, which she used during the session, was on one of the many side streets that surrounded State Circle. It was about a three-minute walk from the Marriott. Still, Kelleher had to get moving. He didn't want to run into McGuire in the lobby and have to try to explain where he'd been.

He jumped out of bed, pulled on his underpants and his shirt, and walked into the living room. Andrea was nowhere in sight. He padded into the kitchen. The note was on the coffee maker:

Kelleher:
I have now made you coffee *and* hot chocolate. You owe me big-time. Sorry I'm not here. I forgot we had a seven o'clock meeting. By the way, thanks. And I *will* deny everything . . .

Andrea

Kelleher read the note four times, psychoanalyzing it. Did the "owe me big-time" reference mean that this had not been a one-night stand? Or did the "deny everything" line mean he was to pretend this had never happened? Probably neither line meant anything.

He poured himself some coffee, took it back to the bedroom, and finished dressing. No time for a shower, which he desperately needed. He was about to walk out the door when the phone rang. Instinctively, he started to answer it, before he remembered where he was. Kyler's tape picked up on the third ring and asked the caller to leave a message or to call at her office.

A female voice came on the line after the beep: "Andrea," she said sharply, "I hope you aren't answering because you're en route. If you're still there, pick up." There was a pause, then a click. The voice was vaguely familiar to Kelleher and he tried to think of who on Gordy's staff sounded like that. The strange thing was, the only person he could think of who might speak to Kyler that sharply was Gordy and it definitely wasn't her. He glanced at his watch again: seven-twenty. Andrea had left here before seven. Why would she be late for a meeting five minutes away? He shook his head, confused again, and pushed open the sliding glass door that led to the stairs outside the apartment. Kyler lived on the third floor of a three-story house that the owner had converted into three one-bedroom apartments so that he could charge an outrageous price to three different tenants during the legislative session. The only private entrance to the apartment was by way of the outdoor staircase.

The sun was just coming up as Kelleher walked quickly toward Main Street. He glanced over his shoulder briefly just to make sure the State House was still there. It was, gleaming as it always did in the early morning, and he breathed a sigh of relief. He needed to know that something in his life had not changed since yesterday.

As he walked to the Marriott, Kelleher's mind was in complete chaos. He knew he had just blatantly violated one of the first tenets of journalism: "Thou shalt not sleep with a news source." The fact that Kyler was now the chief aide to the governor, not just the lieutenant governor, made it that much worse. Throw in the nagging questions about Jamelle Tourretta, and Kelleher knew that any good editor would fire him on the spot if he confessed his crime.

Why had this happened? Sure, he'd always thought Kyler was sexy, but so what? He had found plenty of other women attractive who he knew were off-limits because of his job and had never given in to temptation.

But this time was different. He peered out at the water as the Marriott loomed in front of him and tried to piece it together. He knew it had something to do, probably everything to do, with Barney Paulsen's death. It was as if Oz had been invaded. Everything was different now. Like it or not, this session could never be like others had been. The rituals would not be the same, nor would the people practicing them.

A burst of sunlight hit Kelleher squarely in the eyes and, at that moment, so did a revelation. This was IT. This was The Big Hit. Like it or not, this story was going to determine his future. His days of writing stories about Wendell Hoxledeer's bills were over forever. If he broke this story, if he and McGuire figured out who the hell had killed Paulsen, he would take the step up he had been searching for. But if he blew the story, he was finished here. The *Herald* would reason—correctly—that if he couldn't make The Big Hit after six years, it was time to send him back to the minors. Or to another paper.

That didn't make what Kelleher had just done any less unethical. But at least it helped him understand *why* he had done it. He had walked out to the seawall to figure what the day had meant and had found the answer— Kyler. If the rules had been the same, if he had still been just a State House reporter covering another session, he never would have ended up in bed with her. For that matter, if the rules had all been the same, if Barney Paulsen were still alive, she never would have *gone* to bed with him.

But it had all changed now. For good. The idyllic life he had led in Annapolis had ended the moment the lights went out in the House of Delegates. Like it or not, he would be leaving Oz soon. The only question now was, where was he going?

It was seven twenty-seven when he walked into the lobby. Fortunately, McGuire wasn't downstairs yet. He waved to Mike, the front-desk clerk, who gave him a big grin, as if to say, "Big night, eh?" Rather than wait for the elevator and chance running into McGuire, he took the steps up to the fifth floor. The hallway was empty. He sprinted to his room, opened it, and was changing clothes almost before the door shut. He was in the lobby at seven thirty-five and was surprised to see McGuire walking through the front door as he arrived.

"Where were you?" he asked.

"I knew you'd be a couple minutes late just on general principle, so I brought the car down from the garage." She looked up at him. "Couldn't you have shaved?"

He had completely forgotten about that in his rush to get back downstairs. "Give me a minute, I'll go back upstairs. . . ."

"No, no time for that," she said, reaching into her purse. She walked briskly to the gift shop and returned thirty seconds later with a disposable razor and a small can of shaving cream. "It may be rough without water, but it'll do."

"While I'm driving?"

"While *I'm* driving. The deal was seven-thirty."

He groaned loudly. Actually, though, he didn't mind the idea. He wasn't sure he could keep his eyes open all the way to Washington anyway.

CHAPTER 7

NEWSPAPER POLITICS

The traffic on Route 50 was awful. Kelleher, having cut himself twice trying to shave, had a splitting headache by the time they hit the D.C. city line. The sun, so bright on his walk back to the hotel, had faded and raindrops were splattering the windshield. Kelleher had always been amazed by the fact that traffic came to such a complete halt in Washington whenever the weather was the least bit inclement. Snow was impossible; rain merely unbearable.

It was nine on the dot when they pulled into the garage next door to the *Herald*. Kelleher needed about six aspirin, six cups of coffee, and at least six hours of sleep. Instead, he got to follow McGuire up the steps, around the corner, up the street, and into the Willard lobby. By the time they reached the door to the restaurant, he was breathing hard.

"Thought you were in shape," McGuire said. She was breathing hard too.

"I guess we're all getting older," he said with a grin.

She shot him a look as if to say, "What the hell does that mean?" but let it go. They walked into the restaurant, heading directly for the back corner table where Wyn Watkins liked to hold court in the morning. No one could do a power breakfast quite like the *Herald*'s executive editor.

The table looked like an afternoon editors' meeting was in progress. Watkins sat at one end, flanked by managing editor Byron Tompkins and Tom Anthony. Tony Quintal was next to Anthony, with Jane Kryton and her assistant, Bob Lynch, next. Opposite them sat national editor Shana Owings and two of her reporters, Mike Estes and Howard Franks. Estes was the number two national political reporter; Franks the number two White House reporter. Their presence, Kelleher decided immediately, was not a good sign. It meant national was planning to try to take over the story.

Wyn Watkins stood up to greet McGuire as she and Kelleher approached the table. Watkins thought himself something of a ladies' man, a laughable thought as far as Kelleher was concerned, although it was true that Watkins turned up at social events with very young, very beautiful women on his arm. All that proved to Kelleher was that money could buy company—if not happiness. Watkins had been married and divorced three times.

He threw his arms around McGuire, kissed her grandly, and said, "Wonderful work last night, Maureen." McGuire gracefully slid from his embrace and said softly, "Bobby did most of the spadework, Mr. Watkins." To say that another reporter had done "good spadework" was one of journalism's ultimate compliments: spading meant digging, as in digging up the story.

Watkins regarded Kelleher suspiciously for a moment before shaking his hand and saying, "You too, Kelleher." Kelleher swallowed his real response, smiled, and said, "Thanks, Mr. Watkins." His friends at the *Post* always told him that Bradlee was "Ben" to everyone in the newsroom. Kelleher suspected that Watkins might have a heart attack if one of his reporters ever called him Wyn.

The two Annapolis reporters made their way around the table, shaking hands and exchanging hellos with everyone. There was a ritual going on here, one that would likely turn into a full-scale riot as the metro and national staffs fought for the story. Kelleher and McGuire would be expected to sit and watch quietly while their editors divided up the turf. Kelleher wished he had called in sick.

A waiter poured coffee as they sat down. "We waited for the two of you before ordering," Tony Quintal said pointedly, wanting to make sure Watkins noted that they had been a few minutes late.

"Yes, sorry we were late," McGuire said. "With the rain, the traffic was just brutal. We left at seven-thirty and still needed ninety minutes to get here."

"What is it without traffic?" Shana Owings asked politely.

"Forty, maximum," Kelleher answered.

"Going one hundred miles an hour," the ever-helpful Quintal threw in.

"No, it's thirty-five going one hundred miles an hour," Kelleher answered, still looking at Owings rather than Quintal. "It's forty driving the speed limit."

The waiter intervened conveniently at that point to take orders. Once he had ordered his eggs Benedict—what else? Kelleher thought—Watkins pulled his chair closer to the table and said, "Okay, let's talk some strategy here."

"Before you start, Wyn, I'd just like to reiterate that I thought Bobby and Maureen did fantastic work last night," Tom Anthony said. "We're way ahead of everyone on the story right now."

Watkins nodded and charged on. "But what we have to do today is figure out how to stay ahead on the story. Tom, Shana, what have you two come up with?"

Typical Watkins, Kelleher thought. Rather than ask the two reporters who were *there* where the story was taking place, he turned instead to two editors whose major forays outside the office were meetings like this one. Owings jumped at Watkins' question before Anthony could open his mouth.

"Well, Wyn, there's no doubt we're going to need lots of help from Bobby and Maureen on this," she said, as if the story belonged to national. "Mike is working his sources around the country to put together a more complete picture of Paulsen—who he was, how he was thought of, and, of course, what might have led to this. Howard is going to take the Gordy perspective, try to put something together on where she may fit in nationally down the road."

Kelleher felt nauseated. He looked at McGuire, who pursed her lips to indicate he should keep his mouth shut. Anthony was talking now. "If Howard is going to work Gordy, he might start out by reading the profile Bobby and Maureen produced today," he said. "I doubt if he'll find too many new angles to work once he's read that. As for Paulsen, he wasn't much of a national figure, but go right ahead and see what you can find."

Owings glared at Anthony without a trace of subtlety. He had taken her attempt at an end run and, for all intents and purposes, told her to stick it. Kelleher had always liked Tom Anthony.

"Well, how do you two want to divide this up?" Watkins said.

Kelleher had heard enough. "Excuse me, Mr. Watkins, may I say something?" he said. Watkins looked down the table at him as if he were a servant who had sat in someone's seat.

"What is it, Kelleher?"

"With all due respect to all of you and the planning you need to do here, it seems to me that there's only one story that really matters in all this."

"Gordy," Shana Owings said triumphantly.

"No," Kelleher said, perhaps too emphatically. "What matters is who *did* it. This is a murder and we have to solve it."

Watkins laughed. "Don't you think the police might want to do that, Kelleher?"

"Mr. Watkins, you don't understand," Kelleher said, no doubt digging his grave a little deeper. "Right now I don't think they know any more than we do. Maureen and I both have sources we can work, and if we don't actually solve the thing ourselves, we can certainly be the first ones to write it. *That's* the story. The rest of it is political blather."

"Political blather, is that what you call it?" said Estes, whose life was political blather.

"Mike, you know what I mean. We write political analysis stories all the time. People run for office every year. A governor gets murdered in this country every *fifty* years."

Anthony looked at Watkins. "He's right, Wyn. I'd be glad to have national study all the political implications of this and let the two kids we sent to Annapolis keep working on the legislative session. Let Kelleher and McGuire work the murder."

"Just a second." It was McGuire. "I'm not disputing what Bobby says. But there are some political stories we've been working on that I don't want to give up."

"You don't have to give them up, Maureen," Anthony answered. "Maybe this thing will be over in a couple of days, who knows? But I do think you and Bobby are the ones who should be working on it right now, don't you?"

McGuire didn't look happy with that notion, which surprised Kelleher. Maybe she saw this as an opportunity to do some work with the people on the national desk.

"Maureen, I think Tom's right," Watkins said. "You and Kelleher work the police story. We'll leave the local politics to the Montgomery and Prince Georges reporters for now. They'll like that idea. And Shana, your people can hunt around for the national implications to this story."

He regarded Kelleher coolly. "Does that meet with your approval, Mr. Kelleher?"

Kelleher knew Watkins was telling him that even though they had been forced to go along with his idea, he had spoken out of turn. "I think it's a great idea," Kelleher said, swallowing his tongue instead of telling J. Wynton Watkins to fuck off once and for all.

The rest of breakfast was phony small talk and questions about what to work on for Saturday's and Sunday's papers. The only thing agreed on was that McGuire and Kelleher would be responsible for any news on the case and would put together a Sunday piece re-creating the events of Thursday and examining where Gordy might lead the legislature as governor. After that, if the murder was still unsolved, they would turn over the local political reporting to their backups.

They all walked back to the newsroom in the rain after breakfast. Kelleher could tell that McGuire was sulking. He couldn't imagine why she was so tense, but he was sure he'd find out later.

As they got off the elevator and the editors headed off, he said quietly to McGuire, "Will you make some calls on Tourretta?" They had agreed in the car coming down that mentioning Tourretta to the editors would be foolish. After all, it was little more than a wild guess at this point and they didn't want anyone pushing them to produce a story where perhaps none existed.

"I'll see what I can find out," she said and headed off to the ladies' room. Kelleher paused at the front of the newsroom to check his messages. There were quite a few, including one from Susan Sanders. He had completely forgotten to call her about the noon news. He walked to his desk and called the in-office answering machine in Annapolis, just in case Kyler or Sims had called there. Neither one had. He picked up a copy of the last edition that was sitting on his desk. It was poor form to read your own stuff in the newsroom, so he decided to go to the bathroom, where he could have some privacy.

It was just after eleven o'clock now and the office was slowly coming to life. Kelleher could think of no place in the world that he loved being in more than a newsroom. Even with all the Byzantine politics of the *Herald*—or any newspaper, for that matter—there was a shared feeling you had with the other people there that you couldn't have anyplace else. Everyone did the same thing, in one form or another, shared the same hopes, dreams, and fears. Everyone spoke the same language. As he walked down the hallway to the bathroom, he passed several other reporters. Each had a word of encouragement: "Good work last night; great story, Kelleher; unbelievable stuff, huh, Bobby?"

The message was loud and clear: it was a tough story, a long day and a long night, and he and McGuire had come through. Kelleher liked nothing better than being in the newsroom the day after a big story. Even McGuire admitted she didn't hate it. "Taking bows," she called it.

McGuire was waiting for him at his desk when he returned. "I spoke to Jamelle Tourretta," she greeted him.

"And?"

"She was in Annapolis hoping to meet with Meredith Gordy after the speech. Your theory that Kyler was lying is right. Kyler had set the meeting up but hadn't told Gordy."

"How come?"

"Seems that Gordy has distanced herself from FFF since my series. You remember she was still in the Senate then and was very critical of their methods."

"Yeah, so?"

"Well, Kyler goes way back with Tourretta. First met her in college."

"Wait a minute; Kyler's a lot younger than Tourretta, isn't she?"

"Six years. Tourretta was in law school, Kyler was an undergraduate. They were both members of NOW at Northwestern. That's how Kyler ended up working at FFF when she came to Washington. Anyway, Tourretta's giving a speech Sunday at your beloved alma mater. She was hoping to convince Gordy to show up at the speech as a kind of public extension of an olive branch. FFF has backed away from their seduction tactics and is just working to find and promote female candidates these days. Tourretta wants Gordy back in the FFF fold, so to speak, and this was going to be a start."

Kelleher rocked back in his chair. McGuire was sitting on his desk, sipping what had to be her sixth cup of coffee.

"How much coffee have you had today?" he wanted to know. Usually, she asked *him* that question.

"Too damn much. You think we need to follow up on this Tourretta thing any further?"

He shrugged. "I don't know. Her story makes sense, I guess. But I wouldn't mind talking to Kyler about it again, just to see if she tells the same story."

McGuire hopped off the desk. "Let me put it this way: If Tourretta's lying, I guarantee you she's on the phone with Kyler right now making sure their stories match. She's no dummy."

"So I've gathered. You know, UVA is playing Maryland on Sunday afternoon in Charlottesville. Did Tourretta say what time she was speaking?''

''Noon, in the student union building.''

''Hmmm. The game's at four: Maybe if nothing else is cooking I'll take a drive down there and hear her speak. I'd sort of like to meet her anyway.''

''And you wouldn't mind going to the game either, would you?''

''No, as a matter of fact, I wouldn't. Let's see what shakes out.''

''In the meantime, we need to think about a story for tomorrow.''

''I was just thinking that. Why don't you call Tom Wyman and some other state-police types and I'll call Alan Sims.''

''Fine.''

''One more question.''

''Shoot.''

''Why did you get so upset at breakfast about the notion of letting the politics go for a few days so we can work the murder story? That's the front-page story in all this.''

McGuire hesitated. ''I know that, Bobby. But I just don't like the idea that here we have a chance to write something the national people will notice and we're stuck writing what really amount to glorified cop stories.''

Kelleher nodded. His theory had been correct. ''Maureen, first of all, you don't have to impress national. You're there already. Second, the cop story *is* the story—no matter what anybody in this newsroom tells you.''

''I hope you're right,'' she said, ''on both things.''

''I'm right. Go call Wyman.''

He dialed Alan Sims's direct line at the office. No answer. He dialed the number for Sims's secretary. No answer. He tried the main number at the State House. He got a tape informing him that the state government was closed until eight A.M. Monday. Next, he tried Sims at home. This time he got his answering machine. He left a message asking Alan to call him at the office in Washington and hung up.

That done, he tried Kyler and went through the same frustrating sequence, although this time he didn't waste any energy with the call to the main number. Kyler was probably in with Gordy, but he didn't think calling her there was such a hot idea. It might embarrass Kyler and being embarrassed might annoy her. In any event, Kelleher felt that their next conversation should be face-to-face.

Sitting around the office working the phones was a nice way to while away a rainy day, he decided, but it wasn't very productive. He decided to head back to Annapolis with a stop on the way in Bowie, just in case Sims was home and not answering the phone. Given the mood he'd been in the night before, Kelleher thought that was a distinct possibility.

He explained his plan to McGuire, who wasn't thrilled. "We're going to have to come up with something for first edition," she said. "Be back here or in the office up there by five o'clock so we can talk."

Kelleher saluted and went off to convince Kryton to sign out a company car to him, since they had driven down in McGuire's car. Normally reporters weren't allowed to keep cars overnight, but in this case Kryton figured they could make an exception. "Just don't get in an accident, okay?" she said, none too optimistically.

Driving through northeast Washington, traffic was horrendous, and it was two o'clock by the time he pulled into the circular driveway outside of Sims's house. He rang the doorbell three times, then waited for a response. He was about to head around back to see if Sims was asleep in his basement rec room when the door opened. Sims, dressed in a T-shirt and sweatpants, was standing there.

"You've been here all day, haven't you?" Kelleher demanded.

"I was too hung over to go anywhere this morning," he said. "Now I'm just too disgusted with the world to go anywhere."

"Anything new disgust you?"

Sims did his best to smile. "Would you like a beer?" he asked.

"I thought you'd never ask."

Sims led the way downstairs to the basement, which he had designed himself. It had a large, comfortable rec room with a bar, a second room big enough to hold both a pool table and a Ping-Pong table, and a third room that served as an office. Whenever Kelleher envisioned his dream house, it had a basement like this one.

Sims walked behind the bar and took out two beers. "I guess one won't kill me," he said as he tossed a can to Kelleher. "Although when I woke up this morning I vowed never to take another drink of any kind."

Kelleher sat in an armchair. "So, are you really going to stay on and work for Meredith?"

Sims sat down on one of the couches. "I suppose," he said. "At least until Kyler becomes so impossible that I have to leave. I told her I'd give her a final decision after her speech Tuesday night."

"Monday night."

Sims shook his head. "No, Tuesday. She met with Cutler and Weiland this morning and they convinced her the legislature should have a day to get back to normal before she spoke to them. I hate to agree with either of those assholes, but I think they're right. The first time she walks into that chamber as Governor Gordy will be traumatic for everyone—including her. A day of adjustment is a good idea."

Kelleher nodded and plunged ahead to the real reason for his visit. "You find out anything new today?"

"Bobby, I thought you came out here to see how I was feeling," Sims said with mock hurt in his voice.

"Actually, I did," Kelleher said. "But . . ."

"But you've got a job to do. I know. Did you check out Jamelle Tourretta?"

"Maureen did. She came to town to try to talk Gordy into showing up at a speech she's giving Sunday in Charlottesville. She's looking for some kind of rapprochement with Gordy."

"You buy that?"

"Any reason not to?"

"Don't know. But I do know she was sitting right behind one of the suspected shooters."

"Wait a minute. How do you *know* where she was sitting? And how do you know who the shooters are?"

"Don't know," Sims said. "Don't know anything for sure."

"Yeah, but you've got an idea. Come on, Alan, what did the cops tell you?"

"Off the record?"

"Fuck, no. What good does off the record do me? What do you know?"

"Bobby, you put this in the paper, the cops will know I gave it to you."

"How can you be sure of that? Maureen might be getting it from one of her state-police sources right now."

"No way. Not this. None of her sources even knows about this. I guarantee you that."

Kelleher sighed. He was in a tough position. Sims clearly knew something important. He couldn't afford to walk out of here without knowing what it was. But on the other hand, if he agreed to put it off the record and then found it out somewhere else—from Kyler perhaps?—or if McGuire learned it, he would have a hard time convincing Sims that he hadn't violated their agreement.

"Can we compromise?" he asked finally.

"How?"

"Put it on deep background. If I can get someone else to tell me, I can use it."

"No good. You can't repeat this anywhere. At least not tonight." Sims sighed, which seemed to set off his hangover. He began rubbing his temples. "I'll tell you what. You keep it out of the paper until Monday and I'll give it to you. By then, enough of the cops will know about it that I'll be protected and you'll have the weekend to try to follow up on it."

"Yeah, but by then other guys might have it."

Sims shrugged. "Best I can do."

"One condition," Kelleher said, not willing to give up entirely. "If we find it out somewhere else, I'll call you. If I can convince you we really have another source, we can use it."

Sims looked at him closely. "You wouldn't try to fake me out, would you?"

"Alan, I've known you too long for that."

"Okay. Deal." Sims stood up and walked across the room to his desk. He reached inside and pulled something out of it. He stood with his back to Kelleher as if trying to be sure he was doing the right thing. Finally, he turned around and walked back to Kelleher. "Look at it for a minute, then I'll explain," he said.

He handed him a photograph. Apparently it was a picture taken of the gallery during Paulsen's speech. Kelleher could see a red-headed woman whom he assumed to be Tourretta sitting smack in the middle of the gallery in the second row.

"Where'd you get this picture?" he asked. "Why would anyone be taking a picture of the gallery while Paulsen was speaking?"

"Look a little closer. That's actually a photograph of a TV still frame. Maryland public television was taping the speech. The producer went for a shot of Helen Paulsen early on, then pulled back to show the entire gallery."

"So the Maryland public TV people know about this."

"No, no, calm down, Kelleher. The cops just asked them for a look at the tape. They have no idea they found anything."

"What's to prevent them from figuring this out?"

"Figure *what* out? Just looking at the picture, you've got nothing without the ballistics report."

"Finally we cut to the chase. What the hell did ballistics tell you?"

"Look at the picture again. Count in six seats from the left, eighteen seats from the left, and six seats from the right in the front row. Paulsen got hit by bullets from three different guns. You already knew that. What we know today is that the shots almost surely came from those three seats. We could be off by one seat on the two side seats, but not likely. The guy in the center seat we *know* is one of the shooters. The other two are likely.''

"Even so, Tourretta sitting right behind the guy doesn't make her part of the conspiracy.''

"True enough. But it does put her that much closer to it. *Very* close to it.''

Kelleher had put the picture in his lap while Sims was talking. Now he picked it up and peered at it again. "Any leads on the shooters?'' he asked.

"Not so far. The cops are going through every file the FBI has.''

Kelleher was staring at the guy in the center seat, the one sure shooter. Like the other two, he had a heavy beard. But his face was somehow familiar.

"What are you staring at?''

"I'm not sure. This guy in the middle seat, he looks kind of familiar, like I've seen him some . . . Holy shit! It's Jimmy Dumont! Fucking Jimmy Dumont!''

"Who the hell is Jimmy Dumont?''

Kelleher put the picture down, got up, and walked behind the bar for another beer. He was suddenly wired; the exhaustion that had been following him all day was completely gone.

"Jesus, Alan, this really makes it crazy. Jimmy Dumont was the goddamn grand dragon of the Ku Klux Klan when I was a student at UVA. This guy is so fucking crazy right wing it isn't even funny. If he's really one of the shooters there's absolutely no way Jamelle Tourretta is involved in this thing. There cannot possibly be two human beings farther apart politically on the planet earth than Jamelle Tourretta and Jimmy Dumont.''

"Whoa, Kelleher, time-out here a second. You're telling me that there was a living, breathing branch of the KKK on the campus of the University of Virginia in the eighties?''

"Yes and no. It was supposed to be a secret but it became a fairly highly publicized story. Burned crosses started showing up around campus: one in front of the black fraternity, another in front of the dorm where most of the athletes lived—a lot of them black, obviously—another one outside the union one night when Ed Koch was giving a speech.

"I found out from one of the guys on the football team that there was this crazy guy who lived in his dorm named Jimmy Dumont. Dumont was telling people he was the grand dragon of the KKK for the state of Virginia. Turned out he had maybe six other guys. I went to him, told him I'd heard this, and he admitted the whole thing, showed me his robes and everything. He dropped out of school at the end of that semester, I think he was a junior at the time, and said he was going to join one of those fundamentalist churches to save the world from bleeding heart liberals, niggers, and Jews—although not necessarily in that order."

"You sure this is him?"

Kelleher walked back over to the picture and studied it again. There just wasn't any doubt. He would recognize those crazed-looking eyes anywhere. "If I'm Bobby Kelleher and you're Alan Sims, this is Jimmy Dumont. I'm that sure."

Sims stood up and walked to the phone. "Hold it," Kelleher said, "what are you doing?"

"I'm calling the cops."

"No, wait a minute. Let's talk about this first. You want me to hold off until Monday about the picture and the ballistics report. Okay, fine, then at least give me until Monday to try to track Dumont down."

Sims shook his head. "Can't do it, Bobby. We're talking about a guy who killed the governor of Maryland. I can't hold the cops up two days on tracking him down."

"Why not? Look, Alan, I don't want the guy running around loose either but the fact is, he's clearly not a crazed killer. He's part of a carefully planned conspiracy. That means he's hiding somewhere, not running around loose shooting at people."

"*You* said he was crazy."

"Yeah, but politically crazy, not Son of Sam crazy."

"He's already killed once, Bobby."

"Killed with two others and run. Killed and left his weapon behind. Very carefully shot one person and got out. Come on, Alan. If you aren't going to let me write for tomorrow, you hold off too. Give me until Sunday night at least. Not even Monday morning, Sunday night."

Sims let go of the phone and sat back down. "This is craziness. What if he does do something else? How will that make us both feel?"

"I'll tell you what, Alan. I'll get Tommy Montagne, our FBI guy, to check him out. If he has any kind of rap sheet that indicates random violence at all, you call the cops right away."

"You give me your word on that?"

"Absolutely."

Sims let out a deep sigh. "Which now brings us to the next question. If your guy Dumont really is the shooter, then what the hell is the motive? Okay, Barney was a liberal, but Gordy is even *more* liberal."

"It's much weirder than that, Alan. At least Paulsen was a man. There's no way Jimmy Dumont, at least the Jimmy Dumont I knew, would be involved in a conspiracy to make a woman governor."

"Guess what, pal?"

"I know. But there's also no way that Jamelle Tourretta and Andrea Kyler would ever be involved with someone like Dumont. What Tourretta told Maureen must be true." That idea, the notion that Kyler really wasn't involved in all of this, made Kelleher smile, the first real smile he'd had in what felt like a very long time.

"Why are you grinning like an idiot?"

"No reason. Listen, I have to go. I told Maureen I'd check in with her by five and I want to call Montagne, get him to check out Dumont."

Sims stood up. "Call me right away if he finds anything."

"You have my word."

━ ━

It was raining even harder when Kelleher left Sims standing at his front door and raced to his car. It was such a cold and driving rain that going outside seemed like about the stupidest thing in the world. Driving from Washington to see Sims, the rain had depressed Kelleher, making him think all sorts of morbid thoughts about Barney Paulsen and the inevitability of death. Now, though, as he steered carefully back to Route 50, he barely noticed the rain. The mystery of who had killed Barney Paulsen had taken a confusing twist, but in doing so it had exonerated Andrea Kyler. Life suddenly seemed full of promise, even if he was totally baffled by the stunning re-entrance of Jimmy Dumont into this life.

Kelleher still remembered going to Dumont's dorm room on a day much like this one to confront him. Jimmy Dumont was a little guy, perhaps five feet eight and 150 pounds, but his eyes shone with the kind of intensity Kelleher remembered seeing in film clips of Charles Manson. There was an insanity in those eyes, especially when he looked right at Kelleher and told him that the world must be controlled again by white Anglo-Saxon Protestant males because no one else was fit to run it. He had certainly never figured Dumont as a killer, though; he hoped his theory that he wasn't dangerous—at least dangerous to civilians—was correct.

He steered his car carefully down Rowe Boulevard and parked on State Circle. With the government shut down, no one would be ticketing. Even running just a few yards from the car to the office, he got soaked. Fortunately, he had his sweats in the office. He changed into them and lay his clothes out on the couch to dry before dialing McGuire's number at the office.

"Where the hell have you been? It's almost six o'clock."

"Calm down, will you? Getting around in this weather isn't exactly easy, you know."

"Have you got anything I can add to this story? Watkins isn't exactly thrilled that I haven't given him anything new."

Kelleher thought for a moment about what he could add without violating his agreement with Sims. "Well," he said finally, "you can say that police sources are seeking three white males and they remain baffled about the motive behind the conspiracy."

"You sure about that?"

"Oh, yeah." Kelleher was very sure about it and he knew that information like that would get Watkins off McGuire's back—at least a little bit.

"You got anything else?"

"Yeah, a lot, but nothing we can use today. Finish writing for first edition, then call me back."

"You in the office?"

"If I'm not here I went back to the hotel to shower. I'm soaked."

They hung up and Kelleher checked the messages. Most were dull but there *was* one from Andrea Kyler. "Call me when you can, I'll probably be in the governor's office working with Meredith. Tell the trooper you're my brother. I told him I was expecting a call from him."

Kelleher immediately dialed the governor's office and identified himself as Andrea Kyler's brother. She came on the line thirty seconds later.

"Where are you?" she asked.

"The office."

"I'll call you back in ten minutes."

Fifteen minutes later, the phone rang. "Hi. I'm sorry I had to run out that way this morning."

"Not a problem. What are you doing tonight?"

"Working. There's going to be a memorial service Monday morning. Meredith has to give the eulogy. That means we have to come up with two speeches—one for the eulogy, one for Tuesday night—by the end of the weekend, and Meredith wants it all done *now*. She's hyper as hell."

"Understandable."

"You guys dredge up anything new on the murder today?"

"I was just going to ask you that question myself."

"That's logical, I suppose. Bearnarth just briefed Meredith. Seems like they've ID'd two of the shooters through the FBI."

This was something new. "Really?"

"You hadn't heard that then."

"No. You got names by any chance?"

"If Bearnarth had them, he didn't give them to Meredith. But apparently the FBI is putting out APBs."

"I love it when you talk like that."

"Shut up, Kelleher."

"If I shut up do you think I can see you tomorrow night?"

"It really depends on how much work we get done during the day."

He took a deep breath, then let it out with his eyes closed. "Andrea, if you don't want to see me you can just say so."

"Kelleher, why do all men have such fragile egos? I called *you*, remember? I would like to see you very much, although I think we have a lot of talking to do."

"You're right about that."

"By the way, I heard Maureen talked to Jamelle Tourretta today."

"Yeah, she did as a matter of fact. How'd you know that?"

"Jamelle called me right after she hung up with Maureen. She wanted to be sure I had straightened things out with Meredith."

"And did you?"

"I told her the whole story. She was a little bit pissed off that I didn't tell you both the truth yesterday, but I explained to her how sensitive Jamelle was about it."

"So she's obviously not going to Charlottesville Sunday."

"Obviously."

"Well, I may go."

"Really?" There was surprise in Kyler's voice. "Why?"

"I'd like to meet Jamelle Tourretta, if only to see if she's everything she's supposed to be. There's also a basketball game that afternoon."

"You can get away with all this going on?"

"Not sure yet. But I'd like to."

"Well, if things are sane by tomorrow night, I might go with you, if that's all right. I told Jamelle I'd try but that I probably couldn't make it."

"It's all right. I'll call you tomorrow afternoon."

"Remember, you're my brother."

"What's my name?"

"Well, I've got eight of 'em so you can basically take your pick."

"I didn't think *anyone* had eight brothers."

"All big strong farm boys, so mind your manners around me."

"I never pictured you on a farm either."

"Lawrence, Kansas. I have to go. Call me tomorrow afternoon."

She clicked off. Kelleher sat with the phone in his hand for a moment trying to picture Kyler on a farm with eight brothers. He wiped that mental picture from his mind and dialed Tommy Montagne, hoping he would be in the newsroom.

"Montagne."

Kelleher had never met a police reporter who answered the phone any other way other than by saying his last name. Personally, he always said hello. If someone was calling on his direct line, the odds were they knew who they were calling.

"Tommy. Kelleher. You on deadline?"

"Writing for Sunday. What's up?"

"You got any friends at the bureau who could tell if there was an APB out for someone in the Paulsen shooting?"

"Probably. You got a name?"

"Maybe. Actually, there seem to be three shooters and they've apparently ID'd two of them. I have only one name, though: Jimmy Dumont."

"I saw in your story that they thought there were three shooters. Spell the guy's name for me."

Kelleher did. Montagne promised to call him back as soon as he could. It was almost seven o'clock, which was supposed to be first-edition deadline. He called McGuire and told her what he had learned from Kyler.

"I'll go ask Jane to push the deadline back," she said. "You start writing a new lead there."

Kelleher thought about calling Alan Sims before he started to write but decided to wait until after deadline. He was two paragraphs into the story when the phone rang.

"Good news and bad news," Tommy Montagne said. "The good news is, you're right, there *is* an APB out on two guys. I can confirm that for you. The bad news is, neither one of them is named Dumont and I can't get them to give me the two names.''

"How come?"

"Something about not wanting them to see their names in the newspaper. Seems silly to me. I'll work on it some more tomorrow. Maybe by then they'll have made an arrest.''

"In which case, everyone will have it. What the hell, though, this is good. I got one last favor I should have asked you before. Can you get someone over there to run Dumont's name and see if he turns up anywhere?"

"Already did that. I figured if you had the guy's name, you'd want to know about him. They've got a sheet on him but it's all right-wing political stuff. No arrests.''

"Hasn't ever done anything violent?"

"There was some cross-burning stuff when he was in college and he's been involved with some group that's trying to get the First Amendment repealed. I think we've written about those guys before. You might check the library on that.''

Kelleher had heard about that group. In fact, he had once looked up clips on them because Myron Cutler had been pushing a bill that would have changed Maryland's libel laws, making it nearly impossible to write anything about a politician. Kelleher had wanted to write a story about right-wing politicians who tried to chip away at the First Amendment whenever they had the chance. He had never gotten around to writing the story, though.

"Listen, Tommy, I really appreciate this," he said to Montagne. "You saved our ass.''

"Do me one favor then?"

"Byline?"

"Hell, no. Just the opposite. Keep my name off the story. If it shows up, big shots at the bureau'll know one of their people talked.''

"That's easy. You got it.''

"I'll call you tomorrow if I get anything new.''

Kelleher hung up admiring Tommy Montagne even more than he had before. Montagne was an old-fashioned reporter who believed his job was to make the newspaper as good as it could be and not worry about who got credit for it. There weren't a lot of guys in the business that secure.

He was halfway through his story when the phone rang again. "I think I've got something you can use tomorrow," Alan Sims said.

"APB on two guys?"

"Very good. So, I'm not your only source. I'm proud of you."

"Any way you can get names?"

"No, but I can tell you one of them is *not* Jimmy Dumont."

"I know. There's also no sheet on him at the FBI except for some of his radical political activities. Apparently his latest thing was wiping out the First Amendment."

"Yet another reason why shooting Barney to make Meredith governor makes no sense."

"It may be that Meredith has nothing to do with this."

"What do you mean?"

"I don't know. It's just that Jimmy Dumont and Meredith Gordy do not make a match in any way, shape, or form."

"And you're completely certain that was Dumont in the picture?"

"Completely. I wish we could get names on the other two, though. It might fill in a lot of blanks."

"Check me tomorrow."

Kelleher sighed, realizing he would have to wait to learn more. The other line was ringing. He looked at his watch: eight-ten. He knew exactly who it was."

"Five minutes," he said, without waiting to hear a voice.

"Not a minute more," Jane Kryton said. She did not sound amused by his clairvoyance. "They're screaming over on the news desk."

He raced through the rest of the story and sent it exactly five minutes after hanging up with Kryton. He wondered what—if anything—the other papers had. He was tempted to break the code of competing reporters and call Kenworthy and Frece but he resisted. If they had nothing and asked him if he had something, he would have to tell the truth—and that wouldn't be such a good idea. The phone rang again. This time it was Tom Anthony.

"Bobby, this is damn good but isn't there any way you can get names?"

"Tom, I'm trying but apparently the FBI is playing this very close to the vest. Even Montagne can't get them to talk."

"Stay with it," Anthony said.

McGuire called almost as soon as he hung up with Anthony. "You bailed us out there with the stuff on the two shooters," she said. "Sims give it to you?"

"Uh-huh." That was a lie really, since Kyler had told him first but he wasn't yet prepared to deal with McGuire on the subject of Andrea Kyler.

He did fill her in, though, on the picture Sims had showed him, the ballistics report, the deal he had made with Sims, and the fact that he had recognized Jimmy Dumont in the picture. After he had filled her in on who Dumont was, she asked him if he was certain Sims wouldn't go to the cops with his name.

"If he does, then we just go with the ballistics report, the picture, and Dumont's name," he said. "But I don't think he'll do it. Alan's a man of his word; at least, he always has been. I don't think he'll go to the cops until Sunday night. Unless something happens between now and then."

"Like what?"

"Well, the arrest of the other two shooters. They might ID Dumont at that point. Who knows?"

"So what do we do for Sunday?"

They agreed to meet in the office by three o'clock to write the overview piece they were supposed to produce. Before then, Kelleher would keep checking with Montagne and his state-police sources on the IDs of the two shooters. McGuire would call Jamelle Tourretta one more time to see if she had ever heard of Jimmy Dumont, unlikely as that was, but also to find out if she remembered anything she had seen him do or say before the lights went out. Kelleher also suggested McGuire talk to Tom Wyman in case he might be able to get the names of the two shooters for her. If there was any way to do something for McGuire, Wyman would do it.

"Drive carefully coming home," McGuire said. "The roads are supposed to be awful. Traffic is brutal all over."

"I promise, Mother," he said. He hung up feeling good about the work they had done that day, confused as hell about the Paulsen murder, and excited about Andrea Kyler. He wished there was some way the two of them could be together at that moment, curled up in front of the fireplace in her apartment.

He stood up, stretched, and realized how tired he was. There was really no point driving home now with the weather so lousy and the traffic so bad. He decided to go back to the Marriott, take a hot shower, and order room service. As tired and wet as he was, that sounded almost as good as curling up with Kyler.

Almost.

CHAPTER 8

DEAD ENDS

*T*he Marriott was packed when Kelleher arrived there. It usually was on Friday nights, which was when the political crowd moved out and the Naval Academy crowd moved in. Every weekend, the midshipmen and their dates, dressed to party, moved into the hotel just as the politicians and the reporters who covered them moved out. Walking through the lobby, looking at all the shining young faces, Kelleher felt old and lonely, a little bit, he suspected, like someone who has outlived his peers. Kelleher hadn't outlived anyone, he had just stayed in Annapolis on a night when all his peers had gone home.

Once he was in his room and under the shower, he found his mind jumping from fantasies about Andrea Kyler to nagging confusion about Jimmy Dumont. Dumont made no sense, not in any of the equations Kelleher could come up with. He realized he needed to know more about what Dumont had been doing in the ten years since they had last crossed paths.

His best starting point would be back where they had first met: UVA. Although Dumont had not—as far as Kelleher knew—ever graduated, the alumni office might have kept track of him, if only to try to hit him up for money. Ann Roberts, who had been arts editor of *The Cavalier Daily* while Kelleher was sports editor, worked in the alumni office. Kelleher and Roberts had dated after graduation, when he was still living in Richmond. Occasionally, they still ran into each other at basketball games. She might be willing to open her office on Sunday if he drove down there. She might even be able to get into the registrar's back records, which might—or might not—turn up some clues.

It was worth a try. Once he had called room service, Kelleher called Charlottesville information and got Ann's number. He didn't think she would be home on a Friday night but he figured he could leave a message. To his surprise, she answered on the first ring.

"Why, if it isn't the only man I ever really loved!" she said when she heard his voice.

Ann Roberts was from Lumberton, North Carolina, and had learned at a very young age that men respond to flattery. She was a classic Southern debutante, an only child who described her family's politics by saying, "My daddy would just as soon shoot a Republican as vote for one."

Underneath the practiced Southern charm, Ann Roberts was one of the smartest people Kelleher had ever met. And yet, she categorically refused to try anything more challenging than raising money for UVA. Kelleher suspected that Daddy Roberts had probably instilled in his daughter the notion that doctors and lawyers and MBAs were supposed to be men, not proper young ladies. Proper young ladies were supposed to *marry* doctors and lawyers. The fact that Ann was now twenty-nine and still single was probably sending shock waves through Lumberton society.

"Listen, darlin'," he said, falling into the Southern accent that always seemed correct when talking to Roberts, "I need your help."

"Can't help you from a hundred miles away," she replied, another of her favorite lines.

"I don't doubt that," he said. "But it is your knowledge I'm needing. You remember Jimmy Dumont?"

"Jimmy Dumont . . . Jimmy Dumont . . . did I date him? No, wait, he was the crazy guy you wrote about, the KKK guy. Sure, I remember him. Of course."

"I need to find him."

"Hold on, Bobby. Let me think a minute. I swear I saw his name in the paper not that long ago. But I'll be damned if I can remember where."

Kelleher was now on the edge of the bed. "Are you sure, Ann? What kind of paper? Alumni news, a real newspaper?"

"A real newspaper, I'm pretty sure. I just can't remember."

"Maybe in your files or the registrar's files there's something that will trip your brain."

"I'll take a look Monday morning."

Kelleher was shaking his head vehemently as if she could somehow see him. "No, not soon enough. Can't you go in there tomorrow?"

"I've got five hundred alumni coming in for the day. I'm sitting here right now making final plans."

"What about Sunday? I was thinking of coming down Sunday. Maybe we could meet and go in there together."

"Are you buying me brunch?"

"Breakfast. I have to go hear Jamelle Tourretta speak at noon. I'll meet you at ten and then we'll go eat at Charlie's after we get done in your office."

"Why in the world would you go hear that *awful* amazon woman speak?"

"Part of the job, dear."

"All right, but we eat first. You know I need my nourishment. Charlie's at ten, *then* we go to the office. It's easier for you that way anyhow, you'll be right on campus for the speech."

She was right. "Make it nine-thirty just to be safe," he said.

"That means you have to leave your house at seven-thirty."

He sighed. "And you know how much I love getting up in the morning. But for the chance to see you, I'll do it."

"A chance you've avoided consistently for five years."

"Come on, Annie, I'd have to take a number and get in line again, you know that."

"Oh, I know. The line is right outside my door now. Can't you hear them pounding?"

She sounded a little bit sad. Kelleher didn't like hearing her that way. Ann Roberts was one of those people he always thought managed to stay happy. He couldn't deal with an in-depth conversation about the trials and tribulations of life right at that moment, though.

"I'll see you at nine-thirty Sunday," he said, ending the phone chat.

"Bring lots of money." She clicked off.

Kelleher noticed that someone was pounding on his door. It was room service. "Thought you'd gone out or something, sir," the waiter said when he opened the door.

"Sorry," he said. "My mind isn't all here tonight."

He turned on the news while he ate and was gratified to hear one of the anchors say, "*The Washington Herald* reports in its first edition tomorrow morning that the FBI has issued an APB for two unnamed suspects in the shooting death of Governor Barney Paulsen.'' He smiled and flipped to Channel 2. Susan Sanders was in the middle of her report. She was sitting on a set that had a mockup of the State House behind her. Normally, she would have done her report from the State House lawn or the front steps, but tonight she was in Baltimore.

''And while the police continue their investigation, Governor Gordy has announced that she will ask the legislature to postpone its *sine die* adjournment by one day and use that day to confirm her choice for lieutenant governor. She says she doesn't want to use any of the legislature's time on the appointment of her successor, since Governor Paulsen's death has already put the legislative schedule way behind. Gordy says she is happy to continue with Senate President Myron Cutler as her number two in command for the rest of the session and added that she would consider Cutler seriously for the lieutenant governor's post.''

Kelleher hit the mute button so he could continue to look at Sanders without listening to her. This was typical TV reporting, he thought. Myron Cutler had as much chance of being Meredith Gordy's lieutenant governor as *he* did. Come to think of it, less chance. At least he and Gordy agreed politically.

He drifted off into a restless sleep interrupted by constant dreams. Barney Paulsen, Andrea Kyler, Maureen McGuire, Alan Sims, Jimmy Dumont, and Ann Roberts kept appearing in different roles. None of them turned out well. Kelleher kept waking up, then drifting back to sleep. His last dream, in which Barney Paulsen's ghost kept trying to tell him, in a voice so soft that Kelleher couldn't hear, who the killer was, was interrupted by the ringing phone. He stared at the clock on the desk: it was after nine A.M. He had finally fallen into a real sleep.

He picked up the phone, convinced it would be McGuire. It was Jane Kryton. She didn't even bother to say hello, which wasn't a good sign.

''Have you seen the *Post* yet?'' she snarled.

Kelleher groaned. That question could only mean that Kenworthy had beaten them on something. Something big. ''What have they got?'' he asked hoarsely.

''Let me read it to you: 'FBI sources confirmed tonight that Jamelle Tourretta, executive director of Females for Freedom, the radical feminist group, was questioned in New York Friday in connection with the murder of Maryland Governor Barnard A. Paulsen.'

'' 'Although no charges have been filed against Tourretta, sources say that she was seen in the gallery on the day of the shooting. What's more, the two suspects the FBI is now seeking both worked at one time as bodyguards for FFF at rallies. Tourretta told agents that she was in Annapolis for a meeting with Andrea Kyler, a former FFF employee who now works for Governor Meredith Gordy. She categorically denied any connection to the shooting. Reached by the *Post* late tonight, she again denied any connection to the shooting and added, "Barney Paulsen was one of the few governors in this country who was a true friend to the women's movement. Even if FFF did believe in this sort of violence, Governor Paulsen would be the *last* person we would think of taking any action against!" ' "

Kryton paused. "You want more?"

"No, I can read it and weep myself. You talk to Maureen already?"

"I can't find her. She must already be up and out somewhere. Did you guys know anything about this?"

Kelleher considered lying but finally decided to tell the truth, even though it made him and McGuire sound much worse than a lie would have. He admitted he'd been tipped about Tourretta by Sims, that McGuire had spoken to her Friday, and they had believed her story. "Which, of course, may be completely true," he said, knowing that reasoning sounded pretty flimsy.

"True or not, Watkins called Anthony at home first thing this morning when he heard WTOP quoting the story on the radio. Kenworthy got this very late, Bobby, probably after hearing about your first-edition story. It didn't get in until their last edition. But Watkins is going off the wall. In fact, I don't think it's a very good idea for us to tell him that you guys knew Tourretta was there and didn't follow up."

"We did follow up, Jane."

"Not enough."

"I know." He was almost tempted to tell her about Jimmy Dumont to explain why it was impossible for Jamelle Tourretta to have been involved. Now, though, there was yet *another* twist to the story: the other two shooters had once worked for FFF. That certainly didn't fit with Dumont. Kelleher decided to hold off on telling Kryton about his college acquaintance, even though that meant he and McGuire would take their lumps. He realized they were in a delicate position: balancing the insatiable nature of newspapering, the demand to advance the story every day, against the need to use the available facts to get the full story.

Right now, Kelleher knew the first thing he had to do was meet the demands of the newspaper, specifically the demands of J. Wynton Watkins, who was not going to be at all happy that the newspaper run by Ben Fucking Bradlee had now advanced the story one step farther than his own reporters had. Just two days had passed since Barney Paulsen had been shot, but to Bobby Kelleher it was starting to seem like weeks, even months.

Looking for Alan Sims, Kelleher walked briskly to the State House. The back door was locked, so he headed to the front and jogged up the steps. At the top, he turned around and looked down Rowe Boulevard. The government buildings sparkled in the morning sunshine. He was still in Oz but he was beginning to think that maybe the Wicked Witch was going to win in this version of the movie.

The state police still had the metal detector set up at the front door. He cleared it without any problem but found the steps leading to the second floor blocked. His press ID did him no good. "Sorry, sir, no press upstairs today," a very young and very polite trooper told him.

Kelleher retreated to the basement, hoping to try the elevator trick that had worked for him on Thursday. The troopers were onto it, however; the elevator was covered. Kelleher ducked into the pressroom, still empty at this hour, and dialed Sims's direct line.

"Yes, Kelleher," Sims said, sounding bored.

"How'd you know it was me?"

"Because five people in the world have this number and the only one other than you who has it who knows I'm here is my wife, and I just left her forty-five minutes ago."

"You should be a reporter. You happen to see *The Washington Post*?"

"I have a fax of the story right here on my desk. It wasn't in the edition I get at home so someone sent it to me from downtown."

"I'd kind of like to see it myself."

"Where are you?"

"Basement. Pressroom. Should I come up?"

"No. The whole staff is in this morning. Walk down to the harbor. I'll meet you in ten minutes."

Kelleher used the extra couple of minutes he had—the harbor was a five-minute walk—to call Rich Murray, the sports information director at UVA. Murray had been the SID when Kelleher was a student and was always good about getting him press credentials when he came to a game.

"To what do I owe the extreme pleasure of this call?" Murray asked. "Could it have something to do with the presence of the Maryland Terrapins tomorrow afternoon here in Charlottesville?"

"Actually, Rich, I just miss seeing you," Kelleher said, playing the game he and Murray always played.

"Then you have finally forgiven me for not getting you more ink in the papers when you were an undergraduate?"

"Not yet, Rich, but I'm getting closer."

"Should I put your name on the parking list?" he asked.

"That would be great. You know, someday you may actually be forgiven."

"I will look forward to it."

He jogged to the harbor after hanging up with Murray and found Sims already there, sitting on a bench they both liked because of the view. "You want some coffee?" Sims asked, holding up a paper cup. Kelleher realized he hadn't had his morning caffeine yet and gratefully accepted. Along with the coffee, Sims handed him Kenworthy's story. At least Tom had credited the *Herald* with breaking the story about the APB on the two suspects. It was tough to hate Kenworthy even on mornings when he made your life miserable.

"So, you got any ideas?" he asked Sims when he had finished reading.

"Not a single fucking clue," Sims said. "The cops are convinced it's Tourretta and FFF. I would be, too, if it weren't for what you said to me about Dumont. Are you *sure*, absolutely fucking *certain*, that's who it is?"

Sims reached into the envelope in which he had been carrying the *Post* story and produced the picture again.

"Look one more time, Bobby," he said softly, as if speaking to someone who couldn't admit he was wrong about something.

Kelleher stared long and hard at the face. There just wasn't any doubt. "It's him, Alan, I just know it's him."

Sims sighed. "This whole thing would make a lot more sense if it *weren't* him."

"Believe me, I know that. But murdering Barney doesn't make any sense to begin with. To assume that figuring it out is going to make sense is probably a mistake."

"That is the most confusing and sensible thing you have said in the last two days."

They both laughed, probably for the first time since the assassination. It was a relief. Kelleher relaxed momentarily. The sun had warmed to the point where sitting on the bench was quite comfortable. But sitting on the bench wasn't going to get any questions answered.

"Can you get me up to the second floor?" he asked Sims.

"As long as you've got a reason to go up there that has nothing to do with me."

"Tell them I have an appointment with Kyler."

Sims eyed him for a moment to see if he was joking. "Kyler? Wouldn't you have a better chance if you said Gordy?"

"Just say Kyler."

Sims stood up. "Oh, Bobby, you *are* full of surprises, aren't you? Come on, I'll get you up there. After that, you're on your own."

━ ━

"I have an appointment with Andrea Kyler," Kelleher said to the trooper on duty outside the governor's ceremonial room. His heart sank as the man looked up. It was his new best enemy from Thursday, Trooper Stern.

"How'd you get up here?" Stern demanded.

"Try paying attention. I'm Bobby Kelleher from the *Herald* and I have an appointment."

"I know who you are," Stern said. "And no one told me anything about you or any reporter having an appointment with anybody. So why don't you just turn around and go back to the basement where you belong."

Kelleher had all sorts of clever responses for Stern's venom but decided to withhold them for the moment. "Look, Trooper, why don't you simply buzz inside and ask Ms. Kyler if I have an appointment?"

Stern shook his head nastily. "I have strict orders not to disturb them. When they come out I'll tell them you were here, and if by some chance they want to contact you, they can."

"Sorry. That's not good enough," Kelleher said. "I have an appointment and I'm going in."

Stern stood up. "Maybe *this* is good enough," he said. "You got until the count of five to get out of here. After that, I arrest you for trespassing."

Kelleher was getting bored with these arrest threats but he also knew that Stern was the type to go through with it. So without answering, he turned and walked out of the room. Ten yards down the hall was a door that led directly into the governor's outer offices. It was used strictly as an exit for staff members. Kelleher knew it wasn't locked, since he often used it to leave after interviews. It was a convenient shortcut.

He knew he was taking a risk but it was a worthwhile one, if only to prove to Stern that there was at least one person in the state of Maryland who knew he was full of shit. Kelleher slid two steps to his right, yanked the staff door open, and darted in, hearing Stern's "Hey!" as he did so. Kelleher took two quick steps into the office, tripped over a chair that was sitting between desks and gracefully went flying, landing right at the feet of Captain Larry Bearnarth, who was sitting outside the door to the governor's inner office.

"Kelleher, what the . . ." Bearnarth said. He was interrupted by Stern, who burst through the door, gun drawn. The trooper raced to where Kelleher was sprawled, pointed the gun straight into his face, and sneered, "Okay, jerkoff, now you *are* going to jail."

Bearnarth stood up and dropped the newspaper he had been reading— the *Post*, Kelleher noted with just a bit of anguish. "Stern, what the fuck is going on here?" Bearnarth demanded.

"This asshole came in here claiming he had an appointment," Stern said. "I told him to get lost and he tried sneaking in the back door as if he thought I wouldn't see him. What do you think I am, buddy, stupid?"

This time, despite the gun pointed at him, Kelleher couldn't resist. "I don't even think you're *that* bright, *buddy*." Stern took a menacing step forward, but Bearnarth jumped in between them.

"Calm down!" he ordered. "And put the damn gun away before someone gets hurt. If the guy said he had an appointment, why the fuck didn't you check? That would have been easy enough, wouldn't it?" When Stern didn't answer, Bearnarth pressed the point. *"Wouldn't it?!"*

"Sir, my instructions were that no one was to disturb . . ."

"If someone says they have an appointment, you check it out, for Christ's sake," Bearnarth said, anger rising in his voice. "Now go back to your post. I'll handle this."

"But, Captain, he disobeyed a direct order. . . ."

"Stern, I'm giving *you* a direct order. Get the fuck out of here!"

Controlling his fury as best he could, Stern turned to go. Kelleher, still on the floor, took a final swipe. "Better learn to take orders before you start giving them to everyone, Stern," he said.

"Shut up, Kelleher!" Bearnarth yelled, clearly sick of the entire situation. Kelleher immediately shut up. Once Stern was gone, Bearnarth walked to the phone, dialed a number, and said pointedly, "Mike, I want you to send relief up here for Stern. And for crying out loud, don't be assigning people with absolutely no goddamn experience up here."

He hung up and looked at Kelleher. "Larry, I'm sorry," Kelleher said, finally standing and brushing himself off. "But that guy isn't just inexperienced, he's an asshole."

Bearnarth nodded. "He's got some kind of hard-on for the media, I think," he said. "We'll keep him away from you guys, although, to tell the truth, Kelleher, I don't think anyone expected any media up here today. Now, have you really got an appointment with someone or were you just bluffing?"

Kelleher shrugged. Bearnarth was not the president of the media's fan club by any means, but he understood the give-and-take that was part of the job. "Larry, I *think* you'll find that Andrea Kyler's expecting me. If there are a bunch of people in there, though . . ."

"Just Andrea and Miss . . . I mean, Governor Gordy. Damn, that's hard to get used to."

"I know. And I really am sorry about . . ." He waved his hand in the direction of Stern.

Bearnarth nodded mutely and pushed the intercom button. "Bobby Kelleher is here to see Miss Kyler," he said. As he spoke, Kelleher's nerves acted up: what if Gordy got angry with Kyler for talking to the press? But his worries seemed groundless when the door to the governor's office opened and he saw Gordy standing there with a bemused grin on her face.

"So, Bobby, still bluffing your way through life?" she said.

"Well, actually, Meredith . . ."

"You can explain inside," the governor broke in. "Miss Kyler will see you now."

Kelleher walked in to find Kyler sitting with her feet propped up on one of the chairs next to the fireplace. She was surrounded by books and notepads.

Kelleher was beginning to understand. Clearly, Kyler had told Gordy about what had happened between them. That surprised him. Even though a staff member going to bed with a reporter wasn't as bad from an ethical standpoint for the staff member as for the reporter, it still wasn't very good business.

Gordy was still standing. "Bobby, would you like something to drink?"

"Coffee?"

She disappeared into the little pantry that adjoined the office and came back a moment later with two mugs. "You take anything in it?"

"Black is fine. I'm sorry to interrupt, but I need some advice and direction as much as anything."

Kyler stood up. "Meredith, I think I know what Kelleher wants. And I think it's better for him to get it from you." When Kelleher didn't argue, she went on. "I'm going back to my office to look up those two quotes we were talking about. Bobby, if you need me when you're finished, I'll be in there."

"Is fifteen minutes enough time for you?" Gordy asked Kelleher.

"I hope so."

Kyler put her shoes on and walked out without casting even a glance at Kelleher. Gordy sat down and indicated that Kelleher do the same.

"You want to know about Jamelle Tourretta, I assume?" she said.

Kelleher put his coffee down and nodded.

Gordy suddenly popped up out of her chair and started pacing. "Look, Bobby, strictly background here, but what the hell am I supposed to think? Tourretta shows up in the gallery and Barney gets killed. Andrea, the person I trust most in the entire world, lies to me about it, then tells me Jamelle came here to talk politics with me. Next thing I know, the FBI is questioning Tourretta and has an APB out on two men who used to work for her. Andrea swears she knows nothing about any of this, but frankly it scares the hell out of me. Too many things add up right now. How the hell can I be governor if I find out someone committed murder to put me here?"

Kelleher made a snap decision. "Meredith, things don't add up quite as much as they seem to."

"What the hell does that mean?"

Without mentioning the picture, he told her that he knew who the third shooter was, then explained who and what Jimmy Dumont was. As he talked, her brow furrowed and she stopped pacing.

"I don't know if I find that comforting or not," she said when Kelleher was finished. "It just makes no sense."

Kelleher agreed. "But it does make it at least possible that both Tourretta and Andrea are telling the truth," he said. "To find out, all we have to do is find Dumont and the other two shooters."

Gordy smiled. "You want to believe Andrea's telling the truth as much as I do, don't you?"

Kelleher caught himself blushing.

"How did this come up?" he asked. "I mean about her and me. Did she walk in and announce it?"

"Actually, she was late for our staff meeting Friday morning. Afterward, she told me why. She said it was one of those right place, right time sort of things. I don't think she felt badly about it, if that's important to you."

"I felt badly about it."

"As a man or as a reporter?"

"Kind of hard to separate the two in my case. As a man it was definitely right place, right time. As a reporter, it couldn't possibly have been worse place or worse time. Especially given the Tourretta situation."

Gordy held up her coffee mug as a way of asking Kelleher if he wanted more. He really didn't but he nodded yes anyway. He wanted to see where this discussion was going to lead. Gordy returned with coffee for both of them, sat down again, and took a long sip.

"It seems to me," she said, "that this is one of those strange, if not unique situations in which the politician and the reporter need to work together. We both need the answer to the same question: is Andrea Kyler involved in the murder of Barney Paulsen?"

"Which means we have to find out first if Jamelle Tourretta is involved."

"Any ideas?"

"Maybe. I was thinking of taking a drive to Charlottesville tomorrow to hear that speech she wanted you to go to. It will also give me a chance to try and see if I can track down Dumont. I have a friend in the alumni office who'll help me out."

"After the *Post* story, Tourretta's speech will probably be a mob scene."

"True enough. But maybe I can get Andrea to help me arrange to talk to her afterward."

"What good do you think that will do you? Do you expect her to confess?"

Kelleher shook his head ruefully. "Unfortunately, I'm not quite that irresistible. But there's a decent chance that if she lies to me, I'll know. At least I'll walk away with a gut feeling. Right now, I haven't got one. The facts lead in too many different directions."

Gordy stood up and walked to her desk. "This is my direct line at the Governor's Mansion," she said, handing him a piece of paper. "They asked me to move in there last night for security reasons. Call me if you find out anything interesting. We should finish the two speeches by midday tomorrow so I'll be there most of the afternoon.''

Kelleher stared at the card for a moment. ''Where's Helen Paulsen?''

''At their beach house. She didn't want to be around here at all. Understandable. She'll be back Monday for the funeral.''

Kelleher slipped the phone number into his wallet. Gordy put a hand on his shoulder. ''Bobby, I truly hope this Jimmy Dumont character is the one. For all our sakes.''

Kelleher nodded, mesmerized for a moment by Gordy's eyes. ''I'll call you,'' he said. He shook hands with Bearnarth and thanked him on the way out, then walked out the same back door through which he'd entered. Looking left, he saw that Stern had been replaced by a different trooper. Smiling rather smugly, he walked around to Kyler's office, which was still in the lieutenant governor's suite. She hadn't moved yet. No one was in the outer office, so he walked right in. She was sitting at her computer writing when he walked in.

''Role reversal, huh?'' he said, pointing to the computer.

She smiled wanly and pushed back from the computer. ''So, do you think Tourretta and I are lying about why she was here Thursday?''

One thing about Kyler, Kelleher thought, she never beat around the bush.

''I don't think *you're* lying,'' he said, wondering if that was hope as much as belief. ''But the fact that you *did* lie Thursday is making it a bit tougher on Meredith.''

''I know. It wasn't one of my more intelligent decisions. But I can honestly say I wasn't really myself that day.''

''I noticed.''

She glared at him for a moment, then stood up and came around the desk. In her shoes, she was almost as tall as he was. ''I do owe you an apology for telling Meredith about what happened,'' she said. ''That should have been between us, especially since it could be very awkward for you.''

''Wouldn't be a bit awkward,'' he said. ''I'd just have to decide whether to resign or wait to be fired.''

She laughed nervously and poured herself some coffee. ''Then I guess it's fair to say our little encounter Friday morning was a one-time thing.''

It was said as a statement but clearly delivered as a question. Kelleher sat down on the couch and crossed his legs.

"Part of me is incredibly drawn to you, even just sitting here right now. But, Jesus, Andrea, the way things stand right now, the whole thing is impossible." When she didn't say anything, he shrugged his shoulders and said, "Unfortunately, one of my worst traits is that I can never admit that anything's impossible."

She looked at him intently, then said, "Maybe we should try to see each other tomorrow night, at least to talk."

"I'd like that. But I'm going to Charlottesville tomorrow. And I could use your help."

"My help?"

"With your friend Jamelle. She's going to be mobbed by reporters down there as sure as I'm sitting here. I want ten minutes alone with her. Can you arrange it?"

"I should probably tell you no, that we aren't that close," she said. "But the truth is, the answer is yes, I can arrange it. What do you want me to tell her?"

"Tell her I'm an honest reporter who'll tell her side if he's convinced it's the truth."

Kyler shook her head. "She won't talk to you to tell her side. She doesn't care much about that. I'll just tell her I think you're a good guy and she should talk to you."

"How close *are* you to her?"

Kyler stood up again and walked to the fireplace. "She was my mentor, still is in a lot of ways. I met her in college. She was in law school, I was an undergraduate. She was the most extraordinary person I had ever met—in every way. I've never had trouble meeting men but I was a wallflower compared with Jamelle. She was like a magnet. The funny thing was, she told me she never had a date in high school. She was so embarrassed by her size that she walked around slumped over in the baggiest clothes she could find.

"Then, as a freshman in college, she took a required gym class and everyone in the class wanted to date her. One look at her in a T-shirt and shorts, I guess, and they all went crazy. After that she got into bodybuild-ing, and by the time I met her she was very proud of her body. And her strength.

"She was also brilliant. Number one in her class in college and in law school. I was the girl next door, straight off the farm."

"In Lawrence, with all the brothers."

"Exactly. My daddy was the football coach and all my brothers played football. I was head cheerleader and dated the quarterback."

"Of course."

"Jamelle showed me a world I never dreamed existed. She took me out of the cornfields. Heck, the only reason I even went to Northwestern was because I broke up with my boyfriend senior year and I didn't want to go to UK when he was going to be there."

"UK?"

"Sorry. University of Kansas. That's where all my brothers went too."

"So you went to the big city and found out all sorts of things your daddy never told you about."

"You got it." She laughed. "When my father found out I had marched in a pro-choice rally my sophomore year he threatened to stop paying my tuition. I told him to go ahead, I'd just work part-time and go to school part-time."

"Did he cut you off?"

"No. He never really could say no to me. I was his little girl."

"And now?"

"He died the year after I graduated. Cancer. My brothers are all convinced I'm a dyke because of NOW and FFF. Except for Bobby. He's the youngest, a year younger than me. We're still close."

"Bobby?"

"Yeah, I know. Freudian, right?"

Kelleher smiled. Andrea Kyler shook her head. "I'll call Jamelle for you. Are you home tonight? I'll call and let you know what's going on."

He nodded and walked across to where she was standing. Her arms were folded on her chest. Very lightly, he kissed her on the lips.

"I *do* believe you," he said and walked out, leaving her standing there, arms still folded.

CHAPTER 9

DEAD OR ALIVE

Naturally, Kelleher was late getting back to the office. Just as naturally, Maureen McGuire and Jane Kryton were not happy with him.

"I hope you're late because you have something," McGuire said as he shucked his jacket. "Watkins is off the wall. He says he can't understand how the Tourretta thing got by us."

"You and Jane didn't tell him, did you?"

"No, but we better come up with something new for tomorrow."

Kelleher called Tommy Montagne at home. "I've got calls in all over," Montagne said. "So far, nothing. If I hear anything, I'll call you right away."

McGuire had talked to Tom Wyman, who told her the police and the FBI thought they were closing in on the two shooters they had ID'd and were hoping that those two would finger Tourretta after they had been arrested. "Right now, that's the lead," she said.

That wasn't likely to thrill Watkins but unless they came up with names or the FBI made an arrest it would have to do. The next two hours were spent writing the overview piece; re-creating the scene on Thursday, showing how lives had changed in the wake of Paulsen's death. Kelleher handled that piece while McGuire wrestled with the news story. This was their way—that which needed to be done quickly, he did; that which required bleeding over every paragraph, she did. When he finished the fast story, he would come and work with her on the tough one, sometimes rewriting the lead.

When Kelleher finished his piece and hit the ''done'' button so that Kryton could begin editing it, he moved to read over McGuire's shoulder. Five paragraphs into the story, she was already rehashing old news. It wasn't her fault, though; that was all they had.

''Dammit, this is frustrating,'' he muttered.

She nodded. ''I know. But what else can we do? It isn't our fault the FBI hasn't made any arrests.''

''I'm almost tempted to tell them about the Dumont stuff just to get them off our necks.''

''No, no.'' She shook her head so that her hair fell down into her eyes. ''Bad idea. For one thing, we can't write anything based on your ID. For another, you'd have to tell them about the picture, and your deal with Sims is not to use that until tomorrow, right? We just have to grit our teeth, get through this, and hope we can come up with something really substantial for Monday's paper.''

He knew she was right. And yet he wondered what would happen if they woke up tomorrow morning and found that Kenworthy or Frece had gotten the names of the two shooters. He walked to his desk and dialed Sims's office again. No answer. He dialed his home number. No answer again. He waited until the tape came on and then said, ''Alan, if you're there, pick up. It's Kelleher.''

Sims was there, as Kelleher had suspected. ''What's up?'' he said.

''Nothing, absolutely nothing. That's the problem. Have you heard anything at all from your cop pals about the two shooters? We basically haven't got a lead right now and I think Watkins is going to go nuts when he reads what we have.''

''All I know is the FBI says they think they've got a bead on both guys. But they haven't got them yet. Your FBI guy can't get you names?''

''No, goddammit.'' Kelleher was thinking, as he talked, of a way to strengthen the lead. Sims had just confirmed what Wyman had told McGuire. If they retooled the first sentence to imply that the FBI was close to an arrest, maybe they could keep Watkins at bay.

''Alan, if we wrote something like 'FBI and police sources said yesterday that the arrest of two suspects in the shooting of Governor Barnard A. Paulsen was imminent,' would we be off base?''

"I would just throw in the word *believed* before 'imminent,' to protect yourselves."

Kelleher nodded. "Maybe that'll save us for twenty-four hours. Thanks."

"Hey, Kelleher," Sims said. "What would you do without me?"

"I don't even want to think about it."

He hung up and noticed Tom Anthony reading McGuire's work. That wasn't a good sign. Anthony was normally very laid-back about seeing leads. If he was checking this one out it was on orders from above. He walked back over to McGuire's desk.

"Tom, I think we can strengthen that lead a little bit," he said.

"I hope so," Anthony said, tension in his voice.

"Give us ten minutes."

Anthony walked away, back over to Watkins's office, Kelleher noticed. He sat down and told McGuire what Sims had said. She agreed that while it wasn't earth-shattering, it was helpful. They reworked the lead together, went through the story, and sent it to Kryton just before the six-thirty P.M. page-one deadline. Stories slated for the front page had to be in an editor's hands at least thirty minutes earlier than other stories.

Kelleher was about to get yet another cup of coffee—his fourteenth, by his calculations—when the phone rang at his desk. It was Ann Roberts. "Are you still going to buy me brunch even if you don't need me tomorrow?" she asked.

Kelleher was too tired, too nervous, and too close to deadline to do schtick, even with his old friend. "Ann, what the hell are you talking about?" he snapped, sorry for his tone as soon as the words were out of his mouth.

"Well, if you're going to take that approach, I won't tell you why I called."

"Sorry. I'm sorry. Really. It's been a very long day."

"Well, this may make it longer or shorter. Jimmy Dumont is in Charlottesville."

"*What!* Where?! How do you know?"

"One step at a time here," she said. "You remember Katie Brighton, my co–arts editor? Well, she's here for the weekend with her husband. Anyway, they're staying out at The Boar's Head and, as we speak, I'm cooking dinner for them."

That was all wonderful, Kelleher thought, but what the hell did it have to do with Jimmy Dumont?

"Anyway," Roberts continued, "don't lose your patience with me, because I'm getting to the point."

"Good."

"You never change, do you? Anyway, Katie and Bill—that's her husband—called me last night right after I hung up with you to confirm plans for tonight. I mentioned that I had just talked to you and you were coming down Sunday and all that, and that I was going to help you try to track down everyone's favorite Klansman, Jimmy Dumont."

"You didn't tell her why, did you?"

"No, no. I just said it was for some story you were doing on right-wing politics. Anyway, Katie walked in here just a few minutes ago and said, 'You'll never guess who we saw out at The Boar's Head this afternoon.'"

Kelleher held his breath. "Not . . ."

"Yup, Jimmy Dumont. She said when they were checking in a man with a heavy beard was at the front desk asking if someone could come to his room to start a fire, that he didn't have enough wood. Katie said she kept staring at him, wondering why he looked familiar, and then she realized it was Dumont. She said she almost said something to him but he looked at her so funny it scared her, so she didn't say anything."

"Jesus! She's sure?"

"How sure were you when you saw the picture?"

She was right, of course. Jimmy Dumont had a face you never forgot, even with an added beard. He was about to ask Ann Roberts for more help, when he heard a voice calling his name.

"Kelleher!" It was Tom Anthony. He was standing outside of Watkins's office, waving at him. McGuire and Jane Kryton were already walking in that direction. Kelleher shivered for a moment, knowing what the meeting was about. He put up a finger to Anthony to indicate he needed one minute. *"Now!"* Anthony bellowed, very uncharacteristically.

"Bobby, are you still there?" Ann Roberts was asking.

"Yeah. Listen, Ann, are you going to be home? Let me call you back in a few minutes; I have to go into a goddamn meeting."

"I'll be home all night."

His mind was racing as he sprinted across the newsroom. If he could just get to Dumont the whole story might blow wide open. The only thing to do, clearly, was get out of there as fast as possible and drive to Charlottesville. First though, Watkins had to be dealt with.

He was sitting behind his desk, feet up, holding what was obviously a printout of their story. Anthony, Tony Quintal, Kryton, and McGuire were already seated. "We're just waiting on Shana," Watkins said.

What the hell did they need Shana Owings for? This had nothing to do with national's part of the story. Before he could ask the question, Shana Owings walked in without a word and sat on the couch next to Anthony.

"Okay," Watkins said. "Now that we're all here, let's talk. Kelleher, McGuire, I've read your story. I'll give you this, you've done everything possible to milk it into something viable. But as a great man once said, you can't make chicken salad out of chicken shit, and that's what this is."

"Wyn, it may just be that there isn't any real news today," Anthony said.

Watkins slammed the desk with the printout. "You mean like yesterday?" he said, voice rising. "Look, Tom, I know how hard they've both worked. I don't fault the effort here. It may just be that we need more bodies. Or it may just be that we need more experience."

"That's really not fair," Kelleher heard himself say, wishing at the same moment that he hadn't.

"Excuse me, Mr. Kelleher?" Watkins said, turning toward him.

"Mr. Watkins, we *did* get beaten on the Tourretta thing. But that's the first goddamn piece of news of any kind that *anyone's* gotten us on."

"And I suppose you think the *Post* and the *Sun* are going to have stories in the morning that say nothing—like this one? You think Bradlee isn't sitting over there right now telling his people that one story isn't enough? You think the *Sun*, which thinks it *owns* Maryland politics, isn't going to come back with some kind of big story? Come on, Kelleher, grow up!"

Kelleher knew there was some truth in what Watkins said. Certainly, he couldn't sit there and swear that neither the *Post* nor the *Sun* would have something in the morning. But deep down, he didn't think they would. And he was more convinced than ever that the key to this story lay with Jimmy Dumont. Still, he couldn't say that yet, so he did the smart thing— for once—and said nothing.

Watkins walked behind his desk and sat down again. "Okay, here's what we're going to do. Shana, who have you got who can dive right in first thing in the morning?"

Shana Owings crossed her legs and leaned back on the couch. Clearly, she felt that she now controlled the situation. Tom Anthony looked miserable. Kelleher felt as if he and McGuire had let him down.

"I can get you Roche and Tyler," she said to Watkins.

Kelleher almost gagged. Tammy Roche was, without question, the least competent person on the national staff. She had been hired away from *The Boston Globe* a year ago, for big money, in order to satisfy Watkins's lust to have someone from Harvard on the national staff. She had a Harvard degree, all right; the problem was, she had no clue about how to work a story. She had been a party reporter at the *Globe* and if she had been hired to do that at the *Herald*, she would probably have done just fine. Instead, she was assigned to the White House, where she wrote, for all intents and purposes, party stories. Everyone joked that it was a shame she hadn't been around when Reagan had been president, because she and Nancy Reagan would have become best pals.

Tim Tyler was a perfectly competent, anal-retentive economics reporter, who would, no doubt, make five hundred phone calls by noon tomorrow and return to announce that he had learned from several key sources that Barney Paulsen was indeed still dead.

Kelleher looked at McGuire for reaction to this news. She said nothing. It was Tom Anthony who spoke up. "So, Shana, how do you think Tammy Roche will crack this case—throw a party for all the suspects and lock them in a room until someone confesses?"

"That's enough, Tom," Watkins said sternly. Tammy Roche was not only his hire but someone he clearly had a thing for. Kelleher couldn't help but wonder what it would be like to watch the two of them kiss, since both carried their noses so high in the air it would be difficult to get them down far enough to execute a proper lip smacker.

"How will this work?" McGuire asked in her own polite way.

"I want the two of you to take them to lunch tomorrow," Watkins said. "Brief them on where you are, who the key sources are, and set them up with people who aren't sources who'll talk only to one of you. Spread yourselves out, get to work, see what you come up with."

"And who moves the stories?" Anthony asked, meaning who had editorial control.

"For now, you and Shana work together, Tom," Watkins said. "But if we don't see some real progress soon, I'll just turn the story over to national. If your reporters have to become legmen for the more experienced reporters over there, so be it."

Kelleher didn't want to believe what he was hearing. Forty-eight hours after they had been heroes, he and McGuire were now being told that if they didn't break something major in another day, they were going to be reduced to running quotes for the likes of Tammy Roche. He would quit first, that much he knew. Still, to argue with Watkins right now would be futile. What he wanted to do was get the hell out of here and on the road to Charlottesville. He certainly wasn't going to hang around for any lunch the next day, though there was nothing to be gained by announcing that here.

"Any questions?" Watkins asked.

Kelleher had all sorts of questions, answers, and comments rolling around in his head, but he said nothing. He stood up, walked out the door without acknowledging anybody, went straight to his desk, and was about to dial Ann Roberts again when he saw the expression on McGuire's face as she flopped down into the chair at her desk. Kelleher hung up the phone. Out of the corner of his eye, he could see Shana Owings talking to Tammy Roche.

"So," he said to his partner, "are we getting fucked or what?"

She sighed. "There's no doubt we're getting fucked, but that's not really the point. The good news is that they've given us two incompetents. All we have to do is give them a bunch of people to call, and keep working the story ourselves. They'll never come up with anything."

Kelleher realized that was true. In a way, Owings had done them a favor. If she had put someone like Tommy Montagne on the story, he might very well have broken it in a day or two. Of course, it wouldn't bother Kelleher that much if Montagne was the one who broke the story. Some writers you worked *with*, others you worked *against*. It didn't matter whether you were on the same newspaper or not. Kelleher would rather see Tom Kenworthy or John Frece break this story than have Tammy Roche break it. That was a blasphemous thought, he realized, but true nonetheless.

"Well, you've got lunch by yourself," he said to McGuire. "I'm going to Charlottesville."

McGuire shook her head. "Not a good idea. You don't show for lunch, it'll get back to Owings and she'll go right to Watkins."

He was about to explain to her why he had to go, when Tammy Roche sauntered over. "So, I hear we're going to be partners," she said.

Kelleher had disliked Tammy Roche within thirty seconds of meeting her. She had an air that said, "I'm better than you." She clearly thought that every man who laid eyes on her couldn't resist her charms and she just as clearly thought herself smarter than everyone else. She had short, stylishly cut blond hair, a pretty good figure—Kelleher was forced to admit—and wore about $50,000 worth of clothes to work every day. This being Saturday, she was in blue jeans, but they were the designer type that cost $150 a pair.

Much to Kelleher's relief, McGuire responded to Roche before he could. "Tammy, we're going to need all the help we can get," she said, smiling her best phony smile.

"So I understand," Roche replied, her voice filled with sarcasm. "Well, where should we brunch tomorrow?"

Brunch? Kelleher thought. Of course. They would *do* brunch. Tammy Roche didn't eat meals, she *did* them.

"Might as well go to the Willard," McGuire said.

Roche rolled her eyes. "I get so bored with the Willard. Can't we go someplace a bit more interesting?"

"Look," Kelleher said, unable to stay silent any longer, "this isn't a social occasion. This is work. The Willard is the easiest place so that's where we'll go." He didn't know why he was getting so upset, since he had no intention of even showing up for the lunch, or *brunch.*

"Believe me, Kelleher, if this were a social occasion, you and I wouldn't be eating together," Roche said, giving him an icy look.

Kelleher actually smiled. "Well, Tammy, I'm glad we can agree on something."

He walked away before it got any uglier and found an empty desk he could call Ann Roberts from.

"Boy, I thought you had given up on me," she said when she answered.

He didn't even hear her. "Look," he said, "I'm going to drive down there tonight. I'll go straight to The Boar's Head to see if I can find Dumont."

"You need a place to stay?"

He hadn't even thought about that. But staying with Ann wasn't a great idea. Judging by what she had said about her social life the night before, they both would probably be tempted to do something they would regret in the morning.

"I'll get a room at The Boar's Head."

She laughed. "No way, Bobby. The whole town is sold out. Alumni weekend plus the basketball game tomorrow. You can stay with me. Don't worry, I'll behave."

"But will *I*?" He said it more to be polite than anything else. It was the right thing to say, though.

"You always were a sweetheart," she said. "Drive carefully and call me when you're through. I'll give you directions to my house. You've never seen it, you know."

"I know," he said, embarrassed, since she had been in it for five years. "I guess you never invited me."

"Good try."

"How late will you be up?"

"Don't worry about it. Just call me."

There are some people in your life, Kelleher realized, who will be your friend no matter what. He had not been a very good friend the past few years, partly because he knew that to get romantically involved with Ann Roberts again was a mistake for both of them: they were just too different. And yet, if they were to go out to dinner and drink some wine, they would almost inevitably end up spending the night together. She still seemed to find him attractive and there was no doubt about how attractive *she* was. Rather than face all that, Kelleher had shied away from her in recent years. Now, he had sort of burst in upon her life again and her response was "How can I help?"

If you made five friends like that in a lifetime, you were lucky. As Kelleher hung up, McGuire, whom he also considered one of those five friends, walked over, having finally gotten rid of Roche.

"So," she said, "noon at the Willard?"

He shook his head. "I can't," he said. "A friend of mine just called me from Charlottesville. She says Jimmy Dumont is down there."

"What in the world are you talking about? How did she even know we were looking for him?"

Kelleher explained his call to Ann Roberts and her subsequent call to him. "That's a long way to go on a wild goose chase," McGuire said. "I mean, how likely is it that this woman really saw the guy?"

"More likely than you know. Anyway, I have to go there to hear Tourretta speak."

"And to see this old girlfriend?"

Kelleher made a face at her. "Normally, you'd probably be right. But in this case, I can honestly say I wish it were someone other than Ann who was involved. It just complicates things."

"By the way, Tommy Wyman tells me you spent quite a bit of time in Andrea Kyler's office this afternoon."

Kelleher was going to kill Wyman when he had the chance. McGuire was looking at him as if she had caught him looking up someone's dress. But Kelleher was nothing if not fast on his feet.

"Gordy sent me to her," he said. "She's going to try to set me up to talk to Tourretta tomorrow."

"That took forty-five minutes?"

"It did. I talked to her for quite a while about Tourretta and FFF. I'm not as up to speed on them as you are."

"And she talked to you?"

"I suspect she was trying to cast things in as positive a light as possible, especially knowing that I know she lied the other day."

That seemed to satisfy his ever-curious partner. "Call me when you get to Charlottesville," she said. "And for crying out loud, be careful. If this Dumont character is as crazy as you say and he really *did* kill Paulsen, he's dangerous. Don't do anything heroic."

Kelleher, having escaped the cross-examination, stood up and kissed her on the forehead. "I won't be out late, I promise," he said.

▬ ▬

Kelleher knew the route to Charlottesville better than the one from his bed to his bathroom. He had no idea how many times he had driven west on I-66, gotten off at Gainesville to pick up Route 29, then taken that eighty-five miles through the towns of central Virginia before turning right at University Hall. From the *Herald* garage to U-Hall, without traffic, the trip was exactly two hours if he kept the speedometer just under sixty-five the entire way. Anything over sixty-five and the Virginia state police were apt to nail you.

Normally, Kelleher reveled in this drive. During the daytime, the last hour was as pretty as anywhere in the country, the mountains rising up on either side of the highway. It was also a homecoming for Kelleher every time he pointed the car toward UVA, a return to the scene of many of the happiest moments in his life.

Not this time, though. The road was dark and still slick from Friday's all-day rain, and Kelleher was hardly in the mood for nostalgia. He stopped at the McDonald's in Warrenton for a Big Mac and a cup of coffee—he was up to sixteen—and pulled into Charlottesville just after eleven o'clock. Throughout the trip, his mind wandered from subject to subject: one minute he was figuring out a way to approach Jimmy Dumont, the next he was fantasizing about Andrea, the next he was trying to decide how to deal with what was going on at the newspaper. Annoyingly enough, Ann Roberts and Susan Sanders also popped into his head on more than one occasion.

He drove past U-Hall, the parking lots empty and quiet, across the little bridge, and made a right toward The Boar's Head Inn, which was a little more than a mile down the road. Kelleher turned into the winding drive leading to the reception area of the hotel, still undecided as to exactly what it was he wanted to do. As he pulled the car to a halt, he made a decision: do whatever comes naturally and hope. Maybe even pray.

The lobby was quiet when he entered but he could hear music coming from the bar. He nodded toward the guy at the front desk and walked directly to the house phone.

When the operator picked up, Kelleher asked to speak to Jimmy Dumont.

"I'm sorry, sir, I don't have anyone by that name," she said. He asked her to try under James or Jim. No and no. No Dumont at all registered in the hotel. Kelleher should have figured as much. If Dumont *was* there, he wouldn't be registered under his real name. He thanked the operator and walked up to the front desk. The guy working there, whose name tag said "Chris Mills," looked to be about his own age. Kelleher wondered if he had been at UVA at the same time he had been there.

"Can I help you, sir?" Chris Mills said formally, which was not an encouraging start.

"I hope so," Kelleher said. "I'm supposed to meet a friend of mine here. I'm sure he's checked in, because I talked to him this afternoon, but your operator says she doesn't have his name."

"What name did you ask for when you spoke to him this afternoon?"

"I didn't. He called me and said he was checked in and we agreed to meet here in the lobby at eleven o'clock. I suppose I should have asked his room number."

Chris Mills wasn't paying attention to him. He was locked in on two women in spangly party dresses who were walking across the lobby. Kelleher, looking for any opening at all, turned and looked as they went by. He didn't get much of a look, but he acted like he had.

"Not bad for a Saturday night in Charlottesville," he said in a man-to-man conspiratorial tone.

Mills laughed. "You walk into that bar, you'll get a real eyeful," he said. "I've been working since noon and the talent parade today has been amazing."

Working since noon. That struck a chord. Chris Mills might very well have been here when Katie Brighton saw Jimmy Dumont. "Listen, Chris," he said, "maybe you saw my friend this afternoon. He told me he was coming down to the front desk as soon as he hung up with me, to try to get someone to bring some firewood to his room."

Mills nodded. "What's he look like?"

"Short, maybe five-eight. Stocky. Dark. Heavy beard. If you didn't know him, you might think he looked a little bit crazy."

Chris Mills was nodding as he finished. "Yeah, I remember him. Definitely."

He punched a couple of buttons on his computer. "He's not registered under the name Dumont, though."

"He's not? That's weird. What name is he under?"

Chris Mills smiled that annoying hotel smile at him. "I'm really sorry, sir. I can't tell you that."

"You can't tell me his *name*? I thought you just couldn't tell me a room number."

"If you give me a name, I can ring the room for you," Chris Mills said. "But if you walk up here and describe a guest to me, I can't just give you a name. Suppose you came up and described some great-looking woman. I couldn't just give her name out, could I?"

The asshole had a point. Still, Kelleher plowed on for another moment. "I understand what you're saying," he said, trying to keep it as friendly as possible. "But clearly, this isn't that kind of situation. I mean, if the guy wasn't a friend of mine, how would I know he was coming down here to ask for firewood this afternoon?"

"I still can't give you the name. I'm sorry."

Kelleher looked at Mills for another second to see if there was any chance he was going to change his mind. There wasn't. His wallet was in the car. Maybe a bribe was his next move. Two more women were walking through the lobby and the clerk was again distracted. That gave Kelleher an idea—a better idea than a bribe.

"Sorry to have bothered you," he said to Mills, smiling as if the rebuff were no big deal.

"No problem at all," Mills said, his eyes fixed on a tall blonde.

Kelleher turned and walked out to the lobby. He was still driving the *Herald* car he had checked out Friday and there was a phone in it. He pulled his notebook out of his jacket pocket, double-checked Ann Roberts's phone number, and dialed.

"Are you still entertaining?" he asked without saying hello.

"Depends on what kind of entertainment you're looking for."

He had walked right into that one. "Thanks, Henny. Do you still have guests?"

"No, they've gone back to the hotel. Where are you?"

"At the hotel. And I need your help."

"*More* help?"

"A lot more. For this one you'd be more than justified telling me to go to hell."

"Not a first. What do you need?"

"I need you to put on something really sexy. . . ."

"Why, Bobby, after all these years . . ."

"No, no, that's not it. I need you to flirt with someone for me, get something I can't get."

"Like what?"

"Like Jimmy Dumont's room number. He's not registered under his own name and the front-desk clerk won't tell me the name he *is* registered under. But I suspect if someone who looks like you asks him real nice, he may give it up."

"Oh, really."

"Every woman who walks through the lobby, he's all over them with his eyes. And I venture to say no one has walked through the lobby who comes close to you."

"Bobby, you're groveling. Stop it. What should I wear?"

He sighed. In a way, he almost wished she had said no. This was so far beneath her. But . . . "Something low cut and short."

"Hooker-type stuff, you mean."

"Well put."

"You're about eight minutes from my house. I'll be dressed by the time you get here."

She was as good as her word. And whether he had been groveling or not, he'd told the truth. Ann Roberts dressed up was still one of the most stunning women Bobby Kelleher had ever met. "I'm amazed I can still fit into this dress," she said, greeting him at the door with a peck on the cheek.

The dress was light blue, showing lots of cleavage—something Ann Roberts had in ample quantity—with a slit up one leg. The light-blue pumps went with the dress perfectly.

"Will I do?" she said.

"Oh, yeah," he said, swallowing hard. "You'll definitely do."

He briefed her on the way back to the hotel, speeding. It was close to midnight and he had no idea what time Chris Mills's shift ended. The overnight person would have no way of knowing who Jimmy Dumont was.

They pulled back into the hotel parking lot. "Maybe you better wait here," Ann Roberts said.

He shook his head. "No. I may be willing to put you through something as awful as this, but I won't put you through it without someone at least keeping an eye on you. There's an entrance right next to the bar. I can walk up the hallway and be right around the corner watching while you talk to my friend Mr. Mills."

"The key is getting the room number, right?"

"Absolutely. If you get that, I'll do the rest."

She snorted. "You always take the easy jobs."

She got out of the car and walked toward the front entrance. He raced quickly around the back, was suddenly seized by fear at the thought that the door might be locked, and breathed a deep sigh of relief when he found it open. He walked up the hallway until he came to a public phone. He picked it up and pretended to be using it just as Ann walked into the lobby. Mills was still working at the front desk. Kelleher saw his eyes go wide as Ann approached him.

"*Hello* there," he said, a greeting quite a bit different from the one Kelleher had received an hour ago.

"Well, hi," Ann said, her best Southern accent rolling off her tongue. "I am in need of help."

"And I am the man to help you," Chris Mills leered.

"Oh, I hope so." She was leaning across the desk, giving Mills the view of a lifetime. "I want to leave a note for one of your guests. I met him here this afternoon at lunch. He asked me to have brunch with him here tomorrow and I said yes, but to tell you the truth, I'm having second thoughts. He seemed just a bit strange to me. I mean, I like meeting new guys, but I think maybe I'll take a pass on this one."

"What's his name?" Chris Mills said.

Ann was almost whispering now. "Tell you the truth, I'm not sure," she said. "That's why I didn't call. I only live just down the road. I was on my way to a party at a friend's house so I thought I'd stop and leave a note."

"How are you going to do that when you don't know his name?"

"Well, actually, he was standing right at this desk when we started talking and I was hoping you'd know him. It was John or Jim or something. Maybe you saw him: very dark, heavy beard, about my height?''

Kelleher's heart sank when he saw Mills's eyes narrow suspiciously. ''You know, you're the second person in the past hour to ask about this guy.''

Ann took a step back as if horrified. ''You don't think he spent the afternoon here just hitting on every woman who came by?''

The desk clerk laughed, clearly disarmed. ''No, this was a guy. A friend of his. Least he said he was.'' Mills was looking at his computer the way he had done when Kelleher was there. This time the outcome was different though.

''His name's Jim Tourretta. Room seven.''

Kelleher almost gasped out loud when he heard the name Dumont was registered under. Either the guy had a very strange sense of humor or the trail was a lot hotter than he thought it was. Ann had somehow managed not to change expression.

''Can I borrow a piece of paper?'' she asked.

''Sure can,'' Mills said. ''Now where did you say that party was?''

She smiled. ''You know where Bynoe Road is, back toward UVA? It's number twenty-four. We'll be there until *very* late.''

''I'm off at one.''

She finished writing the note, smiled wonderfully one more time, and said, ''I'll still be there, Chris.''

She turned and walked out. Kelleher waited long enough to watch Mills follow her out the door with his eyes. He hung up the phone, dashed out the back door, and ran to the car. It had gotten very cold, but he hardly noticed. Ann was standing by the car, waiting, shivering.

''This is not a night for a dress like this one,'' she said.

He opened the door, switched on the engine, and turned the heat all the way up. Then he hugged her. ''You missed your calling, baby,'' he said. ''You should have been an actress.''

''Or a stripper,'' she said wryly. ''I *hate* it when men look at me that way. That's why I never wear this dress anymore. I just hate it.''

She was shaking from the cold, the fear, and the experience she had just been through with the hotel slimeball. ''I'm sorry,'' he apologized, hugging her again. ''I really am sorry.''

''Did you hear what he said?'' Her voice was very small. ''Room seven?''

''I heard. And is there really a party going on at twenty-four Bynoe?''

''There *is* no twenty-four Bynoe.''

He laughed, delighted that she had played Mills for a fool, and started to back the car out of the parking spot.

"What are you doing?" she asked. "Where are we going?"

"I'm taking you home. Then I'm going to come back and see if I can talk to Dumont."

"Oh, no you don't. I got you that room number, I'm going with you."

"Ann, I may be a big enough jerk that I'll let you go through what you just went through, but I'm not a big enough jerk to jeopardize your safety. This guy may be armed, may be crazy, and he's definitely very dangerous."

"And so who are you, Bruce Willis? Why don't you call the police?"

"Can't. I'd have to tell them about the picture I was shown and I can't do that for twenty-four more hours."

"So what'll you say to this armed, crazy, and dangerous guy?"

"I'm hoping he remembers me from college. He told someone back then he thought I was fair to him. If I act as if this is all a coincidence, nothing to do with Paulsen, maybe he'll talk to me."

"It's very risky, Bobby. But it's less risky if someone's in the car waiting to call the police if something goes wrong."

He looked at her, studying. She was completely recovered physically and emotionally, it appeared, from dealing with Chris Mills. She was also right. Having her along could be very helpful. If she had been McGuire, there would be no question about her going with him. Ann Roberts deserved the same respect he would show McGuire.

"Okay," he said. "But stay in the car out of sight."

"I won't do anything unless I have to," she said.

They drove around to the rooms, which were set apart from the main building. He parked several doors down from number seven. "If you hear anything that sounds violent, call the police," he said, trying to sound confident that nothing like that would happen.

She nodded, then leaned forward and kissed him lightly on the lips. "For God's sake, don't be a hero," she said. McGuire had said the exact same thing to him several hours ago.

Kelleher got out of the car, looked around to see if anyone was in sight, walked up to room number seven, and knocked lightly. No answer. He knocked again, harder. He pounded a third time. Nothing. Shit, he thought.

Kelleher returned to the car. "What now?" Ann asked.

"First, I'm going to try and call the room," he said. "If he doesn't answer the phone, that means he's not there almost for sure."

"And then?"

"I'm gonna try to get a look in there. I can pick that lock easily."

"Where did you learn to pick locks?"

"I know a lot of lawyers." Actually, he had learned it from his pal George Small, in high school. George Small was a schoolyard basketball player who never went to college, never got out of Baltimore. Kelleher imagined he was probably dead now. But in high school, he and George had played together every day and been pals. And George had taught him how to pick locks. It was not that difficult.

"Don't you think you'd be better off just waiting for him?"

"Maybe. But I doubt it. If I can get a look at the room, I might have a much better idea of just what I'm dealing with. Plus," he grinned at her, "I've got a lookout."

She shook her head. "I think you're nuts."

"Of that," he said, picking up the car phone, "there is little doubt."

He dialed the number for the hotel and asked for Jim Tourretta in room seven. He let the phone ring four times and hung up before the operator came back on to take a message.

"You ready?"

"Ready for what? What do I do?"

He turned on the engine, backed the car out of the space he was in, and drove down four spaces, pulling into a spot right in front of room seven's window. "When I leave, slide over into the driver's seat," he told her. "You see any car coming in this direction, flash the headlights right at the window. I'll pull the curtain open once I get in there. Any car'll have to come from up there by the main building, so if you flash as soon as you see one, I'll be able to get out before it pulls up."

"Will you see the lights?"

"I hope so. I'll keep an eye out."

She sighed again. "I haven't liked any of this," she said. "But I *really* don't like this."

"I know," he agreed. "But sometimes you have to take risks in life. Something tells me this is one of those times."

She said nothing. He patted her on the shoulder and got out of the car again. Just to be sure, he knocked on the door twice more. Still no response. He pulled a file out of his pocket—he had carried one ever since he had learned to pick locks; sometimes he picked them on bets. This was a little more serious.

The lock gave way easily. There were no lights on in the room. To be certain the room was empty, he said aloud, ''Mr. Tourretta?'' If by some chance Dumont was in the room, he might be able to pretend he was hotel security. ''Mr. Tourretta?''

No answer. He groped for a light switch and found one. Flipping it on, he was greeted by the sight of an unmade bed, an open suitcase sitting on the floor in front of the fireplace, and, on the mantle over the fireplace, a pistol. Dumont was either very careless, very cocky, or very stupid.

Kelleher walked over and checked the gun. Not being an expert on guns—he had actually never before held a real one in his hands—he decided not to mess with it. He'd heard too many stories about guns going off by accident, so he put it back on the mantel. Then, glancing at the window every few seconds, he began going through the suitcase.

There was the usual assortment of clothing, enough for a fairly long trip, Kelleher guessed, and plenty of newspaper clippings from the previous two days. The subject of every clipping: the shooting of Barney Paulsen. Underneath the clippings was a notepad. The letters ''LOL'' were inscribed at the top.

LOL? What the hell does that stand for? he wondered, examining the pad. There were two phone numbers on it. He was reaching into his jacket for his notebook when he saw the headlights flash. Once, twice.

Kelleher jumped to his feet, forgetting the pad. He took three quick steps across the room to the door. Too late. A key turned in the door. Kelleher dove for the bed, trying to roll under it. Even at his quickest, he wouldn't have made it in time.

''Move one muscle and you are a very dead motherfucker.''

He hadn't heard the voice in ten years, but he knew in that one sentence it was Jimmy Dumont. And, without looking up, he knew there was a gun pointed at him.

''Not moving,'' he said. It was easy to stay still. He was as scared as he'd ever been in his life.

Dumont crossed the room to where he was lying on the floor and put the gun up against his head. For a split second Kelleher thought Dumont was going to blow his head off right there and then. He heard himself gasp in terror.

''Roll over on your back,'' Dumont ordered. ''And hold your arms straight up over your head. Move very slowly, asshole.''

Kelleher followed his instructions, nearly moving in slow motion to be certain he didn't make a mistake. Dumont patted him down thoroughly, grabbing his crotch and giving a hard, painful squeeze as he did. Kelleher cried out in pain but was terrified enough—and smart enough—not to make any quick, instinctive movement.

"Okay, now, very slowly stand up. And keep your arms up over your head."

Kelleher obeyed, knowing the gun was right on him the whole time. When he got to his feet, he found Dumont standing just outside an arm's length away from him, gun pointed right at his head, a broad grin on his face. The eyes, as always, were wild and frightening.

"I've got to hand it to you, Kelleher," Jimmy Dumont said, "you're better than I thought. I didn't believe you'd have the smarts to get into my room."

Kelleher wasn't stunned that Dumont remembered him. But he was fairly shocked that Dumont didn't seem very surprised to see him.

"You been expecting me, Jimmy?"

"If you'd called ahead, I would've had champagne waiting." Dumont grinned his wicked grin, then motioned him to a chair near the fireplace. "Sit down there for a minute, Bobby boy."

Kelleher was praying that Ann had called the police. At this stage, losing the story meant far less to him than losing his life. Kelleher was no coward, but he had absolutely no interest in dying young.

Dumont came over and stuck his face very close to Kelleher's, his breath reeking of gin. He was also in desperate need of a bath.

"Bobby boy, you never were too bright," Dumont said. "What you should have done was stuck to playing basketball with all those nigger friends of yours."

As a kid, Kelleher had permission from his parents to hit another kid if they used one of two words: *nigger* or *kike*. He grimaced when the word came out of Dumont's mouth and Dumont noticed.

"Don't like that word, do you, Bobby boy? Nigger. *Nigger.* Ugly word, isn't it? Well, you won't have to hear it much longer."

"I don't think shooting me here would be one of your better ideas, Jimmy."

"Oh, Bobby boy, it would be a very *bad* idea. I agree. And I appreciate your concern. So, instead, why don't you stand up and walk nice and slow over to the door. Don't open it until I tell you to, just walk."

Kelleher stood and walked to the door. If the police didn't show soon, he would have to make some kind of move. But Dumont was no fool. He made sure to stay out of Kelleher's reach. He was clearly very practiced, very professional. Kelleher knew he needed to stall. *Where the hell were the police?*

"Before we go, can you just tell me one thing?" he asked.

"One last wish?" Dumont smiled. "I'll grant it. Go ahead and ask."

"Why Barney Paulsen? He was a nonentity, no matter how much you disagreed with his politics. And by killing him, you put someone even more liberal into power. A woman, no less."

Dumont moved close to Kelleher, sticking the gun hard into his ribs. "I'll give you one last thought to ponder during these final minutes, Bobby boy," he said. "That bitch will never sign a bill into law."

Kelleher felt a chill run down his spine. "What does that mean?" he asked, almost not wanting to know the answer.

"It's nothing for you to worry about, cause you ain't going to be around to worry about it." He poked the gun into Kelleher's ribs again. "Now, open the door very slowly and turn left. My car's five spaces down."

Kelleher was desperate to stall some more. "Just tell me one more thing: why didn't you kill Gordy on Thursday when you had the chance?"

" 'Cause somebody fucked up," Dumont said, his voice laced with disgust. "Now quit stalling, Kelleher. I may not want to shoot you here, but if I have to, I'll knock you cold and carry you to the damn car. Would you prefer that?"

If he was going to die, Kelleher probably *would* prefer that, yes. But he wasn't giving up on himself just yet. Prodded by Dumont, he pulled the door open, hoping against hope to find himself staring at a well-armed police officer. No such luck.

He walked outside and turned left. Dumont was pressed up against him, gun still in his ribs, which were beginning to throb slightly. His car was still parked where he had left it. But there was no sign of Ann. For a second, Kelleher had the panicked thought that Dumont had seen her flashing her lights and had done something to her. That was impossible, though. He'd gotten to the door just seconds after he'd seen the lights.

"Okay, Kelleher, it's this one," Dumont said, pressing something into his hand. "Open the trunk with this key."

"The trunk?"

"Where'd you expect to be riding, Bobby boy, up front with—" Dumont screamed in pain just as Kelleher felt the gun drop away from his ribs. He turned in time to see the madman, a stunned look on his face, collapse into a heap, his eyes rolling back into his head. Standing behind him, looking terrified, was Ann, holding what appeared to be a potted plant. She was frozen, the pot gripped in both hands, having just smacked Dumont on top of the head with it.

"Did I kill him?" she asked.

Kelleher knelt over Dumont, feeling for a pulse. It seemed strong. There was a little blood coming from the spot where Ann had clobbered him, but he was clearly alive. "Where the hell have you been?" he asked. "I thought you would have called the police by now."

"I couldn't get your damn car phone to work!" she yelled back. "You forgot to give me the code! He caught me completely off guard, Bobby. He drove up with his lights off, I didn't see him until he walked past me, then I had to wait to flash the lights until he started into the room or he would have seen me. After he went in and the phone didn't work, I started to go into the hotel to call the police, but when nothing happened after I'd been trying the phone for a few minutes, I figured you were either hiding or he was going to take you someplace. I didn't think he'd kill you here, so I decided to take a chance and wait to see if you came out. I was afraid if I left to go into the hotel, you might leave and I'd lose you completely. So I found this damn pot and . . ."

Kelleher didn't know whether to laugh or cry. He had a feeling he was about to do both.

"What now?" she said.

Kelleher looked around. Apparently, no one had heard or seen them. If he called the police and waited at the scene, he became part of the story. He would also have to explain why he'd broken into Dumont's room rather than call and tell them what he suspected.

"Check and see if he left the door open when we came out," he said to Ann, who'd put on a coat now that she didn't have to display her body to any more leches. She walked over, pushed the door, and it swung open. Their first bit of luck so far. Kelleher grabbed Dumont's arm and lifted him up onto his shoulder. Short as he was, he was extremely heavy, especially as dead weight. Kelleher's knees almost buckled, but he managed to carry Dumont back into the room and stretch him out on the bed.

"I'll get his gun," Ann said.

"*No!* Leave it right there. There are no fingerprints on it. Just leave it where it is." That reminded him of the gun on the mantel. It had his fingerprints all over it. He would take that with him. Not wanting to take any chances, Kelleher pulled one of the sheets off the bed and tied Dumont to one of the bedposts. Then he took the other sheet and tied his leg to the bedstead. He pulled the phone out of the socket and checked Dumont's pulse again. It was fine. His breathing was slightly labored but steady.

He walked to the mantel and grabbed the gun. He was tempted to leave the newspaper clippings as evidence, but he was afraid the police might get his fingerprints off them somehow. He wanted to remove any evidence that he had been there.

"Come on," he said to Ann finally. "Let's get the hell out of here."

"Do you have any idea what you're doing?" she asked.

"I certainly hope so."

He couldn't call Maryland from the car phone, so he waited until they were back at Ann's house. Then he dialed Alan Sims. It was, he knew, two-thirty in the morning, but he had no choice.

"Hello?"

"Alan, wake up, it's Kelleher."

"Kelleher? Bobby, what's going on? What time is it?"

"Late. Alan, listen to me. I found Dumont and he's definitely one of our guys."

"Where? How do you know? Where are you?"

"I'll tell you all about it later. Just listen carefully. You have to call your cop pals. Have you got a pen? Write this down."

There was some thrashing around at the other end of the phone. "Okay, go ahead," Sims said.

"Tell them to send the Virginia state police to The Boar's Head Inn, room seven. You got that?"

"Spell *Boar's*."

He did. "Dumont's there with a pretty good bump on the head. He's okay, though, and he's tied up."

"*What*? You hit him on the head?"

"No, I didn't, as a matter of fact. But tell them to arrest him and charge him with the murder of Barney Paulsen. They'll see when they look at him that he's the guy in that middle shooter's seat."

"The Virginia state cops haven't got that picture."

"But *your* guys do. They make the arrest, then he's extradited to Maryland."

"What the hell happened, Bobby? I mean . . ."

Kelleher cut him off. "Not now. The guy may come to and figure out a way to get untied and then I'll never forgive myself. Or he might be hurt worse than I think. I doubt it, but you gotta get the cops moving on this fast."

"Okay, okay. Where do I call you back?"

Kelleher hesitated, then gave him Ann's number.

"You got a room number?"

"It's a friend's house."

"I'll call you."

Kelleher hung up and sat back on the couch. Ann had disappeared up the stairs. Now, she was coming back down wearing a bathrobe. "I just had to get that damn dress off," she said. "Do you want coffee or something to drink?"

"Coffee would be wonderful," he said, getting up and following her into the kitchen.

"What did you do?" she asked.

He told her. He also told her about his exchange with Dumont inside the room, and the fact that Meredith Gordy was in real danger. "There's no question he didn't work alone. The other two shooters are still out there somewhere and I'm sure there are others involved, too. Ann, he *knew* I was coming."

"Are you sure?" She poured the coffee in a mug that said "YOO-VEE-AY" on it and handed it to him.

"Oh, yeah. The fact that he drove up with his lights out makes me even more certain. Why would he do that if he didn't think I might be waiting for him somewhere?"

"Who could have tipped him?"

Kelleher had a theory, although it wasn't one that he liked. "Kyler told Tourretta I was coming to Charlottesville," he said. "Tourretta might have tipped him to be on the lookout for me."

"You really think he might be working with Tourretta?"

"I don't see how. But the only other people who knew about Dumont were Sims and Maureen." He slammed his hand on the counter. "Damn! I never called Maureen to tell her I was okay."

"You *weren't* okay until a few minutes ago. Call her in the morning and . . ."

The phone rang and when she answered it, she broke into a smile. "He was just about to call you. Hang on."

She handed him the phone. "How'd you know I was here?" he asked his partner.

"I didn't," McGuire said. "But I tried five hotels and you weren't in any of them. I took a chance you'd be there. I'm just glad I remembered her name. Now where the hell have you been?"

"It's a long story."

"I have time."

He filled her in. "I'm still waiting to hear back from Sims," he said when he was finished.

"Call me as soon as you do. Then we'll decide what to do next."

The call waiting on Ann's phone was clicking. "This has to be him," he said. "I'll call you back."

It was Sims with bad news. "You didn't tie him up tight enough," he told Kelleher quietly.

"What?!"

"The cops found bloodstains on the bed, sheets tossed on the floor, and the gun outside the door. But no Dumont. No anybody."

Kelleher was horrified. "Oh, God, I should have stayed there. I never figured he could possibly come to *and* untie himself so quickly."

"Well, he can't have gone very far," Sims said. "Unless someone picked him up. His car is still there."

Kelleher's head was throbbing when he hung up a few minutes later. Ann came and sat next to him on the couch. "Got away?" she asked. He nodded, almost imperceptibly.

"I just don't know how it could've happened," he said. "I have to call Maureen back. I feel like a complete fool."

He filled McGuire in on what had happened. They agreed to talk again in the morning to decide what to do next. Kelleher felt confused, hurt, tired, sore, and stupid. Ann patted his hand, her hazel eyes full of concern.

"You look as beat up as anyone I've ever seen," she said.

He looked at her, almost overpoweringly drawn to her. There was no way he could ever repay her for what she had done for him tonight, from the scene in the lobby to saving his life in the parking lot. He kissed her hand and said softly, "You know, I really do love you."

It was a line, only it wasn't. It was exactly what he felt at that moment. She moved closer to him and put her arm around his neck. "I know you do, old friend."

They looked at each other for a moment and then he was kissing her, needing to kiss her. It wasn't the right thing to do; intellectually, he knew that. Emotionally and physically, he wasn't nearly so virtuous. He was starting to untie her bathrobe when she said quietly, "Not here, Bobby."

He reached down, picked her up in his arms—she was considerably lighter than Dumont—and carried her upstairs to the bedroom. As it had been with Andrea two nights earlier, their lovemaking was intense, cathartic, and lengthy.

The only difference was that this time Kelleher didn't sleep when it was over. He lay on his back, staring at the ceiling while Ann curled up next to him. They had known each other for so long, been through so many stages in their relationship. Even when they had dated, there had been an unspoken understanding between them that this was all good fun, certainly nothing serious. They were both so much older now; he'd reached the stage where the idea of sharing his life with someone had become important. Could that someone really be Ann?

And yet, Kelleher had felt many of those same emotions the other night with Andrea, who, by comparison, was a complete stranger. Was he reacting to the *idea* of being in love rather than to actually *being* in love? In both cases, an extraordinary and frightening experience had played a major role in what had happened. First, Kelleher had watched Barney Paulsen die. Then he had faced death himself. In each case his instinct had been to reach out to someone else. For comfort. For relief. For safety.

The most frightening thing about death, Kelleher supposed, was the loneliness of it. Both Andrea and Ann had provided a haven from loneliness on two terrifyingly lonely nights. The question he was going to have to face, once some semblance of normalcy returned to his life, was whether these two nights had simply been an escape from his fears. He believed they were more than that, much more. But if so, how could it have happened with two different women within forty-eight hours?

It was almost six o'clock by the time Kelleher drifted off to sleep. He awoke an hour later in a cold sweat, having dreamed that he was locked in the trunk of Jimmy Dumont's car. Ann was still asleep. He got up to make coffee and take a shower. Making sense of his life, he realized, would have to wait. First, he had to make sense once and for all of Barney Paulsen's death.

CHAPTER 10

JAMELLE TOURRETTA

Kelleher and Ann had just finished their coffee, having studiously avoided any discussion of what had happened between them in the early morning, when the phone rang.

Ann, who had put on a sweatshirt and shorts, shook her head as she got up to answer it. "Has to be for you," she said. "There's not a single living human being who would call me at nine o'clock on a Sunday morning."

She was right. It was Sims. "They found Jimmy Dumont," he announced when Kelleher picked up the phone.

"Fantastic!" The sense of relief was immense. A thousand pounds were lifted off his back and from the pit of his stomach. "Do they think he'll talk?"

"Not likely," Sims said. "They found him face down near a rest stop on I-64—with a bullet in his head. Someone killed him execution-style."

Kelleher suddenly felt nauseated. Not so much at the notion that Dumont was dead but because he knew that would have been the way he would have ended up if Dumont had gotten him into the car. Beyond that, though, the plot had taken yet another unfathomable twist. Who would kill Dumont and why?

Sims sighed heavily at the other end of the phone. "Bobby, I can only protect you for so long. The cops are all over me wanting to know who tipped me about Dumont."

"Alan, I can't be in the middle of this. At least not right now."

"I can protect you for a day or two," Sims said. "But that's it. Now tell me exactly what happened."

Kelleher went through the entire evening's events in detail. When he finished, there was a long silence on the other end of the phone.

"Gordy has to be told right away," Sims said. "She has to be protected if this thing isn't over yet."

"Can you tell her without telling her your source?" Kelleher asked.

"Impossible. She'll demand details. And she's entitled to them. But I think I can convince her to keep the details to herself. She can simply tell Bearnarth there's been a threat made against her. They'll beef up security on her say-so without demanding to know why. At least for now. But the next question is: what the hell are you going to write?"

That was a damn good question, one Kelleher had been pondering in the shower. What was really called for, he knew, was a first-person story detailing what had happened. But he couldn't put himself into the middle of an ongoing story; it would, in effect, take him out of the story as a reporter. That was absolutely the last thing he wanted. He was starting to smell blood. He knew he was close, probably closer than anyone else. And right now, that was all he cared about.

"I'll write about Dumont, about how he and the other two guys were ID'd off the picture, and about his background at UVA and in right-wing political causes." Saying that reminded Kelleher of something he had seen in Dumont's suitcase. "Hey, Alan, do the letters LOL mean anything to you."

"LOL? Sure, Lovers of Life. Why?"

That was it! Kelleher had brain-locked the night before! Lovers of Life was the extreme right-wing group that was trying to dismantle the First Amendment as part of its campaign to stifle the pro-choice movement and the liberal media. What do you know, Kelleher thought. It seemed the LOL had turned to murder as part of its campaign to prove how much it loved life.

"Alan," he said, "Dumont had a notepad in his suitcase that said LOL on it. The cops must've found it when they checked his room."

"Holy shit," Sims said, suddenly excited. "Finally, this thing makes sense. Who is Maryland's most visible LOL member?"

They both said it together: "Myron Cutler!"

If Meredith Gordy were to die while the lieutenant governor's office was still vacant, the Senate president was next in line to be governor. Senate President Myron Cutler.

"Jesus, Alan, do you think Cutler? . . ."

"Cutler's a jerk, Bobby, but he's no murderer."

"Right now, we've got to assume anything's possible."

"I understand that, but my guess is Cutler's just a foil. What the cops have to do now is catch these other two shooters before they turn up dead, too."

"You think that's possible?"

"My guess is Dumont's dead because someone figured out he was about to get caught. Two days ago, the FBI thought it was right on the tail of the other two guys. Now, they've lost them. Judging by what happened to Dumont, there may be a reason."

Kelleher felt himself shudder slightly. "There's a lot of people getting dead here," he said softly.

"Do me a favor, Bobby, and don't become one of them."

He called McGuire after he finished with Sims, told her about Dumont's death and Sims's plans to warn Gordy. McGuire was just as unnerved by this turn of events as he had been.

"Come back here right now," she said, almost shouting. "Come into the office and we'll tell the editors what's happening. They'll get us out of this national staff crap and you can write from here, safe and sound."

It was tempting, Kelleher had to admit. Being back inside the *Herald* building would make him feel a lot safer. But something told Kelleher he needed to talk to Tourretta. He still didn't know why Dumont had been registered at the hotel under her last name, unless it was part of LOL's plot to make Tourretta look suspect. Beyond that, he was still mystified by the fact that Dumont had seemed to be expecting him.

By his unofficial count, only five people had known he was coming to Charlottesville: Meredith Gordy, Andrea Kyler, Maureen McGuire, Ann Roberts, and Alan Sims. And Kyler—at his request—had passed that information on to Tourretta.

He definitely needed to look Tourretta in the eye and ask her some questions and see what kind of response he got. So he told McGuire he would stay for the speech, write his story from the pressroom at University Hall, then drive back to Washington.

She was exasperated. "You aren't making sense," she said. "Clearly, you're in some kind of danger. Get the hell out of there, Kelleher. Don't use Tourretta as an excuse to hang around and pop that babe of yours one more time.''

That one really stung. It also wasn't true. "I'll call you at the office,'' he said, "*after* I see Tourretta.'' He slammed the phone down, angry at Maureen McGuire for one of the first times in his life.

Ann had been upstairs while he'd been on the phone; she came back down the stairs dressed for a run, carrying her running shoes.

"You'll be gone by the time I get back?'' she asked.

He looked at the clock over the mantel. It was after ten. "You don't want to go with me to the speech?''

She shook her head. "I've got things to do, people to entertain at the basketball game. And you've got work to do, too. Just promise that you'll call me every so often to let me know you're okay?''

"I'll call you tonight, I promise.''

She put a hand on his cheek. "You don't owe me anything or have to make any promises, Bobby. Just call. I can't follow you around with a potted plant every day, you know.''

He laughed, kissed her hand, and she was gone. He wished he could just stay there and wait for her to come back. But that wasn't possible. He had to go see Jamelle Tourretta.

▬ ▬

It was about a ten-minute walk from U-Hall, across The Lawn, which was the heart of the UVA campus, to the union. They were playing touch football on The Lawn, a sight that always made Kelleher nostalgic. It was hard for him to believe that nine years had passed since he had last played a touch-football game here.

The auditorium was mobbed when Kelleher got to the press entrance. There, he found Tom Kenworthy waiting in line to have his ID checked. Seeing Kenworthy reminded him that he hadn't checked the *Post* or the *Sun* yet. Presumably, if either paper had broken anything important, McGuire would have given him the bad news.

"Where the hell have *you* been?'' Kenworthy asked him as he walked up.

"Probably the same places you've been, except for Friday night when you broke this Tourretta thing.''

"I just hope she doesn't want to fight me,'' he said.

"I didn't see the *Sun* this morning,'' he said. "Frece have anything?''

Kenworthy shook his head. "We all had the same story, more or less.

But I heard driving down this morning that they found the *third* suspect somewhere in Virginia, face down with a bullet in his head. They didn't release a name, though."

Kelleher knew the name: Jimmy Dumont. And now he knew that Sims's theory was right. Whoever was behind all this had killed the shooters.

"Frece coming?" he asked Kenworthy, trying to remain calm.

"Told me yesterday, no. They're sending someone from Baltimore. Don't ask me why."

They'd reached the table, where two young women wearing FFF straw hats were sitting.

"Did you call ahead?" one of them asked.

"I did," Kenworthy said. "Tom Kenworthy, *Washington Post*."

One of the women had a list. Kelleher wondered if he wasn't going to get in because he hadn't called in advance. "Right, Mr. Kenworthy," she said. "Just sign here and I'll make a name tag for you."

What was this, Kelleher wondered, a cocktail party? "I didn't call ahead," he said. "I'm Bobby Kelleher from *The Washington Herald*."

"Have you got some ID, Mr. Kelleher?"

He produced his ID card. She looked at it briefly, handed it back, and smiled. "No problem," she said. "Just sign here at the bottom of the list." Kelleher breathed a sigh of relief, put his tag on, and followed Kenworthy down the side aisle of the auditorium to one of the front rows that had been roped off for the media. There was another young woman in an FFF straw hat waiting for them there. "Gentlemen, Ms. Tourretta will be meeting with the media in room one forty-one down the hall ten minutes after she's finished speaking," she announced.

Kelleher and Kenworthy settled into their seats. Several other State House reporters were already there, as were a number of TV types. Their camera equipment, Kelleher assumed, was set up in room 141.

"She ought to give you a percentage for turning this into a media event," he whispered to Kenworthy.

"I don't think she looks at it quite that way," he answered.

Another young woman in an FFF hat walked onstage at noon and took the microphone. "Ladies and gentleman, if I could have your attention, please," she said. "If I can have your attention, we'll get started."

The crowd, a full house, quieted. "My name is Missy Mathis. I'm the vice president of the UVA speakers union and campus coordinator for FFF."

Kelleher had heard that FFF had been having trouble remaining viable on a lot of campuses since Tourretta's admission of their seduction tactics. Some thought the group was slowly dying. Fund-raising had gone down the last two years; fewer and fewer candidates had wanted the FFF stamp of approval. That was why it made sense that Tourretta had wanted Gordy there today—to give FFF a Good Housekeeping Seal of Approval. Tourretta had put FFF back on the map, all right—although once again for the wrong reasons.

Missy Mathis was quite pretty, very petite with long light-brown hair. She wore a white blouse, a black skirt, and sensible, low-heeled shoes. She spoke for a few moments about Jamelle Tourretta's accomplishments, about how she had risen through the ranks of FFF to become executive director and had succeeded the group's founder, Amy Coltraine, as its most visible spokeswoman. That was certainly true, Kelleher thought, but it had been Coltraine who had given the group respectability. She was now back in the mainstream, working with NOW, feeling that FFF had become a wayward child she could no longer control.

Missy Mathis said nothing about the seduction tactics Tourretta had brought to the group or its recent problems. Instead, she finished her introduction by saying, "It gives me great pleasure to introduce one of the most important women and one of the most important *people* in America today, Ms. Jamelle Tourretta."

The reaction to Tourretta was mixed. Some applauded loudly; some politely. Some cheered. Others just stared. Kelleher fell into the staring category. Sitting in the third row, he had an excellent view of Tourretta as she walked onstage. Alan Sims had not exaggerated.

She was at least six feet tall and, standing next to the petite Missy Mathis, she looked even taller. She was also wearing a white blouse and a black skirt; Kelleher wondered if that wasn't some kind of FFF uniform. Unlike Mathis, though, she wore spike heels, making her even taller. Her shoulders were broad, her chest was, for lack of a more genteel word, huge. Her legs were solid and muscular but shapely. Even in the spike heels, she moved with remarkable grace, like some kind of giant gazelle, seemingly unencumbered by her size. Her flaming red hair was shoulder length, curly and stylish all at once.

"My God!" Kelleher said softly.

Kenworthy grinned. "First time you've ever seen her in person?"

He nodded.

"Quite a sight. You ready to join FFF now?"

"Where do I sign?" Kelleher said, gradually recovering his composure.

Jamelle Tourretta may have been more impressive as a speaker than she was walking onstage—if that was possible. She spoke eloquently about the feminist movement, about the death of the ERA, and the distressing swing to the right brought on by Reaganism in the 1980s.

"For years, women said, 'Our time will come,' " she orated. "Then they said, 'Now is the time.' What frightens me is that it seems, in many ways, our time has now passed. We have made gains, yes, but in the last few years, we have lost ground. The Supreme Court of Ronald Reagan and George Bush will only hurt our cause more. The treatment of Anita Hill in the Clarence Thomas case is a stunning example of how little most politicians respect women. That is why FFF is more important now than ever. We need to identify and help elect candidates who believe that, for women, the good old days are a myth, that a new day must dawn very soon.

"Women like myself intimidate people," she continued. "I know that. But pleading and cajoling, shouting and begging haven't gotten us what we want, what we deserve. Too often, we women are the intimidated. Maybe it is time we become the intimidators. We can't keep saying someday. We have to say now, immediately, today."

She smiled, looked toward the media for a moment, and went on. "The state of Maryland was struck Thursday by a terrible tragedy. Its governor was murdered. By coincidence, I was present that day. Some would like to imply it was more than coincidence; the facts will prove that to be completely untrue. Tragic as Governor Paulsen's death was, the new governor of Maryland is Meredith Gordy, a woman capable of greatness, a woman who can play a key role in the advancement of our movement."

She stopped again and looked into the crowd. "A woman," she said finally, "who can be president. I pray that day will come soon and I implore all of you to help it come sooner."

She smiled again, rolled up her blouse sleeve and curled her arm into a muscle that would have made Arnold Schwarzenegger envious. "Remember," she said, flexing her arm, "the days when only men could be strong are behind us. Strength is something anyone can have if they want to be strong. Always, we should want to be strong. Thank you very much."

She put her arm down and stepped back from the lectern as many in the audience—almost all of the women—stood to applaud her. Kelleher had taken out his notebook and started scribbling furiously when Tourretta had brought up the Paulsen shooting. He was amazed by what she had said: In one breath she had denied any involvement in what had happened; in the next she had started promoting Meredith Gordy for president.

"You think she has some kind of death wish?" Kenworthy asked as they stood up to leave. "I mean, except for that little disclaimer, she all but endorsed Paulsen's assassination."

"She is," Kelleher said, "an interesting woman."

"In more ways than one," Kenworthy agreed.

They worked their way down the hall to the room where Tourretta was supposed to meet with the media. There were, by Kelleher's count, fourteen camera crews in the room with at least another dozen tape recorders sitting on the table at the front of the room where Tourretta would be seated. He and Kenworthy worked their way around to a windowsill to sit down. Kelleher wondered if Kyler had gotten through to Tourretta.

Missy Mathis walked in to the front of the room, followed by Tourretta and another woman who looked a little bit like a bodyguard. "Why in the world would *she* need a bodyguard?" Kelleher whispered to Kenworthy.

"Ladies and gentlemen, I know you have a lot of questions for Ms. Tourretta," Missy Mathis said. "But she does have a plane to catch, so we're going to have to limit this to fifteen minutes. We appreciate your cooperation."

One of the local TVs asked some silly question about what she thought of Charlottesville and Tourretta answered politely. Then, Tom Daniels, from Channel 5 in Washington, another one of Maureen McGuire's "mannequins," brought up Kenworthy's story.

"Can you confirm that you were questioned by the FBI?" he asked. "And do you have any comment?"

"Thank God," Kenworthy whispered. "I didn't want to have to ask the fucking question."

"I'll certainly confirm that I was questioned by the FBI," Tourretta was saying. "It is amazing to me that I was one of two hundred people in the gallery that day and, as far as I know, the only one to date questioned by the authorities. I'm sure my lawyers will be looking into that in the future.

"I was in Annapolis that day at the invitation of Andrea Kyler, Governor Gordy's chief aide. She has confirmed that for anyone who has asked. I was hoping to meet with *then* Lieutenant Governor Gordy specifically to invite her to attend this speech here today. Obviously, I never got that opportunity.

"I want to make something very clear. Governor Paulsen was very much a friend of the women's movement. I think his record bears that out. But even if he was the absolute worst Neanderthal to ever pull on a pair of pants, FFF would never, I repeat, *never* resort to violence of that or any other kind. One of the first tenets of the women's movement in this country has been to get away from the kind of violence perpetuated by men in the past."

"Why do you think the FBI questioned you?" The question came from someone Kelleher didn't know.

"They put two and two together and came up with three," Tourretta said. "Paulsen is dead; Gordy, someone we at FFF very much support, becomes governor; they point a finger at FFF. The only problem is, they're wrong."

Kenworthy couldn't hold back any longer. "What about the fact that two of the suspects used to be FFF bodyguards?"

Tourretta shot him a look. "I can't comment on that," she said.

"What do you mean *can't* comment?" Kenworthy followed.

"I mean, I *won't* comment," Tourretta said. "No arrests have been made. When they are, we will be exonerated."

Missy Mathis stepped in at that point. "I'm sorry, but that's all the time we have."

Kelleher wondered if that meant he was going to get shut out. But as Tourretta stood up amid all sorts of shouted questions from every corner of the room, another straw hat approached him.

"Mr. Kelleher?" she said, eyeballing his name tag.

"Yes?"

"Please follow me."

Kenworthy was giving him the eye. "What are you up to, Bobby?"

"I really don't know," he lied. "You sticking around?"

"No, going straight back to D.C. I have to write this and see if there's been any movement on the murder. Obviously, this guy showing up dead, whoever he is, gives us all something else to chase after."

Kelleher nodded, feeling a little bit sheepish about not telling Kenworthy that he knew who the dead person was. But that was the nature of the business: on some days you had to pretend your friends weren't friends.

"I'll see you back in Annapolis tomorrow," he said.

"Fran's after session?"

"Jeez, I sure hope so. It would be nice to do something normal again."

Kenworthy laughed. "Tell me about it." He lit a cigarette, waved a hand at Kelleher, and headed for the back door. Kelleher turned to follow the straw hat.

They walked out the door and turned left into an area of the hall that had been roped off to prevent any media from following Tourretta. At the end of the hall was a flight of steps leading to the basement. They went down the steps, made another left, and came to a white door.

"You can go in there," the straw hat said.

For a split second Kelleher felt he was being trapped somehow. But before he could ask any questions, the straw hat had turned on her heel and disappeared back down the hall. Kelleher hesitated for a moment, then pushed the door open.

The room was some kind of dressing room, an area for speakers to come and rest, put on makeup, whatever. Missy Mathis was sitting on one of the dressing tables. The woman Kelleher had assumed was a bodyguard was standing just inside the door with her arms folded. She was as big as Tourretta but with none of the sex appeal. She was just a very large, very hard-looking woman dressed in a work shirt, blue jeans, and running shoes.

Jamelle Tourretta sat in an armchair on the far side of the room talking on the telephone. She had a cigarette in one hand and was speaking so softly that, even standing ten feet away, Kelleher couldn't make out what she was saying. Neither Missy Mathis nor the bodyguard spoke or even acknowledged his existence when he walked in. Kelleher smiled at Mathis, who looked right through him. She had taken off her straw hat and Kelleher could now see that she wasn't merely pretty but quite beautiful. He had just become aware of the fact that he was staring at her when he heard Tourretta hang up the phone.

She stood up and walked across the room to him, hand extended. "Mr. Kelleher, I presume?" she said with a friendly smile.

"For better or worse," he answered, putting out his hand. Her handshake was firm without trying to prove anything. Kelleher suspected that she didn't feel any need to do so. Standing face-to-face with Tourretta was just a bit overwhelming.

"Have you met Missy Mathis and Wendy Paul?" Tourretta indicated first Mathis, then the bodyguard. "Missy's a student here. Wendy works with me." Kelleher nodded at the two women, who continued to ignore him.

"Andrea said you wanted to talk to me," Tourretta went on, still standing a few inches away, towering over him. "What is it I can do for you?"

Kelleher walked over to the dressing table that Mathis wasn't seated on and leaned against it. He couldn't concentrate standing that close to Tourretta. "I need to ask you a few questions."

"If it's about the FBI, you heard my answer. There really isn't anything more to say."

"It's not about the FBI. It's about James Dumont."

She lit another cigarette, offered him the pack, and then handed one to Wendy Paul. She walked back to the chair she had been sitting in, sat down, and crossed her legs.

"Who," she asked, blowing smoke out of her mouth, "is James Dumont?"

"Was," Kelleher said. "The Virginia state police found him face down in a ditch this morning."

"Is that the man we heard about on the radio this morning?" Tourretta asked.

"That's the man," Kelleher said, without saying anything more. "But last night he was registered at The Boar's Head Inn here in Charlottesville under the name James Tourretta."

The FFF leader's eyebrows went up for just a second. "James Tourretta? Same spelling?"

"You got it."

"And you think that makes a connection between me and the assassination."

"I really don't know what to think. But you were sitting right behind Dumont in the gallery on Thursday."

"I was? How do you know that?"

"I'm a reporter," Kelleher said, using the response he always used when he had no intention of revealing how he knew something. "You're sitting one row behind him at the time of the shooting, then he shows up registered in a hotel using your name, and now he shows up dead. You have to admit, Ms. Tourretta, it does raise some questions."

Jamelle Tourretta stood up, took another drag on her cigarette, put it out in an ashtray, and walked over to Kelleher. Since he was leaning against the dressing table she now appeared to be at least nine feet tall.

"I do *not* have to defend myself to you or to anyone else, Mr. Kelleher," she said quietly but firmly. "Andrea asked me to give you ten minutes because she said you wouldn't ask the same tired questions. I have now given you ten minutes and you have yet to raise a question worthy of a response."

She glared at him so fiercely that Kelleher thought she might start a fight. Fortunately, she didn't—because he definitely would have lost. "If you want to drag FFF through this, Mr. Kelleher, you go right ahead. We'll rise above you the way we've risen above people like you in the past."

Kelleher stood up as straight as he could. It didn't seem to make much difference. "I'm not making this stuff up, Ms. Tourretta, I'm just asking you about it. If I just wanted to drag FFF through the mud, I could report what I know *without* speaking to you."

She peered at him, as if considering exactly what to do with him. Then, she smiled. "You're right, I suppose," she said. "I'm sorry to snap at you, it's just that I resent so much being questioned about this. I can see where people might turn coincidence into circumstantial evidence, especially given my feelings about Meredith Gordy. But believe me, Mr. Kelleher, I was just in the wrong place at the wrong time. I was as terrified as anyone when the lights went out."

"What do you remember?" he asked.

She shook her head. "Not a lot that's useful. I can believe what you say about me being right behind this Dumont—is that what you said his name was?—because I remember hearing what sounded at first like very loud firecrackers right in front of me. You know, a *pop-pop-pop* sound. I told the police that. But that's all."

"You don't remember the guy sitting in front of you at all, then?"

"I really don't. To tell you the truth, I walked in just as everything was starting. Wendy here had gotten there ahead of time and saved a seat for me because I was talking to Andrea, trying to make postspeech plans to see Meredith."

She paused to light another cigarette. "The police are *sure* this Jimmy Dumont person was involved? What do they know about him?"

"Not much yet," Kelleher said, not willing to give Tourretta any information. "They're hoping they get to the other two guys still alive."

"Well," Tourretta said, reaching for her coat, "I certainly hope they do, because I'm tired of having this hanging over me. It really isn't fair to me, to the organization, or, for that matter, to Meredith Gordy."

She pulled her coat on and offered her hand to Kelleher again. "If we don't catch this flight, we'll miss our connection back to New York," she said. "I'm sorry for my outburst."

"Perfectly okay," Kelleher said, still trying to make himself taller, without success. "Are you connecting through Richmond or Washington?"

"Richmond."

"USAir?"

"Air Virginia, then USAir," said Missy Mathis, speaking for the first time. "And we've got only twenty-five minutes to get you there."

Jamelle Tourretta looked at Kelleher again. "When you see Andrea, tell her I'll call her later in the week. After things calm down a little."

Kelleher nodded. "Thanks again for the time."

She followed Mathis and Paul out the door while Kelleher stood there in the empty room for a minute trying to figure out what was bothering him. Something Tourretta had said had made him uneasy, but he couldn't put a finger on it. He cursed himself for not having turned on the tape recorder when they started talking.

He pulled out his notebook, sat down at one of the dressing tables, and began reconstructing the conversation as exactly as he could. This was an old tactic of his, something he had done for years, because he had such a good memory. If someone was talking in an uncomfortable situation, he never pulled out a notebook or tape recorder, for fear that it would inhibit them. He would wait until the conversation was over, then sit down and, using his questions as a starting point, put together everything they had said. He was very good at it.

It took him ten minutes to write out the conversation. He read it through but could come up with nothing. What Tourretta had done was really not unusual: she had played dumb at first, then tried to intimidate him. When that hadn't worked, she'd gone the charm route. It was the classic three-step interview and it had ended as they usually ended: with a lot of words, a couple of good quotes, but not a single interesting fact.

"Damn!" Kelleher said, snapping the notebook shut. He looked at his watch. It was almost two o'clock. He needed to get over to U-Hall to call the office and start writing. Since the game was at four o'clock, he would have the pressroom pretty much to himself until three. Then the writers would begin arriving for their pregame meal—Kelleher had never met a sportswriter who would pass up a free meal, no matter how vile it might be—and it would be impossible to work.

He walked quickly back across the campus to U-Hall, stopped at his car to pull his computer out of the trunk, and went inside. As he'd hoped, the pressroom was virtually empty. He exchanged greetings with the ushers, the same men who'd worked in the building when he had played, and set himself up at the desk where the *Herald*'s phone was located.

He called the desk and got Jane Kryton. Her mood was not great. "All I can tell you is, this story Maureen says you have better be good," she said. "Because when Watkins found out you didn't show up for lunch with the national people, he went straight off the wall. Tom Anthony's not thrilled either."

He quickly briefed her on Jimmy Dumont and his political background; on the LOL and on Sims's theory (without mentioning Sims) that the other two shooters might also be dead. He didn't tell her about breaking into Dumont's room, his meeting with Dumont, or any of Ann Roberts's involvement. Even so, she was impressed.

"Congratulations. I think you just saved your ass," she told him. "That's a hell of a story. It kind of shoots down the *Post* story about Tourretta, doesn't it? The only problem we have now is figuring out why the LOL would want to make Meredith Gordy governor."

"Maybe they didn't intend to make Meredith Gordy governor," he said, again leaving out details.

"What the hell does that mean?"

"It means that Myron Cutler is probably the most visible LOL member in the Maryland legislature."

Kryton was silent for a moment. "Are you saying you think Gordy might be in danger even now?"

"I'm saying anything is possible."

"Start writing. The sooner we get the story, the better."

"You got it, boss. How about switching me to Maureen?"

Kryton transferred him to McGuire. "So, did you get anything from Tourretta?" she asked.

"Not really. A lot of indignation, a couple of usable quotes, not much information."

"What'd you think of her?"

He could almost see McGuire grinning into the phone at the thought of his first face-to-face meeting with the FFF amazon.

"Did she do the routine where she stands right over you?"

"Yeah, how'd you know that?"

"She told me that she loves to stand over men and look down at them because it freaks them out. They lose concentration."

"She's got that right."

McGuire laughed. "Listen, I made some calls to check out Dumont and the LOL."

"And?"

"I talked to some guy who's the spokesman for the LOL down at their Lynchburg headquarters. They willingly admit that Dumont was a member a couple years ago but say he hasn't been active in any way other than to pay dues recently. I also talked to Cutler."

"What did old Myron have to say?"

"Pretty predictable stuff. He expressed the usual shock and dismay, said he couldn't believe anyone from LOL would be involved in anything like this, and said he had never in his life heard the name Jimmy Dumont. To quote him exactly, he said, 'Who is this Jimmy Dumont person?' "

Kelleher chuckled. He could heard Cutler saying those exact words. "I'll call you after I file so we can work your stuff in with mine or figure out a sidebar," he said.

He hung up, thinking about snotty old Myron Cutler. And then it hit him right smack in the face.

"Holy shit!" he said. He pulled out his notebook and began reading what he'd written about his conversation with Tourretta. There it was. Just before she'd left she had said to him, "The police are really sure this Jimmy Dumont person is involved?"

He might have had a word or two wrong in there but she had definitely said 'this Jimmy Dumont.' He could still hear her saying it in just the way he imagined Cutler had. Which was all well and good except for one thing: when he had asked Tourretta about Dumont he had referred to him as *James* Dumont. He checked his notes again, then shut his eyes to try one more time to recall the conversation. There was no doubt about it. He had *never* referred to Dumont as Jimmy. She was lying.

He suddenly had another idea. Reaching into his wallet, he pulled out his USAir frequent-traveler card and dialed the number for reservations.

"USAir, Jane Hermann, how may I help you?"

"I need to get some flight information."

"Certainly, sir, how many traveling and where do you wish to go?"

"Actually, I needed to know about a flight this morning."

"Which flight was that?"

"I need to know what you had flying out of New York to Richmond that would have been able to connect to Charlottesville."

"One moment, sir."

Kelleher could hear the tap-tap-tapping of the computer in the background. "Yes, sir, we had a flight that left New York/La Guardia at seven thirty-two A.M., arriving in Richmond at eight fifty-five A.M. From there you could have connected to an Air Virginia flight that left Richmond at ten oh-four A.M. and arrived in Charlottesville at ten thirty-five A.M."

"Can you tell me those flight numbers?"

"Yes, sir. The USAir flight was number 1151 and, wait, let me see, yes, it was Air Virginia 3422."

Kelleher scribbled the numbers on the back of his notebook. "Okay, bear with me one more minute here. This afternoon, going back to New York out of Richmond, what flights do you have?"

"Checking for you, sir." More tap-tap-tapping. "Okay, sir, we have a flight leaving at four P.M., that's flight number 977. It arrives in New York at five thirty-five and then our last nonstop is at seven fifty-one P.M. That's flight 1804 . . ."

He cut her off at that point. "You say 977 leaves at four?"

"Yes, sir. And there are seats available, although it leaves in a little more than an hour."

"Right, that's fine. One more question. Is it possible for you to tell me if a particular person was on those flights this morning?"

"No, sir, I can't do that here. But if you were to call our business office in Indianapolis in the morning, they'd have a record of the flight manifest. They might be able to help you."

Kelleher wondered if he should just ask if Tourretta had reservations on any of those flights. That wouldn't prove anything, though. "Okay. Thanks for your help."

"Thank you for calling USAir."

Hanging up, Kelleher dialed the *Herald* switchboard. He identified himself to the operator and asked her to put him through to Dana Russo, the paper's aviation reporter, at home. Dana was home but she had her hands full. Kelleher could hear at least two children crying in the background.

"I'm sorry to bother you at home," he told her, "but I need help."

"What's up?" she asked, then added, "Dennis, will you get these kids to quiet down?! Sorry, Bobby."

"I need to know if someone was on a USAir flight this morning. You know anyone who can check a flight manifest for you on a Sunday?"

"If I can find the guy, yeah, I think so. What do you need?"

"See if Jamelle Tourretta was on flight 1151 out of LaGuardia this morning. I also need to know if she has a reservation on flight 977 out of Richmond this afternoon. It leaves at four. If she *does* have a reservation, if there's any way to find out if she shows up for the flight, that'd be great, too."

Dana was a good reporter, so he knew her mind was racing. She'd be dying to ask what he had on Tourretta for Paulsen's murder. But she was a total pro, so all she said was, "How about if you call me back at about five? I'm kind of running around."

"That would be fine." If she came up with the right answers, that would be more than fine.

The sound of the Virginia basketball team walking past the door en route to their pregame warmup reminded Kelleher that he had a lot of writing to do. He turned his full attention to his computer.

The story was easy to write: a straight lead described the discovery of Dumont's body two days after he had shown up photographed in a seat which positively identified him as being one of the three Paulsen shooters. Kelleher then went on to fill in details of Dumont's political background.

The only delicate part involved Jamelle Tourretta. If Dumont was definitely involved in the conspiracy, that would seem to clear Tourretta and FFF. But Tourretta's lie that morning left her smack in the middle of the case—at least as far as Kelleher was concerned. Yet, he couldn't write that. Ultimately, he played it conservatively, mentioning that she had been questioned, quoting her angry denial in the speech and her insistence to him that she had never heard of Dumont. He thought long and hard about whether to tip other writers off by mentioning that Dumont had used the name Tourretta while at The Boar's Head.

He finally decided against it, though it pained him right in his journalistic instincts. It was a good, solid note, newsworthy certainly. Any journalism professor would insist on putting it in. But Kelleher was after The Big Hit—and giving up an advantage in that pursuit would be a major mistake.

He had absolutely no qualms about leaving out Dumont's nasty crack that Gordy might never sign a bill into law. If writing something jeopardized someone's safety, you didn't write it, plain and simple. Letting

Dumont's co-conspirators know that Gordy was aware she was in danger might make them more careful. The key here was to keep them off guard, to catch them, and, at the same time, to make sure Gordy stayed alive and well.

The game had already started. Kelleher could hear the crowd screaming as he filed. It was a good, solid story, he thought, although not *the* story. He hoped he would be able to write that one soon. He was surprised when the computer informed him that he had written sixty-three inches. That was a lot, especially in less than two hours.

He called McGuire once the story was in and they decided she should piece together a sidebar summing up the investigation so far, including the confusing dichotomy of first Tourretta and now Dumont being considered suspects on some level. "Be careful not to clear Tourretta," he said.

"What do you mean?"

"I mean she lied to me about knowing Dumont. They're connected somehow, I'm convinced of it."

"Bobby, that's just too crazy. How do you know she lied?"

He told her about the conversation.

"And you're absolutely certain you never once said 'Jimmy' to her?"

"Am I ever wrong about stuff like that?"

She sighed. "Makes absolutely no sense."

She was certainly right about that. "Do me a favor and tell Jane I'll call her from the car phone when I get in range of D.C.," he said.

"Are you leaving now?"

"I have a few more calls to make first but I should be out of here before six. At least I hope I will."

"You going home?"

"I'm going straight up to Annapolis and stay there. The service for Paulsen is at ten in the morning, so there's no point going home."

"Then I'll see you at the service."

He hung up and dialed Sims. He filled him in on what he had written and about his conversation with Tourretta.

"That's certainly an interesting twist, isn't it?" Sims mused. "There isn't a reason in the world for her to lie about Dumont, is there?"

"Apparently there is."

"Sounds like a case for Bobby Kelleher."

"Thanks, ace. And what have you been doing all day?"

"Well, I spent a good portion of the morning bringing the governor up to date on your actions and movements. She'd like to talk to you whenever it's possible. Right now I'm watching your beloved Cavaliers lose to Maryland.''

''Are they losing?''

''Down twelve. They can't hit a jump shot.''

When he heard that Virginia was getting beat, he had an incredible urge to throw something. He knew it was silly that a ball game could make him so crazy. It was ludicrous, really. So he suppressed the thought. Then he decided that maybe he'd kick the desk into little pieces. He was proud of himself when he maturely said good-bye to Sims without having broken anything.

He called Andrea Kyler after that but there was no answer in her apartment and the trooper who answered at the governor's office said everyone had gone home. So he dialed Meredith Gordy's direct line at the Governor's Mansion. She answered it right away.

''Bobby?''

''How'd you know it was me?''

''You and Andrea are the only ones who have this number and Andrea's sitting right here. Where the hell are you?''

He told her and gave her the details of his meetings with Dumont and Tourretta. It was strange for him to be telling her more than he was telling his editors, but what the hell—this had already been a more-than-strange three days.

''Why don't you come here when you get to Annapolis?'' Gordy said. ''Andrea and I will both wait for you.''

''Do you think,'' he said softly, ''that Andrea is above suspicion right now?''

There was a long pause on the other end of the line. ''I hope so,'' Gordy said finally. ''That's one reason I want to talk to you in person.''

''I'll be there in three hours if I don't hit any game traffic.''

The pressroom was now filled. It was halftime. He saw Doug Doughty, who covered Maryland for the *Herald*, and mouthed, ''Score?''

Doughty held up five fingers and pointed his thumb down. Virginia was down five. That was better than twelve.

Gordy was still talking. ''Be careful, will you? It strikes me that it's possible that whoever killed Dumont might very well know that you saw him last night.''

''That thought did occur to me. I'll see you in a few hours.''

"I'll leave word at the police desk downstairs that you're expected."

"Good idea," Kelleher said, wondering if perhaps his pal Stern might have been transferred over to the mansion.

He had one more phone call to make, to Dana Russo to see if she'd gotten anywhere with USAir.

"You find anything?"

"First of all, Jamelle Tourretta wasn't on any USAir flight out of New York this morning. I had my guy check the manifests to see if she might have connected for some reason through Baltimore or Washington. Nothing."

"Interesting. Okay, anything else?"

"Uh-huh. She *did* fly out of Richmond this afternoon."

"Well, that figures. No reason for her to lie about that, I guess."

"But she didn't fly back to New York."

"No? Where'd she go?"

"Baltimore."

Kelleher sat up straight in his chair. If you wanted to get to Annapolis by plane, you would fly to Baltimore. "Are you *sure* she didn't connect there to New York or someplace else?"

"Positive. She had no reservation but she bought a ticket this afternoon at two fifty-four P.M. for a flight that left Richmond at three-eighteen. According to my friend, the flight landed in Baltimore at four-thirty."

"Theoretically, though, she could have connected to go somewhere else on another airline and your friend wouldn't know about it, right?"

"That's true. But there aren't a hell of a lot of places you can fly to out of Baltimore without going on USAir."

"Dana, I owe you one, a *big* one."

"Just do me one favor."

"What's that?"

"Quit using the word *genuine* in your copy all the time. I swear, you haven't written a story the entire legislative session that hasn't had the word *genuine* in it at least once."

"Really?"

"You just got through writing for tomorrow, right? Pull your story up on the screen. I'll bet you a dollar you've got *genuine* in there somewhere."

He turned his computer back on, called the story up, and began scrolling. The fifth paragraph began with, "Dumont's death leaves the police and the FBI with a genuine dilemma."

He groaned. "I owe you a dollar *and* lunch."

He hung up, still frowning at his computer screen, when a sudden roar reminded him where he was. The game had to be almost over. On his way out, he stopped just to quickly glance at the court. Time was out—for TV, no doubt—and Kelleher could see on the scoreboard overhead that Maryland had extended the lead to nine with 7:37 left.

"Damn!" he said, shaking his head. His team should not be losing at home to Maryland. He walked dejectedly out the back door that led to the press parking lot. Maybe by next weekend this would all be over and he could drive down for the Duke game. Then again, maybe not.

The temperature had dropped at least twenty degrees since he'd arrived at U-Hall in midafternoon. The air had that presnow feel that Kelleher hated. He hoped it would hold off at least until he reached Annapolis.

He got in the car, turned up the heat, and switched on the broadcast of the game. Virginia had cut the lead to five, with four minutes left. He held out little hope, though. He turned left at the traffic light and headed back up Route 29. It was almost six o'clock. He would stop at the McDonald's in Warrenton again and be in Annapolis by nine.

For the next forty-five minutes, Kelleher completely forgot about Barney Paulsen and Jimmy Dumont and Meredith Gordy and Jamelle Tourretta and The Big Hit. All his attention was focused on the radio as Virginia rallied. First, Corey Alexander, the brilliant guard, hit a three-point shot with three seconds left to send the game into overtime. Then, after Maryland had built a five-point lead in overtime, the Cavaliers rallied again. This time, they scored four points in the last twenty seconds to tie.

On the last play of the overtime, Maryland's Johnny Rhodes went to the basket and, according to the Virginia broadcasters, "looked like he might have gotten hit." Kelleher laughed. If the Virginia guys said Rhodes *might* have been hit, he must have been hammered. "And Gary Williams is going crazy over there," said Tom Maxwell, the play-by-play man. That, Kelleher knew, was no exaggeration. Gary Williams, the Maryland coach, was almost always going crazy. This time, it sounded like he had a case.

They went into the second overtime. Again, Maryland led all the way. Kelleher was beginning to think the game was destined never to end. He had reached the loneliest stretch of highway on the trip, about thirty-five miles north of Charlottesville. With eleven seconds left and the score tied, Rhodes hit a jumper to put Maryland up 105–103. Virginia was out of time-outs so the ball was rushed up court.

"Five seconds," Maxwell said. "Alexander left side, Rhodes all over him. Drives into the corner. Double-teamed! No place to go!" Kelleher was dying. They weren't even going to get off a shot, for crying out loud.

"From the corner, three pointer at the buzzer!" There was a split second of silence and then Kelleher heard a roar so loud it practically jumped right out of the radio. "*Good*! It's *good*! Corey Alexander at the buzzer! The Cavaliers win it one-oh-six to one-oh-five! *What a finish!*" Maxwell was so hoarse Kelleher could barely understand him.

"*Yes!*" he shouted at the radio, shaking a fist, as happy as he could remember feeling for a long time. McGuire was always bugging him about living vicariously through Virginia basketball, but what the hell. You had to take pleasure wherever you could find it. His only regret was that he hadn't been there to see the end of the game.

Kelleher had been so wrapped up in the game that he hadn't noticed the car tucked in behind him. Now he looked up and saw the headlights. He was going sixty-five—ten over the limit but fairly safe. During the daytime, Kelleher didn't mind if someone tucked in behind him. But at night, the lights were distracting. He kept going for a couple more miles, then decided to slow a little bit and let the other car pass him. He tapped the brake lightly to take the cruise control off and let the car slow to sixty. Instead of pulling out to pass, the car behind him also slowed.

"Sonofabitch," Kelleher muttered. He slowed even further, to fifty-five. This time, the trailing car pulled into the left lane. But instead of racing past, the car slowed as it pulled even with Kelleher. "What the fuck is this guy's problem?" Kelleher said aloud, glancing left to see if it was a joke, perhaps, someone he knew driving. It was too dark to see anything, though, other than the shapes of two people in the car.

Kelleher checked his speedometer. Fifty-two. He accelerated again; the other car matched him. It had to be a couple of kids playing a game. He wondered what to do. He didn't want to pull over on this lonely stretch of road. He didn't want to get into a drag race either. He was about to roll down his window to see if he could ask his shadows just what the hell they wanted, when he saw the car suddenly swerve toward him.

"*Jesus!*" he yelled as the car smacked into the front end of his car. "What the fuck's the matter with you?!" he screamed.

Wham! the two cars collided again. It took all of Kelleher's strength not to lose control of the wheel. This was no longer funny. He slammed his foot on the brake and pulled over onto the shoulder. His car limped to a stop as the shadow car disappeared around a curve.

Kelleher breathed a deep sigh of relief. He turned off the engine, sat back in the seat, and pulled off his seat belt. He realized he was pouring sweat. Fear of the unknown again. "Crazy fuckers," he muttered. He took three or four breaths to regain his composure, then got out of the car to see how bad the damage was. In keeping with his luck, it was just starting to snow. He wished he'd gotten a glimpse of the license plate.

The office wasn't going to be pleased with this at all. He could hear Elsie Grisco, the newsroom administrator, now: "What do you *mean* some crazy guy pulled up next to you and started banging your car with his? Couldn't you have avoided him?"

The front end and the left side were banged up badly. He had lost a headlight but still had one left to get home on. He crouched by the left front tire to make sure none of the twisted metal would scrape against it once he got going again.

That was when he heard the car coming. That was also when he saw his life pass before his eyes. The car was coming from the north but it was on *his* side of the highway. As it came around the curve, it was bearing straight down on him. Kelleher screamed, leaped from his crouch, and threw himself across the hood of his car just as the oncoming car smashed into it. The collision sent Kelleher flying off the hood, onto the ground. He landed hard and felt a searing pain in his right arm.

There was no time to worry about that now. Kelleher had finally figured out that these weren't joyriding kids. Someone was trying to kill him. Without thinking about his arm or looking back to see what had happened after the collision, Kelleher scrambled to his feet and sprinted into the woods by the side of the road, running as fast as he'd ever run.

The woods weren't very thick so he was able to move unimpeded. He sprinted all out for what felt like an hour but was probably a minute, not looking back. Finally, he took a chance and glanced over his shoulder. He saw no one. He took a bigger chance and stopped, panting, bent over. He still couldn't see anyone in the darkness but he *could* hear footsteps— coming toward him.

He'd run about four hundred yards and was shaking from cold, fear, and exhaustion. Kelleher ran three miles almost every day but he hadn't run this hard since college. He wondered what kind of shape his pursuers were in. As he was wondering, he heard a gunshot. There was no more time to think. He turned and took off again.

Breathing hard, holding his side, wondering how much farther he could go without collapsing, he came to a clearing surrounded by several clumps of thick bushes. He decided to take a chance—albeit a desperate one—and dove into the greenery. Again he felt the searing pain in his right arm. It hurt so much he almost cried out. Instead, he clamped his hand over his mouth—an act that probably saved his life.

Lying flat on his stomach, he heard his pursuers arrive in the clearing. They stopped, looked around. One of them carried a flashlight. He held it up, flashing it in a circle. Kelleher again put his hand over his mouth, afraid they would hear his breathing. They were standing no more than ten feet away from him. He wondered if they could hear his heart pounding. To him it sounded about as subtle as a bass drum.

"Sooner or later there'll be a ridge. That'll turn him back toward us," one of them said.

"Let's split up," the other said. "You go left, I'll go right." The second person was a woman. Could it be Tourretta? No. He would recognize that voice.

The two of them headed off. Lying there, Kelleher had an idea. He was between the two thugs and the road. If he could get back there, maybe, just maybe, in their haste to pursue him, they had left the keys in their car. If so, he could take off in it, assuming it wasn't badly damaged. His car was clearly out of commission after the collision.

As he was deciding what to do, Kelleher heard one of them coming back. Damn! he thought. Whichever one it was had dropped to his/her hands and knees and was examining the ground. Kelleher understood. He was checking for footprints. If whoever it was knew what he was doing, his prints would lead right to this bush. Sure enough, the thug began moving in his direction. It wasn't going to be long now. Behind Kelleher, the bushes were much too thick to try to run through. Had he trapped himself?

Maybe. The thug was almost on top of him. Kelleher made a decision: one-on-one he might have a chance, particularly if he had the element of surprise on his side. He picked up a stick that was lying next to him. Carefully, he put his right hand down to give himself support—almost crying out in pain as he did so—and tossed the stick over the thug's head, bouncing it off a tree.

Hearing the sound, the thug whirled around. That was the opening Kelleher needed. He leaped to his feet and dove at the thug, who turned back a split second too late. They rolled in the dirt, Kelleher on top, the thug trying to get a hand on the gun Kelleher could feel pressed against his waist. With his free, good hand, Kelleher grabbed for the pistol. The thug was considerably stronger than he was; Kelleher was rapidly losing the leverage advantage he had gained with his initial attack.

Just before the thug could push him away, Kelleher got hold of the gun, swung it as hard as he could and connected solidly with skull. He heard a moan and felt his opponent go slack. He looked down and saw a pool of blood oozing onto the ground. The thought that he might have killed somebody, even somebody who'd been trying to kill him, made Kelleher sick to his stomach. He kneeled down to take a look. As he rolled the thug over, he gasped: It was Wendy Paul, Tourretta's bodyguard.

"Oh my God," he said. The woman's blood was now on his hands— literally and figuratively.

"Wendy! You okay? Where are you?"

It was the bodyguard's partner, who no doubt had heard the scuffling. Kelleher knew he couldn't hang around to find out how badly he'd hurt her. He got up, the gun still in his hand, and sprinted back in the direction of the highway. He was having trouble breathing by now and his arm was throbbing with pain. He heard a shot, then another, and he realized the second thug was close behind him. He wondered if he should turn and shoot back, but he wasn't even sure if he knew how to use the gun.

He kept running. When he got back to the highway, the two cars were still tangled with each other. He jumped into the thugs' car, praying. His prayer was answered—the key was in the ignition. Would it start? He turned the key and heard the engine scream to life. He put the car in reverse and backed it away from his own car. Metal screeched against metal as he did. He was facing the wrong way on the highway, so he backed the car onto the shoulder to turn it around.

As he did, Paul's companion burst from the woods, heading in his direction, gun pointed at the windshield. Kelleher switched into drive and gunned the car forward. The bullet missed the hood by inches. He sped down the highway—in the wrong direction—for a few hundred yards, hoping to survive until he was out of shooting range.

When the car turned around, he saw his pursuer behind the *Herald* car, using it as a shield, hoping Kelleher would drive by where he could get a clear shot at him. Instead, Kelleher drove straight up the shoulder, lights out, his head below the steering wheel, as if he intended to ram his own car. He heard another shot and turned the wheel hard at the last instant to avoid the crash. It worked. The thug had already made a dive for cover.

Kelleher hit the brake hard so he wouldn't hit the median, then slammed his foot on the accelerator. He could see the SOB in his rearview mirror, running back onto the highway—but it was too late to get off one last shot.

It was the happiest moment of Kelleher's life. From the second he had seen the car hurtling at him until just now, he had been fairly convinced he was going to die. Realizing he'd escaped, he began crying and laughing hysterically all at once.

Had this really happened? He looked down at the speedometer and realized he was going ninety. There wasn't another car anywhere in sight. "Get a grip, Bobby," he said aloud, slowing the car to a more reasonable speed. He had never before come so close to dying. He also knew it was distinctly possible he'd just killed another human being.

He noticed that the car had a phone. Would it work? Was he close enough, he wondered, to call the office? Or should he try to call Gordy? Or Sims? Or the police?

He decided on Sims. Sims could get his police buddies working ASAP. He picked up the phone—it worked—and dialed Sims's number. His wife, Mary Jane, answered.

"He just left a few minutes ago," she told him. "Someone called and he said he had to go into the office for a little while."

"You think he's there yet?"

"I doubt it. He couldn't have left more than ten minutes ago."

He hung up and dialed Gordy. She answered on the first ring. "Bobby, you aren't in Annapolis yet, are you?"

"Not exactly, Meredith. I'm still in Virginia. Listen, is Andrea around?"

"She's downstairs."

"Good. Jamelle Tourretta's bodyguard and some thug just tried to kill me."

"*What!* How? Where?"

"I'll give you the details when I get there. In the meantime, ask Bearnarth to tell the Virginia state police to check Route 29, maybe forty miles north of Charlottesville. They'll find my car, a *Herald* car, pretty banged up by the side of the road. They also might find the bodyguard if they check the woods. Unless her partner went back for her, she'll be there."

Gordy was all business. "Anything else?"

"Not for now. I should be in Annapolis in about ninety minutes unless my office tells me to come in there. I have to call them now."

"I'll call Bearnarth. I'll see you soon."

He was dialing the office when he noticed a walkie-talkie that was next to the phone. Then he saw something on the steering panel that said "siren."

"No," he thought. "It can't be." But it was. He pulled open the glove compartment and found the registration. Forgetting about the office, he dialed Gordy back.

"I was wondering why this car phone was so strong," he told her. "Now I know."

"Why?"

"Because the car belongs to the Maryland state police. I'm driving an unmarked police car."

"Jesus. This is getting spookier by the minute. You have the registration?"

He read her the information. She promised to pass it on to Bearnarth immediately. Kelleher wondered if Gordy understood the implication: if there were state police involved in this conspiracy, protecting her would be that much more difficult.

He was already passing into Fairfax County by the time he called the office. A copy aide answered Jane Kryton's phone and he wondered if she had gone home.

"She's right here," the aide said. "But she's real busy. Who's calling?"

"Bobby Kelleher."

"*Kelleher!*" He heard the phone drop and then the aide screaming, "It's him, it's Kelleher!" It was nice to be appreciated.

Three voices seemed to come on the phone at once, all of them screaming. "Where are you? Are you all right? What the hell happened?!"

Finally, it hit him. The state police had found the *Herald* car at the scene, called the newspaper, and reported its condition—and the absence of a driver. It probably hadn't taken long for the office to figure out it was his car. When the babbling stopped, he filled them in on what had happened, including his escape. Tom Anthony was on the line, along with Kryton and McGuire.

"Bobby, I want you to get back in here as soon as you can," Anthony said. "I want a doctor to look at you and I don't want you out there running around if someone's trying to kill you."

"I appreciate that, Tom, but we're too damn close to getting this story.

I'm going to go to Annapolis and see Gordy. I'll be safe in the State House. I promise I'll get a doctor once I'm up there.''

''I want you to write all this for Tuesday. You're part of the story now. A big part.''

He knew that was true and it didn't make him happy. The mention of a doctor reminded him about his arm, which was useless, except for holding the wheel steady while he punched the telephone buttons. To distract himself from the pain, he reviewed exactly what he knew about the case to decide what to do next.

Jimmy Dumont and Jamelle Tourretta were both involved in this, there didn't seem to be any doubt about that. The question was, how could two people who were so radically different politically end up involved in the same conspiracy? That was the real stumper in this whole equation. And then it hit Kelleher, a theory so simple it almost had to be true.

One of the things McGuire had found in doing her background research on Dumont was that he had never really held a job. He kept attaching himself to different radical right-wing causes but had never worked. That meant the guy couldn't have a lot of money. And yet, Kelleher had found him in a three-hundred-dollar-a-night room at The Boar's Head Inn.

Someone had to be bankrolling him. That someone, Kelleher thought, was Jamelle Tourretta and FFF. Tourretta had used Dumont brilliantly. She—or someone in her group—had hired him as one of her three shooters. Kelleher remembered from college that Dumont always bragged about what an expert marksman he was. Tourretta told Dumont the plan was to kill Paulsen *and* Gordy. When only Paulsen ended up dead, they told him a mistake had been made, that one of his fellow shooters had somehow missed. They promised him that they'd go back and get Gordy, and that had kept him in line. He must have realized he'd been had—that's why they killed him.

There was no doubt now that it had been Tourretta who'd warned Dumont that Kelleher was on his way to Charlottesville. There was also no doubt in his mind that it was Tourretta, or perhaps Wendy Paul, who'd shown up after he'd left Dumont and killed him. Sims was probably right that the other two shooters were dead, too. That left no one alive to point a finger at Tourretta.

Except for Kelleher, who'd come too close to Dumont for comfort. Tourretta had figured if she got rid of Kelleher, that would be the end of the story. Which meant she had to try again.

The only disturbing part of this scenario was Andrea. If Tourretta was indeed the mastermind of the Paulsen shooting, did that mean Andrea was one of the conspirators? Very possibly. That thought depressed him.

One part of his theory didn't fit: If Jamelle Tourretta had instructed Wendy Paul to follow him out of Charlottesville and kill him, why didn't she then fly home to New York? Why Baltimore—which probably meant Annapolis? Was she planning a meeting with Andrea? Or was this another step in her master plan: make Gordy governor, pin the rap on the LOL, and then get Gordy back into the FFF fold. Kelleher wished McGuire was with him in the car because she was good at things like this. They would have to sit down at length the next day and decide what to do and—just as important—what to write. Did they go to the police or write the story and let the police take it from there?

The saddest part of the story, Kelleher thought as he wheeled the car onto Route 50 heading north to Annapolis, was what it would do to the women's movement. Once it came out that Tourretta and FFF had turned a movement that prided itself on nonviolence into one with blood all over its hands, the Neanderthals would set the ERA and all the women's-legislation bills way back. The right-wingers would use this as an excuse to—at best—put women's issues on the back burner or—at worst—bury them altogether.

He shook his head in disgust. For someone so brilliant, Jamelle Tourretta was awfully stupid. The whole thing depressed him, wiping out the pleasure he had felt just a few moments earlier when the whole case had come clear in his mind. The Big Hit was right there for him, he knew that, and yet he couldn't help but feel sad about it.

Three miles south of Rowe Boulevard traffic came to a halt. Kelleher groaned. The last thing he needed right now was to sit in traffic with his mind racing and his arm throbbing. That's what he did, though. There was some kind of accident, had to have been. Route 50 had undergone a lot of construction in recent years but on a Sunday night this mess wasn't being caused by construction.

It took him about thirty minutes to get to the spot where he could see all the police cars. There were a few ambulances and fire trucks on the scene, too. Traffic was being pushed into one narrow lane on the left. As Kelleher squeezed by, he rolled down his window to ask the Annapolis cop who was directing traffic what happened.

"Looks like some kind of hit-and-run," the cop said. "Guy went over the embankment but they say it looked like he got sideswiped before he lost control.''

Kelleher could certainly relate to that. He wondered if he shouldn't pull over and play reporter, try to get some more details. On another night he would have, but not tonight. He gunned the car to sixty as soon as he was past the accident and, a minute later, pulled onto Rowe Boulevard. He could feel himself relax just a little as the State House came into view.

He drove the car around State Circle and parked in the spot marked ''reserved for Senate President.'' He would turn the car over to the state police and they could take it from there.

He walked across the street to the gate outside the governor's mansion and buzzed.

''Can I help you?'' a voice asked, coming, Kelleher knew, from the trooper's desk just inside the door.

''Bobby Kelleher,'' he said. ''Governor Gordy's expecting me.'' Saying ''Governor Gordy'' still sounded strange.

''Just a minute, sir.''

Kelleher cooled his heels for a moment, annoyed. Meredith had said she would alert the cops that he was coming. It was too damn cold to stand out there.

The buzzer sounded. Kelleher pushed the gate open and walked through the small yard area where the cars used to transport the governor and top staff parked. The door to the mansion was unlocked. Kelleher walked into the small hallway and presented himself to the trooper at the desk. As soon as he did, he saw the trooper's eyes go wide.

It occurred to him then, for the first time since his escape, what he must look like. In addition to his arm hanging limp, he was covered with dirt and mud and blood. He hadn't noticed until he had gotten out of the car, but he had twisted his ankle at some point and was limping badly.

''You should have seen the other guy,'' Kelleher said, delivering a line he had always wanted to deliver.

''The governor will be right down,'' the cop said.

''The governor is here.''

Kelleher turned around to find Gordy standing in the doorway that led to the main part of the mansion. Kyler and Bearnarth were right behind her.

''My God, Bobby, you look *awful*.''

''Most of it's just dirt,'' he said. He held up his limp right arm. ''But I think I need a doctor to take a look at this.''

Gordy nodded and Bearnarth disappeared in search of a doctor. "In the meantime, you could use a shower and some clean clothes to put on," she said.

"And some food," Kelleher added, remembering that he hadn't eaten anything since leaving Ann's house in the morning.

He followed Gordy up the stairs. Kelleher had never been above the first floor of the mansion. The basement level was the working level. That was where the staff and security were. The first floor was the public level. When the governor hosted receptions or when tours came through, it was the first floor they got to see. The second floor was the living quarters, strictly off-limits. In fact, only a select few of the legislators had ever seen it.

Kelleher wasn't in a mood to feel privileged, though. Having arrived at his destination, he could now feel the exhaustion and pain kicking in. He also wasn't thrilled that Kyler had yet to say a word since he'd come in.

Gordy led him into what was obviously a guest bedroom and pointed to the bathroom. "I'll call downstairs for food. Anything you want in particular?"

"Steak," Kelleher said. "I'm entitled to one, I think."

"I'll bring the doctor in as soon as he gets here."

"Then we have to talk."

"I know."

Kelleher quickly stripped off his clothes as soon as the door closed and gratefully stepped into the shower's soothing hot water. His body was covered with cuts and bruises.

Thinking back to the Virginia woods made Kelleher shudder. Death had always been something of an abstraction to him, something he knew he would face but, he presumed, not for a long, long time. Now, in less than twenty-four hours, he had twice found himself very close to it. Neither experience had been pleasant, to put it mildly. The second time had been far more terrifying than the first. And yet, Kelleher knew that it wasn't over. Unlike a frightening plane ride, a safe landing didn't mean you could go off and tell your friends how scared you had been. In this case, the plane hadn't landed yet—and there was no knowing when it would. Or *if* it would.

Once he told Gordy what had happened, the police might conceivably arrest Tourretta although the evidence against her was still circumstantial. He wondered if her arrest would make him safe. Might her underlings still try to get him? How widespread, within FFF, was the conspiracy?

That brought him back to Andrea. He had to know if she was involved.

And if so, *how* involved. Did she know that Tourretta was sending someone to kill him? That would be heartbreaking. But he had to deal with the fact that it might very well be true.

The hot water helped his arm. Relieved, he suspected now that it wasn't broken. Walking into the bedroom, he found a bathrobe lying on the bed. He put it on and sat down in front of the fireplace. Just as he did, there was a knock on the door. Gordy came in, followed by the doctor.

"Bobby, this is Dr. Jameson," Gordy said.

Kelleher didn't ask where Jameson had come from, he was just glad to see him. Jameson took a look at the arm, asking him where it hurt and how much movement he had. "Well," he said, "I'm going to have to see an X ray, but I don't think there's a break. I'd say you tore some ligaments in your wrist, though."

"That would require a cast?"

"Soft cast," the doctor said. "You should be able to write in about a week or so."

"I'm left-handed."

"Less than a week then."

Kelleher actually laughed at the one-liner, surprised he was able to do so. Jameson gave him some pills for the pain and told him he should report to the hospital for an X ray in the morning.

"I'll leave word, so they'll be expecting you," he said. "You shouldn't be there very long, assuming the X ray just shows the ligaments. If I'm wrong and there's a break, then we'll have to see if you need any surgery. But I don't think it's likely."

He left almost as the food was arriving. Bearnarth was right behind the elderly man who was carrying the tray. "Kelleher, Maureen wants you to call her when you get a chance," Bearnarth said. "She's still in the office."

"Soon as I eat," Kelleher said, eying the steak, which was approximately the size of a small cow. He was sitting down at the table where the food had been placed when another trooper appeared in the doorway, tugging on Bearnarth's arm. The two of them disappeared. Gordy had been watching the doctor as he examined Kelleher. Kyler was nowhere in sight.

"Where's Andrea?" he asked as he began to attack the food.

"She has some things to finish for tomorrow morning. I told her I wanted to talk to you alone before you talked to her."

"She understand why?"

"I think she does. After I told her what happened to you, she told me that she still didn't believe Tourretta was involved in Barney's murder. When I then asked her why Tourretta would send someone to try to kill you, she just said, 'I have absolutely no idea.' The fact that she *doesn't* have an answer makes me more inclined to believe she's telling the truth."

"I think you may be right. I hope so, anyway. But I'm convinced this is a Tourretta/FFF deal all the way."

"Really? Even with Dumont . . ."

She didn't finish the sentence because Bearnarth had come back into the room and was standing between them. His face was ashen. "Governor, I'm sorry to interrupt."

"What is it, Larry, what's wrong?"

He held a piece of paper that appeared to be something off the police wire. Bearnarth looked to Kelleher as if he was going to cry.

"Governor, I don't really know how to say this."

"Come on, Larry, what is it?" Gordy said, standing up to face him.

Bearnarth took a deep breath. "Governor, Alan Sims has been killed. In a car accident."

Kelleher felt nauseated and faint all at once. He saw Gordy stumble and thought she was going to fall. Bearnarth grabbed her and helped her back to the chair she'd been sitting in. Kelleher, too weak to stand, heard himself say, "Larry, you're certain? No doubt at all?"

"I went and checked it myself before I came in here. The ID is positive. He was dead on the scene. Apparently his car went off an embankment just outside of town. The only question is why the hell he was coming up here at this hour on Sunday night."

This time, Kelleher did get sick. He lurched out of his chair onto his hands and knees and threw up. He still didn't have much food in him so he ended up heaving like a drunk with the d.t.'s. The accident he had passed on Route 50 had been Sims. The cop said the car had been run off the road, sideswiped by a hit-and-run. That was the *exact* same MO Wendy Paul had used on him in Virginia.

He started trying to talk too soon and began heaving again. The cop who had brought Bearnarth the information was kneeling next to him, trying to give him water. Bearnarth was doing the same with Gordy. He looked up and saw Andrea Kyler in the doorway. She was crying. Were the tears real? he wondered.

His breath was coming back. Even so, Kelleher couldn't face the idea that Alan Sims was dead. He forced himself to analyze the situation, so as not to deal with his emotions.

"Meredith, listen," he said, still gasping for breath, sitting on the floor. Gordy's eyes were glazed but she looked right at him when he spoke. "Listen," he repeated. "This wasn't an accident. They killed him. I talked to Mary Jane a little while ago. Someone called Alan to come up here. It had to be a trap. Then someone ran him off the road, the same way they tried with me. Only with Alan, it worked."

Gordy looked at Bearnarth. "That what happened?"

Bearnarth nodded. "It was hit-and-run," he confirmed. "The car was sideswiped, went over that embankment back toward the Route 450 exit."

"Those murderous fuckers," Gordy said. It was the first time Kelleher had ever heard her swear. "I want Jamelle Tourretta arrested and held on suspicion of murder. And if she objects, bring her to *me.*" She whirled on Andrea. "If you know anything about all this, you better tell us right now! I'm through being patient. This has already gone much, much too far."

"Meredith, I swear to you . . ."

"Don't swear anything to me. Did *you* call Alan Sims? Did you set him up? It had to be someone he knew."

Kyler was shaking her head vehemently. "No, no, Meredith. I'm telling you I don't know anything about any of this and I honestly don't believe Jamelle does either. I can't swear to Jamelle's innocence but I can swear to mine."

Kelleher jumped in. "If Jamelle's not involved, Andrea, what was her bodyguard doing out there in Virginia trying to kill me?"

"Bobby, I don't know. Maybe she was acting on her own. That's why I won't *swear* she's not involved. Are you *sure* it was Wendy Paul?"

"Absolutely positive."

"It makes no sense, I admit that. But does it make sense that Jamelle Tourretta would be involved with this Dumont guy and the Lovers of Life? I mean, my God, Bobby, where's the sense in *that*?" She was crying now, though trying not to. She brushed her cheeks with the back of her hand.

"There *is* no sense in it," Kelleher said. "Which I think was the plan all along." He proceeded to walk Gordy, Kyler, and Bearnarth through his theory: Tourretta and FFF used Dumont as their decoy, then eliminated him when it looked as if he might fall into the wrong hands—Kelleher's or the police.

"I want Tourretta off the streets now, wherever she is," Gordy said grimly.

"She flew into Baltimore this afternoon," Kelleher told her, watching Kyler closely as he spoke. Her face registered nothing when he delivered this information. "I wouldn't be shocked if she's in Annapolis somewhere."

Gordy shot a look at Kyler. "You know anything about that, Andrea?"

"I really don't, Meredith," Kyler said. "There's no reason for you to believe me, but I really, really don't."

Gordy stood up. "Larry, I want Tourretta found and arrested. In the meantime, has Mary Jane Sims been told about what happened yet?"

Bearnarth shook his head. "I was going to go and do it myself," he said.

Gordy shook her head. "I'll do it."

"I'll go with you," Kelleher said.

"I don't think you should, Bobby." Gordy's voice was quiet but she had again assumed command. "For one thing, I suspect you're going to have a story to write. For another, I think you're safest if you stay here tonight."

"What about you?"

"If your theory's right, I'm not in any danger, am I?"

He had to concede that. She was also right that he would need to write a story about Sims's death. It was almost ten-thirty. He could still make second edition. That thought made him feel guilty. A good friend of his was dead and he was thinking of a deadline.

"How much did Alan know about all this?" Gordy asked.

"He knew everything I knew except for the attack in Virginia."

"That would explain it, wouldn't it? They figured they'd get rid of both of you at the same time."

"But how did they *know* that Alan knew?" Kelleher asked.

Gordy had an answer for that one. "You said the car that attacked you was a state-police car. My bet is that one of the state troopers who Alan thought was a pal of his is part of the conspiracy."

Horribly enough, that made sense. Kelleher looked at Bearnarth. "Have you got anything on that car yet?"

"Yeah, we do." Bearnarth grimaced. "It was assigned to one of the women who works security at the Court of Appeals."

Kelleher and Gordy looked at each other. "A woman?" they both said.

Bearnarth nodded. "The other person who attacked you, are you sure it was a man?"

"I sure thought so," Kelleher said. "But I couldn't swear to it. Paul's so big, I suppose I could've mistaken her for a man in the dark."

"She has a very husky voice," Kyler put in. "If you heard her talk, you'd swear she's a man."

Gordy headed for the door. "We'll talk more when I get back," she said.

They left him alone. Kelleher picked up the phone and dialed McGuire's number. There was no answer so the phone automatically switched over to the desk. Kelleher asked the copy aide if Maureen was around anywhere.

"Right here," he said.

"Bobby." McGuire came on, sounding breathless. "You heard about Sims?"

"Yeah. It's on the wire?"

"About twenty minutes ago. You think it's connected to what happened to you? It has to be, doesn't it?"

"No doubt. They ran him off the goddamn road." He took a deep breath. "I wonder who coaxed him out of the house. Maybe they can trace the call or something."

"What do you mean?"

He told her about his call to Mary Jane Sims. "Can you write all this?" she asked. "Jane says they can push the deadline to eleven-thirty."

"Only problem is, I don't have my computer. It's in the car I left by the side of the road."

"Can you make it to the office?" she said. "Or are you too sick?"

"I can get there," he said. "But I can dictate the thing just as fast. It's a very straight story."

"How much do you pin on Tourretta?"

"Right now, all I can say is that there's no doubt Sims was murdered and that it's almost for sure connected to the Paulsen murder. But I can't say who did it. Hey, is there any word on whether the Virginia cops found Wendy Paul?"

"Nothing."

"If something comes up, let me know."

"Absolutely. Do you want to meet for breakfast in the morning before the memorial service?"

"I have to see the doctor first thing. Let's just meet at the State House. I'm exhausted."

McGuire switched him into dictation and he concocted the story, wishing he could lay out his theory on Tourretta's guilt. That would have to wait another day, though. When he was finished, he had them switch him back to Kryton.

"I'm reading it right now," she said. "This is so sad. Where does all of this end?"

"That's the million-dollar question," he said and hung up because he thought he might start to cry.

He drifted off to sleep, dreaming that Jamelle Tourretta was chasing him through the woods. The dream ended when she caught him. What happened after that Kelleher didn't know. As soon as she got her arms around him, he woke up in a cold sweat.

CHAPTER 11

STAYING ALIVE

Kelleher was still sleeping fitfully when he felt a hand on his shoulder. He snapped awake with a start and found Andrea Kyler standing over him.

"What the hell?" he mumbled. "What time is it?"

"Just after six," she said. "I'm sorry. But you were sound asleep when I came in last night and I have to talk to you."

He sat up, rubbing his eyes. The painkiller the doctor had given him had worn off and his wrist was throbbing again.

"What do we need to talk about?" he said, stifling a yawn.

"Us."

He laughed cynically. "Don't you think your timing's a little bit off?"

She shook her head. "No, that's exactly my point. I couldn't sleep last night knowing you might think I had anything to do with what happened to you and Alan."

Alan. The memories of the previous night came swimming back to him. Alan Sims really was dead. He hadn't dreamed that. The thought that he would never see him again made him feel profoundly sad all over again.

She took his head and turned it so that he was looking her right in the eye. "Listen to me, Bobby. I *am* close to Jamelle Tourretta. I'm not going to try to tell you that isn't true. But *if* she's involved in all this and if your theory's right, I'm not part of it. I give you my word."

His instinct, looking into her eyes, was to believe her. But was he reacting logically or emotionally? He knew what McGuire would say. That he was getting softheaded.

"I really don't know what to believe right now, Andrea," he told her. "All I know for sure is that someone I liked and respected is dead and whoever killed him is trying to kill me too. Until I resolve that, I can't think about you and me or anything along those lines."

She stood up. "I understand," she said. "But try not to think the worst of me. When this is over, I think we have . . ." She paused, looking for a word.

"Potential?" he said softly.

She smiled. "That's the word." Then she spun and walked out.

Kelleher couldn't sleep after that encounter. He got up and showered and came back to find clean clothes—where they came from, he had no idea—stretched across one of the chairs. He got dressed and walked downstairs. Gordy was sitting at the table in the mansion's huge kitchen, drinking coffee.

"Do you want breakfast?" she asked.

"Just coffee," he said, sitting down. "How did it go with Mary Jane?"

She shook her head. "Not good. We had to get a doctor to come in and sedate her. She was hysterical."

"Understandable. I still can't really believe it."

She took a long sip of coffee. "Neither can I. I sat up all night wondering if I want to be involved in all of this anymore."

Kelleher leaned forward. "Meredith, if you get out, it's one more good person gone from a business that needs good people."

"Bobby, if FFF killed Barney to make me governor, how can I possibly continue? I'd be giving them what they want."

Kelleher looked affectionately at Gordy. She really was that rarest of the rare: a politician to admire. "Meredith, if Tourretta really did this, there won't be any FFF to speak of when things are over. You owe it to yourself, to the people of this state, hell, to Barney Paulsen, to stay on and be governor."

Gordy laughed. She stood up to pour more coffee just as Bearnarth walked in. "You know what you sound like Bobby? A politician."

Kelleher groaned. "Please, anything but that."

"Don't worry," Gordy smiled and patted his hand. "You'll snap out of it." She looked at Bearnarth. "Got something?"

"Yeah, I do," Bearnarth said. "The Virginia cops found Wendy Paul's body. They had trouble in the dark but as soon as they got some light, they found it.''

"Body?" Kelleher said. He had to put the coffee down; his hands had started to shake.

"She's dead," Bearnarth said. "But the good news for you is you may not have killed her."

"How can that . . . I creamed her with her gun. What else could've killed her?''

"How 'bout a bullet through her head.''

"Jesus!"

"Her partner, right?" Gordy asked.

"Probably," Bearnarth said. "We figure he decided trying to get her out of there was too tough. Rather than take a chance that she might come to at some point and be convinced to talk, he finished her. For what it's worth, Kelleher, she was probably alive when you left her.''

Kelleher was still shaking. He looked at Gordy. "These people obviously don't like to play around," he said. "They kill each other, too.''

"Which is why I'm putting a tail on you," Bearnarth told him. "They're gonna try for you again.''

Kelleher shook his head. "Look, Larry, I appreciate that and I'm not trying to be brave or anything here. But I'm going to be in very public places all day today. A tail would be obvious. Other reporters would notice; they're too smart not to. I'd like to avoid that for at least twenty-four more hours. By Tuesday, I'm sure I'll have to write what happened to me, which means I'll have to start giving interviews. That's it as far as work's concerned. So give me at least one more day to be a reporter.''

Bearnarth looked at Gordy, who said, "You promise to stay in public places all day? You won't try to play hero?''

Kelleher laughed. "You're starting to sound like Maureen. I promise, Mother.''

She nodded to Bearnarth, who shook his head. "It's risky, Kelleher. There are too many dead bodies around already.''

Kelleher tried to take a deep breath. It wasn't as easy as it should have been. "Just find Tourretta," he said. "She's the key.''

Bearnarth put his arms out helplessly. "We've been looking for her all night, believe me.''

"Your guys have any idea who called Alan yet?" he asked.

"None. We asked Mary Jane if she had any clue but she was too hysterical to answer. All she said was he hung up and said he had to go to Annapolis, he'd try to make it as quick as he could."

"She said Annapolis, not the office?"

Bearnarth pulled out a notebook. "She said Annapolis. That make any difference?"

"Maybe not. But then again, maybe." He drained his coffee. "Long day ahead. I better get going."

"Stay in touch," Gordy said.

Kelleher leaned down and gave her a peck on the cheek. "I promise," he said. "And I won't stay out late tonight, either."

"Yes, you will," Gordy said. "It's Monday, remember."

On Monday, the legislature didn't go back into session until eight o'clock at night. Usually, Kelleher would wander into the office at midmorning to check his mail, perhaps have lunch with a friend, and then drive up to Annapolis at about four o'clock. After a quick check to make sure none of the committees were having an ad hoc meeting—sometimes late in the session they would do that to try to get some work done with nobody around—he would go back to the hotel, unpack for the week, and go for a run. After that, most of the reporters would meet for dinner and then wander over to session. Rarely did anything newsworthy take place on Monday night. The session was little more than an excuse to get everyone back to town in order to go out afterward. Kelleher loved Mondays, the tradition, the notion of everyone in a community coming together again after the weekend. As he walked out of the mansion gate, Kelleher had a feeling that those days were behind him.

The morning was cold, bright, and clear as he walked to the hospital. The doctor was right—he had a slight ligament tear. They fitted him with a soft cast and he headed over to the House office building. If this were a normal week, he'd be making these rounds on Tuesday morning and he would stop en route to the floor to see Alan Sims.

Over and over in his mind he tried to figure out who could have called Sims last night and lured him onto the highway. Andrea was an obvious candidate, but he wanted to believe she was telling the truth. If not Andrea, who? Maybe one of the state troopers Sims had been tight with. At least *one* cop was involved in this plot; maybe another had been the traitor. Kelleher made his swing through the House offices a brief one—

almost no one was in; most of the legislators were driving up from their homes for the service—then walked briskly back to the State House.

The security was as tight as, if not tighter than, on the few occasions when he had covered events at the White House. The general public was not allowed in at all. Those with invitations had to present them *and* identification to get into the building.

Kelleher ran up the State House steps only to learn that the media were being admitted to the building by the basement door. There, an ID would get you as far as the pressroom. To be admitted to the House chamber for the service, a special pass was needed from Tom Stallworth, the president of the State House Correspondents Association.

Kelleher certainly wasn't going to complain about extra security at this point. He walked around the corner to the side entrance and waited patiently to show his ID and pass through the metal detector. Stallworth, organized as ever, had passes ready and waiting for the local regulars. Members of the national press would receive credentials on a first come, first served basis and only after all the regulars had been taken care of. Tom Mercer from NBC was objecting loudly to this arrangement when Kelleher walked in.

"Who are you to tell me whether I can or cannot cover something?" Mercer was saying to Stallworth.

"Your crew is guaranteed a spot in the balcony, so you'll have pictures," Stallworth said. "But I can't deny people who cover this place every day a spot. You'll have to be patient."

Kelleher, thankful he wasn't Stallworth, grabbed his pass and went up the back steps to the House lounge. As he expected, another security checkpoint was set up there.

"I'm sorry, sir, no one is allowed up here before nine forty-five," the young trooper posted there told Kelleher.

"I don't want to go in," Kelleher explained. "But I do need to find Tom Wyman."

"And who are you, sir?"

"Bobby Kelleher from *The Washington Herald.*"

"Wait right here."

The trooper disappeared into the House lounge and came back a moment later.

"If you'll wait for a minute, Lieutenant Wyman will be right out. He's finishing up a planning meeting."

"Thanks a lot." Kelleher made a note to himself to tell Wyman how helpful the trooper had been. He always believed that if you bitch when someone gives you a hard time, you should be thankful when someone goes out of their way to be helpful. This guy could easily have said "He's in a meeting" and shooed Kelleher back to the basement.

Wyman came out soon after, a cup of coffee in his hands. He looked five years older than he had on Thursday afternoon—which, Kelleher realized, was beginning to feel like it *had* been five years ago.

"What's up, Bobby?" Wyman asked in a tired, sad voice.

"You got a minute?"

"Just about. Come on back here."

He led Kelleher back to the lounge. As he had done on so many other mornings, Kelleher poured himself coffee. Today, there would be no newspaper reading, though. They sat in two chairs in the far corner of the room.

"Tommy, someone got Alan to leave his house last night with a phone call."

Wyman nodded. "I know," he said. "Bearnarth told me."

"I hate to say it, but I think it might have been one of your guys. You know that one woman has already been tied to the case."

"Yeah, I know. Jackie Roane. They think she was with that FFF woman they found this morning. Everyone's looking for her. You think there might be someone else involved?"

"I don't know, but it had to be someone he knew and someone he trusted. Mary Jane said the conversation didn't last more than a minute. That means someone must have just said, 'Alan, get up here,' or something like that, and he took him at his word."

Wyman made a face. "I'll check into it, see if any of Alan's friends are acting funny. It's a little bit like finding the old needle in the haystack, though."

"I know."

The two men looked at each other. Kelleher could feel tears welling up in his eyes. Wyman looked like he was about to cry too. "I don't know how much longer I can go on, Bobby," he said. "Paulsen's death was hard to take but politicians know there are risks. Alan, though. What did he ever do? All he's ever been . . . all he ever was . . . was a good, honest man."

Kelleher couldn't continue this conversation. He stood up to go. Never in his life had he spent more than ten minutes with Wyman without being asked about Maureen McGuire. Today, nothing. He patted Wyman on the shoulder and walked out of the lounge. He wanted to go back to the office but he knew that trying to get back into this building would be almost impossible.

Instead, he went back downstairs and called to see if there were any messages on his tape. One intrigued him: it was from Chris Mills, the lecherous front-desk clerk at The Boar's Head. He dialed the number Mills had left. It was the hotel switchboard. He asked to speak to Mills.

"Chris Mills."

"Mr. Mills, Bob Kelleher returning your call."

"Ah, yes, Mr. Kelleher. I assume that was your voluptuous friend who coaxed Mr. Tourretta's room number out of me."

Kelleher sighed. The guy was calling to give him a hard time. Okay, he thought, be polite and get it over with.

"Look, I'm sorry, Mr. Mills, but . . ."

"No apology necessary. I figured out who you were when I read the newspaper this morning. I also figured out that Mr. Tourretta was really this Jimmy Dumont they found shot to death. Obviously, there are very serious things going on here."

"Yeah, I guess there are."

"You know, if you'd just told me your name, you wouldn't have had to go through that whole thing with your friend. You and I were in school together. I remember when you wrote for *The Cavalier Daily*."

Kelleher laughed. "I didn't think anyone remembered back that far."

"Well, I do. But that's not why I called. I think I may be able to help you. Reading your story, I had the sense that there's still some suspicion that Jamelle Tourretta's involved."

"What about it?" Kelleher said, being careful.

"Well, I have a guy here, one of my security staff, who may have seen her here that same night."

"When?"

"He says it was about two in the morning. You should probably talk to him directly. Can you get back down here?"

Kelleher smelled a trap. "I'm not sure. Can't you just tell me what he said?"

"Yeah, I can. But I suspect you'll need to talk to him directly before you print anything."

"Why are you calling me instead of the police?"

"My guy won't talk to the cops. He's an illegal. But he's scared and he feels like he should tell someone what he saw. When I read your story this morning it was obvious to me that you have a pretty good handle on what's going on. That's why I called you."

"I'm glad. But it's not as obvious to me how good a handle I have on all this. Tell me when your guy saw Tourretta."

"Like I told you, it was about two A.M. He was making his rounds when he saw the door to room seven open. That's the room Tourretta, er, Dumont was in. Anyway, my guy didn't think anything about it, but the next thing he sees is someone coming out of the room carrying someone over their shoulder. He starts to say something, then he sees that this person is carrying a gun in their free hand."

"He must have pretty good eyes to see all this in the dark," Kelleher said.

"There's a light right over the door to each room, remember? She was standing right in the door. That's how he saw that it was a woman. A woman with long red hair."

Kelleher kept listening.

"Our security guards work unarmed," Mills continued. "My guy didn't want to take this person on. She had Dumont, I guess it was Dumont, slung over one shoulder and the gun in the other. He got out of there. This morning he came looking for me. Said he had to talk to someone."

It was just a little too pat for Kelleher. A guy he had humiliated—with Ann's help—calls out of the blue offering help if he could get back on Route 29. Then again, he didn't have much else to pursue. He was running out of angles *and* time.

"Look, Mr. Mills, I appreciate your calling me. Right now I have to go into the memorial service for Governor Paulsen. Can I call you back at this number in a couple of hours?"

"If I don't hear from you by noon, I'll figure you aren't interested."

Kelleher hung up and sat staring at the phone, completely baffled. He was frustrated: the story was so close he could feel it on his fingertips. But he didn't have it yet.

"Well, stranger, it's certainly nice to see you in one piece."

Kelleher turned to see McGuire walking into the pressroom. He was extremely glad to see her. She came over and hugged him, holding him for a good twenty seconds longer than her usual hug. "You scared the hell out of me last night," she said.

"Me too. Listen, I just got a very strange phone call."

He explained to her about Chris Mills, about Ann Roberts's role in acquiring Dumont's room number. McGuire had a big grin on her face when he finished.

"Major cleavage, huh?"

He nodded his head. "Yes, Maureen. Did you remember to sharpen your claws this morning?"

She laughed. "Sorry, I couldn't resist. I think you're right, though. The whole thing reeks of setup. This guy sounds like someone who could be bought for a couple hundred dollars."

He was sure she was right. And yet . . .

"I'll decide what to do after the service," he said. "Let's get upstairs before they lock us out."

He meant it as a joke but they were the last two reporters admitted to the chamber. The doors were shut and locked at precisely ten A.M. The state police had already announced that the doors to the House would remain locked throughout the service and during Gordy's speech. That way, if anyone had any ideas about *anything*, they would be unable to slip out.

Kelleher walked through the school desks to his perch on the railing, convinced he'd be told to move. To his surprise, no one said anything. The rituals were much more somber than they'd been the previous Thursday. When introduced, the senators walked in quietly. No ovation, no jibes back and forth. The same thing happened when Gordy entered. Once everyone was in place, the back doors of the chamber swung open and there was Barney Paulsen's casket.

Two state troopers wheeled it up the aisle as everyone stood in silence. Seven pallbearers followed the casket. Kelleher's throat caught when he saw the open spot where the eighth pallbearer—Alan Sims—should have been. *Alan Sims was supposed to have been there.*

The minister was from Paulsen's church in Baltimore. He said several prayers, then introduced Meredith Gordy.

Meredith was warm, funny, and strong. Whether people agreed or disagreed with him, few people disliked Barney Paulsen. Even fewer would have wished him dead. The silence, the mourning, was all real. But the new governor made everyone in the room feel better. She talked about the first time she'd met Barney Paulsen—he thought she was Meredith

Gordy's *secretary*. She remembered trying to educate him on the importance of women's issues, and his willingness to listen and try to learn.

"He became for me both a friend and a counselor. I think he learned from me; I *know* I learned from him. Barney Paulsen never tried to be anything he wasn't; he knew exactly what he was and who he was and he was proud of it. He stood for the right things in politics and as a human being."

She paused and said softly, "I miss him."

As Gordy spoke, Kelleher found himself staring at Andrea. She sat where Gordy normally sat during Paulsen's speeches. Wyman had told Kelleher that they'd offered that seat to Myron Cutler since, for the moment, the Senate president was the acting lieutenant governor. Cutler had said he would sit in the Senate president's seat because that was the job he had been elected to. Kelleher found that surprisingly human.

If Gordy's speech affected Kyler, she didn't show it. She sat with her legs crossed, arms folded, staring intently at her boss. The look on her face was so blank Kelleher wondered if she was even listening. Kelleher prided himself on his ability to read expressions. But there was no way to read a blank page.

Gordy finished her prepared text. She cleared her throat, hesitated, and plunged forward. "I walked in here intending to say nothing about Alan Sims," she said, just a bit of a tremor in her voice. "I thought perhaps it inappropriate in that we are here this morning to honor Barney Paulsen.

"But these two tragedies are so clearly connected, just as these two men were so clearly connected in life, that I feel as if I must say something.

"We are all victims right now, perhaps not in the tangible sense that Barney and Alan have been victims, but we are victims. Not only because they are gone, but because of the terror we all feel right now. Those who have committed these horrific crimes *will* be brought to justice, that much I pledge. When they are, we must be absolutely vigilant in our pursuit of swift justice. There can be no rationale, no justification for these crimes. No cause in the world is worth the waste of life we have seen these last few days." Gordy looked around the chamber. "For Barney and for Alan, thank you."

No one moved. Then, from the back rows, the applause started. It built swiftly until everyone on the floor was standing. They were standing in the gallery too. Even the media, which always prided themselves on staying detached, stood to applaud Meredith Gordy. She had expressed the anger that everyone felt, and everyone reacted. Kelleher was crying, embarrassed by the tears until he looked around him and saw there weren't many dry eyes in the House. Kenworthy was crying. So was Frece. He looked at Kyler. Her face was still blank.

Everyone remained standing as the casket was rolled back out. It had been a catharsis; they all needed to deal with the loss they had suffered, the anger they felt. To Kelleher, Barney Paulsen's death had been sad, but it hadn't cut him open emotionally. Sims's death had. Perhaps he'd allowed himself to get too close to a source but Kelleher felt no shame in that. If you are human, you cross that invisible line once in a while.

Kelleher took a deep breath. Having admitted to himself that he was human and fallible, he now had to get himself together and return to his reporter mode. McGuire had volunteered to follow the funeral procession to Baltimore. That would leave Kelleher time to write his story about the events of the previous evening.

And to figure out what to do about his friend in Charlottesville, Chris Mills.

As soon as the casket had exited the chamber, most of the reporters began scrambling for the door. Kelleher had to explain about his cast to everyone—"got knocked down playing hoops," he said. He then stopped McGuire in the lounge as she was heading for one of the processional media vans.

"I hate doing things like this," she said. "I hope you know that."

"I know. I owe you one. But writing this first-person story about last night isn't going to be easy. I'm not exactly thrilled about having to do it."

"But you know why it has to be done."

"Absolutely. Someone tried to kill me. That has to be reported. This is the only way to do it—unless *you* write the story, which doesn't make any sense since I was there."

"Go be a star," she said and raced off after Kenworthy, who was also heading for the van. Frece came up behind Kelleher.

"That was a hell of a story this morning, Bobby. How'd you ID Dumont? The cops swear they didn't release his name to anybody until today."

"Lucky break, John, nothing more," Kelleher said, not wanting to share any more details. Even with Alan Sims dead, Kelleher felt obligated to protect him as a source. He wasn't really sure why. It didn't matter much anymore. But he felt he should carry out his promise to his friend.

He walked back to the office. The sun washed over the city; Annapolis was truly Oz at moments like this. Kelleher didn't even notice. As soon as he was inside the office, he sprawled in a chair and dialed the office of alumni affairs at the University of Virginia. He had to go through two secretaries before he reached Ann Roberts.

He was half expecting a crack about the fact that he had broken his promise to call her last night, but she wasn't in a joking mood. "I just heard about Alan Sims on the radio," she said. "You have to get police protection. If they went after him, they'll definitely go after you. They must know that you know at least as much as he did."

Ann Roberts was too damn smart, Kelleher thought. Even if he didn't tell her about what had happened on Route 29, he wasn't likely to assuage her fears. He tried anyway. "I know what you're saying," he said. "Believe me, I intend to stay in very public places until all this shakes out."

"Do they have any idea who killed your friend?"

"Not really. I'll explain the whole thing to you later. Right now, I have to ask for your help again."

She sighed. "Have I ever denied you anything?"

He told her about his call from Chris Mills. "I need to get a sense if this is on the level or some kind of setup," he said. "Even if it's a setup, *you* won't be in any danger. Have them meet you in the restaurant at The Boar's Head for lunch. The *Herald*'ll buy. Rent a tape recorder if you haven't got one."

"You think Mills will go for this?"

"Only if he's on the level. If he says no, that proves it was a setup of some kind."

"You mean a setup to try and kill you, don't you?"

"I have no idea. Can you do it? Do you have time?"

"I *should* tell you to go to hell and remind you that you call me only when you need help."

"But you'll do it?"

"I'll do it, Kelleher—but don't ask me why."

"I'm not that stupid."

He dialed Mills back as soon as he hung up with Ann. He explained that she was a part-time reporter for the *Herald* and could be at The Boar's Head in forty-five minutes to meet for lunch.

"We can't do it at the hotel," Mills said. "Too many people will want to know what's going on."

Kelleher was about to tell Mills to take a hike, that he wasn't sending Ann anywhere that wasn't very public, when Mills said, "How about The Aberdeen Barn?"

That was a surprise. The Aberdeen Barn was Charlottesville's best steak house. A *very* public place. "Fine," Kelleher agreed. "I'll tell her to meet you at The Aberdeen Barn at twelve-thirty."

"She won't be wearing that same dress, will she?"

"I sincerely doubt it," he answered, feeling guilty once again about making Ann meet with this sleazebag.

When he called her back, he gave her the details. "Let him tell it to you without leading him," he said. "And try to get a sense of whether it sounds like his lines have been rehearsed."

"Yes, boss. I understood the first time. How much space have I got?"

"Funny. You were a reporter once, you can do this."

"I was an *arts* critic."

"It never hurts to broaden ourselves, Ann."

She snorted. "I'm plenty broad enough."

Ba-boom. "Call me as soon as you're finished."

"You got it."

"One more thing," he said, the words coming out before he could think of what to say next. "I really will make this up to you. I promise."

"I told you, Kelleher, never promise anything."

CHAPTER 12

OZ

Once he began to write, Kelleher felt himself relax. Writing was always therapeutic for him; it was one thing that always seemed to come easily.

This story was one that wrote itself. He didn't have to be clever or melodramatic; all he had to do was describe what had happened to him. That was plenty dramatic enough. Unlike other stories, he didn't have to pause to check quotes to make sure he had told both sides. There was only one side to this story: his.

He was about a thousand words into the story—just at the point where he saw the headlights in his mirror—when the phone rang. Looking up, Kelleher could tell by the angle of the sun that it was almost late afternoon. He looked at his watch: three forty-five! He still had a lot to do. It was Ann Roberts on the phone.

"How'd it go?" he asked.

"Well, this guy Chris Mills definitely wants to date me," she said. "What do you think, is he my type?"

"Funny. What happened?"

"I'll send you the tape Fed Ex so you can listen yourself. But my reaction is that this little guy is either a very good actor or very, very scared by what he saw Saturday night."

"You think he's on the level?"

"Let me put it this way: Mills asked me if you thought the whole thing was some kind of joke or setup. Do you bring that up if that's what you're doing?''

"You might if you're *very* smart. But I don't think Mills qualifies in that category. My guess is Tourretta probably did kill Dumont and that this guy saw her.''

"I want to tell you one thing, Bobby, and I'll admit I may be way off base here. I've done a lot of reading on the women's movement, on NOW, and on the start-up of FFF.''

"And everything you've read about them says they're nonviolent.''

"Militantly nonviolent, if that's possible. One of the points they make is that men have always solved the world's problems with guns and violence and it's time to change all that. But this is a bloodbath. It doesn't fit.''

"No, I guess it doesn't. But it's still the only answer that makes any sense.''

"You may be right. But it still doesn't add up to me. Everything I've ever read about Meredith Gordy says she would have been a star without anyone taking such radical steps. I just don't see the need for this kind of violence.''

"No reasonable person would. But clearly we're not dealing with reasonable people here.''

She sighed. "Well, you're the reporter. I just have a feeling you should keep chasing the Dumont side of the story, too. Don't ask me why.''

"I won't.''

"But you *can* do one thing for me.''

"Anything.''

"Write my name down on the back of your notebook so maybe, just maybe, you'll think to call me once a day until this is over. I really *do* worry about you.''

He nodded. "I'll do it,'' he said. "I'm sorry I didn't call last night.''

"Apology accepted, Kelleher. Again.''

He was smiling when he put the phone down. Ann Roberts, it seemed, could always make him smile. He had no time for happy thoughts, however. Jane Kryton had told him that the big-shot editors wanted his story in the office by four o'clock so it could be lawyered. It was now four-fifteen and he wasn't even halfway through. He sat down and began writing again. It wasn't five minutes later when the phone rang.

"You almost done?''

It was Jane. Of course. So he lied. "Just about. I'm struggling a little bit writing in the first person.''

"I understand. But people are getting antsy here. They're planning to splash it very big on page one. Go as fast as you can."

Going fast was not a problem at all. It was the length of the story that troubled him. By the time he pushed back from the computer he had written a little more than three thousand words. But he wanted to put in every detail. If the editors thought something was superfluous, they could take it out. He didn't think they would. He knew that identifying Wendy Paul as Tourretta's bodyguard/assistant would send the *Herald*'s lawyers into an apoplectic fit since her presence in the woods pointed the finger heavily at Tourretta. But the facts were the facts.

He was finishing the story when he heard a banging on the door. "Who is it?" he asked before opening it.

"Christ, it's me," Maureen McGuire said. "Why have you got the bolt on?"

"Old age," he answered, letting her in. "How was your afternoon?"

"Awful. The speeches at the grave site went on forever. Helen Paulsen broke down completely and had to be carried out. The story will be easy but it was a miserable time."

"I'm almost finished. I'll give you a hand."

It was nearly six by the time he filed. Once his story was in, he leaned over McGuire's shoulder and helped her put her story together. They were almost finished an hour later, when the phone rang.

"*Washington Herald*," Kelleher said.

"Bobby? Wyn Watkins."

"Mr. Watkins? What's up? I mean, what can I do for you?"

"You've already done plenty, Bob. Your story's magnificent. The writing is vivid, the reporting that led to it superb. I just wanted you to know I'm proud of you."

"Thank you, sir," Kelleher said, hearing the click as he reached the word *sir*.

"What was that?" said McGuire, pausing to look up.

"Watkins. He loved my story. Said he was proud of me."

McGuire grunted. "Two days ago he was ready to make us into errand boys for the national staff. Sunday morning he was ready to *fire* you when he found out that you were in Charlottesville. Now you're a goddamn hero. Some business we work in, huh?"

Kelleher grinned. "Let's finish your story, then get something to eat."

"Chick N Ruth's?"

"Perfect."

They sent McGuire's story a few minutes later, then walked down to Main Street to Chick N Ruth's Delicatessen, which was almost as much of an Annapolis landmark as the State House. Once, it had been at the center of state politics. Back when Marvin Mandel was governor, he ate breakfast every morning in the same booth there. If you wanted to talk to the governor, the best place to do it was in the morning at Chick N Ruth's.

Things had changed when Mandel was forced out of office after being convicted of mail fraud, but the tradition of naming sandwiches after politicians continued. Kelleher ordered the Fred Weiland kosher salami, while McGuire asked for the Meredith Gordy corned beef. They sat in Mandel's old booth by the front door while Kelleher recounted Ann Roberts's meeting with Chris Mills and the security guard.

"Sounds like this guy's telling the truth," McGuire said, munching on her sandwich. "The big question we have to answer next, I think, is just how involved your friend Andrea Kyler is."

"What do you mean, *my* friend?"

"Oh, come on, it's been written all over your face for days. I never once heard you call the woman anything but Kyler. For the last four days you've called her Andrea a dozen times and you've gotten a little moon-eyed every time her name's come up. Face it—you've got that lovesick look to you."

"Come on, I'm not lovesick." He grinned sheepishly. "Likesick, maybe, but not lovesick."

"And what about this Ann woman?"

He stopped grinning. "We're just longtime pals."

She shook her head. "Trust me on this. You don't run around putting your life on the line for an old pal."

"*I* would."

"Okay then, old pal, pay for dinner and let's get to session."

"Anything for an old pal," he said, throwing twenty dollars on the table. He felt better than he'd felt in four days. Not only was he Wyn Watkins's hero—at least for the next few hours—this was starting to feel like a real Monday night. Dinner with McGuire, a walk up to the State House for session, and then Fran's. At least for the moment, he was back in Oz.

━ ━

The House lounge was buzzing when they arrived. The funeral service had been truly cathartic. To the legislators, it was time to get back to business—and play—as usual. They had now had four full days to deal with Paulsen's death. Only a few of them knew Sims well enough to really be shaken up by his murder. They all figured, no doubt, that it was just a matter of time until all of Paulsen's attackers were arrested, so why not enjoy the last six weeks of the session?

McGuire glanced around the lounge and shook her head. "Nobody here I want to talk to," she said. "I'm going to head over to the Senate."

"Lots of people *there* to talk to," he said.

"Yeah, well, that's true. But at least there I feel like I'm working."

"If you're done first, come here. If I'm done, I'll come there. Then we'll go to Fran's."

"Bobby, I don't know about tonight. I'm wasted."

"So am I, but who knows when we'll have another Monday in Fran's."

She smiled. "You know, Monday night in Fran's isn't *quite* as big a deal to me as it is to you. If I never have another one, my life will somehow swim forward."

"I understand that," he said. "But come on. Do it for your old pal."

She frowned but he knew he'd won. "For an hour," she said.

"My friendship is worth a whole hour? I'm flattered." He knew he would talk her into staying longer when the time came. She went off to the Senate while he poured a cup of coffee. Mike Benroove, a legislator from the Eastern Shore, was standing by the coffee maker when he walked up.

"Hey, Kelleher, you seen the page du jour?"

Benroove's thoughts rarely strayed from the topic of sex. New pages arrived in Annapolis each Monday night and Benroove—who could have been a TV mannequin if he wasn't a politician—had taken some considerable pride in his ability to make a move on each week's new victim. Rumor had it he actually kept a tally somewhere. Kelleher and McGuire had talked about trying to write that as a story but had held off, partly because it would be awfully tough to prove and partly because they knew the story would make them pariahs in the entire legislature. It would be breaking the code.

"Which one?" Kelleher asked as politely as he could.

"You'll know when you see her." Benroove actually winked. "Tall blonde. I have to figure out how to get her to Fran's tonight."

"Why don't you just ask her?"

Benroove looked shocked. "You know I don't do that," he said. "It would be undignified for a member of the House to do that. But *you* could ask her."

"Uh-hunh. I'm just a member of the undignified media."

He walked away before the conversation went any lower—if that were possible—and walked into the House. Weiland was gaveling for quiet. Announcements were made—there would be a memorial service for Alan Sims on Thursday. A number of bills were whisked through preliminary readings. Several resolutions, one sending condolences to Mary Jane Sims, were passed. Finally, it was time for various members of the House to rise and request personal privilege to put their shock over the death of Barney Paulsen into the record. When a legislator asked for "personal privilege," it meant that he or she wished to address a topic that did not directly pertain to what was being discussed on the floor. It was used most often in situations like this. Kelleher wondered how long Weiland would let it go on. There wasn't any serious business to conduct tonight, but if all 141 delegates felt they had to prove that they were sorry Barney Paulsen had been killed, the session could last until midnight.

"Chair recognizes the delegate from Anne Arundel."

Kelleher looked up and saw Wendell Hoxledeer rising. This would really be the height of hypocrisy, given Paulsen's open disdain for Hoxledeer. "Think Wendell will cry and try to get on television?" Kenworthy whispered.

"In a New York minute," Kelleher answered.

"Mr. Speaker, personal privilege, please?" Hoxledeer said.

"Proceed, sir."

"Mr. Speaker, members of the House, I rise tonight not to praise our late governor . . ."

"But to bury him," Kenworthy murmured.

". . . but to express my true feelings about him, and, for that matter, about our new governor, Meredith Gordy. Mr. Speaker, I would not wish anyone dead, not Governor Paulsen, not Governor Gordy, but if I were to stand up here and tell you I'm sorry the governor is dead or feel any pain because of it, I'd be lying."

Weiland's face turned a deep, furious red. "Sir, you are totally out of order!" He was almost screaming. "I will not tolerate that sort of talk in this chamber!"

"Mr. Speaker, I am speaking on personal privilege. . . ."

"Totally irrelevant, sir. Personal privilege does *not* give you or anyone else the right to make demeaning and derogatory comments about *anyone,* much less about our late governor and our current governor. If you do not relinquish the floor immediately, I will have you removed."

"Mr. Speaker, with all due respect, you have absolutely no right . . ."

"*Try me!*" Weiland roared.

The House was completely silent as Hoxledeer considered his options. "Mr. Speaker," he finally said, "this is not the end of this incident, I promise you."

The entire room was buzzing as Hoxledeer sat. Weiland gaveled for order. A few more members rose to put in their two cents about Barney Paulsen. No one was listening, though. Hoxledeer had stolen the show—which was exactly what he had intended to do all along.

"What do you think?" Frece asked, walking over to Kenworthy and Kelleher.

Kelleher shrugged, looking at his notes. "You gotta give it a couple graphs. Guy stands up and basically says he's glad the governor's dead, you have to write it."

Kenworthy nodded. "Six-inch box, somewhere inside. If it was anybody else, it would be worth more. Even so, everyone who picks up the paper tomorrow reads that story."

Kelleher looked at his notes one more time. Even for Hoxledeer this was wild stuff. "You think we need to talk to him?" he said.

"Boy, do I hate that idea," Kenworthy said.

Before Kelleher could respond to that, he heard someone calling his name. He looked up to see Buzz Ryan, the chairman of the Appropriations Committee, trying to get his attention. Ryan was pointing toward the lounge, meaning he wanted to meet back there to talk. "Them too," he mouthed, pointing at Kenworthy and Frece.

The three reporters retreated to the lounge. Ryan came in a moment later. The eulogies on the floor had resumed. "You guys are going to write it, aren't you?" he said.

"Write what?"

"That Hoxledeer crap. All he's trying to do is get his name in the paper, you know that."

Kelleher put an arm around Ryan. He was a short, pleasant Irishman, impossible not to like. His friends enjoyed saying that since he'd become chairman of Appropriations his name had been changed to "powerful committee chairman Charles E. (Buzz) Ryan," since he'd been referred to that way so many times in print.

"The guy stood up on the floor of the Maryland House of Delegates," Kenworthy said, "and, for all intents and purposes, said good riddance to Barney Paulsen. How the hell can we not write that?"

"Just don't," Ryan said. "If you all agree not to write it, nobody gets scooped."

"And what happens when our editors see it on TV or hear a cut on radio?" Frece said, shaking his head. "You know all those guys are going to run with the thing. We'd love not to write it. But we have no choice."

Ryan shook his head, disgusted. "And you wonder why people think the media are a bunch of jerks." He stalked back onto the floor.

Kelleher watched him for a minute, then shook his head. "You know something, guys," he said. "He's not totally wrong."

Kenworthy and Frece said nothing. Maureen McGuire walked into the lounge. "They still yammering on about Barney?" she asked.

"Oh, yeah," Kelleher said. "Except for Hoxledeer. He's glad he's dead."

"What?"

"Come on, I'll tell you about it while I call the desk," he said, walking to one of the phones in the back of the lounge. In a fit of conscience, Kelleher did something he almost never did: he talked down a story. He explained to the desk—Kryton had gone home so Phil Sowickey, the night editor, was in charge—that Hoxledeer really was just pandering for attention. Sowickey had been inclined to give him twelve inches; Kelleher talked it down to eight. Then he dictated the story quickly to a dictationist, pointing out that most members of the House saw Hoxledeer's speech as nothing more than a crude play for attention.

Take that, Wendell, he said to himself as he hung up, figuring Hoxledeer would soon be up on the floor ripping him once again. That was fine, Kelleher thought. After all, you judge a man by his enemies.

▬ ▬

The House was just breaking—mercifully—when Kelleher finished dictating, so he joined McGuire and the two of them worked their way out of the lounge and down the back stairs. At the bottom, he heard a familiar voice calling his name. He looked up to see Susan Sanders standing there, hands on hips.

"Remember me?" she said, smiling.

"Actually, I just told Maureen that I was going to try to find you before you went to Fran's," he said, being careful not to be so stupid as to add, "right, Maureen?" That would make it much too easy for her to make a liar out of him. She seemed content to just watch, so he barged forward. "Turns out, you saved me a trip. Are you going to join us?"

He was hoping she'd be too proud to accept the last-second, bail-out invitation. No such luck. "I have to go do a stand-up on the lawn." Her hands were off her hips now. One of them was on Kelleher's shoulder. "I'll meet you down there, though, if you promise to save me a seat."

"Consider it done."

"Oh, Bob, I don't know if I can *wait* fifteen minutes to see you again." McGuire was doing a hot-breathed imitation of Sanders. "I certainly hope you can squeeze me into your social schedule, between Miss Charlottesville and the news source you've been banging."

The last line was a major blow. "Are you trying to get me to go kill myself or something?" he asked.

"No. I'm just trying one last time to get you to think with your brain and not your you-know-what."

He had to admit the comment was not totally out of line. They walked down to Fran's, Kelleher freezing without his coat. Once the sun had gone down, the temperature had dropped considerably. He smelled snow in the air again.

Fran's was packed, more crowded than Kelleher could remember it at any time during the session. Once upon a time, Fran's had been jammed with legislators, lobbyists, and reporters almost every night, Monday to Thursday, and completely overflowing with "civilians" on Mondays. That had changed with stricter drunk-driving laws and the media's penchant for reporting on the personal lives of politicians. David Jackson had written a landmark story on nightlife in Annapolis in the mid-eighties, describing, among other things, a committee chairman urinating on a corner just off Main Street at two o'clock in the morning.

That didn't happen very often anymore. Now Monday was the only night when a crowd turned up at Fran's—and often people just did a walk-through to show their faces, then went home. But showing up at Fran's at some point was still part of the ritual of the legislature. For years, the Montgomery County delegation had held their delegation meetings on Monday night. That practice had been abandoned because the Montgomery legislators were ridiculed so often for never showing up at Fran's that their leadership decided it was costing them votes. Even in the sober nineties, it was better to be thought of as a lush than a nerd if you wanted to succeed in Annapolis.

The back booth in the corner was always unofficially reserved on Monday night for the media, and McGuire and Kelleher joined the group there. Kenworthy had already ordered scotch and soda. McGuire, sticking to her vow not to stay long, insisted on a Perrier. Kelleher asked for scotch, knowing he'd better not get drunk. If he did, he was capable of falling prey to the charms of Susan Sanders. That was the last thing he needed right now.

The drinks arrived and they were all ordering food when Susan walked in. She had changed from the stylish suit she'd been wearing to go on the air into a very sexy red skirt. McGuire elbowed him in the ribs when she saw her walk in, and whispered, "You're done, Kelleher."

"No way," he mumbled, trying his best not to stare.

Before McGuire could say anything else, Susan made it to the table. "Is there any more room here?" she asked. There wasn't, but all the men at the table began maneuvering to *make* room. Susan ended up right across from Kelleher.

A waitress came up to see if anyone wanted another drink. "I'd love a glass of chardonnay," Susan said. Kelleher thought McGuire was going to throw up.

"So," Susan said, "finally we get a chance to talk."

Not exactly. Just as she sat down, the band began to play. One of the best things about Fran's—and one of the worst things—was that it was almost impossible to talk once the band started. Tonight, Kelleher considered it a blessing.

That didn't prevent Susan from talking. She wanted to know how Kelleher found out about Jimmy Dumont, how he knew that Sims had been murdered, when everyone else had reported his death as an accident, and who he thought had *really* killed Paulsen. Kelleher kept his answers fairly short, especially since McGuire rolled her eyes every time he opened his mouth.

Food—simple, good, and plentiful—arrived and everyone ate. The moment she finished her scallops, McGuire stood up. "I'm outta here," she announced. "I *have* to get some sleep."

"Stay another thirty minutes," he said.

"Not a chance. I said an hour, it's been an hour." She clapped him on the shoulder. "You are officially unchaperoned." She smiled at Susan, who couldn't hear a word she was saying over the band. "I'm sure you won't miss me one little bit."

As soon as she was gone, Susan Sanders indicated the packed dance floor and asked, "Would you like to dance?" Kelleher hesitated. But he enjoyed dancing, even with the light cast he had on, he was halfway through his second scotch, and it was still too early for Kyler to show up. So, he figured, why not?

As they walked onto the dance floor, Kelleher could hear some of his friends hooting in the background. The band was playing "Smoke on the Water," a good seventies dancing song, and Susan was into it very quickly and very enthusiastically. Kelleher wasn't a bad dancer, but he wasn't in this woman's league. She had every move he had ever seen plus a few more. Her hair was flying and so was her skirt, exposing her impressive legs. Glancing at the tables around the dance floor, Kelleher could see a lot of staring going on. He would have been doing the same thing if he had been sitting there.

The third song was "What I Did for Love," which Kelleher knew by heart. That was the way it was at Fran's: at least once every four songs, the band played something slow. Susan immediately stopped her gyrating and put her arms around him. It was not, by any stretch of the imagination, unpleasant.

He could feel himself smiling dopily as they moved around the floor—until the moment when he looked up and saw Andrea Kyler walking, with several members of Gordy's staff, to a booth. She was looking right at him. He felt sick to his stomach. There was nothing he could do right then except wait for the dance to be over. It ended, in Kelleher time, about three hours later. He kept staring at Andrea. She wouldn't look at him. The last lyrics finally died out.

"That was great," he said hurriedly to Susan. "I need a break, though. You wear a guy out."

"Let me go to the ladies' room and I'll meet you back at the table."

He thought for a minute about going directly over to Andrea, but decided that was a bad idea. Miserable, he returned to the table. Kenworthy had a huge grin on his face.

"My only regret is that Maureen didn't stay to see this," he said. "She would be so proud. Her little boy and the TV star."

"Oh, shut up," he said, unable to think of anything wittier. He had become quite sober the moment he spotted Andrea. "I have to get rid of her without hurting her feelings."

Kenworthy shook his head. "The only way you're getting rid of that babe is when you say, 'Honey, it's time to get up and go to work,' " he said.

"Why isn't she after a legislator or one of the TV guys?"

"They didn't have the big scoop this morning, pal. Anyway, what the hell are you complaining about? Who are you to look a gift bimbo in the mouth?"

It was a good point. Only not with Kyler there. Kelleher had to think of something, Susan was coming back to the table. He had an idea—a clumsy one perhaps—but it was the best he was going to come up with.

As soon as she sat down, he took her hand—she smiled when he did—looked into her eyes, and said, "Susan, listen, don't hate me but I have to do a little bit of work right now. I've gotta go ask Andrea Kyler about something in my story for tomorrow. Will you give me five minutes?"

"Only if you promise not to run off with her," she said, smiling.

Kelleher almost choked on that one. "Not likely," he said finally, lightly pulling his hand free.

He felt like a fool. But he had executed step one. Step two was to walk across the dance floor to where Andrea and her group were sitting. The good news was the band had taken a break so he wouldn't have to shout to make himself heard. Naturally, when he reached the table, the entire group looked at him as if to say, "What the hell do you want?"

"Kyler," he said, reverting to calling her by her last name for the sake of those listening, "can I talk to you for one minute? I need to make sure I have something about tomorrow's schedule straight."

"Kelleher, I didn't come in here to talk to reporters," she answered coldly.

"I only need one minute."

She smiled at her companions and stood up. "If I'm not back in sixty seconds," she said, "come and get me."

She and Kelleher walked to the corridor leading to the restrooms, where there was a little bit of breathing room. "You're down to forty-five seconds," she said before he had even opened his mouth.

"Okay, okay, I know how tough you are," he said. "Look, I don't want to sound like a cliché, but I can explain what you just saw."

"Explain? Why would you need to explain? Bobby Kelleher dancing with a TV bimbo isn't exactly a headline, you know."

"Andrea, give me a break. You know how I feel about you. . . ."

"Whoa, wait a minute, Kelleher. I don't even know how I feel about you, so how the hell can I know how you feel about me? You don't owe me anything, I don't owe you anything, so don't do this little-boy-lost routine on me."

"Okay, fine, but regardless of what you feel or don't feel, we need to talk."

"Call me at the office in the morning."

Kelleher's patience ran out. He grabbed her by the arm and pulled her toward him, forgetting—and not caring—about who might be watching.

"Listen to me. Just about everyone in this town who knows what the hell is going on thinks you're part of this conspiracy, that you helped put together the plot to kill Barney. Even Meredith thinks it and she knows you better than anyone. I may be the *last* goddamn person still willing to believe in you. So don't give me this 'call your office' bullshit. By the time I call there you may be in jail."

For the first time in his life, Kelleher saw just a trace of fear in the smoldering dark eyes. She didn't try to pull free of him. Instead, she seemed to collapse in his direction.

"We can't leave together," she whispered. "I'm already going to get a hundred questions about why the hell I'm even talking to you. I'll stay thirty more minutes and leave. You wait a little longer, then I'll meet you at my apartment."

She turned to walk back to the table, had a thought, and turned back to him. "One more thing, Kelleher. If you're planning on getting laid tonight, I'd suggest you stick with Madonna over there. This is business."

"Fine," he said coldly. "I'll bring a tape recorder."

He regretted it as soon as he said it. She was just being the old Kyler, to prove there still *was* an old Kyler. There was no need for him to respond the way he had. He walked into the men's room, needing time to think about how to escape Susan Sanders as gracefully as possible.

By the time he walked out, he had a plan. He pushed his way through the crowd to the bar and waited until he could catch Joe Tonelli's eye. Tonelli had been bartending at Fran's for ten years and knew all the regulars. That certainly included Kelleher.

"What do you need, B.K.?" Tonelli asked.

Kelleher put twenty dollars on the bar. "I need a scotch and a glass of chardonnay," he said. "But more important, I need your help."

Tonelli shrugged. "Name it."

"In forty-five minutes, say twelve-thirty, I want you to come find me, either back at the table or on the dance floor, and tell me that someone from my office is on the phone up here. Can you do that?"

"Not a problem," Tonelli said. He picked up the twenty dollars and handed it back to Kelleher. "Keep the money, Bobby. I'll hit you for some basketball tickets next month."

"Deal."

He walked back to the table with the drinks. "Are you trying to ply me with liquor?" Susan Sanders asked.

"Whatever works," he said with a laugh.

Kelleher nursed his drink, not wanting to lose control of his senses. He needed to kill time, so he asked Susan where she grew up, how she'd gotten into television, what she liked about the job. She had just gotten to the part where a college classmate had suggested a tryout for the on-campus cable TV station when Kelleher noticed Andrea Kyler get up to leave. He looked at his watch: twelve-ten.

"And then, six months ago, I got the offer to come to Baltimore to cover politics," Susan was saying. "That was what I'd always wanted to do, so I figured I'd give it a shot. Of course, I never *dreamed* I'd be involved in a story like this one."

Kelleher sensed someone standing behind him. He looked up to see a leering Mike Benroove. "Hi, Susan," he said, flashing his eighty-seven teeth.

"Hello," she said politely.

"Like to dance?" Benroove asked.

Under normal circumstances, Kelleher would have been angry at Benroove's trying to hit on someone he was sitting with. Now, though, he was hoping Sanders would say yes.

"No thanks," she said, causing Kelleher to smile in spite of himself. "I'm kind of busy right now."

Kelleher should have let Benroove slink off, but he couldn't resist. "What happened to the page du jour, Benroove?"

Benroove turned red. Leaning down, in a whispered voice, he said, "Come on, Kelleher, cool it with that." He glanced over at the dance floor. "Anyway, she's over there."

Kelleher looked at the dance floor, where a very tall blond girl was dancing with one of the male pages. Kelleher knew the kid, seventeen at the most, was a page because he was still wearing his yellow page's jacket.

"Oh, come on, Benroove. You can certainly handle a seventeen-year-old, can't you? Give the kid a lollipop and send him home."

"Fuck you, Kelleher," Benroove said, walking away.

Kelleher was about to explain the Benroove legend to Susan Sanders when Joe Tonelli walked up. "Bobby, I'm sorry to interrupt, but there's a call for you at the bar. I think it may be your office."

Kelleher rolled his eyes in disgust. "Jesus, can't I escape them for a couple of hours?" He stood up, shook his head, and smiled at Susan. "Be right back," he said and followed Tonelli to the bar.

He picked up the phone, which Tonelli had taken off the hook for effect. "Just in case she walked up here with you," Tonelli said. "I gotta tell you, Bob, I don't know why you're trying to get away from that one."

"Long story," he said, picking up the phone. Tonelli had dialed one of the sports-score tapes. He talked to the tape—Indiana had lost to Ohio State and North Carolina had beaten Clemson for the two thousandth time in a row—for a few minutes, then put the phone down. He waved to Tonelli and walked back to the table.

He sat down, shaking his head angrily. "I can't believe this," he said. "I have to go back to my office. I wrote this big story for tomorrow and they've completely fucked it up on the desk. I've got to rewrite the whole middle section."

"What happened?"

"Too boring to get into, believe me. Screwed-up editing, basically. I have to get it fixed for the last edition."

"Will you come back down here when you're finished?"

He looked at his watch. "If I get finished before last call, I'll come back. But don't wait on me. These editors are so stupid, I don't know how long I'll be. I can't believe they screwed this one up."

He stood up, then leaned across the table. "I'm really sorry, Susan. I'll make it up to you another night. Okay?"

"Promise?"

He remembered what Ann Roberts had said to him about promises. For once, he listened to her advice. "There are a lot of nights left in the session," he said, a pretty good nonanswer, he thought.

He waved good night to Kenworthy, Frece, and the others. Kenworthy wasn't letting him get away that easily, though. "Where are you going?" he asked. "It's still early."

"Screwup in the office," he said. "Believe me, Tom, I'm not running off after a story."

That was partly true, he thought. At least it wasn't as blatant a lie as the one he'd told Susan. He walked out of the bar, kicking himself for putting himself in a position where he had to act like such a jerk.

It was snowing and Kelleher felt wistful as he slipped and slid across Main Street, turned up King George Street, and headed for Andrea's apartment. Twice, he thought he heard footsteps behind him. Twice, he turned and found no one. He was half-frozen by the time he carefully negotiated the steps leading to her building. She answered his knock immediately.

"I'm making hot chocolate," she said. "You want some?"

"That sounds great," he said. "Do me a favor and give me a couple aspirin with it, though."

"Too much scotch?"

"Just enough that a couple of aspirin can't hurt."

She walked back into the living room carrying two mugs of hot chocolate. With her shoes off, she was several inches shorter than Kelleher, which he liked. She sat down on the couch, curled her legs under her, and smiled. "So, what did you do with Miss Baltimore, tell her to wait for you in your room?"

"Are you and Maureen related or something?" he said, sitting down next to her on the couch and accepting the mug she handed him. "I admit, I've gone after some not-too-deep women in the past, but honest to God I haven't pursued this woman at all."

"You haven't exactly run away from her, though, have you?"

He smiled triumphantly. "I'm here right now, aren't I?"

That finished that topic of conversation, much to Kelleher's relief, since he knew there was a grain of truth in what she was saying. He popped the aspirin into his mouth and sipped the hot chocolate.

"Okay," Kyler said. "Let's get down to it. What makes you think I had anything to do with Paulsen's murder?"

Walking over, Kelleher had considered his strategy. Should he come right at her with his theory or work around the edges? He hadn't really decided, but now, sitting on the couch, he abandoned all the games. He told her that he thought Tourretta had used Dumont as a decoy and then killed him when he had outlived his usefulness.

"Tourretta is the mover and shaker in this deal," he said. "Someone inside had to help her set the whole thing up. No one in Annapolis is close to her the way you are. Two plus two equals four, I'm afraid."

She sat for a moment, saying nothing. "So Meredith thinks I plotted to commit murder? And you do too?"

He shook his head. "Emotionally, neither one of us wants to believe that. But intellectually, we're searching for answers. I need answers from you, Andrea.''

She stood up and walked to the small liquor cabinet in the corner of the room. "I have a sudden urge to drink," she said. "You want something?''

"No thanks." He stood up, walked behind her, and put his hands on her shoulders. "You have to tell someone the truth sometime," he said softly. "Everyone is expendable to Tourretta, that much is obvious. Tell me what's going on before she gets to you.''

For a moment she didn't answer. Finally, she turned around to face him. Tears were brimming in her eyes. "Sit down," she said, pointing to the couch. He walked back and she sat down next to him.

She sipped her drink and took a deep breath. "I *am* involved," she said after what seemed like an eternity. "But it isn't the way you think.''

He could feel his heart pounding very hard. He wondered if someone was watching all this, if he had been set up. Were the doors locked? Or was someone already in the apartment?

"What the hell does that mean?" he said, finding his voice.

She finished the drink and put it down. "Jamelle *was* plotting to make Meredith governor," she said, choosing her words carefully. "And I was helping her with that plan. But the plan I was involved in didn't include murder.''

"What did it include? How else do you get Barney out of there?''

Kyler smiled ruefully. "Easy. The old seduction routine. Barney and Jamelle had crossed paths before at an FFF fund-raiser in New York. He had a couple drinks and made some kind of pass at her. You know how he was with a couple drinks in him.''

Kelleher nodded. Everyone knew Barney liked two things: liquor and women.

She continued. "Jamelle was in town last Thursday to see *Barney*, not Meredith. That's why I lied when you two asked me about it in her office that night. Meredith didn't know anything about Jamelle coming to Annapolis. By then, I was totally confused.''

The plan, as Kyler laid it out, was simple: Helen Paulsen was leaving for New York right after the speech to spend a couple days shopping and going to theater. Tourretta was going to have dinner with Paulsen at the mansion, ostensibly to talk FFF politics. Both of them knew that wasn't what it was really about, though.

"I helped arrange the meeting," Kyler said. "Again Meredith knew nothing, of course. Once Jamelle hit the sack with Barney, it would have been over quickly. She plays the tape back for him, he resigns, citing health reasons, and Meredith is governor."

"How could you all be sure he wouldn't call your bluff, simply say that he'd made a horrible mistake, apologize, and denounce FFF for going back to their old tactics?"

"Barney couldn't have handled that kind of publicity, you know that. He would rather be out of office than be publicly humiliated that way."

"So, when did the plan change from seduction to murder?"

"I'm pretty sure now the plan always *was* murder. When I saw Jamelle in the gallery, I was surprised. I thought she'd show up after the speech. But I figured she liked making herself noticeable, and that was that. The next thing I knew, the lights went out and I heard Weiland scream when he got hit, because he was sitting right next to Meredith."

"So you never knew they were going to kill Barney?"

"Never. I swear it. It didn't take me long to figure out what had happened, though. Jamelle called a meeting the next morning—that's where I had to go when I left you that day—to discuss what to do next. I almost didn't go, but I wanted to confront her."

"And?"

"And she told me if I opened my mouth, I'd be implicated. She said I didn't know enough about their plan to get anyone but myself arrested. I would end up in jail and they'd never build a case against anyone else."

Kelleher suddenly remembered the voice on Kyler's tape that morning. It had been Tourretta.

"You were late to that meeting," he said.

"How do you know?"

"Tourretta called here. I heard her voice on the tape."

"Yeah, I was late. I was driving around trying to decide what the hell to do. I almost went straight to Larry Bearnarth, but I didn't have the guts. And, I guess there was still a small part of me that *wanted* to be unsure. When I went to the meeting, I knew."

"Who else was involved?"

"Beth Bevans. She helped recruit the cops. There's the one who's hiding out now, Roane. And at least two others. I don't know who they bought off to plant the guns and help with escape routes."

"You think one of them lured Sims out of his house last night?"

"Possible, I suppose. God, Bobby, Meredith doesn't think I did *that,* does she?"

"Meredith isn't sure about anything right now. Tell me what Jamelle said at that meeting."

She sighed again. "They were going to wait a couple days and then tip the cops to where Jimmy Dumont was. Let him take the fall along with the LOL. They had told him the plan was to get Paulsen and Gordy so that Cutler would be governor. For that and twenty-five thousand dollars he went along. Dumont was pretty money starved, according to Jamelle. They put him in the center seat because that was the main spot to get Paulsen from. They told him the two guys in the corners had a better angle at Gordy. That was why Weiland got winged, to make it look like they had gone for Gordy and missed."

"That's pretty damn good shooting."

"Jamelle only uses the best."

"So the plan was, Dumont gets caught, brags that the whole thing was an LOL plot, and the LOL takes the fall while Tourretta brings Gordy, now a national figure, back into the FFF fold."

"Exactly. And it might have worked if you hadn't recognized Dumont's picture and showed up at his doorstep. I guess Jamelle figured she had no choice but to get rid of him since she didn't know how much you knew or had told him."

"But now, they're all messed up. Everyone's convinced FFF killed Barney. Tourretta's going to be charged with murder as soon as the cops find her."

"Not necessarily. Finding her won't be easy, for one thing. The plan now, according to Beth, is for Lovette and Williamson, the other two shooters, to turn up dead in a couple days with a suicide note next to their bodies."

"And the note will say?"

"That they killed themselves because they and Dumont failed in their mission to make Cutler governor; that they had made things worse by making Gordy governor and therefore couldn't live with themselves."

"And Tourretta thinks people will buy that crap?"

"Apparently. Dumont's history as a fanatic will help, I guess."

"Do these two guys know this is going to happen to them?"

Kyler shook her head. "No. In fact, right now, they're hiding out with Jamelle. She's going to wait a couple days so Meredith can give her speech tomorrow, emerge as a big hero, and then they'll drop the bomb that it was the LOL, not FFF, that pulled this off.''

Kelleher stood up. Now *he* needed a drink. There was no way Jamelle Tourretta was going to pull this off. Or was there? Just thinking about what she'd done—and was planning to do—made him feel queasy.

"Right now there are only two people," he said slowly, "who know enough to stop Tourretta from pulling this off.''

"You and me.''

"Exactly. Which means we have to do something to protect ourselves before they come after us.''

"You think they have to kill us?''

"Maybe they're going to wait until they knock off the two shooters. Or maybe they'll take care of all four of us at the same time. But it'll happen.''

He held up the scotch bottle to ask if she wanted more. She shook her head. "So what do we do?'' she asked.

He sat back down on the couch. "Well, the most obvious answer is to go to the cops. But it may be that we aren't completely safe doing that. We don't know who or how many of them are involved. I think there's really only one way to get this over with once and for all.''

"And that is?''

"Put the story in the newspaper, just like you told it to me here. Once it's all out in public, Tourretta probably won't be able to get rid of the two shooters. Even if she does, we'll have the FBI protection by then and her plan to turn all this on the LOL will be finished.''

"Do you think you could get the story past your lawyers?''

He moved closer to her on the couch and gently put a hand around her neck. "Only if you go on the record. No anonymous source. You, Andrea Kyler, telling the whole story.''

She sighed and looked into his eyes. "If I do that, the *best* thing that happens is I go to jail as a conspirator in the original plot and as an accessory for my silence the last few days.''

"That's all true. But what's the worst thing that happens if you *don't* talk?''

She looked at him quizzically, then said, "We die?''

"Bingo.''

She put her head on his shoulder. "What is a nice girl like me doing in a place like this?'' She pulled her head up. "There really isn't any choice, is there?''

He shrugged. "Andrea, I'm not real big on melodrama but this isn't just the safe thing to do, it's the right thing to do. There's a bloodbath going on here. We can end it before it gets bloodier."

"I hate what Jamelle has done to FFF. It was an important group."

"It may be again someday. But only after she's taken out of the picture."

She nodded her head, tried to talk, but could only make sobbing noises. Kelleher put his arms around her and held her, feeling her racked with tears. After a few minutes, she said, "Stay here tonight?"

He responded by kissing her, gently at first, then emotionally, the two of them clutching and grabbing. He picked her up—a bit clumsily because of the cast—to carry her into the bedroom, and Ann Roberts flashed through his mind. For a split second, he felt guilty, but she was unbuckling his belt even as his mind was back in Charlottesville. The vision disappeared and he unzipped her dress, slid out of his pants, and rolled onto the bed with her.

They both screamed with relief and ecstasy the first time. After that, it was quieter, full of the kind of intensity that comes when two people sense that this may be an ending rather than a beginning. Kelleher finally fell into a deep sleep, dreaming he had called Ann Roberts to confess what he had done. She started to cry and wouldn't stop.

He woke up, staring at the ceiling, and said to himself, "fucking egomaniac." He looked at the clock by the bed: five twenty-two A.M. Next to him, Andrea was sleeping soundly. He fell asleep again, so heavily that when he woke he had the sense for a minute that he had dreamed the entire evening, that Andrea had never really poured out the whole story. He looked at the clock again to confirm where he was. It was almost seven-thirty. He rolled over to wake Andrea and—déjà vu—found the bed empty.

She never finishes what she starts, he thought and pulled himself out of bed. He put his pants on and headed for the kitchen, expecting to find a note. Sure enough, it was there in the same spot.

Kelleher:
Sorry, I did it again. This time I really *do* have a staff meeting, honest injun. Write the story. It's the right thing to do. Stay out of dark alleys today; no need to be heroic. Call me later . . .

Andrea

He wondered if he should call Gordy's office to be sure she had really gone there. No, he thought, bad move. But a moment later he was dialing the phone. The worst move at this point would be to get careless.

"Governor's office. Trooper Stern."

Damn, Kelleher thought, what was that SOB doing back upstairs?

"Andrea Kyler, please," he said, sounding as casual as possible.

"She's in a meeting with the governor. Can I take a message?"

Kelleher thought about that for a moment. He wondered if Stern had *seen* Kyler go into the meeting or had just been told she was in there.

"No, no message," he said. "But you actually saw her go into this meeting, right?"

"Who is this?"

"Tim Maloney, Prince Georges chairman. I'm supposed to meet with her in a little while and I wanted to be sure she was there."

"Oh yeah, right, Delegate Maloney, okay, sorry. I thought you were one of those asshole reporters. She went in thirty minutes ago. I'll tell her you called when she comes out."

"Fine." Kelleher figured if Andrea was baffled by that message, so what? If he told Stern not to give her the message, he might start blathering. He hung up, feeling clever for having outwitted his pal Stern. Of course, outwitting Stern was not exactly grounds for a Pulitzer nomination.

More important than any byplay with Stern was the simple fact that the deed was all but done. The bad guys were going to be caught and he was finally going to have The Big Hit. This morning's story had been a good, solid hit. Tomorrow would be the big one. *The Washington Herald* would break the story on the murder of Barney Paulsen and help send the killers to jail. Stories didn't get too much better than that.

He had a sudden urge to call Ann Roberts and tell her what was going on but he stopped himself. For one thing, that wouldn't be a good idea, blabbing *this* story around. For another, he didn't feel like explaining to her how he had come to get the story. He still had some serious sorting out to do about his feelings for Ann and Andrea. He was as confused now as he had ever been.

If he couldn't tell Ann, he could at least tell his partner. He would insist that they co-byline the story. After all, they'd worked on it together from the beginning. She had been too good a friend for too long for him to even think about not sharing this with her. He started to call her, then decided to walk back to the Marriott and tell her in person.

He pulled his clothes on, raced out the door, and almost killed himself trying to run down the steps, which were now coated with snow and an underlayer of ice. It had snowed most of the night; Annapolis was covered in white. A white Oz. He didn't even feel the cold as he waltzed down Main Street to the hotel.

Oz was his again. He could leave it now with no regrets. Well, one regret: Alan Sims. The only business left undone was finding out who had called Sims on Sunday night. If there was anyone he wanted to come face-to-face with, it was that person. Whomever it was had to have been someone Sims considered a friend; that made it that much more sickening.

He walked into the Marriott lobby and saw McGuire standing at the front desk. She had her coat on. "You going out?"

"Just getting back. I went for a walk. I'm checking messages. So, which one was it last night?"

He smiled. "Andrea."

"Well, congratulations. I thought sure the blonde was a done deal. Was it worth your while?"

"More than you can imagine," he said, ignoring the chiding tone in her voice. "Let's get breakfast and I'll tell you."

They went upstairs to the restaurant and sat at a table overlooking the harbor. He told her the whole story—except for the part about going to bed with Andrea. She could figure that out on her own.

"You did it, Bobby," she said when he was finished, grinning broadly. "You really did it. You cracked the whole goddamn thing open! You're going to win the Pulitzer Prize!"

"Calm down," he said, playing her role for once. "Let's not get carried away. Anyway, *we're* going to win whatever we're going to win for this story because it's going to carry two bylines."

"Don't be silly. You broke it."

"Wrong. I couldn't have gotten it without you. I wouldn't have even survived this long at the newspaper without you and you know it." He reached across the table and grabbed her hand. "We were about to go down together on Saturday. Now we'll fly together tomorrow. No argument. We'll write it together."

She actually looked a little misty-eyed, something he'd never seen before. "Andrea's right about you," she said, wiping her eyes quickly as if he wouldn't notice. "You really *do* have potential. Let's go call Kryton and tell her."

They did exactly that, then walked to the State House for the morning sessions of the House and Senate. Yes, all was well in Oz. The wicked witch would be dead—or at least in police custody—soon. The good witch—Gordy—would reign as governor. Dorothy—Andrea—still had some problems to sort out, but he was sure they could be handled. And Kelleher and McGuire could live happily ever after.

Of course, Kelleher still had to figure out whom he wanted to live happily ever after with.

CHAPTER 13

BETTER READ THAN DEAD

Kelleher was so caught up in what he was going to write for Wednesday's paper that he completely forgot what he had written that morning—and the inevitable response to it. As soon as he walked into the House lounge, he was besieged by other writers wanting to talk to him about his experience in the Virginia woods. Part of him reveled in the attention; another part was tremendously uncomfortable with it. One of journalism's cardinal rules was that you don't ever become part of the story. In this case, he rationalized, he had no choice. When Kelleher heard Weiland gaveling the House to order he forced himself to play bad guy.

"I can't talk anymore now," he insisted. "I have to go to work."

Susan Sanders, who'd been standing at the back of the circle of reporters, approached him as the crowd broke. "You really weren't joking about that story, were you?" she said.

"Well, it was a fairly big deal," he said, not wanting to lie any more than he had to. He had already done enough of that the previous night.

"Will you come on camera for a couple of minutes after the House breaks?"

He owed her that one. She told him where her crew was located outside the building and he promised to show up after the House recessed for the morning. He had this sudden dread about what it was going to be like on Wednesday, after he and McGuire wrote *the* story. This one had been nothing compared with what they had now.

Walking into the chamber, he spotted Kenworthy and Frece sitting over by his rail.

"So, how's it feel to be a hero?" Kenworthy said.

"Two parts good reporting, four parts luck," Frece said.

"Luck?" he said, indignant.

"Of course, luck. If you weren't lucky enough to have Tourretta send someone to try to kill you, you couldn't have begun to write that story."

"And it wouldn't have that human drama element," Kenworthy put in.

"Fuck both you guys," he said, laughing. "I hope you get lucky enough to have someone try to kill you someday."

This was part of the ritual of the business: you never really congratulated another reporter on a big story; you just gave him enough of a hard time that he knew you were jealous as hell.

Kelleher settled himself onto the rail as Big Jim Immel rose to give his committee's report. How long had it been since Immel had stood up for Wendell Hoxledeer and gotten Kelleher all excited? A week? A month? A year? It felt longer. He wondered if he would ever be able to get excited about the goings-on of the legislature again. After the past six days, it all seemed so mundane.

"By the way, hotshot, I've got a scoop for you," Kenworthy whispered as Immel began reading bills.

"What's that?"

"Your little blond friend from Baltimore didn't stay lonely for long after you ran out last night."

"Who?"

"Benroove."

"Oh, come on, tell me anything, but not that."

"He was back at the table about twelve seconds after you left. Twelve seconds after that, they were on the dance floor. Maybe fifteen minutes after that they were walking out the door."

"Guess I broke her heart, huh?"

Kenworthy laughed. "Well, you could make the case, I suppose, that you drove her over the edge."

"Good point. At least I saved some poor page from the guy."

No one was listening to Immel as he finished up. The floor was full of life, people standing in little knots, whispering. Kelleher could see a number of delegates holding the *Herald,* showing one another his story, he imagined.

McGuire came into the chamber just before the House broke. "Nothing cooking with any of the Senate committees?" he asked.

She shook her head. "Not a thing," she said. "I just talked to Tommy Wyman. He said the FBI thinks it has a bead on Tourretta."

"Where is she?"

"In New York somewhere. They think they may have her in custody before this evening."

"Which would mean we could tie the whole thing together tonight."

"If we're lucky. We need to get an early start on this. Why don't you make a quick sweep of the House committees after lunch, and I'll check out the Senate for a while. Then we'll meet back in the office."

"Fine. What's lunch?"

"Bob Bonnell. It's a date I made last week. No way out of it."

Bob Bonnell was Myron Cutler's administrative aide. He was the *Herald*'s best source—specifically McGuire's best source—when it came to Cutler and the Senate.

"No problem," he said. "I'll just grab a sandwich and eat in the office."

She shook her head. "I don't think that's such a good idea. As far as we know, you're still in danger. Don't spend any time alone. You can't eat with Kenworthy and Frece, 'cause you'll want to blab the whole story. Do your celebrity thing, then take one of these guys to lunch. I'm sure you'll have no problem finding someone looking to eat for free."

There was little doubt about that. Legislators were notorious for their willingness to accept freebies—from anybody. When it was time to eat, many of them went in search of a "sponsor," usually a lobbyist or a reporter who was willing to buy them an expense account meal. It was a great deal for everyone: the lobbyist charges his clients, the reporter charges his newspaper, and everyone eats for free.

Weiland gaveled the House into recess and Kelleher was immediately surrounded again. He answered questions for ten minutes, then excused himself. He found Mike Allen standing next to him. Allen was Gordy's press secretary, a short, nervous man who redefined the word *neurotic*. Allen was not only afraid to fly—in a business that demanded it—he also didn't like *driving*. With Gordy moving up the ladder, Allen, who appeared overmatched before, was now well over his head.

"Governor Gordy wants to know if you can come up and have lunch with her," Allen said to Kelleher.

Kelleher smiled. He would certainly be safe enough up there.

"Give me fifteen minutes," he said. "I have to go do a quick TV interview."

"But . . ." Allen spluttered as Kelleher walked away.

He went outside, found Sanders, and did his two-minute bit—resisting the urge to bring up Benroove's name. Why act like he cared? His ego could handle the bruise. He left Sanders, walked back inside, and found Mike Allen waiting at the bottom of the steps.

"This is easier than you having to fight your way through all the security," Allen said. "They're sweeping the House right now just to make sure there aren't any stray guns or weapons lying around."

Allen maneuvered him through all the various checkpoints and troopers, then walked him in through the back door to the governor's suite—the one Kelleher had made his unceremonious dive through on Saturday. Kelleher was surprised when he walked in to find Gordy alone. He had expected Andrea to be there, too.

"Andrea coming?"

"Working on the speech," Gordy said. "We're also trying to figure out what's going to happen to her after your story comes out."

"She told you?"

"Everything. I was disappointed in her but relieved she didn't know anything about the plan to murder Barney."

"You believe her, then."

Gordy nodded. "I do. She's not a criminal. She knows she has to resign, but she feels good that telling the truth should bring this nightmare to an end finally."

"I sure hope so," Kelleher said, sitting down. There was a plate heaped high with cold cuts on the table in front of the fireplace. "So, Governor, what's up?"

"Nothing," she said, shrugging. "I just figured this was as safe a place for you to have lunch as any. Until your story's on the street, there may still be some danger."

"You and Maureen really *do* think alike," he said.

She laughed. "Speaking of the women in your life, what do you think will happen with you and Andrea now?"

"I honestly don't know the answer to that, Meredith," he said finally, putting together a roast beef sandwich. "I think we both have strong feelings for each other but I think we need some time. The past six days haven't been the best environment for romance."

"That's a good point," she said.

Gordy stood up, went to the pantry, and returned with two mugs of coffee. "So what do you do after all this is over?"

"I'm not sure," he said. "Maybe the paper'll promote me to the national staff. I don't think I can cover the legislature again. If they don't promote me, I don't know. Maybe I'll go to law school or something. Try to learn a real skill."

Gordy laughed. "You in law school? Get serious. Bobby Kelleher, if there's any human being who was put on this earth to be a reporter, it's you. You live for all this. If they didn't have newspapers, you'd go door to door screaming at people, 'Hey, did you hear what happened in Annapolis today!' "

Kelleher grinned at that notion. "I suppose you're right. Sometimes, though, it gets so frustrating. Not now, of course, but some of the time. . . ."

Gordy stood up. "You find a job that doesn't have frustrations, call me," she said. She walked to her desk and sat down. "Go back and write that story. And tomorrow, when the network shows call you, don't forget you knew me when."

He laughed and stood to go. "I'll see you tonight," he said. "Remember, I have to knock on everyone's door and tell them all about your speech when it's over."

She rolled her eyes. "Talk about the sublime and the ridiculous all in one day . . . You get to break the story on Barney's murder on the one hand and you get to tell people that Meredith Gordy pledged to carry out Barney Paulsen's legislative package on the other. What a day!"

"Meredith, if I were the reporter you say I am, I'd use that quote."

He thanked her for lunch and left. It was time for the House committees to begin meeting, so that's where Kelleher headed.

At the House office building he walked down the long hallway on the first floor, checking the committee rooms. There were six House committees and they all met on the first floor. The delegates' offices were on the second, third, and fourth floors. All around him, Kelleher saw the faces of Annapolis: the lobbyists, the staff members, the hangers-on who showed up to testify on nearly every bill that came up for a public hearing.

There were actually people who did just that, spent ninety days wandering from committee room to committee room exercising their right to express their opinion on any and all legislation that came before the Maryland legislature. Kelleher had been tempted to do a story on them but always backed off because doing it would mean he would actually have to *talk* to those people. He couldn't stand the thought.

For no reason at all, Kelleher walked into the back of the Judiciary Committee's hearing room. Ellen Feiner was Kelleher's favorite committee chairman. She was from Brooklyn, a classic New Yorker with a New Yorker's sense of humor. Whenever Kelleher was really bored he just walked into Judiciary and wrote down Ellen Feiner one-liners.

Kelleher sat down in the back row, rather than make himself conspicuous by walking up to the press table, and listened as a middle-aged woman explained why a bill that would make a one-year jail sentence mandatory for anyone convicted of drunk driving was a good idea.

Kelleher was about to get up and leave when Morgan Lamont slid into the seat next to him. Lamont was the highest-paid lobbyist in Annapolis, making about $750,000 per session. Kelleher believed that Lamont would lobby in favor of shooting first-graders who were late for school if someone paid him to do it. He was a pretty good source, but Kelleher didn't have the stomach to suck up to him. He left that to McGuire, who could get Lamont to tell her anything by merely saying good morning to him. Kelleher wished he could escape but Lamont had seated himself in the corner and he was trapped.

"Well, Kelleher, I never figured a hero like you would be reduced to covering this stuff on the day of his big scoop," Lamont said.

"Yeah, well, that's the way it is, Lamont," Kelleher said.

Lamont smiled. "You aren't listening to any of this. Why are you here?"

"More important, why are *you* here?"

"Next bill," he said. "They're trying to make automobile dealerships include in their advertising how many cars they have available at an advertised price. You know, they say nine thousand nine hundred and ninety-nine dollars and then you get there and there's one car at that price with no radio and no air-conditioning and everything else on the lot is fifteen grand."

"Sounds like a good bill to me," Kelleher said. "You can't possibly be here to try to pass it?"

Lamont shook his head. "You know me better than that. I'm here for the automobile guys."

"Of course. You're here to kill it."

"Already *have* killed it," Lamont corrected, grinning. "I've got all the votes I need with two to spare. This is just a formality."

"Jesus, Lamont, you are amazing. What are you getting paid, fifteen grand for buying a couple of these sleazeballs dinner?"

"Twenty-five," Lamont said. He loved to brag about his fees. And why not? They were a matter of public record anyway.

"Well," Kelleher said, "before you get up there and make me nauseated, I'm getting out of here."

If Lamont was insulted, he didn't show it. "I'd get out of here too if I were you," he said. "Before that Tourretta broad shows up and kicks the shit out of you for saying she killed Barney."

Kelleher laughed. "I don't think she's likely to show up here."

Lamont shrugged. "Maybe not. But she may sue the hell out of you now that those two guys who did the shooting have turned up dead."

Kelleher sat up very straight. "What two guys? What are you talking about?"

Lamont smiled, pleased he knew something Kelleher didn't. "You didn't hear about this? It was on the radio. The second and third shooters turned up dead this morning near the Inner Harbor in Baltimore. Double suicide, the cops think, and . . ."

"There was a note," Kelleher interrupted. "Saying they killed themselves because they blew the whole thing by not killing Gordy, too."

"I didn't hear about the note," Lamont said. "But you did know about it, then?"

"Right, yeah, I did," Kelleher said, standing up and pushing past Lamont. He could feel himself sweating profusely. The plan was in full swing now and Tourretta and friends weren't far away. Baltimore was a thirty-minute drive from Annapolis. They could be here right now for all he knew.

It took him five minutes to half walk, half run back to the office. Every few steps he swiveled his head to make sure no one was behind him. His heart was racing. McGuire was waiting for him when he walked in.

"You heard?" she said, seeing the look on his face.

"Yeah. You talk to the desk?"

"Uh-huh. I told them what Andrea said, that this is all part of the plan."

"What did the note say?" Kelleher asked.

McGuire shook her head. "That's the one strange thing. The note just says, We deserve to die. The cops say it's a double suicide, but they aren't pinning anything on the LOL just yet."

Kelleher sat down in his chair. Tourretta was smarter than he had thought. "If they spell it all out in the note, maybe everyone gets suspicious," he said. "This way, they make it harder. Eventually, though, everyone figures out they were in it with Dumont and killed themselves because they didn't carry out their mission."

"But who killed Dumont then, if the cops decide it wasn't Tourretta?"

"I haven't figured that one out yet," he said. "But I'll bet Tourretta has."

McGuire nodded. "In any case, we better start writing. This thing is going to be pretty tough to explain."

He picked up the phone. "I know that. I want to call Andrea, just to make sure she knows what's going on. If the two shooters are dead, we must be next."

"Good idea," McGuire said. She walked across the room, locked and bolted the door.

He called Andrea's office but was told she'd gone to a late lunch. He left a message, then called her apartment and left a message on her tape telling her to call him immediately.

He sat down to write and found that his hands were shaking. Why? He really didn't expect Jamelle Tourretta to come charging in here, gun drawn. Her plan—whatever it was—had to be more subtle than that. She couldn't *possibly* pull this thing off. He knew that—but did *she*? Apparently not. She was evidently still trying.

He began playing with different leads: "The death of Maryland Governor Barnard A. Paulsen was part of a complicated plot designed not only to make Meredith Gordy governor, but also to lay the blame for the killing on the extremist right-wing group Lovers of Life," Kelleher wrote. "Gordy, who succeeded Paulsen last Thursday, knew nothing of the plot, launched by Jamelle Tourretta, executive director of the radical feminist group Females for Freedom."

McGuire, who'd been on the phone, looked over his shoulder. "Good," she said. "Perfect."

"Who were you talking to?" he asked.

"Bearnarth," she said. "He's putting special protection on Andrea right away. And he wants you to be sure not to go anyplace alone in the meantime."

"I promise," he said, meaning it. His heart was still racing.

Kelleher was jumpy the rest of the afternoon. Every time the phone rang he hoped it was the cops saying they had Tourretta. Most of the time, it was the office, wanting to know when they could see a lead. Kelleher wrote the story through once—it was more than three thousand words long—then he and McGuire went through it paragraph by paragraph, making sure the picture was complete and that there was no confusion in anyone's mind about who all the various players were. He still hadn't heard from Kyler.

Just after four o'clock there was a knock on the door. Kelleher froze. McGuire went to get it. "Find out who it is," he hissed.

"Who is it?" she asked.

"Federal Express."

Sure it was, Kelleher thought. "Tell them to leave it there at the door," he said. "They have our signatures on file."

McGuire repeated that request. Kelleher looked out the window. There was a Federal Express truck parked outside. Still, that didn't necessarily mean anything. "The guy's gone," McGuire said, staring out the peephole."

"Be careful," he said. "There might be someone else waiting in the hall."

She opened the door, picked up the envelope, giggled, and walked back into his office. "It's from your friend in Charlottesville," she said, tossing him the envelope.

Of course. It was the tape Ann had promised to send. Kelleher opened the envelope. There was a note attached to the tape.

> Bobby:
> See if you agree this guy's telling the truth. You were always good about stuff like that. I've checked our Dumont files, just for the heck of it. Did you know that he was once arrested for trying to break up an FFF rally three years ago? Might be worth checking him out some more. By the way, Chris Mills called me *twice* last night. You don't owe me *one*, you owe me about *six*. *Be careful!*
>
> Love,
> Ann

Kelleher smiled as he read the note. Maybe tomorrow he would have time to check Dumont out a little more, but he had a feeling it wouldn't matter. Still, he appreciated Ann trying. And he did owe her a lot more than one.

"Advice for the lovelorn?" McGuire asked.

"Cute. She says Dumont once broke up an FFF rally. You think that could mean something?"

"It means Dumont didn't like FFF. But that's hardly a scoop. Come on, let's finish this."

They went back to work and, by five o'clock, they had a story Kelleher thought they could be proud to put their names on. It laid out the entire plot in painstaking detail. "I have to admit," he said as they were sending it into the paper, "that I'd feel a hell of a lot better if Tourretta were in custody."

"She will be soon," McGuire said. "After our story shows up tomorrow morning . . ."

She was interrupted by the phone. Kelleher picked it up. It was Andrea. "Where have you been?" he asked, slightly annoyed that she'd taken this long to get back to him.

"It's been crazy," she said. "Did you write the story?"

"Just finished it."

"Including the part about the two shooters turning up dead?"

"You bet."

"Can I see it? After all, it is my political obituary."

He grimaced at that. "Sure you can. Why don't you come by here? Or I can bring it with me to the speech tonight."

"I have a better idea. Why don't you bring it by my apartment?"

"You mean after the speech?"

"I mean now."

Kelleher frowned. Something was going on here. He could understand Andrea being interested in what the story said, but they both knew that being alone together now—with Tourretta still on the loose—was a bad idea. And yet, she was suggesting it.

He wanted to think that she was just being naive but he knew that was impossible. She just wasn't that way. So he stalled.

"We still have to hang here for a few more minutes while the lawyers read this thing," he said. "Why don't I call you back when we're done?"

"I'll be right here," she said.

He hung up and looked at Maureen, who had been scrolling through the story on the computer screen, but listening to the conversation too. "What's the deal?" she asked.

"I don't know, but something's up," he said. "She wants me to come by the apartment and show her the story now. The whole thing screams *trap* at me."

Maureen picked up the phone and began dialing. "That's exactly what it sounds like to me," she said. "Let's see what Bearnarth thinks. Meantime, you call the office and find out what the deal is with the lawyers. Jane said they have some questions already.''

Kelleher knew that was inevitable. Having a story lawyered was always a nightmare. The questions usually were of the ''Are you sure the sun set in the west?'' variety. Still, he knew on a story like this they had to be dealt with. He dialed Kryton, who put Chris Jones, the ultimate Yalie WASP lawyer type, on the phone, and for the next fifteen minutes they wrestled. By the time they were finished, McGuire was off the phone with Bearnarth.

''What'd he say?'' Kelleher asked, happy to be rid of Jones.

''He agrees that it sounds like something is up,'' she said. ''The problem is, there's really only one way to find out for sure.''

''Go over there.''

''You got it. Larry says if you don't want to, they can just go themselves and tell Andrea you were suspicious. Without a warrant, though, they can't search the place to see if Tourretta or any of the others are there.''

''But if I go in and don't come out after a few minutes, they can show up guns drawn, so to speak.''

McGuire shook her head. ''The more I think about it, the less I like it. What if you walk into an ambush or something? There might not be time for the cops to arrive.''

''Not likely,'' he said. ''Tourretta's too smart to just start shooting people in the middle of a residential neighborhood. She'll have something more clever than that cooked up.''

They looked at each other. He shrugged. ''Call Bearnarth back and tell him we'll give it a shot. As long as I know the cops are right outside, I don't mind going over there.''

''You sure?''

''No, but I'm too curious not to. I also want to find out what the hell Andrea is up to. I thought she was playing straight with me this morning.''

''Only one way to find out, I guess.''

Kelleher dialed the apartment. Andrea answered on the second ring. ''I'm having a little trouble with the desk,'' he said. ''The lawyers are screwing around. No big deal. I just need a few minutes extra.''

''Fine,'' she said. ''Take your time. I'm not going anywhere.''

He was glad to hear that. He hung up in time to hear McGuire saying, ''Okay, fine, we'll do it that way.''

She hung up. ''So, what's he say?''

"He's going to have the place staked out. His men will be there within ten minutes. You go over there. I'll call you, let's say about five minutes after you arrive, and say the desk just called with a question I couldn't answer. If you come to the phone and say, 'Hi, Maureen, what's up?' I'll know you're fine, there's no trap, and there are cops outside watching the place. If you say, 'What's the problem?' I'll know you're in trouble. At that point, the cops, as they say in the old westerns, surround the place."

Kelleher took a deep breath. This was getting more frightening by the moment. "Bearnarth really thinks this will work?" he said. "What if it's an ambush? What if someone just takes a shot at me going in?"

McGuire shrugged. "He does. But we can always just call him back and have him send his guys in now."

Kelleher didn't want that. If the cops went bursting into Andrea's apartment, she would take that to mean he didn't trust her. More important, this might be their best chance to flush Tourretta out.

"Okay," he said. "Let's do it Bearnarth's way. It'll take me five minutes to get there. You call me in ten."

He walked to the printer in the corner of the room and picked up the printout they had automatically made when they had finished the story—just in case the computer glitched in sending. He folded it up and stuck it into his jacket pocket.

"Wish me luck," he said.

She put her hands on his shoulders. "Don't worry about a thing," she said. "It's all going to be over soon."

He walked out onto the street and was hit in the face by the wind. First thing tomorrow, he told himself, he was going to buy a coat. Enough was enough.

He walked around the circle to King George Street and turned to walk the half block downhill to Andrea's apartment. He was trembling when he reached the bottom of the steps, and he knew it wasn't from the cold. His lips were dry and his heart was racing—again.

He paused on the street and looked around. No one. Had Bearnarth sent his men over? They were probably just staying out of sight. He stalled a moment longer, then started gingerly up the steps, remembering his near-fall on the way down that morning.

At the top of the steps, he knocked twice on the sliding glass door. Andrea pulled the curtain back to look to see who it was. Then, slowly, she opened the door.

"Hi, there, remember me . . ."

He never finished the sentence because suddenly, she pushed him, saying, "Go, go, run . . ."

Before Kelleher could respond, someone reached from behind Andrea, grabbed him by the lapels, and viciously yanked him into the apartment. He rolled over, started to scramble to his feet, but stopped and froze when he saw a gun two inches from his mouth.

Kelleher squinted for a second, then looked past the gun to the person holding it: Trooper B. D. Stern.

"Nice to see you again, asshole," Stern said.

Kelleher almost laughed out loud. If there was anyone he was delighted to have turn out to be a bad guy it was Stern. Delight turned to fear, however, as he quickly realized what was going on.

Behind him, a voice came from the hallway. "Welcome, Mr. Kelleher. It's nice to see you again."

He turned his head just far enough to see the speaker: Jamelle Tourretta.

Bearnarth had called it. Having carried out part one of her plan, Tourretta had come to Annapolis to carry out part two. Andrea, still sitting on the floor, too stunned to move, had been used to set him up. There was another woman with Tourretta. She was also in a police uniform. "You two met a couple of days ago in the woods," Tourretta said. "This is Trooper Roane. You were rude enough to steal her car."

Roane sat down on one of the bar stools. Roughly, Stern pulled Andrea off the floor and shoved her onto the couch. "You too," he said, pointing the gun at Kelleher again. "Sit over there with her."

Kelleher glanced at his watch. McGuire should be phoning any minute now. There was no reason to panic. He decided to repeat that to himself: No reason to panic. Right. "So, what now?" he asked Tourretta. He was glad to hear his voice was steady.

"If you'll be patient for a couple more minutes, Mr. Kelleher, you'll understand everything. That much I promise you."

Kelleher looked at Andrea, wishing he could tell her that the cavalry was just around the corner. Instead, he pulled the printout from his jacket pocket. "You might want to read that," he said to Tourretta, putting it on the coffee table.

She picked it up, looked at it for a moment, smiled, and tossed it back to him. "You write well," she said.

Kelleher had to give her points for staying cool. "That story's already in the computer system at *The Washington Herald*,'' he said, thinking she might have misunderstood. ''Nothing you do will keep it out of print.''

''I have no intention of doing anything about it,'' Tourretta said calmly.

There was a knock at the door. Kelleher didn't quite understand that. Surely the cops didn't think they could just walk in and ask everybody to put their hands up? Or did they?

Tourretta checked the curtains, smiled, and slid the door open. ''Right on time,'' she said.

Who could it be? Beth Bevans? Another cop involved with Tourretta?

A man with bleached-blond hair and a hard look stepped through the door and hugged Tourretta. ''Good job,'' he said to her. ''You did very well. Of course, so did our little friend here.''

Kelleher recognized the voice at the same instant the ''little friend'' he was talking about walked through the door. The double shock almost made him pass out: the voice belonged to Jimmy Dumont; the friend in question was Maureen McGuire.

━━ ━━

Kelleher was as close to speechless as he had ever been in his life. As soon as McGuire stepped inside, Tourretta slid the door closed. McGuire wouldn't look at him. She sat on one of the bar stools and stared blankly into space.

Kelleher forced himself to turn his attention to Dumont. His jet-black hair was almost white and considerably shorter than it had been. His beard was gone and he wore wire-rimmed glasses. If not for his voice, Kelleher would never have recognized him.

''Figured it out yet, Bobby boy?'' he asked with a nasty grin.

''You're dead,'' Kelleher said, too shocked to think of anything more to the point.

''Don't think so,'' Dumont said.

''The guy with the bullet in his head in Virginia?''

''Had all my identification on him. Driver's license, a couple of old credit cards, even my social security card. He was also built a lot like me and looked like me. No reason for the cops to do any ID check since it was obvious it *was* me.''

''But why?''

Dumont looked at his watch. ''We've got some time here, so there's no reason not to tell you. Jamelle, you get into the bedroom and start getting dressed, though.''

Tourretta nodded and headed for the bedroom. It was obvious to Kelleher, even in his dumbfounded state, that Dumont was in charge of this operation. He looked over at McGuire again. She was staring at the curtains. One thing Kelleher was now certain of: there sure as hell weren't any cops coming to the rescue.

"Okay, Bobby boy, from the top, here's the deal," Dumont said. "I'm afraid you won't live to tell this story but I want you to know it's nothing personal. If you hadn't shown up in the wrong places at the wrong times, you'd a been fine."

"Maureen," Kelleher said. She didn't answer or look at him. "Maureen," he repeated, very gently. Still no response.

"Maureen," Dumont said, "look in that refrigerator and see if there's something for me to drink." Shocked, Kelleher watched her go the kitchen and return with a Coke and a beer. Dumont took the Coke. McGuire still wouldn't look at Kelleher.

Dumont took a swig of his soda, looked at Kelleher, and said, "Be a reporter, Bobby boy, ask me the questions."

Kelleher was too bewildered to know what to ask. He wanted to know about Maureen, how the hell she could be involved in this. But he couldn't even bring himself to ask. He was afraid to even think about it, afraid he'd get physically ill. So he went back to the beginning. Concentrate on the facts. Try to make sense of things, he said to himself. Stay away from emotions. "This was your deal from the start, the LOL?"

"Right."

"Then you wanted to kill Paulsen *and* Gordy."

"Right again."

"But somebody missed Gordy."

"Just barely. But that's where all the fuckin' trouble began."

"Is Myron Cutler in on this, too?"

"Absolutely not," Dumont said. "He's a dues-paying member of the LOL but he doesn't know anything about any of this."

"And is 'this' all about making him governor?"

"Yup. We want to get SB one forty-four passed this year so he can sign it."

"SB one forty-four?" SB was short for Senate Bill. The number was familiar to Kelleher but he wasn't sure why.

"It's the bill Cutler's tried to pass the last two years that requires legislation separate from the governor's budget before any abortion funding can be authorized."

Kelleher remembered it now. The year before it had been SB 87. He'd done a story on it. It was Cutler and the right wing's backdoor play to take abortion funding out of Paulsen's hands. By forcing separate legislation, the conservatives could bring tremendous pressure to bear on legislators who didn't want a pro-choice label. Of course, as long as Paulsen was governor, the bill had no chance. Even if it passed both the House and Senate, he would have vetoed it. But if Cutler were governor . . .

"All this bloodshed is about SB one forty-four?" he asked incredulously. "All these people dead so you can make it harder for poor women to get abortions?"

Dumont stood up and stared menacingly at Kelleher. "I don't expect you to understand what this is about, Bobby boy. But even you know that right to life is about a lot more than poor women and abortions."

No sense arguing, Kelleher thought. He had always tried to stay away from the pro-life fanatics who came to the legislature every year to lobby against abortion funding. Dumont was no different from them—except he was *really* crazy.

"So what happened after you *didn't* get Gordy?"

"What happened was that you had the misfortune to recognize me. I found out you were coming to Charlottesville looking for me but didn't count on your girlfriend bopping me on the head. Jamelle didn't realize you'd be smart enough to bring her with you. We'd already decided I had to be 'killed' to take you off the scent. I would have already been gone and dead before you got there if things had worked out. But they didn't. Jamelle was still in the process of finding someone to play me."

"So when you turned up dead, it looked like Tourretta killed you and that pointed the finger at FFF. Just to be sure, you paid Chris Mills to convince me someone saw her carrying you out of the room. You had to try to get rid of me and Alan Sims because we knew too much and might figure that out at some point."

"Right you are, Bobby boy." God, Kelleher hated the taunting tone to his voice. "Only Trooper Roane here and Wendy Paul botched the job on you."

"Okay, I understand all of that," Kelleher said. "But what the hell are you planning now? You kill Andrea and me and blame that on FFF, too?"

"That's the easy part," Dumont said. "The tougher part is getting rid of Gordy."

Kelleher's eyes went wide. "Wait a minute. You're still planning to kill Meredith?"

"We sure as shit are."

Kelleher laughed. "You've got no chance. The security in there is airtight."

"It sure is, Bobby boy. Only a fool would try to walk in there with a gun tonight."

Kelleher thought about that one for a split second and then it came to him. They'd done it again. Somehow, they had already gotten a gun inside the chamber.

"There's a gun in there already," Kelleher said, knowing he was stating the obvious. "But how?"

In reply, Dumont nodded toward McGuire, who was still immobile on the bar stool. "I think it's time your friend Maureen tells you her part in all this. But make it quick," he said to her. "We don't have much time."

McGuire barely moved her lips. "You tell him," she said tonelessly. "I don't have anything to say."

Kelleher started to get up off the couch because he wanted to grab her and shake her but Stern, standing a few feet away with the gun still in his hand, made it clear such a move would not be tolerated.

"I'd like to hear it from you, Maureen," he said to her and with that McGuire finally looked at him. Her eyes were red, her face blotchy. "I don't think I can, Bobby," she said.

"Try," he told her, the word coming out firmer than he intended.

She took a deep breath and glanced at Dumont. He shrugged as if to say, Do what you want. McGuire got off the bar stool, picked up one of the chairs that went with the couch, and pulled it over so she could sit right across from Kelleher.

"There isn't time to tell you the whole story in a way so you can begin to understand what I've done," she said. "No version will justify it anyway."

"Try," he said again. "You owe me *that* much."

"She doesn't owe you a fucking thing, Bobby boy," Dumont sneered, returning from the kitchen. "But if you want to tell him, Mo, go ahead."

Kelleher felt slightly sick when Dumont called her Mo. The only other person who ever called McGuire that was her brother Mike.

McGuire sighed. "I was never involved with these people," she said, waving her hand to indicate Stern and the rest. "My involvement's with Jimmy."

"What!" Kelleher screamed. "You and him? No way, Maureen, I'm not buying that. . . ."

She held up a hand as a way of stopping his hysterics. "Hear me out," she said. "You've got the wrong idea. This wasn't a matter of choice."

"What the hell does that mean?"

"He's my brother."

Kelleher moved his lips to try to respond to that one but nothing came out of his mouth. Jimmy Dumont was Maureen McGuire's brother? He looked at both of them, searching for family resemblance. If it was there, he couldn't find it. Maybe somehow she meant something else.

"What do you mean, exactly, by 'brother'?" he finally managed to say.

"Usual thing, Bobby boy," Dumont answered with a laugh. "Same mom; different pop. I grew up using my real father's name. My mom remarried after she and my dad split and had Maureen and Mike. If you look real close, we've got the same eyes."

Kelleher stared for a moment but still picked up nothing. Recovering, he turned on McGuire again. "That still doesn't explain getting involved in something like this—unless you're as crazy as he is."

"You're right," she said. "I never intended getting involved. I never really saw Jimmy after he dropped out of UVA, after the cross-burning stuff. Every once in a while our mother would hear from him, looking for money, but that was it.

"Then, when I started to have some success as a reporter, he started calling me every once in a while. He never asked me for money once he became a bigwig in LOL, but he asked for information, like advance notice on where FFF or NOW or Planned Parenthood was planning a convention or meeting or what hotel a politician was staying in during a campaign stop.

"I knew he was up to subversive stuff, breaking up rallies, dirty tricks and all, and I would try to put him off. But he was always making these veiled threats about what might happen to my career if people found out we were brother and sister, even half-brother and -sister."

"What did you think would happen?"

"What do *you* think would happen? You know how our business is. I would have been finished forever as a political reporter. They'd have said I couldn't cover conservatives because my half-brother was a radical right-winger and I might be too close to him. If I said I couldn't stand what he stood for, the conservatives would label me a liberal.

"Even if I said, 'Look, I've hardly spoken to the guy for ten years,' I would have been reduced to covering acid rain or something equally exciting.''

"So that's why you insisted on checking up on Dumont's family. You didn't want me doing it because I probably would have found out the truth.''

She took a deep breath and nodded.

"So all of this was to protect your goddamn career? You think that's some kind of fucking excuse?''

"It excuses nothing. To use a Kelleher phrase, I fucked up. Big-time. The only thing I can say is that for a long time nothing bad ever came of the information I gave him.''

"Until now.''

"Until now.''

"What was it?''

"The map of the State House that told them exactly where the power switches were and how they could get to them. Jimmy called me about two months ago and said he needed me to get some maps from the state police. I told him no way, that whatever he was up to, that was too close to home and sounded too dangerous.

"He went into his routine about telling people at the newspaper he was my brother. This time, I stood up to him. I told him enough, I'm done. I told him I wasn't playing this game with him anymore.''

"And?''

"And he said, 'Fine, let's stop playing games. Let's get serious. You wouldn't want anything to happen to our little brother, would you?' ''

"Why the hell didn't you just go to the police?''

"That's a question I'll have to try to answer the rest of my life. But I panicked. I knew damn well that brother or no brother, Jimmy was capable of that kind of violence and so were his people. They would have killed Mike. I didn't want to live with that kind of fear. So I made a deal with him. I told him I'd get the map for him if he promised me he would never, ever call me again. I said whatever prank he was planning, if he pulled it off, I would turn him in the second he called me again.''

"And you figured it was just a prank he was planning?''

"Bobby, I swear to you, the absolute worst thing I imagined was nothing close to what they really did. I thought about giving Jimmy the map and then tipping Bearnarth, but he told me if I thought about double-crossing him there'd be hell to pay.

"So I got him the map. It wasn't very hard. I told Tommy Wyman I was working on a story on the history of the State House, that I needed a bunch of maps that showed where things were and when they were built, improved, remodeled. I ended up with about twenty-five maps. One of them was the one they needed."

"And you never figured they were up to something violent?" He was yelling, afraid he might start crying. He closed his eyes, forcing himself to remain calm. McGuire, who knew him so well, waited until he was under control before continuing.

"Not until a few minutes before Paulsen's speech, when I saw Jimmy walk into the building. I knew he never went on any of these escapades himself. Always sent people, ever since that FFF rally he was arrested at. Remember the story your friend Ann turned up? Jimmy got beaten up by the police there and he told me that would never happen to him again. When I saw him going up the steps to the gallery, I knew something big was up. But even then, I never figured murder.

"It was already five minutes to two, though. The only person I could find to try to warn was Andrea. I tried to tell her she had to find a way to postpone the speech, to keep Paulsen and Gordy out of the chamber."

Kelleher's mind suddenly flashed back to the day of the shooting and the sight of McGuire and Kyler in animated conversation at the top of the steps. He had thought it was a routine political conversation. Never had he been more wrong in his life.

"Obviously, Andrea didn't listen," he said, glancing at Kyler.

"I thought she was onto something involving Jamelle and Paulsen," Andrea said. "That's why I put her off. I just wanted to get the speech over with."

Kelleher turned back to McGuire. "And you knew nothing about Tour-retta and . . ." It was hard for him to say, ". . . your brother?"

"Nothing. She played me for a fool for years. Just like everyone else, I guess. I found out she was involved the next morning."

"At the same meeting Andrea was at?"

"No, absolutely not. Andrea didn't know I had anything to do with this until just now. After Barney was shot, I couldn't find Jimmy. He got the hell out of there right after the shooting. I called him, left a message telling him I knew he'd done this and I was going to the cops."

"Why didn't you do it right away? Why didn't you tell *me*, at least?"

"Panic, I guess. Hysteria. I was going to do it, I just needed to think about how—and what it would mean. But when I got back to the hotel after I left you that first night, there was a message from Jamelle. I called her; she told me she had to see me right away. I said impossible, it was four o'clock in the morning. She then said, 'Maureen, I don't think you understand what's going on here. If you don't come and meet me right now, your brother will be dead before the sun comes up. And if you try to call the police, he'll be dead before they get to Mike's apartment.'

"I couldn't take a chance. I went and met with her. That's when I found out she was involved with Jimmy. She told me the two shooters who worked with Jimmy that day were outside Mike's apartment. If I went to the cops, Mike would end up dead and I'd end up in jail as an accessory to murder, which I clearly had become. She also told me I had one more job to do for them and then they'd leave me alone forever."

"And you *believed* that crap?"

She didn't answer.

"So what was this 'last' job?"

"It was *two* jobs. Get Jimmy a press ID card so he could get on the floor tonight. And they told me if you didn't show up here by six o'clock tonight, Mike would be dead."

Kelleher was pouring sweat by now. McGuire had trapped herself. She hadn't wanted the whole thing to become ugly. Now, it had gone way beyond ugly. And if Dumont and Tourretta pulled this thing off tonight, it wouldn't end here for McGuire, that much he knew for sure.

McGuire got up from the chair and walked to the sliding glass door; she stood there with her back to Kelleher. Dumont, who had listened to the whole story from the bar stool, walked up behind her and put a hand on her shoulder.

"Don't feel bad, little sister," he said. "It's almost over now."

Violently, she pushed his hand away. "Fuck you, Jimmy," she said. At least she and Kelleher could agree on that.

Dumont just laughed his loud, cackling laugh and walked back to the bar stool.

"One more question," Kelleher said, dreading the answer. "Who made the call to Sims?"

McGuire hung her head.

"*Jesus*, Maureen, *Jesus!*" he screamed.

"I had a choice," she said, her voice pleading for some sort of under-standing. "You and Alan or Mike."

"Bullshit. That's bullshit and you know it. Why didn't you go to Bearnarth?"

"How?! They were watching me every minute. The minute I contacted him, they would have been after Mike. That's why they kept the two shooters alive until today. I knew they were watching him the whole time."

"So you just gave up."

There were tears in her eyes now. "I didn't give up. I made a choice, Bobby. I got into something I couldn't get myself out of."

"And you still aren't out of it," he said. "You think this is the end, even if they pull this off?"

Before she could answer, Tourretta came back into the room. She was wearing a strapless black dress slit up the left leg almost to her hip, and matching high-heeled pumps.

She shook her head at McGuire. "Purging yourself, Maureen? Have you told him yet how we're going to, as he puts it, 'pull this off' tonight?"

"There isn't time for that," Dumont said, standing up. "It's almost seven o'clock. Bobby boy, I'm sorry to bring this little session to an end, but we've got to get going."

Kelleher looked at Andrea, whose eyes were wide with fear. He felt the same way. Were they going to kill them right now? Right here?

"Hang on," he said, stalling, although he had no idea what he was stalling for. "At least tell me what you're going to do."

Dumont shrugged. "Simple, really. There are two guards posted in the subbasement outside the main control room, as a precaution because of what happened last week." He nodded toward Tourretta. "I think Jamelle can handle them, don't you?"

"How will she get down there?"

"Beth Bevans gets her inside the building, then escorts her to the elevator. The rest she takes care of."

"So she pulls the lights again. But there's no way your shooter will get out of the gallery this time even if you already have the gun planted."

Dumont smiled. "Gun isn't in the gallery. It's taped underneath one of the desks where all you reporters sit. And I'll be sitting in that seat when the speech starts. The lights go out, I grab the gun, shoot Gordy from no more than twenty feet away, drop the gun, and calmly walk out the back door in the confusion, never to be seen again. If someone does figure it out, guess who they'll be looking for? A mysterious reporter from the *Herald*. Jimmy Dumont is dead, remember?"

"Fingerprints?"

"Lead casing on the gun."

Oh, my God, he thought. *This could actually work.*

"One last question," Kelleher said, still buying time. "How do you pin all this on FFF?"

"Simple. Jamelle, who is going to disappear for a long, long time after tonight, sends a letter to the police, confessing to the whole plot. She says that you, Gordy, and Andrea all had to die because you'd figured the whole thing out and were going to turn her in to the cops."

"What about the story in the paper? Why kill us if the story's already in the paper?"

"Turns out Jamelle didn't know about it before she killed you. You end up a hero in death, Kelleher—even though the truth is that your story just makes it easier to sell our version of events."

Kelleher felt sick to his stomach. He had been suckered, set up, trapped in every way. He probably *would* win a Pulitzer for dying heroically in pursuit of the story. Only he had the story *wrong.*

Dumont looked at his watch again. "Enough socializing. Jamelle, Stern, get them into the bedroom and set up."

Stern walked over and took Andrea by the arm. Tourretta stood over Kelleher. "Easy way or hard way, Mr. Kelleher, it's up to you."

Kelleher looked at her in dismay. Even if there hadn't been others in the room who were armed, taking her on one-on-one would probably be futile. He got up and looked at Maureen once more. "You'll never live with yourself, Maureen," he said.

She didn't answer. He followed Stern and Andrea down the hall, Tourretta right behind him. Dumont pushed past them and went into the bathroom while Stern guided Andrea to the one chair in the room, pulled some rope from his pocket, and began tying her to the slats.

"Mr. Kelleher, lie on the bed on your back, please."

"What are you going to do?"

"I'm going to tie your hands and feet to the bedposts. If you cooperate, you'll die painlessly. If you don't, you'll die very painfully."

Kelleher wasn't sure he cared which way he was going to die—but the reality that he *was* going to die was beginning to make him shiver.

"Can I ask one more question?" he said.

"If you ask quickly while you're getting onto the bed."

"How can a group called Lovers of Life justify so much death?"

"Sometimes you have to make sacrifices for a cause," she said seriously. "If six people die to ultimately help save thousands, well, that's the way it is."

"So you believe in all this? The whole FFF deal was a front right from the beginning?"

"From day one. I was Jimmy's first recruit, right after he left UVA. I heard him speak in Chicago. You see, Mr. Kelleher, your problem is you underestimated Jimmy. You thought just because he wasn't a smart-ass liberal like you, that he couldn't possibly be as smart as you. Turns out you were wrong."

Kelleher wasn't really listening as she talked. His mind was racing, trying to figure out an escape. Once he and Andrea were tied up, they were as good as dead.

His back was to her as she finished her answer. Now, he turned to face her, shrugged helplessly, and sat down on the bed. He swung his legs up as if to meekly lie down—and saw his chance. Her concentration had wavered for just a second. With all his might, he pulled his feet back. He kicked her as hard as he could, square in the face. Surprised and off balance, she let out a scream and toppled backward, losing her balance in the high heels.

Following through on his kick, Kelleher bounced off the bed and was out the door before Stern, on his knees tying Andrea up, could move. Kelleher sprinted into the living room. McGuire was sitting on the couch and Roane was in the kitchen. As he raced to the sliding glass door, McGuire didn't move. He grabbed the door and yanked at the handle.

It was stuck. A second desperate yank slid it open. And then, just as quickly, it slid back the other way. Kelleher turned to find Tourretta behind him. He turned again and tried to push the door back open but she was too strong, the door wouldn't budge. Kelleher was no fighter, but he had to try. He turned and swung a fist in her direction. She blocked the punch easily, and hit him in the midsection, doubling him over. The next thing Kelleher knew, everything was upside down. Tourretta had flipped him over her shoulder. Kelleher was dizzy and woozy, and his ribs were killing him.

He heard Dumont come into the living room. "What the hell . . . ?"

"I'm sorry, Jim, I'm sorry," she said. "He surprised me. He's stronger than I thought."

Even woozy, Kelleher almost laughed at that one. It had taken her about six seconds to overwhelm him, and he was stronger than she thought?

"Get him onto the bed. Tie him up real tight and let's get going," Dumont barked. "It's almost seven-thirty."

Tourretta walked back down the hall. Upside down, Kelleher could see that Andrea was now tied up and gagged. "Okay, Mr. Kelleher," Tourretta said, "I'm going to put you on the bed now. Make one false move and I promise you, you'll wish you were already dead."

She swung him down onto the bed and quickly tied him up, arms and legs lashed to each bedpost. She pulled the gag extra tight. Kelleher could see a dark welt forming above her eye. Dumont, walking in behind her, looked at the bruise.

"Maureen!" he called. McGuire, with Roane right behind her, obviously to make sure *she* didn't try anything, came in. "Give her some makeup to put on that bruise. There's no time for ice."

Tourretta, McGuire, and Roane left. Dumont stood over Kelleher and grabbed his cheek—hard. "You get an *A* for effort, Bobby boy. But ultimately you failed." He held the cheek for a second, then let go and turned to Stern.

"You straight on what to do?" he asked him.

Stern nodded. "Pillow for him, pills for her, right at eight o'clock, then get the car and bring it around to the side door to pick up you and Jamelle."

"Good. Make sure you don't leave too soon and make damn sure nobody sees you." Dumont turned to Kelleher again. "Well, Bobby boy, this really is good-bye. Remember, though, you're dying a hero."

He walked out. Kelleher heard the sliding glass door open then shut. He could barely move, Tourretta had pulled the rope so tight. He could turn his head just far enough to look at his watch. It was seven thirty-five. Barring a miracle, he would be dead in twenty-five minutes, apparently suffocated by the pillow his head was now resting on. Andrea and Meredith Gordy would be dead soon after that.

For some reason, he found himself thinking about how Ann Roberts would take the news. If he had listened to her, instead of doing his macho "I'm the real reporter routine," he might not have blown the story—not to mention his, Andrea's, and Meredith's lives. He wanted to cry, scream, hit something. Someone. Himself most of all.

"Asshole," he said into his gag, so intently that Stern heard him.

"What's that?" Stern asked. He stood.

Kelleher shook his head, meaning, "Nothing."

"You try to say another word and I promise you a lot of pain before you die," he said. Andrea was starting to cry. Stern took a handkerchief out of his pocket and dabbed her eyes for her. "*You* I'm sorry to see die," he said. Andrea didn't try to say anything.

As the minutes passed, Kelleher stared at the ceiling, trying desperately to think of *something* he could do. He twisted his head again. It was seven fifty-five. He began to feel nauseated. Five minutes. God, how could this have happened?

He couldn't just lie there and let Stern calmly kill him. He had to get the gag loose somehow, start screaming hysterically, then pray that someone on the street somehow heard him and sent for help. It was a ridiculous long shot, but what else was left?

He swallowed hard to prepare himself for as loud a bellow as he could manage. As he did, he thought he heard the sliding glass door open. His ears pricked up. So did Stern's. He wasn't hearing things. Stern pulled his gun out and put it right next to Andrea's head.

"One move from either of you and she's dead on the spot," he whispered.

Kelleher heard footsteps in the hallway. He shut his eyes and prayed that it was the cops.

"Who's there?" Stern said again, fear creeping into his voice.

"It's me, Stern. Roane," a voice said from down the hall. "Calm down, will you?"

Kelleher felt himself pouring sweat. Even though she was trying to make her voice deeper than normal, Kelleher knew it wasn't Roane. It was McGuire. Stern didn't get it, though, which was understandable. He hadn't worked with McGuire every day for three years. His hands, gripped tightly around the gun, went slack.

"Jeez, Roane, what's the prob . . ."

He never got the last word out because he suddenly went reeling backward as something, thrown from just outside the door, crashed into his head. As Stern fell to the floor, Kelleher saw that it was a toaster. McGuire, who had been a pretty good softball pitcher once upon a time, had thrown it from just outside the door and had cracked him solidly on the side of the head. Dazed and bleeding, he went down. Even so, he still had the gun in his hand.

Kelleher finally had his gag loose enough so he could almost talk. "Hit him again!" he screamed. McGuire had charged into the room as soon as

Stern fell, and she picked up the toaster and swung it again, even as Stern, moving in what looked like slow motion, raised the gun and pointed it at her.

Kelleher heard the gunshot at the same instant he heard the *crack* of the toaster making solid contact with Stern's head. He reeled backward; the gun fell out of his hand. McGuire let out a scream and staggered back across Kelleher on the bed. She was clutching her stomach; Kelleher could see a bright pool of red forming.

Andrea started trying to scream now, too. Stern was woozy, but not out. The gun was lying on the floor a few feet from him. "The gun, Maureen, can you get the gun?!" he screeched.

Maureen lurched forward onto the floor, picked up the gun, and pointed it at Stern. She listed from side to side as the blood from her wound oozed from her stomach.

"Untie my hands," Kelleher said. Shakily, Maureen followed his instructions, putting the gun down on his stomach as she did. She was working as fast as she could but that wasn't very fast. She got one hand untied as Stern got to his knees. He was still trying to collect his senses. Kelleher was tempted to tell McGuire to hit him again but was afraid she might pass out doing it. He couldn't quite reach across to untie his other hand; she would have to do it.

"Other hand!" he said. "Quickly!"

She was bleeding all over him. She got the second hand untied and then fell on top of him, exhausted by the effort. Stern was getting to his feet. Kelleher reached across Maureen and grabbed the gun. He had no idea how to shoot it but he couldn't let Stern get to it. Stern lunged at him. Kelleher swung the gun with all his strength and caught Stern smack in the face. He collapsed in a heap, moaning, right on top of Maureen.

Kelleher's feet were still tied to the posts at the end of the bed. Using all the strength he had, he rolled Stern off him onto the floor. More gently, he moved Maureen, then leaned forward to untie his feet. Just as he got loose, Stern got himself back onto a knee. Kelleher grabbed the gun tighter. Stern was now on the far side of the bed. Even half-conscious, he turned toward Kelleher, smirking. "You can't do it, asshole," he croaked.

"Watch me," Kelleher said. He held the gun with both hands, pointed it right at Stern's chest, and squeezed the trigger. He had never shot a gun before in his life and the explosion shocked him. Stern's body lurched backward against the wall, blood spewing everywhere.

Kelleher dropped the gun onto the bed, rolled Maureen over. She was barely conscious. "Dumont's still in there, isn't he?" he said, wishing he could stop the bleeding.

She nodded weakly. "Got away from him in the lounge with all the people in there," she whispered. "He had no time to follow me. They disconnected the phone here, so he couldn't call Stern to warn him I was coming. But they're still going to do it."

Gently, he laid her back on the pillow. He looked at his watch. It was two minutes after eight. Gordy would enter the House chamber in three minutes and begin her speech at eight-ten. No doubt, that was when the lights would go out.

As quickly as he could, he untied Andrea. "Find a phone somewhere and call the cops," he said, gasping for breath. "Tell them what Dumont looks like and to grab him at any cost. Then call an ambulance for Maureen."

"And you?"

"If you can't get to the cops in time, I've got to try to stop Dumont."

He raced down the hall, through the living room, and out the sliding glass door, which Maureen had left open. He took the steps carefully. It was snowing again and the run up the hill to State Circle was slippery. By the time he hit the circle, Kelleher was almost out of breath. He rounded the bend to the front steps, gasping. He looked at his watch again: seven past eight. "Oh, God," he said and began plowing up the twenty-three steps to the front door of the building. He was almost doubled over by now but he couldn't stop. He raced through the metal detector, hearing the cop yell, "Hey! ID! Where's your ID?!"

"Later!" he screamed, almost too breathless to get the word out. He turned right and charged down the hallway. Here, he caught a break. Tom Wyman was on the door to the lounge. He could see Wyman grinning as he charged toward him.

"Gee, Kelleher, they're starting in there, you better . . ."

Kelleher said nothing, just waved a hand and kept going. He didn't even dare look at his watch. He turned left, took one last deep breath, and hurtled through the lounge. As he passed the door where staff entered, he could see the legislators taking their seats. Gordy had just been introduced. He had no more than ten seconds.

"Holy Jesus!" he screamed and dove for the press door, yanking it open. There was a cop standing there.

"Hold it," the cop said, just as everything in the chamber went black. Taking advantage of the cop's surprise, Kelleher used his last ounce of strength to shove him aside. He had seen Dumont sitting in the front school desk, poised and ready. The screaming started as soon as the lights went out. Wildly thrashing through the desks, feeling various arms and legs as he went, Kelleher was aware of shouting all around him. Dimly, he could see Dumont a few feet from him. He had moved into position and was rising from his crouch to take aim. Kelleher glanced over his shoulder and could barely make out Gordy, frozen on the podium. Desperately, he launched himself full bore at Dumont, throwing himself at him and the gun.

He heard himself scream, *"No!"* and just as he piled into Dumont, he heard the gun go off. They both tumbled to the floor. Kelleher heard a thud and more screams, and then everything went black.

*B*obby? Bobby? Can you hear me, Bobby?"

The brightness of the lights forced him to shut his eyes as soon as he opened them. When he reopened them, everything was blurry. He heard the voice again. "Bobby? Come on, Bobby."

Slowly, his eyes began to focus. He could see Larry Bearnarth kneeling over him. It started to come back to him. He was lying flat on his back, staring at the vaulted ceiling of the House chamber.

"Larry," he said. His voice was only a whisper. "Meredith?"

"Right here," he heard a voice say. Meredith Gordy was standing behind Bearnarth, a look of concern on her face. "What do you think, Tony?"

Tony Langloh, one of the delegates, who was also a doctor, was standing next to Bearnarth. "He may have a mild concussion," Langloh said. "I can't be sure. Other than that and a few cuts, he's fine. A night in the hospital might be a good idea. But other than a headache in the morning, he'll be okay."

"He's used to headaches in the morning." That voice belonged to Kenworthy, who was apparently right behind Gordy.

"What happened?" Kelleher asked, his mind slowly coming back into focus.

Gordy kneeled next to him. "What happened is you saved my life," she told him. "You got your hand on the gun just enough to force him to shoot high. The bullet went into the seal of the state of Maryland, right over my head.''

Kelleher groaned, feeling the searing pain in his bad arm. ''Cops have him?'' he asked.

Gordy nodded. ''Cops have everyone. Tourretta was arrested when she walked out the door and there was no getaway car. Roane gave herself up a few minutes ago. So did Beth Bevans. Stern is dead. Andrea is upstairs right now telling the FBI exactly what happened.''

He wasn't sure he wanted to ask the next question. ''Maureen?'' he said finally.

Gordy clutched his hand tightly. ''I'm sorry, Bobby.''

He felt himself starting to cry. Gordy continued clutching his hand. All of a sudden, it struck him: he hadn't been in contact with the paper for hours. What had happened? Had their blatantly inaccurate story blaming FFF for the Paulsen murder run in the first edition?

''Time,'' he said. ''What time is it? My newspaper. I have to call!''

''Easy,'' Gordy said. ''That can wait. You have to go slowly.''

Kelleher felt himself becoming hysterical. ''No. I can't! I have to call. Our story. It's wrong. They can't run it.''

He heard Kenworthy again. ''They must have held first edition after what went on here.''

''Do they know about Maureen? Does Mike? I have to call. Meredith, help me.''

Gordy looked at Langloh. ''What do you think, Tony? Can we sit him up?'' she asked.

''See how he feels,'' Langloh said.

Slowly, Kelleher sat up. He felt nauseated, but he swallowed hard and said, ''I'm fine. Please, get me to a phone.''

''Stand up slowly, Bobby,'' Langloh said.

He did—and almost fell over. Bearnarth and Kenworthy steadied him. He noticed that the chamber was almost empty. ''How long was I out?'' he asked.

''About fifteen minutes,'' Bearnarth answered. ''We evacuated immediately in case Dumont had accomplices.''

Shakily, Kelleher started to the door, still aided by Bearnarth and Kenworthy. Gordy, Langloh, and two troopers followed. One was Tom Wyman. He looked to Kelleher as if he'd been crying. They got him into the speaker's office just as a coterie of police came out the door with a handcuffed Dumont. For a split second they came face-to-face.

The sneer was still on Dumont's face. "It's not over, Bobby boy," he hissed. "There's plenty more just like me who believe in what's right. God will get you for this."

"I'll take my chances," Kelleher said.

The cops led Dumont to the back steps. Kelleher could hear all sorts of commotion down the hall; the rest of the media were being held back. They went into the speaker's office. He dialed Kryton's line. A copy aide answered.

Kelleher was still weak. One of the cops brought him water. He drank gratefully. "I need Jane," he said, his voice now improved to a rasp. "It's Kelleher."

"Kelleher!" the copy aide screamed. A split second later, Kryton was on the line.

"Bobby, is it all true?" she said. "The wires say you saved Gordy."

"I guess I did," he said.

"Where's Maureen? Why hasn't she called in? We've got fifteen minutes to figure out what to do with your original story. They stopped the presses two minutes before it would have gone."

Kelleher gulped. They still didn't know about Maureen. He had missed humiliating the paper by two minutes. "Jane," he said, trying not to choke on the words, "Maureen's dead. She saved my life."

Jane Kryton said nothing.

"Jane?" he said.

"I heard," she replied, the life having gone out of her voice. "What happened?"

"Not now," he said. "No time. You have to kill our story completely. It's totally wrong. Run wires on the attempt for first edition. I'll sub it for second. The guy behind this whole thing was Jimmy Dumont, it was all an LOL plot."

"LOL? What about FFF? Tourretta? *Dumont?!* Dumont's dead!"

The wires hadn't been given Dumont's ID yet either.

"Tourretta was LOL all the way. A plant to destroy FFF. Dumont's not dead. He was the shooter tonight. I'll explain in my story."

"Can you write? The wire bulletin said you were unconscious."

"I'm okay. I'll try to dictate as soon as I can."

He hung up and looked at Gordy. "You think I can see Andrea?" he asked.

The governor nodded and, with the police surrounding them, they headed for the back elevator. Langloh was still watching Kelleher closely.

"You feel faint at all, you tell me," he said. Kelleher nodded. He wasn't going to faint. Not yet, anyway.

From the elevator, they walked directly to the governor's suite. Below, on the first floor, Kelleher could see chaos. They walked into Gordy's office. Andrea sat on the couch with two men in suits. FBI, Kelleher assumed.

"What have you decided?" Gordy asked.

"We're going to have to take her into custody on suspicion of conspiracy," one of the suits said. "She can probably get out on personal recognizance in a couple of hours. Assuming her story checks out, she'll probably get nothing more than probation or a suspended sentence. That's just a guess, though."

"Can I talk to her alone for a minute?" Kelleher asked. The FBI man looked at Gordy, who nodded.

"Technically, the answer to that question is no," he said. "But I think we need to go call in. Should take us about five minutes."

Andrea was staring at the fireplace. "Thank God you saved Meredith," she said. "By the time I found a phone, all I got was someone saying all hell had broken loose on the House floor. I had no idea what had happened until I got here."

"What happened to Maureen?" he asked quietly.

She shook her head sadly. "I called for the ambulance and went right back to the apartment. I think she was probably gone by then. When the medics got there, they couldn't find a pulse. They tried to bring her back, but it was too late."

"Poor Mike," he said. "I've got to make sure someone talks to him in person before the story hits the paper."

"Do you have to tell the whole thing?"

He nodded slowly. "I'm afraid so." He managed a flicker of a smile. "Maureen would never forgive me if I held back on a story."

She got up and put her arms around him. He let it all go. When he finally stopped crying he realized his time with her was almost up.

"So, Kyler," he said, finding his voice, "what next?"

She put a hand on his cheek. "Well, my friend, I think this is the part where I tell you that I think I could love you someday but right now I have to get away, go start over again. Square one–type stuff."

He forced another smile. "Might have been fun, you know," he said.

"*Was* fun, Kelleher," she said. "Might be fun again someday." She kissed him lightly on the lips and he reached for her. But the door had opened behind them.

"I'm sorry, Bobby," Gordy said, leading the FBI men back in.

Andrea squared her back and winked at Kelleher as an FBI man handcuffed her as gently as possible, and led her out the door. True to form, with a last bit of pride, Andrea Kyler never looked back.

When she was gone, he was left alone with Gordy. "The phone's there," she said, pointing to her desk. "It's all yours. I have to go meet with your colleagues to tell them what happened."

"Andrea have time to tell you?"

"A synopsis. I'll send someone to get you an ice pack."

She left and Kelleher sat down at the governor's desk. There was blood all over Oz. Andrea was going back to Kansas. He dialed dictation. Slowly, painfully, he dictated the story. Each word hurt him, cut him open a little more. It took ninety minutes.

When he was finished, the dictationist told him to hang on as she switched him to another line. Wyn Watkins came on. "I'm reading this right behind you, Bobby," he said. "I know you're sick about Maureen. I am, too. But you've done brilliant work. Brilliant."

"I blew it, Mr. Watkins," he said slowly. "I had the story wrong."

"Never got into print, Bobby. *Almost* doesn't count. Not in our business."

The phone clicked. Kelleher sat there, staring into space. He had been incredibly lucky tonight: lucky to be alive, lucky the wrong story hadn't been splashed across page one, lucky he had come off looking like some sort of hero rather than a fool.

But the past few days had cost him. They'd cost him a lot. Alan Sims was dead. A woman he thought he might love was walking out of his life. And the woman who knew him better than anyone was also dead. It was time for him to leave Oz, too. Where to, he didn't know. He did know that he would miss it.

He was sitting on something that was uncomfortable. He reached into his back pocket. His notebook, through it all, was still there. He turned it over and there on the back he saw the name Ann. He had written it there as he had told her he would, to remind himself to call her.

He reached for the phone and started to dial. He got through the first five numbers and stopped. He hung up. Not yet. Maybe tomorrow. Or the day after.

ACKNOWLEDGMENTS

I want to thank the people who made it possible for me to do this book. Esther Newberg and Peter Gethers showed remarkable patience dealing with someone struggling to write his first piece of fiction. My wife, Mary, humored me during this effort in spite of her belief that Bobby Kelleher, and sometimes his creator, are more or less incorrigible. I also want to thank my old Annapolis friends Tom Kenworthy, Luiz Simmons, Tim Maloney, Buzz Ryan, Dickens Doyle, and Ben Cardin for their assistance in helping me remember what life in Oz was really like.

ABOUT THE AUTHOR

Running Mates is JOHN FEINSTEIN'S first novel and fifth book. His first three books were on college basketball: *A Season on the Brink,* the best-selling sports book of all time; *A Season Inside,* also a national best-seller; and *Forever's Team,* the critically acclaimed story of the 1977–78 Duke University basketball team. Last fall, his chronicle of life on the professional tennis tour, *Hard Courts,* shot to number four on *The New York Times* best-seller list.

Mr. Feinstein, a 1977 Duke graduate, spent eleven years at *The Washington Post* (two of them covering Maryland politics) and has worked as a special contributor to *Sports Illustrated.* His stories have also appeared in *Sport, Inside Sports, The Sporting News, The National, TV Guide,* and *Reader's Digest.* He has won twenty U.S. Basketball Writers awards and three National Sportswriters and Sportscasters awards as Washington writer of the year. His work has appeared in *Best Sports Stories* seven times and he won an American Bar Association Certificate of Merit for investigative reporting in 1980.

Currently he is a contributing editor to *Tennis* magazine and *Basketball Times,* a contributor to *The New York Times,* a commentator for National Public Radio, and a regular on ESPN's *The Sports Reporters.* He is a past president of the U.S. Tennis Writers Association and is now president of the U.S. Basketball Writers Association. He is also a visiting professor at Duke University.

Mr. Feinstein lives in Bethesda, Maryland, and Shelter Island, New York, with his wife, Mary.